William Wyatt Gill

Selections from the Autobiography of the Rev. William Gill

William Wyatt Gill

Selections from the Autobiography of the Rev. William Gill

ISBN/EAN: 9783744664646

Printed in Europe, USA, Canada, Australia, Japan

Cover: Foto ©Raphael Reischuk / pixelio.de

More available books at **www.hansebooks.com**

William Gill

SELECTIONS

FROM THE

AUTOBIOGRAPHY

OF THE

REV. WILLIAM GILL

(Author of "Gems from the Coral Islands").

BEING CHIEFLY

A RECORD OF HIS LIFE AS A MISSIONARY IN THE SOUTH SEA ISLANDS.

PRINTED FOR PRIVATE CIRCULATION.

LONDON: YATES AND ALEXANDER,
LONSDALE BUILDINGS, CHANCERY LANE, W.C.
1880.

CONTENTS.

CHAPTER I. PAGE

Family History 4

CHAPTER II.

Tiverton. 1817—1825 5

CHAPTER III.

London. 1830—1835 8

CHAPTER IV.

Turvey. 1836—1838 23

CHAPTER V.

Voyage of the "Camden." 1838—1839 31

CHAPTER VI.

Arrival in Africa 37

CHAPTER VII.

Arrival at Sydney 45

CHAPTER VIII.

Arrival at Samoa 50

CHAPTER IX.

Arrival at Rarotonga. 1839 57

CHAPTER X.

The Report of the Murder of Rev. J. Williams ... 70

CHAPTER XI.

Native Teachers—Teava and Tupe 78

CHAPTER XII.

Visit to Mangaia, 1841 93

CHAPTER XIII.

Second Visit to Mangaia, 1842 117

CHAPTER XIV. PAGE
Mission Work in the Adjacent Islands—Hervey Group 120

CHAPTER XV.
Third Visit to Mangaia 139

CHAPTER XVI.
Building of Institution at Avarua, and Chapel at Arorangi ... 149

CHAPTER XVII.
Arrival of the New Mission Ship, "John Williams," and State of the Mission in 1845 154

CHAPTER XVIII.
Visit to Mangaia, 1845, with Newly Appointed Missionary ... 163

CHAPTER XIX.
Destructive Hurricanes 179

CHAPTER XX.
Visit to the Islands of Western Polynesia, 1846... 188

CHAPTER XXI.
Mission Work, 1847 to 1852—Rev. and Mrs. Buzacott visit England 241

CHAPTER XXII.
Commercial and Religious Progress 251

CHAPTER XXIII.
Return of Rev. A. Buzacott, and Commemoration of the Thirtieth Anniversary 264

CHAPTER XXIV.
Preparations for a Voyage to England ... 271

CHAPTER XXV.
England 279

CHAPTER XXVI.
Conclusion 314

. . . .

They are not to our love,
But to the home above,
  Taken by Thee.

Gently translated, they
  Pass out of sight,
Gone as the morning stars
  Flee with the night:
Taken to endless day,
So may I fade away,
  Into Thy light.

G. Rawson

SELECTIONS

FROM

THE REV. W. GILL'S

AUTOBIOGRAPHY.

CHAPTER I.

MY great-grandfather was born at Culmstock, Devon; he was a wool-comber, a business of some importance in his time. He died at a good old age in 1790.

My grandfather was born in 1756, and spent the early years of his life in Culmstock. He followed the same business as his father. He removed from Culmstock to North Tawton, where he married. He died in May, 1819, aged sixty-three.

My father was born at North Tawton in 1789. At the age of fourteen he was apprenticed to the trade of tanner and currier at Crediton, and at the age of twenty-two years he removed to Totnes, where he was married on April 6th, 1812.

My mother was a native of Harberton, a village near Totnes; her parents were attached members of the Church of England, and were much esteemed by the inhabitants. Her maiden name was Bartlett.

I was born January 14th, 1813, at Totnes. The difficulties in connection with the Trades Union about this time compelled my father, under the auspices of the Union, to leave Totnes on a visit to London. His duties called him to visit many towns until he settled in Cambridge, where, for two years, he resided with his family.

A combination against the Union in December, 1816, necessitated a return to London, and, after a short stay there, my father decided to return to Devonshire. In 1817 my parents removed from Totnes to Tiverton; we were settled until 1828, when we removed to Brentford, and thence to London, the future home of the family.

CHAPTER II.

TIVERTON. 1817—1828.

MY early memories of Tiverton, Devon, were very pleasant. Tiverton had many educational advantages; there were two good college schools, and two or three good boarding schools. I well remember the kind care of the principal and teachers in the school where I was a pupil. I had no excessive fondness for study, nor any particular aversion; never but once was I punished for carelessness at school, and, in a few years, I made ordinary proficiency—not to distinguish myself as a scholar, but to prepare me for the station in life I was supposed to occupy.

At the age of twelve my father wished me to enter the lace factory. After twelve months' trial, I found that neither the employment nor the general society of the place had any attractions for me. Just at this time my mother made arrangements for a prolonged visit among her relations in the east of Devon, and, to my great relief and pleasure, it was arranged that I and my brother George, who was seven years my junior, should accompany her.

On my return from this tour, and soon after my thirteenth year, I was led to choose the business of cabinet-maker and upholsterer, and was thereupon bound as an apprentice for seven years to one of the largest and most respectable firms in the town, Messrs. Bowden and Sharland. A few months after this the partnership was dissolved, and I was placed under the sole care of Mr. Sharland. Mr. S. was an active Christian man, a member of the Church at the Old Steps Meeting, and one of the zealous teachers in the Sunday School. Mr. S. assiduously instructed me in the business, and Mrs. S. watched with motherly care over my mental and moral improvement. The instruction gained from Mr. S. was of much service to me in after-life. Two or three years before my apprenticeship my mother became a member of the Church at the Old Steps Meeting; this event was a happy one for herself, and blessed in its influence on myself and brothers. By this means we were all early introduced to religious friends and associations.

I well remember the "Old Meeting House" with its high pews, deep galleries, long brass chandeliers holding about sixty or seventy candles on winter evenings. The old place has ever been dear to my memory; it was there I was permitted to begin to understand and to enjoy religious instruction and worship.

Some Unitarian strife among the ministers of the town, and especially in connection with this place, has always marred my otherwise pleasant memories.

The Rev. Wm. Whitta became the minister when these dissensions had ceased, and from him I received much kind attention, which influenced me for good.

I was about ten years old when introduced to a Bible Class conducted by a Mr. Ellis; to him I owe, more than to anyone, the early knowledge and impressions of religion which were fostered into growth in after-life. It was his habit to supplement his Sunday teaching by meeting his scholars every Friday evening for special prayer, and conversation upon the peculiar circumstances of the young men under his care. About two years after my introduction to the class, I was selected to accompany Mr. Robert Ware and Mr. Sharland every other Sunday as helper in the Juvenile Classes at the villages of Chevethorne and Bolham. This was my first attempt at Christian work. The influence of these visits was good, and as I look back on them I often wonder why I was selected to help, but I also feel I had a very simple and sincere delight in the engagement, and trace to it that which led to after public work in the ministry.

When I was fourteen years old, my father, very unexpectedly, was compelled, in consequence of business relationships, to remove from Tiverton to Brentford, near London. This involved the removal of the family also, and necessitated some arrangements which led to the giving up of my apprenticeship indentures. Mr. Sharland in this matter acted with very great kindness and consideration.

On the occasion of my leaving Tiverton, a special service was held in the school, in which I was prayerfully commended to the guidance and care of God. I received many suitable and valuable books as an expression of the teachers' kindness; but no language can describe my deep feelings in this separation. I walked home along "The Causeway" as with a broken heart after the service. My brother George was with me. I felt I was experiencing a heavy trial, but all the memories of my heart in connection with Tiverton filled me with praise to God.

Letters of introduction from the school at Tiverton gave me a position in the school of the Independent Chapel at Brentford, where I was appointed teacher of the second juvenile class. During our stay in Brentford, I filled a situation as manager in a retail leather cutter's business. The place of business was Kingston-on-Thames: young as I was, I was led to accept this heavy responsibility. It was no little joy to my heart that I was enabled to visit Brentford every Sunday, and, of course, returning to Kingston the following day.

These arrangements were continued until the spring of 1830, when our family removed to London.

CHAPTER III.

LONDON. 1830—1835.

My mother was transferred from the Church at Tiverton to that at Barbican Chapel. I at the same time was introduced to the circle of Sunday School teachers there.

My first Sunday in London was in July, 1830. King George IV. was dead, "and lying in state" at St. James's Palace. In company with a young friend, a son of a former acquaintance, I went to see the sight. I confess that I felt that this was a novel way to me of spending the Sabbath, and, while somewhat interested, I felt that I was not at all satisfied. The next Sunday also was spent in "vagrant pleasure," wandering with the same young friend.

Happily, however, during the following week the Rev. Wm. Whitta, my mother's former pastor at Tiverton, sent a special letter of introduction for her and me to the Rev. A. Tidman, of Barbican. This, as it now appears to me, was as the golden link of God's goodness and mercy connecting previous years of youthful experience with all my future years of Christian profession and work.

The following Sunday found my mother a member of Barbican Church. At the same time I became a teacher of a juvenile class, and in a short time my brothers George, John, and Henry were scholars in the Sunday School. Here I soon found a home, and gratefully must I acknowledge the kindness shown me by the Rev. A. and Mrs. Tidman.

Very soon after arriving in London the question of my business pursuits required attention, and just about this time the Messrs. John and Robert Drew, who carried on a large business as tanners and curriers, wished to open a retail business in the West End of London, and, being personal friends of our family, wished me to undertake for them the responsible position and care of the retail department.

This position was accepted and carried on with mutual confidence and esteem until the partnership was dissolved and the business sold.

The Messrs. Drew, however, kindly introduced me to a Mr. Godby, who was desirous that I should conduct a similar business for him in Poplar.

I find an entry in my journal under date of July 18th, 1834, thus:—"Mr. Godby having called yesterday about my taking his shop at Poplar, I this morning specially sought Divine guidance. Mr. Godby came again to-day, and being so desirous of engaging me I consented to go." I remained in Poplar for nearly two years, during which time I came into London regularly every Sunday morning and returned on Monday.

The first Sunday in January, 1832, was one of great interest and importance to me. I was then just nineteen years old, and on this day it was my privilege to join the Church at Barbican. During the previous two years I had profited much under the preaching of the Rev. A. Tidman, and all the associations of the Church and schools had grown in deepening and affectionate interest.

Many kind friends were helpful to me as a youth; some were my elders, and others but little more than my own age. Gratefully do I record some names—Mullens, Challis, Congrave, Dyer, Humphries, Collins, Russell, G. A. Lloyd. Such friends had much to do under God in the formation of my character and its development for Christian usefulness.

Mr. Dyer, who afterwards was a minister in America, was at this time a teacher in the school, and he it was who helped me publicly to decide for Christ, and to join the Church. I have ever had grateful memories of his wise and kind encouragements to me.

While I had very pleasant intercourse with ALL the teachers and friends, and found pleasure in attending with them many meetings for conference and prayer, there were a few select friends with whom it was my delight to associate, who formed what I may call a kind of inner circle of friendship: Messrs. Collins, G. A. Lloyd, H. Russell; Misses Collins, Russell, C. and E. Cunnington, and myself. We had frequent meetings at each other's homes, sometimes for social recreation, and at other times for devotional and religious purposes.

Of friend Collins, I may record that he was very active and prosperous in business, and after my absence from England for sixteen years I found him, when I came home, a useful and influential member of the City Road Chapel; a deacon also, and a superintendent in the Sunday School.

Of my friend G. A. Lloyd, I may record that in October, 1833, he was induced to go out to Sydney, where he became very prosperous as a merchant, and has been several times elected as M.P. (or M.L.C.), and several years he has been a deacon at Pitt Street Chapel, Sydney.

My friend Henry Russell, in 1835, married Miss Cunnington, and went as a missionary to Jamaica, under the auspices of the London Missionary Society.

As the years 1832 to 1835 inclusive were most important in the development of my early mental culture and experimental life, I record a few extracts from my journal:—

"In January, 1833, gave my first address to the boys' Sunday School. The circumstances which led to this my first address were as follow:—It was the good practice in the Sunday School for the teachers and members of the church to give an address every Sunday afternoon.

"From the first, in common with others, I felt instructed and interested by such addresses. Many of the short addresses given by Challis, Mullens, Roberts, Cole, and others have abided in my memory and influenced my heart and life as much or more than many sermons heard during the same period. Most of the addresses were wisely adapted to the scholars. Often while listening to these addresses the thought occurred to me that I might, some day, as a teacher be called upon to take my turn in the duty.

"With the conception of the thought I found myself selecting a text, and I decided that the words of Christ to Peter would be suitable: 'Lovest thou Me?' The work of preparation, thinking and writing, occupied some two months. During this time

I resolved not to mention this work of preparation to any of my intimate friends, from whom I think I kept nothing else secret. Very unexpectedly one Sunday afternoon I was requested to address the boys' school. Thus I was led to prepare for and to practise public speaking. Shortly after this I was chosen to give an address to the girls' school, and not having prepared another I gave the same. This gave me an impulse and encouragement to prepare other short addresses, from such words as 'Christ able to save,' 'The whole world guilty before God,' 'The pleasure of sin for a season,' 'Suffer little children to come unto Me,' 'Flee, youthful lusts,' 'Little children, keep yourselves from idols.'"

With my most intimate friends, H. R. and G. A. L., I felt much drawn and attached to our own place of worship. Rarely ever were we absent morning or evening, and this regularity of attendance I look back upon with pleasure and gratitude. Our dear pastor, Rev. A. Tidman, was much loved by us. His fervent exposition of Scripture, his loving and practical application of invitation, doctrine, and experience, were most impressive, and could not fail to be valuable to such young men as we were.

We were favoured also at Barbican with the occasional services of many of the good preachers of the day; and as I now remember their names, I have a vivid impression of many of their sermons—for example, the Rev. A. Reed preached from "Stand ye in the ways and see, and ask for the old paths, where is the good way, and walk therein, and ye shall find rest for your souls;" the Rev. E. Mannering preached from "Vessels made meet for the Master's use;" the Rev. H. Townley from "When Christ, who is our life, shall appear, &c.;" the Rev. J. Pike from "There is joy in Heaven over one sinner that repenteth, &c.;" the Rev. J. Stratton preached from "He is a Priest for ever, &c.;" the Rev. Alexander Fletcher preached from "There they crucified Him;" the Rev. Dr. Bennett from "Another King, one Jesus;" the Rev. John Morison preached from "From a child thou hast known the Scriptures, &c.;" the Rev. John Burnet from "His Kingdom is not of this world;" the Rev. Dr. Vaughan from "Whither shall I go from Thy presence?"

and the Rev. Dr. Joseph Fletcher from "Thou wilt keep him in perfect peace whose mind is stayed on Thee."

The general influence of these sermons was not only such as to cause pleasure in remembering the texts, but was abiding for good through future years of life; and never do I now read those, and other, texts preached from at that time without associating them with the names of these honoured men.

In looking back on such exercises, I think I can discover the germs and the growth of thoughtfulness which led to much delight in all devotional exercises. Sure I am that in my own case they gave light to the mind, cheerfulness to the heart, and guidance to the life.

I strongly advocate the presenting of short texts of Scripture to the mind and the heart of the young. I have always advised young people, both at home and abroad, to take note of the texts they hear preached from.

I am sorry to find that the good old practice of teachers and others speaking briefly from a short text to Sunday scholars is very much out of fashion now. I have but little faith in the many excuses given as reasons for not doing so. The thing, wisely done, will always insure God's blessing.

My first public speaking before elders and others was at a teachers' meeting, October 15th, 1833, when, for the encouragement of those labouring in the school, I was led to give a Report of a Juvenile Prayer Meeting, which had been established by my brother George, in connection with some of the scholars, but was not known to any of the teachers of the school.

Calling one evening at my father's house, I found to my surprise that a room, which he had suitably fitted up, had been granted to my brother for this purpose. The meeting was then being held. With grateful delight, unknown to my brother, I remained some time outside listening to the reading and prayers.

Certain rules had been agreed to, a copy of which I subsequently obtained, and which I here record:—

1st.—That this Society be denominated the Barbican Sunday School Devotional Class.

2nd.—That it shall be composed of such young persons who are seeking their way to Zion, with their faces thitherward.

3rd.—That no one be admitted as a member unless he has attended one month regularly.

4th.—That none be admitted as a member unless by a majority of votes of the members present.

5th.—That the Prayer Meeting be held every Wednesday evening, to begin at half-past seven o'clock, and to close at half-past eight precisely.

6th.—That the reading of Scripture and prayer be the chief exercises.

7th.—That any instructive book, mutually agreed upon, may be also read.

8th.—That each member preside in rotation.

9th.—That the prayers be short.

10th.—That an extra meeting be held once a month for business.

11th.—That any member being absent for one month be considered as having resigned, unless a satisfactory reason be given for his absence.

12th.—That brothers Edwards and Gill be considered respectively as leader of the singing and secretary.

13th.—That whatever expenses be incurred be defrayed by voluntary subscription.

This Report, which contained other details, very much interested and encouraged all our teachers, and it is pleasing to find, after more than forty years of service at home and abroad, that I can record that most of those youths, so associated in early life, gave themselves to Christ, and that many of them have been engaged in the ministry or in some other works of Christian usefulness.

Besides attending the Sunday School, I find in my notebook records of visitation to the poor and destitute, either alone or in company with some member of the then flourishing "Christian Instruction Society." Also, I was one appointed to join others to give short addresses to the poor people who were accustomed to meet in Golden Lane and Artillery Place.

These services were no doubt stimulating and healthy in the formation of good habits, but still more valuable as means of grace, and while in such a review of the past as I am now making I can see much ignorance and imperfection, I am convinced of this practical lesson, that it is well to employ the little we have wisely and humbly for the good of others.

There will be danger in premature development of youthful piety; it will need to be watered and sustained by growth of love, humility, and faith. Where these are allowed quietly and almost unconsciously to grow it must be an evidence of God's blessing. I have at this time in the review of life numerous illustrations of these sentiments, both in my work at home, and in the islands of the Southern Sea.

Amid these associations and influences, so happy and useful to my early Christian life, I was soon called to the experiences involved in changes and separations of early friends.

In October, 1833, one of my dearest friends, George Alfred Lloyd, was led, with the sanction of his father and mother, to leave England for Sydney, New South Wales. Our friendship was very dear, and it seemed strange to us that he should have consented to go. On Sunday evening, October 27th, a goodly company of us met at his father's house to ask God's guidance and blessing on the undertaking. J. Collins, H. Russell, and I offered prayer, and the good old father gave the benediction. The following evening I parted with my friend. It was a sore trial indeed to our young and tender hearts, and little did we know then all the meaning and the uses of the trial. Soon after Alfred's departure his father died.

Alfred, however, reached his adopted home. He succeeded in business enterprises, and in a year also sent for his mother and family to come to him. There he provided for himself and family a home, and rose to be a man of property and position, and of great influence in all social and religious enterprises, for with all he was a man of God.

On my arrival at Sydney in 1838, I found him settled as a farmer up the country. On my return to Sydney in 1853 he was a merchant of position and a deacon of Pitt Street Chapel.

He visited England in 1858, and laid the foundation-stone of the new chapel, Rectory Place, Woolwich.

Subsequently, he returned to Sydney, became a member of the Colonial Parliament for Newcastle, Financial Secretary to the Colonial Government, and has since held the office of Postmaster-General.

In common with many contemporary merchants he has experienced many changes and vicissitudes, but is firmly attached to truths and principles imbibed in early youth. We have often reviewed the way of Divine guidance, and give thanks for the early influences of Christian associations at Barbican.

It was the practice of the Rev. A. Fletcher, of Finsbury Chapel, to assemble the children of Sunday Schools on Christmas Day. They were gala days and eminently useful, and a means of good to the children of the times. I well remember Christmas Day, 1833, when Mr. Fletcher preached from the words, "The Great Salvation."

The last Sunday of this year has special notice in my journal in reference to the sermon preached by Mr. Tidman from the words, "We spend our years as a tale that is told," and its influence on my heart and feeling.

This year, 1833, had been one of much pleasure and I trust of no little profit. The intercourse with Christian friends had had a formative influence, preparing, as I then little knew, for the years of after-life.

On the last night of the year, in company with friend Russell, I went to the midnight meeting held in the Wesleyan Chapel, City Road. The Rev. Theophilus Lessey gave an impressive sermon from the words, "Behold I come as a thief in the night." Many of our Barbican friends were with us. It was the first service of the kind I had attended. We were all pleased and edified, and with grateful hearts encouraged to go on in the unfolding path of new life.

Attended the early prayer meeting for the new year, 1834, in Barbican Chapel, at half-past six. The place was crowded. It was a memorable meeting. We offered praise. We made our vows, and sought continued grace and guidance.

I find an entry in my journal, that this day I attended the marriage of a friend of my father and mother; the parties were professed Owenites. I was with them till evening; found their minds dark indeed respecting our views of God and Providence. I embraced the opportunity for some plain conversation with them.

This day also, or rather late in the evening, I wrote a long letter to T. C., brother of my friend J. C., on religious matters. As I now review these notes, I am surprised at my boldness; but I thought it right then. God forgave the evil, and blessed the good.

January, 1834.—This is the completion of my twenty-first year. Amid all the changes I have thus far had, my years have been much blessed. Humility and gratitude before God are the true feelings of my heart. Some few trials and perplexities have been allowed to alarm me, but light and hope have been granted. The past year, though gone, yet speaks—its voice tells me of the instability of all earthly things and the uncertainty of all earthly plans; but it also tells me of the faithfulness and love of God. May these reflections abide with me. Henceforth let me dedicate every power and possession to Him who is my Redeemer, and may He daily help me so to do. Amen.

In the month of April, 1834, the situation I had filled as manager in Mr. Drew's retail establishment had to be vacated—most unexpectedly the firm had to make other arrangements, and the business was closed. Thus early did I begin to feel perplexed as to the future plans of life.

But I felt the desire for Christian work growing stronger, and gave my first address in the girls' Sunday-school from the text, "Lovest thou Me?"

This month was blessed to me by a further indication of God's will, and very gradually but surely, my good pastor, Mr. Tidman, who had always taken kindly interest in me, now embraced opportunities, and, as I think I now see, made opportunities to give me something to do at meetings, both for prayer and business. Hence he invited me to the annual meeting of the Religious Tract Society—wished me to accompany him to tea with the Committee of the Irish Evangelical Society, of which he was then the Secretary;—wished me to assist as collector in the public meetings.

These were little things and little thought of at the time; but they yielded much pleasure—a delight in doing something; and I think I now see that they were links in the chain of God's providential guidance towards me.

I heard the missionary sermon preached by the Rev. R. Knill, in the Tottenham Court Road Chapel.

He divided his sermon—I. The Harvest: It was great; II. The Labourers: They were few; III. The Prayer: For increase. Previous to this service, I had strong desires to devote myself to missionary work, but now these desires were matured into a conviction of duty. Up to this time I had not even mentioned my thoughts to my friend H. R.; but now could refrain no longer. In mentioning my convictions to him, I found he also had long had the same desires. We began to feel as living in the opening of a new world. My journal says—"We talked together, we prayed together, we wept together, we resolved together before the Lord."

With these feelings I was gratefully pleased to find myself asked to give another address to the Sunday School, May 18th, 1834. I consented, and took for my text, "God so loved the world," &c.

On the 21st May, 1834, I wrote a letter to my pastor, expressing my desire for mission work, and asking his advice as to entering on a course of study to prepare for that work. The following is the entry under this date: "I humbly submit my case to Him whose wisdom and love will guide me aright, praying, that if He see fit to send me to this work He would make me all He would have me be. When I think of my unworthiness, it seems like presumption for me to aim at being placed in such honour."

The following Sunday services are specially noticed in my journal. Mr. Tidman preached, morning; Isa. xxxii. 2, "Man shall be a hiding place from the storm," &c. Personally I felt this an encouraging promise. In the evening Mr. Tidman preached, what I considered, a testing sermon to me in relation to my recent letter to him; the text was Mark v. 19, "Go home to thy friends," &c.

By invitation, I had an interview with Mr. Tidman, at his

house, in Finsbury Square, on the subject of my letter. He received me very kindly, and, while mentioning many difficulties and hindrances which my peculiar circumstances presented, he encouraged me to use all means at command for mental improvement. He lent me several books.

June, 1834.—Records that friends Henry Russell and Mr. Bright, another Sunday School teacher, had interviews with Mr. Tidman with reference to giving themselves to the work of the ministry.

I find that about fourteen young men, connected with Barbican Church, have been identified with Christian labour.

July, 1834.—Records work in Sunday School, addresses to the Sunday Schools, visitation to the poor and sick, and pleasant Saturday evening prayer meetings.—Also another interview with Mr. Tidman, and another loan of suitable books on the subject of missions.—Also a pleasant week's ramble with H. R., through Sheerness, Gravesend, Milton, Rochester, and Cobham. In this tour of recreation we distributed Bibles and tracts, and spoke on religious matters to many men, women, and children.

August 1, 1834.—Noted as a day of rejoicing—the day of slave emancipation, especially in the islands of the West Indies—where it now seemed likely that my friend H. R. would be appointed for missionary labour.

September.—Records a visit from my mother, who remained a few days with me. The entry has this paragraph: "How kindly these visits are. As I think of all the way she has been led, and of how much I owe to her, I feel more and more love to my mother; may she be helped to make the surrender of me that she may be called to make."

October.—Our friend, the Rev. John Vine, of Bushey, was set apart for missionary work in Jamaica. The service was held in the Old Stepney Meeting House—the Revs. Townley, Tidman, Collison, Knill, and Fletcher took part in the service.

My lodgings being in the vicinity, many school friends visited me to tea and supper. These friendships are remembered as one of the peculiar phases of these years. I don't know how, but so it was, that all the teachers were very kind and very willing to come to see me; these visits were influential for good; many of the friends came four or five miles to spend evenings with me. I now wonder at their kind attentions and loving attachment. Some of the new friends made at Poplar were Messrs. Burrage, French, Temple, Death—Wesleyan Sunday School teachers—who often joined in these gatherings, and through them I gained introduction to their Sunday Schools at Poplar and was often called upon to give addresses.

I am now amazed at the ease with which the journeys to and from Poplar were made. I suppose it was youthful enthusiasm and religious pleasure.

November.—Records, that friend H. R. received letters from the Revs. J. Vine and Alloway, of Jamaica, which decided him to apply to the London Missionary Society to labour there He did so, and was accepted. He married Miss Elizabeth Cunnington, and laboured with good success. I felt, however, that his going to Jamaica was like the breaking of another link in my Barbican friendships; I felt also more and more anxious as to when and where I should be called to labour. H. R. died at his station in the West Indies some time after I had reached the islands of the Pacific.

December.—The entry of this month refers to the illness of Mr. Bright, whose mind gave way so that he was removed from society; to changes in Barbican circles; the close of Mr. Tidman's seven years' labour there; and addresses given to Sunday Schools, all tending to show how events were preparing me for falling in with God's will to go abroad.

Truly I can record, concerning the past four years of my life, that they were specially marked by tokens of God's love and guidance, and personal growth in experience, activity, and hope.

Among the many young men friends associated with Barbican, during 1834 and 1835, was Mr. W. Henry Dyer.

On the departure of H. R. for Jamaica, Mr. Dyer was my constant companion; he was then preparing for the ministry, and soon went to college, and for many years was a most active and faithful minister of Christ. He succeeded the Rev.

W. Jay, of Bath, and has only recently retired from a long and successful ministry.

Early also in this year (1835) my brother George wrote me a letter expressing his desire to profess his love to Christ by joining the Church. This he did; and afterwards gave himself to the work of the ministry, and for sixteen years laboured as a missionary in the islands of the South Seas, and subsequently returned to England and received a call to a Church at Burnley in Lancashire.

My brother Henry also followed his example, and also became a good minister of Christ in the county of Suffolk; and after labouring successfully in the cause of the Bible Society, both in America and in England, died in November 1870.

My brother John also decided for Christ, joined the Church, and, remaining at home, was officially connected with the Parish of St. George's-in-the-East, London.

It will give a further idea of the friendship existing among the teachers of Barbican Sunday School if I extract from my journal the report of a Teachers' Meeting which I convened at my rooms at Poplar. Some twenty-four or twenty-six came down in hired conveyances on Good Friday, April 14th, 1835. Among those present were Messrs. H. Russell, J. Temple, Death, W. H. Dyer, D. Nightingale, A. Nightingale, G. Gill, Burrage, Jefferson, Brown, J. Collins, French, and others; Misses Crook, Turner, Cunnington, Halliday, Burrage, Russell, E. Cunnington, Ross, Collins, Nightingale, and others.

After tea, the meeting resolved itself into one of a free and friendly conversation on a subject previously given: "In what does the glory of Christ's kingdom on Earth consist, and how can it best be promoted by His disciples?"

This was a pleasant and long-remembered gathering; it was the last of many such, and preceded the dispersion of those who composed it to the different paths of our individual lives.

Amid the Christian associations of Barbican School and Church, and through the changes of 1834, my heart was more and more decided to contemplate missionary work. The previous desires excited were deepened, and I had many interviews with Mr. Tidman. Sometimes he met me at his house, and sometimes we took early morning walks in the garden of Finsbury Square.

The arrival of the Rev. J. Williams from the South Sea Islands after sixteen years' labour, and his frequent ministrations at Barbican, tended to deepen and develop my desire for the work.

Early this year Mr. Tidman introduced me to some of the Directors of the Society. I well remember going to see them at the old Mission House, 28, Austin Friars, and subsequently I had more special conversations with Revs. John Arundel and W. Ellis, Secretaries of the Society. These gave me encouragement to apply in the usual way. I had two interviews with the Committee; well do I remember them! Good Rev. Lewis, of Islington, presided; Drs. Morison and Fletcher were among the ministers there.

In reply to the question whether I had any special place to which I wished to be sent, I said I left myself entirely in their hands; I wished time and opportunity for special instruction, and would leave them to decide where to send me.

At the first meeting, the members of Committee inclined to accept me, and send me to the West Indies. This was rather pleasing to me, as my friend H. R. would be there; but, at the second meeting, it was decided to send me to the Missionary Institution, under the care of the Rev. Richard Cecil, Turvey, Bedfordshire, with a view of my going to the South Sea Islands on the return of the Rev. John Williams.

Month after month passed on in attention to these and many other matters in connection with this prospect, and on November 19th, 1835, I left London for Turvey. The Rev. R. and Mrs. Cecil received me most kindly, and so did all the students.

I remember well my grateful praise to God that day, and my prayer for His guidance and help. Among the students at Turvey at this time, and those who afterwards came, were Mr. Lumb, Mr. Stevens, Mr. Hay, Mr. Wilkinson, Mr. Samuel Martin, Mr, Gleg, Mr. Kettle, Mr. Ross, and others. Generally eighteen students were there, and most who were accepted remained two or three years. In the usual course of study, and in the intimate, personal, and family intercourse, I had much delight. Soon, too, I had much exercise in village preaching, and occasionally supplying the pulpit of Mr. Cecil. Under these congenial and favourable circumstances I was permitted to close the year 1835.

CHAPTER IV.

TURVEY. 1836—1838.

TURVEY is a pretty, quiet village, and of much interest as the place where good Leigh Richmond lived so long, and laboured so usefully in the parish church. At his removal there were very many truly experimental Christians in the village, and, had a good Gospel minister been put in the church, no Nonconformist place would have been built.

Among my useful engagements at Turvey was preaching at the villages and sometimes at the towns near. In the morning we usually heard Mr. Cecil. His devotion, his tenderness, his learning, his language, were so valuable to us, that every service, apart from its worship, was a blessing to the heart and a stimulus to the mind.

We generally went to the villages in the afternoon, usually by twos, for both services.

During my two years' residence at Turvey I preached sixty-five sermons—at Bedford, Olney, St. Neots, Newport-Pagnell, and at the villages of Stoke, Harrold, Stagsden, Ashwood, Newton, and Turvey.

While at Turvey we were frequently favoured with visits of good and useful men, friends of Mr. Cecil, to whom we were introduced, and with whom we had free and profitable intercourse—Dr. Bennett, Henry Dunn, Messrs. Bull, John Frost, and Alliott, of Bedford, often came.

The influence of such visits and intercourse was good and highly educational.

In the autumn of 1837 it was decided by the Directors of the London Missionary Society that Rev. John Williams should return to his labours in the Islands. This led to my leaving Turvey six months earlier than I had expected or desired.

During a short visit to London, in the May Meeting of 1836, I made proposals of marriage to Miss Elizabeth Lansborough Halliday, step-daughter of Robert Devonshire, Esq., of Barbican Church. She had gained my affection at the Good Friday meeting already recorded in 1835; and in May, 1836, was not unprepared for a formal offer of hand and heart on my part, and to give her own in return. I had formed a high opinion of her suitability for the work to which I was called, and Mr. and Mrs. Devonshire cordially gave their loving consent; and on September 21st, 1837, we were married at Barbican Chapel, and fully expected to leave England in the following month for the South Sea Islands.

Arrangements, however, in regard to a new missionary ship, desired by Mr. Williams, were not completed until April, 1838.

This delay, though irksome, was unavoidable; but it gave us a better ship than was at first contemplated, and also secured to us some additions to our missionary staff.

On October 12, 1837, I was set apart by public ordination—in Barbican Chapel—to the work of the ministry.

The order of the service was—

Reading the Scriptures and Prayer by Rev. John Young, M.A.

Introductory Address by Rev. John Williams, Missionary.

Questions by Rev. John Arundel, Home Secretary.

Ordination Prayer by Rev. Arthur Tidman.

Charge by the Rev. Richard Cecil.

Conclusion by Rev. W. S. Palmer.

The chapel was crowded in every part, and the service very solemn.

The questions put, and the answers given by me, were as follows :—

"What leads you to hope you are a Christian?"

"Being deeply conscious that the office of the Christian minister demands as an essential qualification a personal experience of Christian grace, I will endeavour to give a concise statement of the grounds on which my hopes of being a Christian are built. I had the privilege of Bible-class instruction in my youth, and have reason to trust that that instruction was blessed in leading me to feel my need of Christ as my Saviour, and in leading me to trust in Him. I was unexpectedly brought away from my godly teacher to this city, and in mercy led to this house of prayer. Here, through the ministry of God's Word, and intercourse with Christian friends, I have been led to make surrender of my heart to God, and to devote myself, as He may direct, to His service.

"I conceive the Word of God is the only standard by which to judge of Christian experience. In this I find it declared that no man can be a Christian until he is born again; that if any man be in Christ, he is a new creature; that a Divine life must be imparted to the soul, and that the evidence of that life will be seen in a corresponding change of feeling and conduct both towards God and man. I hope I know something of this change. I feel in my nature many things opposed to God's will and law; but on the other hand I feel emotions of love to God, and find my chief happiness in trying to love and serve Him. As these are the dispositions produced by the regenerating influences of the Holy Spirit, I would hope I am a Christian.

"Again, the Word of God declares that a Christian places his entire acceptance with God and pardon on the merits alone of the Lord Jesus Christ. I know the tendency of my nature towards self-righteousness, yet I do trust with humble sincerity on the righteousness of Christ for pardon and acceptance. Christ's life, and death, and life in glory are my only trust.

"Day by day I desire to have His wisdom to guide, and His love to help me, so that I may love and serve Him. I therefore trust I may conclude I am a Christian."

"What has led you to think you are in the path of duty called to labour in the ministry of the Gospel among the heathen?"

"This question I consider of much importance. It would be sad, indeed, to go forth to this work without the abiding conviction of being sent by God. My prayer has been, 'Lord, lead me in the way of Thy own appointment; and unless Thy presence go up with me, carry me not up hence.'

"It is the duty of every true Christian to live in some service for Christ, his King and Saviour; but in reference to the particular call to preach the Gospel to the heathen, I have endeavoured to know God's will, by marking the concurrence of desires and convictions which He has inspired with the events of His providence.

"I have reasons, now, after some four years' service, to think God is calling me to this work.

"My particular interest having been excited towards missionary work, I made it known to my pastor, the Rev. A. Tidman, who received me with kindness, and gave me encouragement. By him, in due time, I was introduced to the Directors of the London Missionary Society, and was accepted for the work. After the usual period of instruction under the Rev. R. Cecil at Turvey, I was fully accepted by the London Missionary Society, and have been appointed by the Directors as missionary to the South Sea Islands. In this review of God's gifts and guidance, I think I am in the path of duty in going to the heathen."

"What are your views of the doctrines of Scripture?"

"I believe the Scriptures are a revelation from God, giving a knowledge of Himself and of His will; written by men of God, inspired by the Holy Spirit. The character of the men, the circumstances under which they wrote, the revelations they make, the miracles they performed, and the prophecies they made lead me generally to this belief.

"I believe from this sacred record in the existence of one God—Infinite and Eternal—the only Creator of all things, and the only Lord of Providence.

"I believe, according to the Scriptures, in the Three Persons in the Deity, as Father, Son, and Holy Spirit; but as the Scriptures are silent on the nature of this mysterious union of Three in One, it can only be a matter of faith.

"I believe that God created man in holy, happy, intelligent likeness to Himself. That man in that state was a free, voluntary being—his will and his affections being left to their own free, unconstrained, and accountable exercise.

"I believe that man continued in this holy, happy state of innocency but for a short period; that, willingly yielding himself to the influences of temptation, he disobeyed God's commandments, and rejected His government. In this act of rebellion, I believe, were all the principles of disobedience, and that by it the whole human family were naturally and practically involved in transgression, condemnation, and ruin, and utterly helpless, so far as regarded self-recovery and self-regeneration.

"I believe the Scriptures reveal the plan of God's own mercy; revealed, at first, through the introductory dispensation of Moses and the Prophets, until the coming of Jesus Christ, the Divine Redeemer.

"I believe the Scriptures declare that in Jesus Christ were united the perfect natures of God and man; that by His obedience to God's law, and by His death, He at once became man's sacrifice and righteousness; and by His resurrection the hopes of Christian faith are established, and the justification of the penitent sinner is sure.

"I believe that to be savingly interested in this great salvation men must be convinced of personal transgression, and trust alone on Christ by a living, loving faith. This is, in every instance, the effect of the operation of the Holy Spirit on the mind and heart, and that all such will, through grace, persevere unto perfect redemption in heaven, through Jesus Christ, to the glory of God the Father."

"How do you intend to prosecute your labours among the heathen?"

"In looking forward to the field of labour, and viewing the vastness of its extent, the nature of its duties, and its sacred obligations, my heart has often trembled, and asked, 'Who is sufficient for these things?' And nothing but the conviction that I am in the path of duty, and that my sufficiency is of God, would induce me to go forward in so sacred a work.

"Depending on God's help, it will be my duty to acquire

as good a knowledge of the language of the people as possible, so as to preach, and teach them, the truths and the doctrines of God's Word; so unfold to them these truths as to lead them to abandon idolatry, and to accept the one God of Revelation, and the Lord Jesus Christ as the only Saviour. I hope also to pay good attention to the education of the young, both in secular and religious matters. In the acquisition of the language, I hope to be much aided by our excellent friend and father, the Rev. John Williams, while on the voyage.

"In the administration of the ordinances of the Gospel, I hope to be preserved from all superstitious rites and ceremonies.

"I trust my constant desire will be to live and labour in peace and co-operation with my brethren, and to pay deference to the counsel and the judgment of those whose age and experience claim such deference.

"I hope ever to remember that consistency of character and conduct will be required of me in all things; that justice and mercy, temperance and chastity, patience and humility, are graces and virtues which should be ever reflected in daily life among those where I am to labour; and I hope, by God's mercy and help, so to be enabled to do, and to be persevering and faithful unto death.

"Having made these statements, permit me to address especially those connected with this church and congregation, asking an interest in your prayers and a continuation of your affectionate sympathy. Some of your number are already in the ministry of the Gospel, and may many others be raised up. May the constant presence and blessing of God give you peace and prosperity, and to Him be all praise for ever. Amen."

As usual, in those days, I received a Certificate of Ordination, signed by the ministers who took part in the service. The following is a copy:—

"This commendatory epistle is a testimony to all into whose hands it may come, that William Gill, of London, has prosecuted the studies both of human and Divine literature, and, from his known piety and good morals, has been introduced into holy orders, and, moreover, agreeably to the discipline of the Reformed Churches, by prayer, and laying on of hands of the presbytery, was publicly ordained to the office of preaching the Gospel among the worshippers of false gods.

"Given in Latin and English.

"London, October 12, 1837.

"Arthur Tidman, Pastor.
"Richard Cecil, Tutor.
"William S. Palmer, Pastor.
"Nun Morgan Harry, Pastor.
"James Drummond, Pastor.
"John Hunt, Pastor.
"Charles Mead, Missionary.
"John Arundel, Pastor, and Secretary to L. M. S."

Engagements before Sailing.

After my ordination, unforeseen circumstances detained the Rev. John Williams. One or two ships had been seen, but up to the end of 1837 not one could be definitely fixed upon. At length the "*Camden*" was bought—a West India packet ship of some 250 tons burthen. Various engagements and preparations for the voyage occupied us until April, 1838. During these five months of waiting I was constantly engaged, sometimes attending meetings and preaching for the London Missionary Society, and at other times preaching for ministers in London, and elsewhere. Besides visiting Turvey again, and preaching at Andover, Whitchurch, Merton, St. Neots, Bedford, and Gravesend, in the country, I preached in London; at Stepney Meeting, Old Ford, Bread Street Chapel, Orange Street Chapel, Adelphi Chapel, Honduras Chapel, Horselydown Chapel, Queen Street Chapel, and Barbican and Union Chapels.

On the 1st of April, 1838, I took farewell publicly of the friends at Barbican Chapel. Morning attended the service, Rev. A. Tidman preached; afternoon I had a meeting with the whole school, and in the evening I preached my farewell sermon at Barbican Chapel. Text, Phil. iii. 8, "The excellency of the knowledge of Christ."

Thus was brought to a close eight years of the most happy and important period of my life, conspicuously manifesting the will and love of God in providence and grace.

Departure of Mission Ship "Camden."

The visit of Rev. John Williams to England, during 1835 to 1838, was one of those events which God overrules for the revival of the Church's interest in foreign missions. Mr. Williams had for sixteen years been honoured to extend Gospel missions from the Tahitian Group onward to the Rarotongan and the Samoan Groups, and his narrative of his work, especially in the Rarotonga Island, had been most interesting. Now he was about to return, and was desirous of opening up the groups of Western Polynesia to Christian missionaries. The Directors of the London Missionary Society had resolved to reinforce the mission. Already (in 1835) the Society had sent out the Revs. Murray, Hardy, Mills, Branden, Macdonald, and Heath to occupy the Samoan Islands, recently opened by native teachers. And now, on his return, he was accompanied by Revs. Day, Charter, Royle, Stair, Stevens, Johnson, Thompson, Joseph, and myself.

On the 11th of April, 1838, we left London. Crowds of Christian friends met on London Bridge early in the morning to witness the departure of the "*City of Canterbury.*" This vessel conveyed some 500 friends, with our missionary party, to Gravesend, where the "*Camden*" was at anchor.

CHAPTER V.

1838—1839.

VOYAGE OF THE "CAMDEN."

THE parting with parents and friends was indeed trying, yet there was much to cheer and sustain us. On reaching Gravesend our missionary party was arranged on the after part of the deck of the steamer. Hymns were sung, prayers were offered, and a short address was given. Then came the ordeal of shaking hands and bidding farewell to special loved ones. My dear pastor, and dear brother George, and dear Mr. Devonshire were the last to leave us.

That evening we went as far as Herne Bay, where we cast anchor for the night. The Rev. E. Prout remained with us, and conducted our evening devotions.

On the morning of the next day we again set sail, and reached Dover. Many ministers and friends came on board; and, after many expressions of their sympathy toward us, we held a special service of prayer, and bade them farewell.

On the following morning the pilot left us. By him we sent letters to dear parents and friends.

Some of the letters written by my dear wife at this time, and on many subsequent occasions during the voyage, and while on our station, I have preserved, and desire that they may be copied in this record of our mission life.

The first letter she wrote was when we were off Plymouth, April 14th, 1838.

"MY DEAR MOTHER,—

"As Mr. Prout, who has accompanied us hither, is going on shore, it gives me an opportunity to write just a line, and, from the giddiness I feel in my head, it must indeed be short. I am thankful that I am so well. I suffered yesterday, and the day before, but to-day am much better. I hope, my dear Mother, you have been sustained and consoled in the surrender you have so willingly made. I can say I am quite happy in the prospect that is before me. The struggle in parting was great, but I trust we shall all have reason to rejoice that it was put into our hearts thus to go. The Captain says we have accomplished in three days what ships are often three weeks in doing, that is, getting to Plymouth. Now we have almost a calm, and its comparative ease has, after our illness, set us up again. This morning we had worship on deck; we shall be with you in spirit at to-morrow's services. Be not unhappy on our account. God will still be gracious toward you and us."

* * * *

"Dartmouth,
"*April* 17*th*, 1838.

"My dearest Mother,—

"You will be surprised when you open this to find that we are once again on British ground. On Saturday morning I wrote a line. In the afternoon the wind changed, and the Captain thought it desirable to put into Dartmouth Harbour. On Sabbath evening Mr. Williams and two or three others went on shore, and on Monday several others. Afterwards Mrs. Joseph, Mrs. Day, and myself came on shore. I never would have believed that I should have felt so little fear in a small boat more than a mile from shore. There were many friends to welcome us. I have often heard of Devonshire hospitality, but little expected to experience it so fully in this way."

We remained at Dartmouth until Wednesday evening, when the wind becoming fair, we went on board, bearing with us most grateful recollections of much kindness and refreshing help of Christian friends there.

The following week most of us very, very ill, and were only relieved after we had crossed the Bay of Biscay, on the 24th of April.

On the 26th we were so far recovered and cheerful as to decide on daily plans for study and recreation. We agreed to assemble for worship at eight a.m., to be in class with Mr. Williams for languages at ten a.m., to dine at one p.m. Meet Mr. Williams to read Rarotonga, at three p.m.; to close by singing a native hymn; to take tea at six p.m., and to meet for worship at eight p.m.

This plan was pretty closely adhered to during the whole of the voyage; and, in addition, I commenced translating Watts's "Catechism" into the Rarotongan language, being anxious to gain as much knowledge of the language as possible, so as early to commence my work on the island.

On the morning of April 28th we were off Madeira; Sunday, 29th, off Porto Santo. Had public service on deck, at which we all gathered for the first time since we came on board.

Porto Santo is a small island; it has seven mountains; the highest rises some 2,000 feet.

On May 2nd contrary winds and currents in calms had taken us more eastward than we desired; but we find by observations we are 170 miles from the north-west coast of Africa. This evening commenced a weekly prayer-meeting for all on board who can attend.

On the evening of the 3rd of May formed ourselves into a *church meeting*, with a view to the commemoration of the Lord's Supper. We numbered twenty-eight members. Besides the missionaries and their wives, there were Mr. and Mrs. John Williams, jun., Captain and Mrs. Morgan, the chief mate, the second mate, the steward, the steward's mate, and one of the crew. These Communion meetings were held monthly during the voyage, with the best results.

On May the 5th had a good view of the "*Peak of Teneriffe*," rising 12,000 feet. A belt of cloud encircled it about half way, the other half appearing as in the sky. The weather was very fine, the vessel sailing eight knots an hour, and the thermometer standing at 71°.

Sunday, May 6th.—This was a day of solemn interest. Rev. W. Day preached in the morning, Rev. M. Charter in the afternoon, and in the evening the whole company assembled, and twenty-eight communed in the Lord's Supper; Mr. Williams addressed the communicants, Mr. Stevens addressed the spectators.

Early in the afternoon the poor native Marquesan man died. He had been ill many days, but we had hoped he would have been spared and have been blessed by Gospel truth, so as to have been made a blessing to his countrymen. But God had otherwise ordained. As far as we could we endeavoured to make known to him Jesus the Saviour. On Monday morning, 10.30 a.m., we committed the body to the sea; the ship's bell tolled a quarter of an hour before the service, Mr. Williams gave an address, a hymn was sung and prayer offered; the day was one of much sacred interest, and, we hope, of usefulness to all on board.

Monday, May 7th.—This evening we held a missionary prayer meeting, remembering the missionary meeting about to be held in England, the chief mate and one of the missionaries engaged in prayer, and I gave a missionary address.

Notes from Diary.

"May 10th.—In Lat. of Jamaica, and had many special memories of my dear friend Henry Russell, who is labouring there for Christ; God keep and bless him. We shall not meet again till in heaven we recount the wonders of God's providence, and celebrate the riches of His love."

"May 12th.—Ther. 77°. Wind very high, sea very rough, E. and I very ill. Last night one of the most wearisome nights on board."

"May 13th.—The sea calm, weather fine, all our friends much better. This morning Mr. Joseph preached, and this afternoon I preached from 1 Peter, chap. i., verse 8, 'Whom having not seen, ye love.'"

"May 14th.—We had a little sport to-day in fishing. The heat very trying. Still in the midst of all I wish to improve time, and to-day commenced compiling a Dictionary of Rarotongan and Tahitian words with English meanings. This exercise was useful, and of much value in after-days."

Speak with a Ship at Sea.

"May 24, we crossed the Equator. At noon we were only twenty miles north, and in afternoon were south. Instead of the usual follies observed on board ship on such occasions we, with full consent of all the crew, made the day an occasion of cheerful thankfulness. A holiday was given to the men; nothing being done but that which was needed."

An entry on the voyage thus far made is as follows:— "We have had a favourable passage; rather slow, but no storms, and not more than forty-eight hours' calm. We have not had to use much salt meat. Our health and cheer have been good, better than we could expect on board ship. I am deeply conscious of affection towards England, and dear friends and relatives there; yet it seems strange that there should be so little sorrow or sadness at leaving them all. Surely God has answered prayer, and we should offer grateful praise."

"June 5.—This morning, while at breakfast, we were much excited by the announcement of a ship, about two miles off. The captain hoisted a signal, expressing desire to 'speak' with her.

"It was a cheerful sight, though rather dangerous—so it seemed to us—to see the vessels come so near each other, and then 'lay to.' The large ship, an American whaler, 450 tons, crossed the stern of our little vessel, about twenty yards distant. While the vessels were slowly passing each other, questions were asked and answered by means of ship trumpets, such as—What ship that? Where from, and where bound? We then asked if the captain would take letters, and he, consenting, came on board, and afterwards some of us visited his ship. This was our first venture in a small boat. We found it had been out thirty months. The whaler had no passengers; but thirty-two men as crew. There were two Italians, two West Indians, and four native Marquesans. We gave a supply of tracts, and talked to many of the men about our mission to the heathen, and urged them to attend to religious concerns. All were kind to us, and many seemed much pleased with our visit. We returned to our vessel, and the captain of the whaler returned to his, taking letters that were ready for England. He promised to report our progress and welfare in the 'Missionary Reporter,' on his arrival in America. This exchange of friendship was a pleasant recreation to us."

Progress in Native Dictionary.

During most of the time I had been able so to work on the Dictionary as to complete the letter "R." It required much patience and perseverance to plod on in the work. The doctor sometimes used to scold me for being in the cabin so much. He said *too* much, and sometimes would darken the "bull's-eye light;" but I generally kept my work within the appointed time.

The form of Dictionary was as follows:—

English.	*Rarotongan.*	*Tahitian.*
FAITH	AKARONGO	FAAROO.

CHAPTER VI.

ARRIVAL IN AFRICA.

A LONG, but not unpleasant, voyage of twelve weeks brought us off the Cape of Good Hope. It being the stormy season, the captain decided to double the Cape, as the wind was fair, and made for "Simon's Bay." On Sunday morning, July 1st, at 5.30, we were gladdened by the announcement of being *near land*. On going on deck, it appeared to us that we were dangerously near. The perpendicular mountains rose majestically out of the sea, and soon surrounded us, giving us a placid lake in which to cast anchor. The effect was most exciting and charming. Simon's Town looked very pretty, like an English sea-side village, only that the houses had flat roofs.

We had scarcely cast anchor when an officer from the flag ship, stationed in the harbour, came off to us, and demanded the style of passengers, and cargo. On being answered, "Missionaries and Bibles," he appeared quite confused; but being assured such was the case, he made an official entry as such, and we were then at liberty to land.

As soon as possible the whole ship's company were assembled for a service of thanksgiving to God for His goodness and care bestowed upon us thus far, and to seek His guidance and blessing during our stay.

A letter from my dear wife to her parents will show her feelings up to this date:—

"*June* 27*th*, 1838.

"It is with mingled feelings I now write to you. I feel what it is in reality to be separated from those who are so dear. I cannot sometimes restrain tears of affection, but I know it is possible for nature to weep, while at the same time the spirit has not one feeling of regret, yea, can even rejoice. I do rejoice that God has counted me worthy to be engaged in this embassy of mercy, and my constant prayer shall be, that He may be glorified in us and by us at all times. When I am sometimes depressed on your account, the remembrance of that willing surrender you were enabled to make of one so dear to you alleviates my distress, and dispels all gloom. I am assured the same grace that was imparted, in circumstances so trying, will now, in an eminent degree, be made manifest in binding up the wounded spirit, and pouring the oil of joy into your hearts. You, my dear mother, will feel anxious to know something about our voyage, and to you every incident will be interesting. On April 18th we took leave of our kind friends at Dartmouth. The same day we passed 'Eddystone Lighthouse'—this was my last long look at dear old England, and we felt that we were fast hastening from our country and friends. It is cheering to know that our Divine Friend is with us, and that, while He is the 'confidence of the ends of the earth,' He is the same to those 'afar off upon the sea.' This promise is being verified in our case, for, from the time we left until now, we sing of His mercy and goodness. We have had service twice every Sabbath, and in the evening a prayer-meeting. I have wished my dear mother present many times, just to witness our little assembly numbering about forty persons. We have also a prayer-meeting every Wednesday, and Church members' meetings once a month. These often prove seasons of refreshing. The day we crossed the equator the men had a holiday, and in the morning Mr. Williams gave an address from the Ps. clxvii., 23, 24—'They that go down to the sea,' &c.

* * * *

"On Sabbath morning, July 1st, we were told *land* was in sight. None but those who have been at sea can form an idea of the interest such a sound produces. We were soon all on deck. In the afternoon, about half-past four, we dropped anchor in 'Simon's Bay;' a small boat, belonging to the Government, came off to see who we were, and to make inquiries about our cargo. When Mr. Williams told them it consisted of Missionaries and Bibles, the officers smiled and took their departure. In the evening Mr. Williams and several others went ashore, and Mr. Williams preached in the small chapel; those who remained on board held our usual service. Monday we all went on shore, and it would be impossible to describe my feelings. I had felt very anxious to go, as though I should see some face I knew; but all were strangers; either Dutch, or coloured people; very few English. We went to the house of a Dutch gentleman, where we met with a cordial reception. We then took a long walk, which was very refreshing after being confined on board ship nearly three months without any exercise. We climbed one of the mountains and had a beautiful view of the surrounding country; it was indeed magnificent. In the evening we went to the chapel; it is a neat pretty place, but there was a small congregation. I closed my eyes several times and tried to imagine myself in Barbican, as they sang several hymns and tunes which we used to sing. Mr. Stevens opened the service, Mr. Day preached, Mr. Johnston gave out the hymns, and William concluded. Tuesday we left Simon's Town for Cape Town, twenty miles distant. Mr. Williams had gone the day before in order to send conveyances. We had two vans, each drawn by eight horses. On the way we called at an inn called '*The Shepherd of Salisbury Plain.*' The landlord was an Englishman, and was pleased to see us. The first part of this journey, on the sea beach, was thoroughly delightful. We met a great number of negroes working on the road, and also some convicts. At Cape Town we were met by the Rev. Dr. Phillip, and Mrs. Locke and others; we dined, and then went to our respective places of temporary abode. It was my intention to send more letters with this, by a vessel that is leaving for England to-morrow. I did not like to let the opportunity slip, so you will see that this has been written in a hurried manner. The first part I had commenced at sea. Remember us to all friends, and that peace may reign in your heart continually is my constant prayer.'

* * * *

My journal refers to these particulars in the following summary:—

Cape Town being twenty-four miles distant, we could not send to Rev. Dr. Phillip that night, so many of us landed at Simon's Town, where we attended the Wesleyan Mission chapel, and made ourselves known. We were most kindly received, and Rev. Mr. Williams preached.

After service a Dutch gentleman-farmer and merchant took us to his house, gave us supper, and supplied us with all information needed for our journey to Cape Town. We then went off to our ship for the night.

Early the following morning, Mr. Williams hired a conveyance to take him to Cape Town to announce our arrival, and to arrange for our accommodation. We supposed we might remain two or three weeks before proceeding on our voyage. During the day we rambled up the mountains, saw a Hottentot village of native "kraals," and in the evening held a missionary service in the Wesleyan chapel.

Next morning two waggons came from Cape Town to take our party and baggage there. Each waggon was much longer than our English waggons. Our drivers were young Hottentots. The first seven miles was by the sea, on a wide sandy beach. We crossed the beds of two rivers, which, in the rainy season, are often impassable. At one place we saw heaps of bones of whales and cattle, which had been devoured by the wolves—said to meet here by hundreds at night.

Reach Cape Town.

About three miles on our journey from the sea-beach we came to a roadside inn. We were much amused at the sign of this inn—a painted figure, called "The Gentle Shepherd of Salisbury Plain." Underneath the figure were these lines:—

"Life's but a journey; let us live well on the road,
Says the Shepherd of Salisbury Plain.
Multum in parvo! Pro bono publico,
Entertainment for man and beast in a row.
Lekher kost as much as you please;
Excellent beds, without any fleas;
Nos patriam fugimus! Now we are here,
Vivamus, let us live by selling of beer.
On donne à boire et à manger ici,
Come in and try it, whoever you be."

We were amused much at this learned exhortation, and availed ourselves of lunch at the inn. The landlord had lived here twenty years. He was much taken with our party, and served a good lunch, but we thought him rather high in his charges. Leaving this place we found the road much better than the former part, and we reached Cape Town at 4.30. Here we were met by Rev. Dr. and Mrs. Phillip.

It was with some difficulty that accommodation was provided for our large party, but at length all were located, as comfortably as could be, in houses of friends more or less in sympathy with our Mission.

Cape Town and its Population.

Cape Town is a larger and prettier town than we had expected to see. The streets are built at right angles, very wide, having deep rows of trees on either side, and streams of water flowing towards the sea. The houses are generally three stories high, and the rooms large and airy. There are about 13,000 inhabitants; a large number are Dutch and half-caste. For the English and Dutch speaking people we found an English Episcopal church, and a Lutheran Dutch church, a Dutch Reformed church, and Wesleyan, Independent, and Scotch chapels.

We were surprised to find so little Christian sympathy and effort made to meet the ignorance and degradation of the native population of the town. There is no church or chapel for them, so far as we could learn. Recently one excellent man devoted himself as missionary to their welfare; and it is to be desired that the formal, cold, proud, distant way in which English and Dutch Christians treat the poor Malays and Hottentots and negroes may soon be exchanged for spirit and conduct more consistent with the temper and aim of Christianity. We visited some Hottentot villages near Cape Town, but the people there are distinct from those of the town.

I preserved the following letter sent to my parents—

"*July 15th*, 1838.

"My dear Father and Mother,—

"I did not expect another opportunity of writing, but this morning Captain Ramsey, a most devoted Christian, called to say that he is to leave to-morrow morning at sunrise, and would gladly take charge of letters, at the same time promising that Mrs. Ramsey should call and see you.

"It is Sabbath evening, and we are all lodging at a house where there are but few conveniences for writing, but I feel confident that a letter will be acceptable. You will have heard of our prosperous voyage hitherto. Truly God has answered prayer which has been offered on our behalf. The comfort of our voyage, I think, can never be surpassed, and the winds and the waves have indeed been commissioned with our safety, and we would rely with implicit confidence on the guidance of Him who has so mercifully performed all things for us. On Wednesday last we left Cape Town for Simon's Bay; the expense of lodgings induced us thus to leave earlier than we at first intended. Mr. Williams expected that our vessel would be ready to receive us, but, on our arrival, we found all in confusion and much more work to be done before we could set sail for Sydney. Therefore we have been obliged to engage apartments here, which are even more expensive than at Cape Town. Our visit, on the whole, has been good. We are all refreshed and strengthened by this stay on land, and we have found it good to hold intercourse with friends.

* * * *

* * * *

To-day is Sabbath, and we have had delightful opportunities of Christian services. This morning we attended at quarter-past nine the Wesleyan chapel, where we heard a young missionary of Cape Town; the subject was: 'To you who believe He is precious.' At eleven o'clock we left the chapel and went to the church, where we heard a truly good sermon from the Rev. J. Fraser, a devoted clergyman.

"This evening we again attended the Wesleyan chapel. Simon's Town is but a small place; it has about 18,000 inhabitants, most of whom are Malays, or Negro Hottentots, the other part Dutch. The moral condition of the place is very low; the cheap price of wine and beer is a great evil to the place. Wine may be had at fourpence per bottle, the best is but ninepence, and beer fourpence. You must send out more labourers—the world is given into the hands of the Church. If you could but see what we see here, I am sure you would think with me that England has not done its duty towards this colony. At Cape Town there is a standing army, with slaves; thirty-six are stationed at this small town, but only one preacher of the truth, and he so shackled that he cannot act as he would with the good people of the place. As a nation you are indebted much to Africa.

"We sail on Tuesday morning. May the good hand of our God still lead us. It is now midnight, I must close. I do not consider this a letter, though I shall mark it as one. Kindest love to you both. Be not unhappy about us. God is with us. All is well."

Leave Africa.

After nineteen days' rest, diversity, and recreation, we were glad to find ourselves again on board our ship-home. An addition to our number has been made by Mr. and Mrs. Buchanan, who had been engaged at Cape Town to proceed to Samoa to take charge of normal schools about to be commenced there. We could ill spare room for these friends in our already crowded vessel. But a cabin was fitted up for them in the forepart, and we made the best arrangements we could for their accommodation.

Our stores from England began to fail, and so great was the price of provisions at the Cape that we could not "lay in" all that we really needed.

While at the Cape we were in perplexity with some of the sailors, especially with two young men whose pious parents had gained for them situations on board our ship, hoping the influence would be of good to them. For some weeks before reaching the Cape they had manifested insubordination, and while there they behaved so badly that the captain was led to give them the dismissal they demanded. As missionaries we felt much for these young foolish men. But as passengers, we and the captain were put to the inconvenience of taking two others in Simon's Bay, who by their conduct gave us no little trouble and sorrow.

On leaving the Bay one of the ship's boats got adrift, and going after it in the darkness of night we were in danger, as the wind was high, the sea was rough, and sunken rocks were in our passage.

A Week's Incident of Calm and Storm.

Proceeding on our way nothing of unusual moment occurred to interfere with the ordinary routine of classes, exercise, and cabin duties until during the first week of August, when we were becalmed. Daily we had a large number of sea birds over and around the ship. Mr. John Williams, jun., succeeded in catching a fine molly-mauke, seven feet wide across the wing. After this capture the birds were more shy. One morning Mr. Williams shot a *Cape pigeon*, and in lowering the boat for it, Mr. Williams caught his hand in the ropes and the block, so that in an instant the nail and part of the third finger of the left hand were clean cut off. Before he could be got into the ship he had fainted, and thus the pleasurable excitement of the morning was turned into sorrow and anxiety.

The first Sunday in August, as result of God's blessing on our Bible-class with the crew, one of them wished to make profession of his love to Christ by uniting with us at the Lord's Table.

After a week's calm, we had a change in excess of wind, the ship sailed ten knots an hour, and the sea rose so high as to break over the bulwarks; some who were on deck, at one time, were in danger of being washed overboard.

A Fearful Hurricane.

The night of 8th August was one of utmost alarm and danger. During the day there had been warnings of the approach of a hurricane. The captain had taken the precaution to batten down all the hatchways, to avoid the sea waves rushing below as they broke on the deck. At four in the morning we were alarmed by the flooding of some fifty tons of water on the deck, and all was consternation. Every timber of our little vessel trembled with the bursting of each successive mighty wave. The only safety was in "heaving to," which, to do in such a storm, is considered dangerous. The captain decided to try, and, through mercy, succeeded. One of our sailors, an officer, reefing the sails, became exhausted, and for some time was in great danger. Never shall I forget just peeping up through the "companion staircase" on the boiling, surging sea; it rose mountain high, and the wind howled most fearfully. On looking in Mr. Williams's cabin, I found him sitting on the side of the berth weeping. He scarcely expected we should survive the storm. Passing the cabin of Rev. Thos. Joseph, I found him emptying his large sea-chest of its contents, intending, as soon as he found the vessel going down, to make the chest his coffin!

This storm continued three days and nights; all live stock on deck was washed away. But God in mercy kept us in peace and delivered us.

For many days after the storm we were much exhausted, especially our wives. We did not recover till we entered the "straits," a passage, which we took for convenience, between the coasts of Australia and Van Dieman's Land. Here we had days of fine weather, a fair wind, and much enjoyed the views of the coast of the mainland, and the evening breezes were generally laden with the most fragrant perfume.

CHAPTER VII.

ARRIVAL AT SYDNEY.

On the 10th September, just five months from England, we reached Sydney harbour, where we cast anchor for the night, and the next morning we moved up the cove to a position near the town. From the fulness of a grateful heart we endeavoured to give thanks to God for His constant care and sustaining love, and with loving constraint we made a renewed surrender of ourselves to His service.

Early in the forenoon of the 11th September we were gratified by a visit from the Rev. W. Crook, who was one of the *first* missionaries sent by the London Missionary Society to Tahiti. He came out in the ship "*Duff*." Arrangements were speedily and cheerfully made to receive us and our large party on shore free of charge to the Society.

Our denomination was then very low. The Rev. Mr. Jarrett had left for England, and most of the Independents were in fellowship with the Baptists, under the ministry of the liberal and worthy Rev. Mr. Sanders. Urged by the circumstances of the case, Mr. Williams and others were led to send a letter to the London Colonial Society, commending Sydney to the immediate consideration of the Committee, which led to their sending out the Rev. Dr. Ross, who, for many years, laboured so successfully there, both in the interests of the colony and the islands.

We were detained in Sydney longer than we had wished, awaiting the arrival of ships from England, which were bringing out many of our supplies. The delay, however, was most pleasantly employed in various ways of usefulness, in visiting the churches of the colony, and attending missionary and other meetings.

It fell to my lot to preach every Sunday during our stay and to attend two or three week-evening services.

We saw something of the degraded natives, and were sorry that no efforts had been made to improve their condition. Still more did it grieve us to see the wretched convicts from England. We visited their stations and preached to them.

Visit to Newcastle.

During my stay in Sydney, I visited the friend of my youth, George Alfred Lloyd. He was led to leave parents and friends. The departure was as painful as it was unexpected. One of those events we call mysterious; but God was ruling all.

Alfred had left Sydney, and taken a farm of 300 acres. His widowed mother had joined him on the farm, on the banks of the Williams River, which, at Raymond Terrace, near Newcastle, joins Hunters River.

October 1st found me on board a local steamer, voyaging about seventy miles along the coast to Newcastle. On the morning of the 2nd I was met by Alfred. At his log-house met again Mrs. Lloyd, who, during the past few years, had passed through much trial; but now happy, industrious, and hopeful.

Alfred had taken the farm on five years' lease. His first crops of Indian corn, wheat, and potatoes, &c., were growing, and he had in service eight convicts from Government.

Here I remained a week, visiting farms and taking services at the several stations. Frequently we were out late at night; returning, on horseback, through by-roads and forests. Tales of bush-rangers' outrages sometimes made us feel uncomfortable; but no harm befell us. Our stay there was one of peculiar interest. Often did we review the past of our life with gratitude and praise to God, and in the review we were encouraged to put our trust in Him whose presence would abide.

Early in the morning we left the farm; came in a boat to Raymond Terrace, where Alfred and I again parted. I took steamer at 9.30; reached Newcastle at 1 P.M., and arrived at Sydney at 11.30.

It was our good fortune to attend the *first* Sydney Horticultural Show—a beautiful display of flowers and fruits. Much of the society, and many of the customs and institutions of the place, made us feel as if we were in England; and our stay was doubly pleasant, after so long and tedious a voyage, and especially on the near prospect of our separation from all English society.

Our presence as missionaries in company with Mr. Williams created quite a stir in Sydney, and much interest was excited in all classes of the population in us and in our work. At our farewell missionary meetings the chapel was crowded to overflowing. The Governor was present, to whom Mr. Williams gave a copy of the first edition of the New Testament in the Rarotongan language, and nearly £400 was collected for the funds of the London Missionary Society.

Some ten days before we left, friend Alfred, to our joyful surprise, put in an appearance. He could not resist the desire to see the "*Camden*."

Leaving Sydney.

The 25th of October was to us a repetition of leaving England. The friends of all churches assembled in large numbers. Especial interest was also given to our departure, inasmuch as two excellent missionaries, Messrs. Hunt and Calvert, of the Wesleyan Missionary Society, had just arrived, and were proceeding as the first English missionaries to the Fiji Group. These brethren and their wives were going to the group in the little schooner, "*Letitia*." It was therefore arranged that the "*Camden*" and the "*Letitia*" should drop down to the Heads, seven miles distant, and that the London Missionary Society and the Wesleyan missionaries and friends should follow in a steamer. The largest vessel in the harbour was secured, and well filled with kind Christian friends; we proceeded to our respective vessels.

On leaving, the Baptist minister, whom we had learnt to love, gave out the hymn, "Jesus, at Thy command we launch into the deep." On reaching the "*Letitia*," another hymn was sung, and the Wesleyan minister offered prayer; then the brethren Hunt and Calvert went on board their little vessel. As they left us we sang, "Ye messengers of Christ." At 2 P.M. all our party were put on board the "*Camden;*" last farewells were spoken, and the steamer steamed round us, and while doing so we joined with them in singing our last hymn, "Blest be the tie that binds our hearts in Christian love."

SYDNEY TO SAMOA.

On leaving Sydney harbour the wind failed us, and, the ship drifting towards shore, the captain cast anchor. This was not unattended with danger in forty-five fathoms of water; but it was our only hope of safety from shipwreck. Thus we were all night; but the morning brought us a light breeze, and we were soon proceeding with a fair wind, but rough sea, towards the island.

During this part of our voyage notes from the journal record:—"October 29.—Have had a long talk with a lad from Rarotonga, brought from Sydney. I find, after all my reading and writing in the language during the voyage, that I shall have much to learn before I shall be able to preach to the people. I long to be there and mingle with them, and thus to learn the language."

November 1.—This forenoon fell in with a whaling ship—three months from Sydney, and had only obtained seven or eight tons of oil. We had recently seen a fine shoal of sperm whales. This we told the captain, who soon left us to go in the direction indicated.

November 4, Sunday.—This has been a day of much enjoyment. Mr. Johnson and Mr. Day preached from texts:—"Draw me, and I will run after Thee;" and "Open thy mouth wide and I will fill it." In the evening we held our Communion service. It has been a day of refreshing.

November 17, Saturday.—Calms and light winds continued till yesterday during all this week; we are now, however, sailing at eight knots an hour. On Wednesday we had a pleasant visit to an American ship. There we found a native of New Zealand, whose father was a native missionary. We were pleased to find he could read and write. We invited the captain, and as many of the crew as could leave the ship, to come on board to attend our missionary prayer-meeting. We also found a native from Tahiti, who well knew Mr. Williams. This friendly intercourse at sea was very pleasant. On the following day we fell in with another ship, having on board a native youth of Savage Island. Thirteen years ago Mr. Williams had visited that island; but as yet no entrance has been gained for missions. This youth was much interested in all he saw on board our ship, especially with the crew. He wished to remain with us, but the captain would not consent.

CHAPTER VIII.

ARRIVAL AT SAMOA.

NOVEMBER 23.—This morning, with lovely South Sea weather, and to our great joy, we made Tutuila, an island of the Samoan group. We entered Pangopango harbour. The scenery was most lovely; mountains on either side, some 3,000 feet high, and the sea of the harbour as smooth as a lake. We had not long cast anchor before seven or eight canoes came off to us, bringing the first South Sea Islanders we had seen in their native state. Alas! how degraded! What a contrast to the lovely scenes of land—"where every prospect pleases!" Most of the natives were naked: some few had leaves round their waists. As we looked at them we were much shocked, and were led to doubt whether such as these could ever be instructed and Christianized.

Here we were cheered to find our missionary friends Rev. A. Murray and wife. They had resided here about twelve months, and were just beginning to know the people and the language. Another missionary, Mr. Barnden, was located at Leone, about twenty-four miles distant.

Mr. and Mrs. Murray left England in November, 1835. An eight months' voyage brought them and their necessaries to Samoa, since which time they had had no English supplies. We found them in a most destitute condition—with health much impaired. The birth of their first-born had added to their trials. We cannot too highly speak of the patience and heroism with which our friends bore their trials, and the way in which they spoke of them.

Mr. Murray's was the only house at all fit for occupation. The native houses resembled the roofs of haystacks, with open sides; but, as this was the first mission station we had seen, we did our best to feel interested in the natives. But everything was so novel, and the semi-heathen state of the people more degraded than we had expected, that we felt the need of increased love towards them, and more faith to believe that they could become what we had heard the eastern islanders now were by the reception of the Gospel.

A day or two after our arrival we were invited to meet the chiefs and people. It was the occasion of a feast. Pigs were cooked, and there was an abundance of native fruits. Presents of native food and cloth were made to us, and the chiefs and people who had received the Gospel expressed their gratitude.

November 25, Sunday.—Our new circumstances had led us to anticipate with some interest the services of the day with the few—say 200—natives who then attended. The house used as a chapel had been built for heathen dancing. Most of us attended, but the service was rude and exciting. Many of the natives were all but naked, their attempts at singing were noisy, and the whole, to us, a jargon of an unknown language. I, with others of our number, was very weak and out of sorts; the sudden heat and change of climate—the closeness of the harbour, with mountains 2,000 to 3,000 feet high on either side—the interest and excitement in the novelty of the situation—and use of native food, had quite overcome us. As this was not to be our permanent resting-place, we were not sorry to leave it, and set sail for the Island of Upolu.

Upolu is a large island about sixty miles west of Tutuila. Here we were to leave some of our number, and to await the arrival of a vessel from Sydney which had been engaged to bring down the goods that the "*Camden*" could not bring.

November 27.—Landed at Apia, Upolu. The heat great. Thermometer 89° in the shade. On nearing Apia harbour Rev. Mr. Mills came to us, and gave us a gladsome welcome. He and all the missionaries were in a sad state of destitution, having had no supplies since their arrival. As

4*

soon as convenient we went on shore. A large round house—a "public building"—with open sides, was granted by the chief for our abode as long as we stayed. This house was about ninety feet round, having a fine thatched roof fixed on some twenty posts, and was situated only thirty or forty feet from the beach. It was resolved to divide its area into twelve compartments by divisions of green cocoa-nut branches. A broad space in the middle left us a dining-room and general hall. Under the circumstances this arrangement was pretty comfortable during the day, but at night was almost insupportable. What with the heat when the sea breeze left us, the very heavy rain-like dews, the spray from the sea, the roving about of pigs through the place, the clattering noise of land crabs, and the millions of flies, of which the sand seemed full, we dreaded the time to retire. But this we had to endure nearly six weeks. More than one of our number contracted illness from which they never got well.

December 2.—This morning an attempt was made to preach to natives of a heathen village near, but a hearing could not be gained. At 9 A.M. Mr. Barnden preached to about 300 natives outside our hall, and Mr. Murray preached in the afternoon to a greater number. Mr. Barnden preached in English to us in the hall; Isaiah xxxv. 1, "The wilderness and the solitary place shall be glad for them;" and in the evening we held a prayer-meeting. During the afternoon I took my Bible, and went alone some little distance inland, sat by the side of a fine stream, and there read, thought, gave thanks, and prayed. I tried to realize how many were our mercies; how strange were our circumstances in the presence of these heathen people; and how great the work before us! Our only consolation and hope is in the Lord our strength.

In a few days the whole staff of missionary brethren reached us from their various stations. They were Messrs. Mills, Murray, Hardy, Heath, Barnden, McDonald; Mr. Stair, printer, and Mr. Day.

December 4.—A meeting was held of all the missionaries at which the whole affairs of the Mission were taken into serious consideration, and several important resolutions were passed.

It is encouraging to notice at this early period of the Samoan Mission the good that had attended the labours of the native teachers; so that at the close of 1838 Rev. W. Murray, after two years' residence, was able to write the following interesting letter :—

"With regard to the conversion of souls to God, we are not without encouragement. Our little church consists of fifteen members, who 'adorn the doctrine of God their Saviour;' and many more are professedly, some evidently, under conviction. Among our members are several individuals who afford striking illustration of the power of the blessed Gospel to subdue and transform the vilest and most hardened of mankind. One man, named Tausaga, who formerly lived on Aunuu, a small island close to Tutuila, but who now lives here for the sake of the Gospel, was notoriously wicked—the terror of the place where he lived—the originator of wars—the fomenter of quarrels—the murderer of not a few, and the perpetrator of almost every species of wickedness. At our last church-meeting this person, who affords very unequivocal evidence that he has been created anew, was received into fellowship. It was a most interesting occasion. Almost all present had known him in his former character, and were deeply affected by the wonderful change that had been produced; affected with wonder and admiration at what God had wrought; and they rejoiced to welcome into their fellowship this 'brand plucked out of the burning.' To myself, also, it was deeply interesting and impressive to see with my own eyes those who so lately were hating and murdering one another weeping tears of joy 'over one sinner who had repented.' If there be joy in heaven at the repentance of one sinner in ordinary circumstances, with what emotion must the inhabitants of that blessed world have witnessed this scene!

"The case of another individual, named Taulagi, well deserves notice. The description given above applies pretty accurately to him, only he has been more extensively known, and has carried on his deeds of darkness on a more extensive scale. He is superior to Tausaga in point of talent, and is a much younger man. He is now a teacher, and will, I trust, soon be an efficient preacher of the blessed Gospel. Thus powerfully is the arm of the Lord revealed in this distant land;—revealed in such a way as to arrest the attention of the very heathen, and draw from them the acknowledgment that it must be the power of God, as nothing else could produce such effects.

"The case of another of the members of our little society, Matthew Hunkin, an English runaway seaman, is deeply interesting. I spoke of him in a former communication, as being in a hopeful condition; and I now rejoice to be able to state that ever since that period he has continued to evince the character of a Christian. He was formerly very wicked but is now, and has been for many months past, very decided in his piety; his efforts to promote the faith he once laboured to destroy are untiring. He acts as teacher at Vaitogi, a large settlement about nine miles from Pagopago; comes here every week for instruction; and receives an appointment for the Sabbath, along with the native teachers. His heart is very much set on missionary work, and he is, on the whole, very promising. One native has already been hopefully converted by his instrumentality; and the general influence of his conversion and subsequent conduct on the natives, and also on foreigners living on this island, has been of the happiest kind. O let us not fail to adore the wisdom and goodness of our gracious God in raising up this individual at a time when help was so much needed! and let us be encouraged, too, to persevere in our efforts for the salvation of the vilest and most hopeless of the human race.

"The death of Manga, the old chief who took us under his protection on our first arrival, will, I trust, prove an occasion of good to the island.

"We had hopes that his son Pomare would have succeeded him. Pomare might, indeed, have done so had he wished; but, by the grace of God, his heart is set on another Kingdom, and he pants after honours and distinctions of another kind than those connected with any earthly station, even the most exalted. His eyes have been opened to behold the glories of Calvary, and these have eclipsed 'the kingdoms of this world, and the glory of them.'

"But this will appear more clearly from an account of what transpired at our May meeting, which was held at Leone, on the last Wednesday of the month. The large chapel was quite crowded. After singing and prayer, several individuals successively addressed the meeting. The subject of Missions formed the leading topic, and many earnest appeals were made on behalf of those who know not the Gospel. Amuamu, a chief of considerable importance, formerly a great warrior, and the person who gave brother Williams such a cordial and spirited reception when he first visited Leone, said, 'Let us see that this meeting do not pass like our former May meetings, without any end (result or issue) to it. Let us go to work, and, if we live to see another May, let each come with his offering,—let it be arrow-root, cocoa-nut oil, cinet, native cloth or mats.'

"Pomare, after speaking on various points of interest, said, 'I will now disclose my own desire before this assembly, before God, and before the missionary. I have given my soul to Jesus to be saved by Him; with Him I leave it, and I now place my body at the disposal of the missionary. I am willing to go to any land of darkness to which He may send me. My desire is to die in the cause of Jesus, who was crucified for me. I wish to do the work of God, and I am willing to go to any savage land, or to remain in our own land. I leave it with the missionary; let him choose.' This language would have been affecting from any one; but from one who but a few days before had in his power the most exalted worldly station his native island knows, it came with peculiar weight. Nor was it the language of mere temporary excitement; for, after some days had passed, and having consulted with his wife, Pomare repeated the same sentiments in public, and also to me in private. His wife is a member of our church, and is equally devoted with himself. He is now, with several others, under instruction, and is very usefully employed in teaching and exhorting his own countrymen."

Christmas Day at Samoa.

December 25.—We were still in the native house on the beach, and ill prepared to persuade ourselves that it was Christmas Day. The heat was oppressive, and our social circumstances not much in harmony with an English Christmas. But the wives of the brethren who remained with us contrived to improvise something like a fair dinner for the day. It was resolved that, after dinner, two of the brethren, Mr. Day and Mr. Buchanan, should proceed to their respective stations. The former was proceeding to Faaleifaa, twenty miles distant, and I, glad of the opportunity of seeing the stations, accompanied him under the escort of Messrs. Hardy and Charter. We went in a canoe for six miles, when Mr. Hardy and I landed, and allowed Mr. Day to proceed outside the reef. Mr. Hardy proposed to walk to Faaleifaa, as a shorter way; but before we reached the midway village, Solusolu, the sun had set, and we were quite exhausted. Here we were obliged to remain. The memory of that night is still most vivid: the wild appearance of the natives, kind indeed, but unable to supply us with food we could eat; the hot damp air; the grass floor; and the swarms of mosquitoes. Alas! alas! our hall at Apia was bad, but this could hardly be endured. Seeing my exhausted state, the natives warmed me a cocoa-nut, and brought it me to drink, thinking it would be a substitute for tea; but the very appearance of it made me sick. I well remember a native by my side fanning me all night. The next morning the want of food and sleep had so reduced me that I was carried the remaining two miles to Faaleifaa on the shoulders of a naked native, whose body was much lubricated with oil.

Arriving at Faaleifaa, we found Mr. Day had landed in comfort last night, and, he having our stores, we soon had a good breakfast prepared. After rest and sleep, and *romi-romi-anga* of the legs and arms by a native—a very pleasant operation, akin to "medical rubbing"—I was soon restored.

Mr. Day was kindly received, and had hope of good success among the people. Mr. Hardy preached at three or four villages on our return, and also located native teachers. I was glad indeed to have seen the commencement of Christian work among this people. It gave me an insight into the dangers and difficulties which had to be endured. It impressed me with the necessity of a missionary becoming thoroughly acquainted with the language of the people, and it led me to feel that the hope of all successful missionary labour depended on more faith, and love, and patience than I possessed on leaving England.

December 31.—This last day of an eventful year was one of great sadness. Mr. Barnden, one of the most healthy, active members of this Mission, was drowned. I had gone bathing with him and Mr. Hardy; but, before I was undressed, Mr. Barnden had gone out of his depth. Mr. Hardy ran to his assistance, and I for further help, but it was too late. Our brother was unexpectedly cut off from his work, and the Mission has had to mourn the event. Good old Teava, the Rarotongan, was subsequently appointed to supply his place at Leone.

Our missionary ship "*Camden*" was too small to bring on all our goods to Samoa; it was therefore resolved to charter another ship to bring on those goods left at Sydney; hence our delay in Samoa. But that vessel not having arrived, we left our Samoan beach house, and gladly went on board our own ship—the "*Camden*."

For more than a week we were engaged in mission work among the Samoan Islands, locating missionaries, landing supplies, &c., &c., and on the 17th of January, 1839, were glad, indeed, and thankful to find that we were sailing direct for the Island of Rarotonga.

As I read the incidents of our stay at Samoa, recorded in my journal at the time, I am filled with praise for God's goodness and care, and especially for the advance now made at that Mission.

CHAPTER IX.

ARRIVAL AT RAROTONGA. 1839.

FEBRUARY 4.—It was a lovely South Sea morning. We made the westward of the island, and were thus prevented landing at Ngatangiia. Reaching the leeward off Avarua, we saw a boat coming toward us. The persons in the boat were all neatly clothed, and at first we supposed them to be foreigners; but they were native young men, with the exception of Rev. A. Buzacott and his son Aaron. It was most cheering to see Mr. Williams and Mr. Buzacott embrace each other, after some five years' absence, especially as we remembered that Mr. Williams had introduced Christianity to the island seventeen or eighteen years before. Those young native men were the first-fruits of the Mission. They had been brought up in the Mission schools, and in them we saw the transforming influence of Bible instruction, contrasting them so conspicuously with the heathens at Samoa whom we had so recently left.

The next day we landed at Avarua, and were kindly welcomed by Mr. and Mrs. Buzacott and family, and by the natives. The village was about a mile and a half long, consisting of neat lime-plastered, detached cottages, with gardens on each side the road, and in the middle of the village was a fine chapel. As we entered it we were filled with amazement that such a building should have been raised in these early years of the Mission. It had open pews, a gallery on all sides, and a fine pulpit; all the work of the natives, who, twenty years before, were in a heathen state. It was built to seat 1,400 people. The mission house was a small, neat, plastered building, having only ground floor arrangement, with no ceilings. As this house was too small to accommodate all our party, Mrs. Gill and I were domiciled in the chief's house in the settlement. It was indeed a South Sea palace, two stories high, with ten good bedrooms, and a large hall in the centre.

Makea, the chief, was a noble fellow; every inch kingly in person and in disposition. His redeemed state from heathenism was a grand reward to the missionaries.

The news of our arrival soon spread to all the stations of the island. Multitudes of natives daily came to the mission house to see Mr. Williams and the new missionaries, and to hear the many wonderful incidents he had to tell them of his visit to England—of the printing in England of the first edition of the New Testament in the Rarotongan language, which we had brought with us, and of our new ship, to be devoted to mission work.

A Messenger from Tinomana.

One afternoon, as we sat in the midst of some sixty or eighty natives, we were surprised by the arrival of a messenger from the chief of Arorangi, a village eight miles to the south of the island. As he entered, the assembly received him with great deference. He had come at great speed, and after a few moments' attention to his scanty toilet, and lustily using his large fan, addressing Mr. Williams, he said, "Blessings on you, Williamu. I have a message from Tinomana." "Blessings on you," replied Williams; "what may your message be?" He answered, "Tinomana sends his greeting to you, and he wishes to know whether you have fulfilled the promise you made to him when you left us for England." "What promise?" asked Williams. "You promised to bring out a missionary for Arorangi. Have you done so?" was the inquiry. Mr. Williams, pointing to me, said, "Yes. I have fulfilled my promise; this is he." Instantly the man arose, and gave utterance to his great joy, and said he could not be detained, but must hasten back to Arorangi to tell the good news to the people. We were told that he ran the whole of the way—that some hundreds of the people were assembled to watch his first appearance at the top of the mountain near the station, and to receive the sign of his success. Upon seeing the sign they burst into exclamations of gladness and praise. Surely here was a literal fulfilment of the prophecy, "How beautiful are the feet of him who bringeth good tidings," &c.

I quote from the "Missionary Chronicle" for April, 1840, the following notices of the arrival of the vessel in the Hervey Group:—

"The faith and hope of the churches will be refreshed by instances of the numerous manifestations of Divine mercy which the natives in that group continue to experience under the glad sound of the Gospel. It is generally known that the brethren Pitman and Buzacott, whose labours in Rarotonga for many years past have borne such abundant fruit, have been joined by two of the devoted missionaries, Messrs. Gill and Royle, sent forth with Mr. Williams in the '*Camden*.' The post assigned to Mr. Royle is the Island of Aitutaki, and Mr. Gill has taken up his station at Arorangi, in the principal island, Rarotonga."

Under date of May 11, Mr. Pitman thus writes:—

"Our spirits were highly exhilarated on the appearance of the strong band of missionaries sent out to reinforce our several stations. Welcome, thrice welcome, '*Camden*,' far more than if thou hadst been filled with pearls or diamonds! Sincerely do I pray that these brethren may all prove men of God, counting it their highest honour to live and die in the service of their Divine Master. Surely the powers of darkness must now tremble and gnash their teeth with rage. No doubt this is the case. They have, however, still possession of extensive territories—they are powerful, subtle, and malignant. They will not yield at a word, nor quit without a struggle their strongholds; for strong they are; but blessed be our Rock! they are not impregnable.

"We have every possible encouragement. The Captain of our Salvation leads the way. Shall we then shrink back when dangers threaten, and fear to follow such a Commander? Shall we for a moment despair of success? Despair! for ever let that word be blotted from the Christian soldier's vocabulary. Exercising faith in the Divine veracity, there is no occasion for distracting doubts and fears as to the result of this warfare, for, though I am no prophet, yet of this I am confident, that victory is certain, absolutely certain. It must be so as long as it stands written in the imperishable records of the King of Zion, 'Thus saith the Lord, The Lord reigneth; let the earth rejoice; let the multitude of isles be glad thereof.'"

Adverting to the missionary ship the brethren, in writing to the Directors, remark :—

"The holy zeal manifested by British Christians, in the purchase of the '*Camden*' for missionary purposes, was to us no small source of gratification. Glad, indeed, shall we be to hear that the aim of the Society in providing this vessel may be more than realized ; and that this may be a great means in the hand of God of introducing the Gospel of Christ to every island in the Southern Pacific. May 'Holiness to the Lord' be written on her sails as she traverses this extensive ocean."

The brethren conclude with a brief but comprehensive view of the general state of the Mission :—

"We are happy to inform the Directors that the Lord is still pleased to smile upon our feeble efforts, and to encourage us in our work. Our chapels and schools continue to be well attended, and many have been added to the church, whom we hope have tasted that the Lord is gracious. For the last few years we have been greatly tried in the afflictions of our poor people, and a great number have been called out of time into eternity. It is, however, a pleasing consolation to have hopes respecting the salvation of very many. As far as we have been able to ascertain their views, we cannot entertain a doubt, but to them death has been eternal gain. This will be as gratifying to you, as to us it is cheering and animating."

First Sunday on Rarotonga.

My first Sunday on the island—spent at Avarua—was one of great interest to me. Finding that an early morning prayer-meeting was held by the natives, I went to the chapel. Had I not known a word of the language, the sight of this service could not but be understood as indicating great progress and hope for the future. About 250 natives were present. A middle-aged native presided—a man who, twenty years before, was a warrior, notorious for his cruelty even in the midst of a cruel heathenism. He gave out a translation of one of our well-known Sabbath hymns, then he read a portion of the Psalms, and called on a native Christian of his own age to pray. Two other hymns were sung, and two other prayers were offered. Then the presiding native gave a short address, and closed the service. Three or four such prayer-meetings were conducted every Sabbath morning by the natives at the several stations on the island.

Next to the chapel stood the large and well-planned school-house. At eight o'clock on Sabbath morning 700 children were in it, each class of ten or twelve scholars having its teacher; a hymn was sung, prayer was offered, a short passage of Scripture was then repeated by one of the boys, and a few words of address given by the missionary, after which each class removed to the chapel.

It was a wonderful and overpowering sight, on this my first Sabbath on shore, to see this house of prayer filled with more than 1,600 native worshippers, with but few exceptions clothed in white native cloth; and to remember that only ten years before they were wild, naked heathens; but now subdued, and a goodly number of them thirsting for instruction which should still further dignify and bless them! Mr. Buzacott preached. After the morning service the Rev. H. Royle preached in English in Mr. Buzacott's house. Late in the afternoon, we attended another native service in the chapel, and, in the evening, held a meeting at Mr. Buzacott's house for special thanksgiving and prayer. This was a day of great pleasure—one of many such which we spent on the island.

Only next in interest and importance to the chapel and school buildings was the missionaries' house; with it I was much pleased. It was a neat, commodious, clean, home-like abode. The chief's house was a large, well-built, convenient dwelling, erected by the assistance of an American carpenter. It was well furnished with chairs, sofas, tables, and beds, and the floors covered with fine mats. As we looked at these things we endeavoured to realize the change which had been effected over this people and their habits, by the wonder-working, civilising power of the Gospel of Jesus.

Removal to Arorangi.

We had not been two weeks at Avarua when one morning, quite early, more than 200 men came from Arorangi to take Mrs. Gill and myself down to our station. I had wished to remain with Mr. Buzacott a month or two to make progress in the language, but the determination of the people could not be withstood; so, by the advice of Mr. Buzacott, we consented to go at once. Miss Sarah Buzacott—then about nine years old—went with us, and was of good service for some time as interpreter.

The journey from Avarua to Arorangi was quite a novel sight. A chair was fitted up for Mrs. Gill, and carried by the natives; then followed about 200 men, each one carrying some article. It must be remembered that at that time it was necessary to take out to the islands everything connected with housekeeping, together with furniture, clothes, and English food, sufficient for one or two years. Hence this array of stores, boxes, barrels, furniture, pots, pans, &c., &c. I brought up the rear, riding a horse lent for the occasion by Mr. Buzacott, the people singing, as we proceeded, songs of praise to God for the safe arrival of their missionary.

Arriving at Arorangi we were domiciled in the native teacher's house. Our goods were stored in two rooms, two other rooms were fitted up as bedrooms, and a wide space in the centre was used as dining-room and sitting-room.

A large but rudely built chapel stood in the middle of the village, and a school-house, almost as large, on the opposite side of the road. On Sunday more than 1,400 natives and young people were assembled. We were pleased to find two full services were conducted in the chapel every Sunday, and morning and afternoon schools held with the children. Two morning schools were held every day—at six o'clock for adults, and at eight o'clock for children.

It was most pleasing to find a people only twelve years old in Christian instruction so far advanced, and so prepared and willing to devote themselves to new plans for further improvement.

From the first day I mixed with the natives as much as possible, learning their language, and in less than three months after landing on the island it was my good fortune to read my first address to the people in the native tongue.

"April 28, 1839.—This morning I ventured to read my first sermon. Text, the true and faithful saying: 'Jesus Christ came into the world to save sinners.' I had read the

MS. to an intelligent native first, and was pleased to find that the people understood it pretty well. As I stood up in the midst of so large a congregation to speak in their language, my feelings were indescribable. Through the mercy of the Lord I read the sermon with some degree of composure and freedom, and was encouraged to hope that the people had understood most of what I said."

House Building.

We had not been long at Arorangi when Tinomana, the chief, gave us a good-sized piece of land on which to build a house. The people soon set to work, burning coral block for lime, and cutting wood for the frame of the building.

Availing myself of the assistance of Mr. Thomson, who was with us until he could proceed to Tahiti, I drew some plans for the house. It was raised three feet from the ground, was about one hundred feet long, and sixty feet wide; ground floor only; divided into seven or eight rooms, open to the roof. It had a verandah, six feet wide, front and back. The whole plan was an improvement on anything the natives had seen before. As it was being erected they were more and more interested in the building. It was my good fortune to take a supply of window glass with us—the first the natives had ever seen. When the front doors and windows were opened the wondering people came in great numbers to see its "kākā" (shining) at sunset.

The house took nine months to build, and really did great credit to the poor people, who had had no previous experience of such house building.

Those first months of labour were often very trying both to body and mind. Twice or thrice during the house building we were both ill. Every morning I went to the adults' and children's schools. Some hours each day were spent in attending to the sick of the station, and in preparing medicine. Three afternoons a week public services were held in the chapel. Adult classes—of church members and inquirers—were met three days a week by Mrs. Gill and myself. The work of the house had to be planned, and looked after. These labours, under circumstances of domestic discomfort, with frequent want of proper food, and the exhausting influence of a tropical climate, often induced weariness and sometimes illness. Ships were very unfrequent during those years. Sometimes six, eight, or twelve months would elapse between the visits of ships, especially at Arorangi station, where we lived. Besides the mission ship, I only saw four English vessels at the island all the years we were there. I remember at one time, during those early months, being so weak and undone that, had an opportunity presented, we should have felt justified in taking a voyage either to Tahiti (700 miles) or to Sydney (4,000 miles). But in our trial we sent a messenger to Avarua, and Mr. Buzacott came. He had had some twelve or fifteen years' experience, and was well able to advise. He kindly supplied us with proper medicine, and insisted that we should cease from all work among the natives for a month, and by God's blessing we were restored.

Attempts to teach English.

At this period of the Mission it was thought desirable to make an attempt to teach the youth of the island to read English, so as ultimately to give them the opportunity of studying English books. I went into this plan with zeal and confidence. A class of the most promising lads was selected, and some portion of every day was devoted to their instruction. But in less than a year the plan was abandoned as impracticable, not, I think, from want of ability in the lads, but from want of proper books to learn from, and our want of proper time to give to the study.

I have no doubt that, in the advanced mental improvement of the people, and on becoming more accustomed to Englishmen, many of the young men and women will acquire a good knowledge of English, but no amount of effort would result in its superseding the native language, as was thought probable by some of the Directors. One or two native girls and boys, taken entirely from their homes to reside in the missionary's family, have given good proof of the native ability to acquire an intelligent knowledge of English. A large number of young men who have had two or three years' service on board whaling and other ships, and others who have much to do with foreigners in the markets, find no difficulty in speaking or reading English.

In attempting to advance the young people in general knowledge, I felt the want of school material. Elementary lessons were given in astronomy and geography, which much interested the scholars, and led me to try my skill in map and globe making. A calabásh eighteen inches in diameter was procured, native cloth was pasted over the ends to make it in proper shape, and the whole was covered with writing paper; on this I marked in ink, with sufficient correctness, the continents, islands, and countries of the earth. This primitive instrument, varnished and placed on the pedestal, mightily astonished, and, in some measure, instructed the people.

Institution for Native Pastors.

About this time it was felt that an institution was needed where young intelligent Christian natives should reside under the care of the missionary, and receive such instruction as should prepare them for service as pastors over home churches and as evangelists to the heathen. The Directors had long been convinced that greater efforts should be made to diffuse the Gospel in the South Sea Islands, and other parts of the world, by means of native teachers and evangelists; and, acting upon that conviction, they determined, previous to the departure of the "*Camden*," to attempt a seminary at Rarotonga for the theological education of pious young natives, with a view to their engaging in the missionary work. The feelings with which the brethren Pitman and Buzacott received the views of the Board on this subject are expressed as follows in a joint letter transmitted by them, under date May 23:—

"The wish of the Directors to establish in the islands an institution for the education of young men of decided piety, to be engaged as teachers or pastors, and to qualify them as thoroughly efficient missionaries, we hail with great delight; and, as the Directors have fixed upon Rarotonga for the development of the plan, we hope it will meet with the Divine approbation and blessing. May it please God to qualify, by the powerful energies and special grace of the Holy Spirit, many suitable individuals for such a great and important work."

A suitable piece of land at Avarua was accordingly purchased of the chief. It was fenced round, and a number of detached cottages were built. Twelve or fourteen young men were admitted, and the institution has prospered. During the earlier years the subjects of study were mainly Biblical, sermon and essay composition, with portions of Christian work at the station. Two or three hours a day were devoted to varied works of carpentry, &c.

The new year, 1840, found both Mrs. Gill and myself gaining knowledge of the language, and increasing in interest towards the natives. Most deeply were we touched by the older people's description of their former life in heathenism.

In a letter to the London Missionary Society (January, 1840), of which the following is a copy, a report was given of the first effort of the natives at Arorangi to make contributions in aid of the London Missionary Society, and also some account of natives at work.

"One subject that occupied much of our conversation on our voyage was the importance of constantly urging on the attention of the native churches the duty of relieving the parent Society, and of presenting them with those high motives by which they should be induced, as Christians, to extend the blessings they themselves have received. Notwithstanding all their disadvantages, the members of the churches at Rarotonga have hitherto shown every disposition to discharge those high obligations under which they feel themselves laid both to the church at home and to the heathen round about us. Last year auxiliary missionary societies were first established on the island. One was formed in August last at Avarua, the station of Mr. Buzacott. It was truly an interesting scene, and strongly calculated to encourage the hope that, if their spirit of benevolence be matured by Christian principle, their subscriptions will, at some future time, be no inconsiderable item in the financial report of the Society.

"In September last a similar society was formed at this settlement, Arorangi. On the Sabbath previous to the meeting I took occasion to show the urgent necessities of the heathen, and our duty to render all the assistance in our power, taking as the foundation of my remarks the solicitous cry of the man of Macedonia for help, recorded in the Acts of the Apostles. Early on the day appointed for the formation of the society the chapel was crowded to excess. Services were commenced by singing a hymn celebrating the power and majesty of Jehovah as the only true God, after which prayer was offered for the Divine presence and blessing. Mr. Buzacott, who kindly attended, gave a brief historical account of the parent Society, the first declaration and subsequent prosperity of the Gospel at Tahiti, and the present state and extent of the Society's operations. To these statements the people listened with intense interest, and indicated by the expression of their countenances that their hearts were deeply affected. At the close of Mr. Buzacott's address, Papeiha, the first native teacher sent to these shores, showed that it was their duty to form a branch society to aid the parent Society at home; and, after expressing his hope that they would pay proper regard to that duty, proposed that Tinomana, the Chief of Arorangi, be appointed treasurer for the ensuing year. This being seconded by the elder deacon of the church, it was unanimously carried. The next proposition was that Setephano, one of the chief's sons, be appointed secretary, which was likewise carried; and after the parties proposed had expressed their assent, several other speeches were delivered. We subsequently adjourned to the school-house, the place appointed to receive the subscriptions, and invited the several teachers of the adult classes to bring the collective contributions of his class. Accordingly, each brought his basket of arrow-root, and we found at the close that the whole quantity amounted to 700 lbs. Those who contributed in money brought dollars, half-dollars, and quarter-dollars to the amount of fourteen dollars and a half. Afterwards a large quantity of miscellaneous offerings were presented, of little value in themselves, but pleasing to be received, as showing the disposition of the people, these being their only property. Among them were thirteen fowls, thirteen bundles of 'piere,' dried fruit, thirty-two small, neatly wrought native baskets, forty-two stones, used formerly in the wars, one basket of breast ornaments, and other heathen articles, seven baskets of various kinds of sea shells, by the poor children, and a great number of heathen ear-drops. These contributions remain in the hands of the treasurer, who will dispose of them to the best possible advantage, and forward the proceeds to the treasurer of the parent Society.

"The people with gladdened hearts sat down afterwards to a feast prepared for the occasion, many sincerely praising the Lord, and all counting themselves happy to have lived to see such a day. In the afternoon another service was held in the chapel, in order to give many an opportunity to express the feelings of their hearts, and to exhort one another to diligence and love in the work of the Lord. Twelve or fifteen speeches were delivered, which exhibited much humble gratitude and holy joy on the part of those who, prior to the introduction of the

Gospel, sat in darkness, and revelled in all that can be conceived as polluting and debasing.

"There was one old man present who had been a great warrior, and who in his heathen state seldom appeared *without human flesh hanging on his hook;* but who now, having obtained redemption by Christ, is washed and sanctified, and for many years has united with the faithful in commemorating the dying love of Christ. This poor man, having on his person many scars of his ancient sanguinary conflicts, referred our minds, in the course of the remarks which he made, to the years of darkness which he had witnessed, stating that he had 'lived to behold a new and a wonderful thing—the gathering together of the people to send the Word of the true God to the heathen. It is true,' he said, 'formerly we used to assemble, but it was either to plan attacks of murder, or to flee from attacks made by the enemy; either to devise schemes of theft and pollution, or to carry those schemes into execution. We then met in fear, and with hearts filled with envy and malice, and dared not to assemble our wives and children; but now the darkness has fled, and the true light of the True Sun has shone upon us—Jesus the Lord from heaven. The spears of our wars are lost, and we hold in our hand the sword of the Spirit—the Word of the Lord—we bring with us our wives and our children, and feel that our hearts are filled with love one towards another. We not only love those of our own settlement, but we love all, and are loved by all; and, above all, this day we have met to show our love to those who are as we were, living in darkness, having no God, and no hope; this is a new and a wonderful event, brought about by the great love of God.' After many expressions of gratitude to Divine Mercy, and exhorting others to cherish the same spirit, he most affectionately addressed the young, who listened with much attention, and I trust his exhortations will prove a word in season to many.

"Another old man, a candidate for church fellowship, said, 'I have lived during the reign of four kings. In the first I was but young; we were continually at war, and a fearful season it was—watching and hiding with fear were all our engagements. During the reign of the second we were overtaken with a severe famine, and all expected to perish; then we ate rats and grass, and this wood and the other wood, and many other unmentionable things. During the third we were conquered, and became the prey of the two other settlements of the island; then if a man went to fish he rarely ever returned, or if a woman went any distance to fetch food she was rarely ever seen again.' Here, after referring to many deeds of darkness to which he at that season had been eye-witness, he continued, 'But during the reign of this third king we were visited by another King—a great King—a good King—a powerful King—a King of love—Jesus the Lord from heaven. He has gained the victory—He has conquered our hearts; we are all His subjects; therefore we now have peace and plenty in this world, and hope soon to dwell with Him in heaven. We have done well to-day to meet to make known the fame of this King where the prince of darkness reigns, by sending them that Word of Life which made Him known to us.' Many other speeches were equally pleasing and grateful, as showing the sincere gratitude of the people, and their desire to communicate the source of their joy to others. Commending ourselves and our work to the blessing of Him who will not despise the day of small things, we dispersed with hearts filled with thankfulness and praise."

CHAPTER X.

THE REPORT OF THE MURDER OF REV. J. WILLIAMS.

WHILE pursuing our daily routine of duty, with but very little variety, save our growing interest in the natives and our work among them, we were cheered on the 15th of April by the arrival of a ship. It was the first to bring us letters since we left England. It was a rich treat to have a good supply of news from friends, and of books, papers, magazines, &c. But our joy was mingled with deep sorrow, for by that vessel we heard the report of the murder of our father and friend, the Rev. John Williams, and his companion, Mr. Harris. We had no letters of detail, but only the report of the captain and others. Some days after the arrival of the vessel we found more particulars in a Sydney paper.

In November last, a day or so before his death, he had written the following letter to the London Missionary Society, which will always be read with interest:—

"MY DEAR FRIEND,—

"Being on my way to New South Wales, where I expect to be fully occupied, I am employing my spare moments on board the '*Camden*,' in writing to friends whose many expressions of kindness have indelibly fixed them in the most sincere and sacred affections of my heart. Indeed, the very act of taking up the pen and commencing the letter conveys one in imagination to the place of sacred intercourse, brings you into actual converse with the beloved object of your communication, and calls to remembrance the interesting scenes that live only in the grateful recollections of kindred hearts. But I must not indulge in imaginative correspondence, or give vent to feelings in the expression of which I might speedily fill my sheet. I must recollect that I am nearly 20,000 miles away from you, engaged in a work which is near to your heart, which is constantly in your prayers, and to aid which your possessions are consecrated. Information, therefore, upon the progress of the cause of Christ in these islands, I feel assured, will be most acceptable to you; far more so than a volume of expressions of esteem for your person, or gratitude for your favours. I visited Rarotonga, and am happy to inform you that my truly excellent friend and invaluable brother, Buzacott, entered fully into my views respecting the college. He commenced it immediately with two, and has now eleven, students in it. A large piece of ground has been purchased of Makea, on which to erect the building, and there is every prospect of its succeeding to the extent of our most sanguine expectations. This is a darling subject with me, and I trust I shall live to see it in full and efficient operation. The ground cost 150 dollars. The truly good chief (who is since dead) would not have parted with it for ten times the sum for any other object; indeed, he would not have parted with it at all.

"I could fill my sheet with relating many delightful circumstances about dear Rarotonga; the truly affectionate manner in which the people welcomed me again amongst them; and how they scolded me for not bringing John and Mrs. Williams. The eagerness with which they received the Testaments would have cheered your heart could you have been eye-witness of the scene. The countenance of a successful applicant glistened with delight while he held up his treasure to public view; others hugged the book, while many kissed it; some sprang away like a dart, and did not stop till they entered their own dwellings and exhibited their treasure to their wives and children; while others jumped and capered about like persons half frantic with joy. You will recollect that none are GIVEN AWAY; those who had money to pay for them were the first supplied (the price was 3s.), and in a few days nearly £20 were brought into Mr. B.'s hands. The next were those who had dried bananas or nuts to pay for them; these my dear John was to purchase at the price of a book, and find a market for them where he could. The third class supplied were those on trust; and when some came whose characters were such as to cause some little hesitation, their appeals were pointed and affecting. 'Do let me have a Testament; do let me have the good Word of God; perhaps by reading it my heart may be made better.' Others who could not read, and were slack in their attendance at school, would plead and promise to do better. 'We did not know,' said they, 'that our eyes would ever have beheld such a sight as this in Rarotonga; we shall neither eat, drink, nor sleep if you do not give us the good Word of God.' These are but faint representations of never-to-be-forgotten scenes which occurred at this delightful island.

"At Borabora, too, a box of Bibles was landed by mistake at Mr. Rodgerson's house; the people heard of it, and made applications for them. Mr. R. replied, that Mr. Nott had given special orders that none were to be distributed till he arrived. They immediately exclaimed, 'How do we know that we may live till then! we must have the Word of God;' and much as they fear and respect Mr. R., they would have taken off the roof of his house had he not complied with their demands. You will be pleased to hear *they are paying for the Bibles* they are thus so anxious to obtain.

"The schools at Rarotonga are going on well, the congregations large, and the churches increasing; the only drawback is the great mortality still prevailing at this devoted little island. The deaths at Mr. Pitman's station alone amounted to 260 in one year, while the births were only 60; and at the other stations a similar decrease had been experienced. The good Chief Makea is gone. He was invaluable while he lived; his influence and power, great as they were, were given to God. He died most happy. I never knew a chief I loved so much, or thought so highly of. He will be a great loss to the Mission; but I am happy to inform you his son David is treading in his steps. Thus, my dear friend, we live in a dying world; perhaps this may not reach England before your happy spirit will quit its tenement of clay, and unite with that of my departed friend Makea in praising and loving that Saviour who redeemed you both by His blood. Ere long some friend will communicate to surviving relatives and connections the information of our death; the grand concern should be to live in a constant state of preparation. This I find a difficult matter from the demand incessantly made upon my energies both of body and mind; but I find great comfort from the consideration that many, very many of God's people pray for me, and also that *all* is spent in the *best* of *all* causes.

"I did intend to have said more about the Navigators Islands Mission than I shall have room for; but as I have written to dear ——, and intend writing to Mr. ——, I have requested them to make you acquainted with the contents of my letters; lack of information upon some points will be obtained there. Your invaluable present of books I have divided equally between the Rarotonga and Samoan Missions. Our friends at Rarotonga have not yet received theirs, but to the brethren at the Samoas I have given, I believe, about 180 volumes in your name, and they were to write a letter of acknowledgment to you for them. It is our intention to establish there also an institution for the education of pious natives; which induced me thus to divide your bountiful and invaluable contribution of books between the libraries. Oh, what a luxury it is to do good! what sound philosophy there is in the Bible! What a knowledge it displays of sanctified human nature when it asserts, 'It is more blessed to give than to receive.'

"You will, I know, rejoice with me when I inform you that my dear John is invaluable in the Mission, as is also his intelligent and excellent wife. He has charge, not only of the immediate settlement where he resides, but of ten others, preaching alternately at them, and superintending the labours of the native missionaries who are stationed there. Thus, while he is supporting himself by his merchandise, he is doing the work of a missionary among a population of six or eight thousand people. The great American scientific expedition came to Upolu a week or two ago; by the express wish of the Commodore, John has accepted the office of Consul for the United States of America. By this he will be able effectually to stop the vile and wicked seamen from running away from the ships, and check the wickedness of those on shore.

"I have just heard dear Captain Morgan say that we are sixty miles off the Hebrides, so that we shall be there early to-morrow morning. This evening we are to have a special prayer-meeting. Oh! how much depends upon the efforts of to-morrow! *Will the savages receive us or not?* Perhaps at this moment you or some other kind friend may be wrestling with God for us. I am all anxiety; but desire prudence and faithfulness in the management of the attempt to impart the Gospel to these benighted people, and leave the event with God. I brought twelve native missionaries with me; two have settled at a beautiful island called Rotuma; the ten I have are for New Hebrides and New Caledonia. The approaching week is to me the most important of my life. You would love our dear good captain if you knew him. He is a holy man of God. With sincere esteem,

"I remain, truly yours,
"J. WILLIAMS."

The official report had been sent in a letter by Captain Morgan to the London Missionary Society as follows:—

"DEAR SIR,—

"I have to communicate to you the painful intelligence of the death of your beloved brother and faithful missionary, the Rev. John Williams, who was massacred in the Island of Erromanga, one of the New Hebrides, on the 20th of November, 1839, and of Mr. James Harris, a gentleman who was on his way to England with the view of becoming a missionary to the Marquesas. The event happened the day after we left the Island of Tanna. There the natives received us most kindly, and Mr. Williams remarked he had never been received more kindly by any natives among whom he had been; his spirits were elated to find such a door of entrance opened. In the afternoon we left there three teachers and a son of one of them.

"We proceeded to Erromanga, and hove-to on the south side all night. At daylight we ran down the south side in hope of landing more teachers. The island appeared thinly inhabited; we saw now and then a native or two at a distance. On reaching Dillon's Bay, we saw a canoe paddling along the shore with three men in her, and by Mr. Williams's desire we lowered down the whale-boat, and took in Mr. Williams, Mr. Harris, Mr. Cunningham, myself, and four hands; we spoke to the men in the canoe, and found them to be a far different race of people from those at Tanna, their complexion darker, and their stature shorter; they were wild in their appearance, and extremely shy. They spoke a different language from that of the Windward Islands, so that Mr. Williams could not understand a word they said. He made them some presents, and tried to persuade them to come into our boat. He did not succeed, so we left them, hoping, as Mr. Williams remarked, with favourable impressions towards us. We pulled up the Bay, and some of the natives on shore ran along the rocks after the boat. On reaching the head of the Bay, we saw several natives standing at a distance; we made signs to them to come towards us, but they made signs for us to go away. We threw them some beads on shore, which they eagerly picked up, and came a little closer, and received from us some fishhooks and beads, and a small looking-glass. On coming to a beautiful valley between the mountains, having a small run of water, we wished to ascertain if it was fresh, and we gave the chief a boat-bucket to fetch us some, and in about half an hour he returned running with the water, which I think gave Mr. Williams and myself more confidence in the natives. They ran and brought us some cocoa-nuts, but were still extremely shy. Mr. Williams drank of the water the native brought, and I held his hat to screen him from the sun. He seemed pleased with the natives, and attributed their shyness to the ill-treatment they must have received from foreigners visiting the island on some former occasion. Mr. Cunningham asked him if he thought of going on shore. I think he said he should not have the slightest fear, and then remarked to me, 'Captain, you know we like to take possession of the land, and if we can only leave good impressions on the minds of the natives, we can come again and leave teachers; we must be content to do a little; you know Babel was not built in a day.' He did not intend to leave a teacher this time. Mr. Harris asked him if he might go on shore, or if he had any objection. He said, 'No, not any.' Mr. Harris then waded on shore; as soon as he landed the natives ran from him, but Mr. Williams told him to sit down; he did so and the natives came close to him, and brought him some cocoa-nuts and opened them for him to drink.

"Mr. Williams remarked, he saw a number of native boys playing, and thought it a good sign, as implying that the natives had no bad intentions; I said I thought so too, but I would rather see some women also; because when the natives resolve on mischief they send the women out of the way; there were no women on the beach. At last he got up, went forward in the boat, and landed. He presented his hand to the natives, which they were unwilling to take; he then called to me to hand some cloth out of the boat, and he sat down and divided it among them, endeavouring to win their confidence. All three walked up the beach, Mr. Harris first, Mr. Williams, and Mr. Cunningham followed. After they had walked about a hundred yards, they turned to the right alongside of the bush, and I lost sight of them. Mr. Harris was the farthest off. I then went on shore, supposing we had found favour in the eyes of the people. I stopped to see the boat safely anchored, and then walked up the beach towards the spot where the others had proceeded; but before I had gone a hundred yards, the boat's crew called to me to run to the boat. I looked round and saw Mr. Williams and Mr. Cunningham running; Mr. Cunningham towards the boat, and Mr. Williams straight for the sea, with one native close behind him. I got into the boat, and by this time two natives were close behind me, though I did not see them at the moment. By this time Mr. Williams had got to the water, but the beach being stony and steep, he fell backward, and a native struck him with a club, and often repeated the blow; a short time after another native came up and struck him, and very soon another came up, and pierced several arrows into his body.

"My heart was deeply wounded. As soon as I got into the boat, I headed the boat towards Mr. Williams, in hopes of rendering some assistance, but the natives shot an arrow at us, which went under the arm of one of our seamen, through the lining of the boat into a timber, and there stuck fast. They also hove stones at the same time. The boat's crew called out to me to lay the boat off; I did so, and we got clear of the arrows. I thought I might be able to get the body, for it lay on the beach a long time. At last I pulled alongside the brig, and made all sail, perceiving with the glass that the natives had left the body on the beach. I also ordered a gun to be fired loaded with powder only, thinking to frighten the natives, so that I might get the body; the natives however made their appearance, and dragged the body out of sight.

"Yours, &c.,

"ROBERT C. MORGAN."

At every station the excitement was very great at the report of Mr. Williams's death.

Both by the natives and ourselves, the information was received with deepest sorrow. Never shall I forget the sentiments of grief expressed by the poor people; especially among the aged, who well remember Mr. Williams's first visit to these shores, and his first address to them on the love of God, and always speak of him as the "Oromedua Maata."

One evening on my return from Avarua, the Chief, Tinomana, hastened to our house, thinking I might have heard some further information. He wept much, and said that for the past two nights neither himself nor family had slept; thoughts about "Williamu" had filled their minds. On the Friday afternoon following, at the public meeting of the people, many most interesting and deeply sympathetic speeches were delivered. One poor old man, with streaming eyes, earnestly called upon the people to indulge in deepest grief; "'Twas right," he said, "that they should mourn, and refuse to be comforted. A great servant of God had fallen by the hands of the heathen. We were not to grieve on his account, his spirit was in glory; we were to mourn for the poor widow and her dear family; and especially for the inhabitants of Erromanga. The poor ignorant heathen, let us mourn for them, and pray for them, and do all we can to send them others by whom they shall be brought to the knowledge of God; then with bleeding hearts they would confess their sin, and seek the Saviour."

During this address the whole congregation was deeply affected. Another rose, an ancient warrior, and commenced his address by saying, "Formerly we only knew one kind of warfare, now we know another. The former was the warfare of the servants of the devil with each other, and the devil was their master; the latter was the warfare of the servants of Christ against idolatry and sin, and Jesus was their Master. In the former warfare, the warriors would leave their wives and children, and go forward against the enemy, and frequently fell; but their fall was their shame, and provided not one consoling thought for the widow and the fatherless. How different" he continued, "was the fall of Williamu; he was a warrior, a great warrior; a warrior of Jesus, the Prince of Peace. He left all to engage in this warfare, and he has fallen, but his fall is glorious; his spirit is now in glory, and the land on which he died is sacred. We know God will comfort his mourning widow and family. Let us give ourselves to prayer! Oh, my friends, don't let us cease to pray!"

Another dwelt largely on the deliverance of Peter from prison while the church was praying, and insisted therefrom that our duty was to be very instant in prayer. The last speaker referred to the spread of the knowledge of Christ and His Word by the death of Stephen and the persecution which afterwards arose; and concluded that God would doubtless bring good out of this evil, and that, by the love and power of Jehovah, the blood of Williamu would become the seed of the Church.

These speeches were deeply interesting, inasmuch as they expressed the heart-felt affection and gratitude of the people to him who introduced to them the Gospel; and especially as they exhibited their pity and love towards those by whom his murder had been perpetrated. A few years ago upon hearing such a report, revenge would have been the first emotion of the mind; now they pity the ignorance of the murderers, and pray that soon they may become acquainted with Him whose blood cleanseth from all sin.

The people evinced their ardent attachment to the memory of their father in Christ. At a public meeting held a few days after the intelligence of his martyrdom reached the island, I suggested the erection of a monumental record to their departed friend. Pleased with the thought, the natives unanimously resolved on carrying it into execution; and in June, 1840, a monument, which stands in front of the Mission chapel at Arorangi, was finished. It bears the following inscription:—

"To the Memory of the Rev. John Williams, of the London Missionary Society, who, having laboured upwards of fourteen years at Raiatea, was made the honoured instrument of introducing Christianity to the Hervey and Samoan Islands. In attempting to convey the Gospel to the New Hebrides, he fell a sacrifice, with his friend Mr. Harris, on the Island of Erromanga, to the cruelty of the deluded heathen inhabitants, Nov. 20th, 1839."

We were gratified to witness in the people such a desire to commemorate the character and services of our dear brother Williams, whose heart was full of affection towards them; *but there exist still more enduring monuments of his labours.* Through the power of the Gospel brought by his instrumentality to this land, a nation has been raised from the grossest idolatry to the worship and service of the true God; and not a few, we hope, who first received from his lips the glad tidings of salvation, are now with him in glory.

CHAPTER XI.

NATIVE TEACHERS.—TEAVA AND TUPE.

On the return of the mission ship to Sydney, some natives were taken up, and among them Teava, the first Christian native teacher Mr. Williams took from Rarotonga on the occasion of his introducing the Gospel at Samoa.

Teava.

At a public meeting in Sydney, Teava gave the following speech. He thanked God that the true religion had been taken to Rarotonga. "It is thanks to you also," he said, "because you sent the true Word to our dark land. The sun has now risen upon us. First of all Mr. Williams and Mr. Bourne came to us, when a few received the message. Mr. Bourne came afterwards and baptized 200 persons. Then Mr. Williams came again and lived some time with us, and built a vessel. Afterwards Mr. Williams went to Samoa, and took seven teachers; they were placed with Malietoa at Savaii. On Mr. Williams's second visit to Samoa, I went as a teacher. I was placed with Matetaru at Manono. First, a few became Christians; now they have all turned. Great is our gratitude to you; you have the management of the message, and you have sent it to us. They tell me that your country is only in its infancy, but that you are Britons; in thanking you, therefore, I wish to return thanks to Britain." He then referred in affecting terms to the death of Mr. Williams—"Great was our grief when we knew he was dead, because it was he that first made the Word to grow in our land. This is my message to you, that you have compassion, and send more teachers to Samoa to assist Mr. Heath and Mr. Hardie, and the other message-bearers there, and that you send them to all the lands. You know it is written in Isaiah, that the knowledge of the Lord shall cover the earth, and that then they shall no more hurt nor destroy. We have found this. We called at Tanna, at Niué, and at Erromanga, and they did not hurt us. You know also it is written: 'The harvest is great, but the labourers are few. Pray ye the Lord of the harvest, that He would send forth more labourers into His harvest.' This is a good word, it is my word to you, 'pray ye the Lord of the harvest, to send forth more labourers:' that is the end of my speech."

The Chairman then put the following questions to the natives, which were answered, the first four by Leiatana, the fifth by Fauvasa, and the last by Teava. The natives did not previously know of the questions.—"Q. Why are you a Christian? A. Because I wish to arrive safely and peacefully in heaven.—Q. What reason have you to believe that Christianity is true, and your former religion is false? A. I know that from the Word of God.—Q. What kind of persons ought Christians to be? A. They must do the will of God, and depend upon the blood of Christ.—Q. If persons call themselves Christians, and have not this character, what do you think of them? A. They are all bad men, and the anger of God is toward them.—Q. Who is Jesus Christ? What did He do for the world? A. He is the Son of God. He came down below here to do the will of His Father, and to die for us.—Q. What is necessary in order to constitute a man a true Christian? A. His heart must be changed, and his conduct must be changed."

Among the first converts whom I knew, there were many on Rarotonga who were pre-eminently good and great. One,

TUPE,

was an example of many such.

Mr. Pitman wrote a very interesting account of his character which I desire to transcribe:—

"In the afflictions of our poor people we have been much afflicted; hundreds of them have been called from time into eternity. The satisfactory evidence, however, given by many, very many, of those taken from us, that 'death' to them was 'gain,' is a great alleviation to the grief occasioned by their removal. Death has cut down, with an unsparing hand, high and low, young and old; and we are left to mourn over the devastating effects of this awful visitation. The wise, the good, the useful, the careless professor, and the openly profane, have alike fallen by the devouring sword of this messenger of death. Amongst the number is one of Rarotonga's best men—a most valuable assistant of the Mission in this place, ever since its formation. To me the loss is great, indeed, but I desire to bow, with devout submission, to the righteous decision of Him who cannot err.

"A short account of this good man's religious character, his life, and death will not, I presume, be uninteresting to the Directors. His name was Tupe. He was one of the chief supporters of idolatry in the reign of superstition. But he attached himself to us on our first arrival in this place, in 1827. Ignorant was I then how Providence had gone before in preparing such a valuable assistant in my future labours. In the erection of our first chapel, he was one of the most laborious in the work. Not soon will it be erased from my memory, the joy that beamed in his countenance when it was told him that I intended to remain in this district as their teacher, and that brother Williams would reside in the other division of the island till a ship arrived to convey him to Raiatea. The very first night of our settlement amongst them, he came to our house to make inquiries respecting the truths of the Bible; and, till prevented by disease, scarcely a night passed that he was not present at our friendly meetings for conversation, chiefly on religious subjects. Often, till near midnight, have I sat conversing with him on the 'great salvation.' Nothing, I believe, occupied so much of his attention as the concerns of the soul; nor anything more desired by him than the wide diffusion of Divine truth. Indeed, I may say he was wholly devoted to the temporal and spiritual welfare of his countrymen. Incessant in labour, and indefatigable in his efforts to forward the cause of God, he assisted me in every good work with unwearied diligence, till death.

"He was a man of considerable influence, and, on the establishment of laws, was appointed chief magistrate for this part of the island, which office for twelve years he faithfully discharged. Well do I remember, at a time when we were involved in much perplexity, owing to disputes about land, and all parties were preparing for war, he proposed to go in person to the opposite party and attempt to adjust the points of difference amicably; in doing which he had to pass through a district infested by some desperate young fellows. I stated to him the danger of the attempt, and said that it might probably cost him his life. 'Does the Word of God,' said he, 'justify my proceedings?' I could not but reply in the affirmative. 'Then I go, regardless as to the consequences. God can and will protect me.' He, without a weapon of defence in his hand, passed through the district of these desperadoes, amidst the scoffings and revilings of all. The subject of contention was calmly debated; he returned home, and in a few days, all was quietly settled, and war prevented.

"The unflinching conduct of this good man in passing judgment, his impartiality in the administration of justice between man and man, and his unwavering determination to unite with us in seeking the advancement of 'undefiled religion,' roused some of his inveterate enemies to plot the most cruel revenge; even the destruction of himself and family. This they attempted by clandestinely setting fire to his house, when he and his family were asleep. But He who neither 'slumbers nor sleeps,' mercifully preserved the life of His faithful servant, and of his family. They only escaped, however, with what they had on; everything else was consumed. On discovering the fire, the first thing he endeavoured to secure was, what he considered his greatest treasure, a portion of the sacred Scriptures, viz., the Acts of the Apostles, in the Tahitian dialect; but this he could not effect, and, in attempting it, lost his all. The consequences of this fire did not end here; it communicated to the house of his son adjoining, which was speedily destroyed; then to our large chapel, which also was soon level with the ground. Large flakes of fire passed by and over our own dwelling; but through the timely exertions of the natives we were mercifully preserved from danger. Soon as I saw him, I said, 'Alas! Tupe.' 'O teacher,' he replied, 'the book of God is consumed! My house, my property, never regard, but my book, my book! and, oh, the house of God; will not God punish us for this?' The next morning I had the gratifying pleasure of presenting him with another copy of the book which he so much prized; it was received with feelings of no small delight. What added poignancy to the distress of this good man was to hear many of those who passed by his house when in flames calling out, *E tika kia ka*, 'It serves him right, let it burn.'

"The very first thing which occupied the attention of our valued friend the following day was to see his brother, the chief, and call a meeting of the under chiefs that immediate measures be taken for the re-building of the house of God. 'See,' said he to them, 'the house of God in ruins! What shall we do?' 'Build it again,' was the unanimous reply. *Koia ïa, e tâmâ, mea meitaki*, 'Yes, friends, that's very good,' he said, with joy beaming in his countenance. 'When shall we begin?' he asked. 'To-morrow,' was the universal reply. He then said to me, 'Teacher, be not cast down at what has happened. Let them burn—we will build. Let them burn it again, we will build; we will tire them out: but, teacher, do not leave us in this wicked land.' The very next morning, at sunrise, Tupe, with the old warrior Tuaivi, and Pa, our principal chief, were the first seen passing our dwelling, with their axes on their shoulders, going to the mountains to cut down timber for the erection of another chapel; the whole body of chiefs and people in their train.

"In calling to mind these bygone days, there is a certain something which fills the mind with pleasure of no ordinary kind, and leads the observer of Divine Providence to admire the rich, free, and sovereign grace of God in thus raising up instruments from the rough quarry of nature to carry on His great and eternal purposes of mercy in man's salvation.

"In May, 1833, he was unanimously chosen to fill the office of deacon. How faithfully he discharged its important duties we are all witnesses. Decided piety, deep humility, and holy zeal for the advancement of 'pure religion' were the striking characteristics of our valued friend. This, I believe, no one who knew him would call in question. His knowledge of Divine truth was by no means inconsiderable; and he was eminently qualified for the responsible situations in which Divine Providence had placed him, though he rated very low his own abilities, and almost to the day of his death deeply lamented his ignorance. He often testified, with expressions of the greatest astonishment, to the condescension of God in visiting such a sinful land as this. Conversing with him, as I frequently did, on subjects illustrative of the mercy and compassion of God, he would sit at times for hours in deep thought, and was heard muttering to himself, 'Oh, the love of God! the amazing pity of the Saviour! the depth of the sacred Scriptures! the hardness of the human heart! the exceeding sinfulness of sin!' The Sabbath he reverenced. The Word of God, the house of God, and the people of God, he loved; thereby evidencing that he was a genuine disciple of the Lord Jesus. Unless sickness prevented, or engaged in his official capacity, he was never known to be absent from the house of God at any of its appointed services, either on the Lord's-day, or the weekly evening lecture; nor from our church-meetings for prayer.

"It would not be easy to enumerate the various ways in which our departed friend rendered assistance to me, and to the mission, in the discharge of important duties. Every day in the week he was engaged in some religious exercise; and in the examination of candidates for Divine ordinances he spent no small portion of his time. For this department of labour he was eminently qualified. He connived at the sins of none. This trait in his character early began to display itself. Several years ago, even before he gave evidence of decided piety in himself, our house every night was crowded with people who came to make inquiries respecting the discourses delivered from the pulpit, &c. Observing some more particular in their questions, constant in the attendance at the house of God, and very active in everything proposed for the good of the community, I, one night as we were sitting alone, made inquiry into their characters, and said, 'I hope by their attaching themselves to us, and their ready acquiescence in putting down existing evils in the land, that they are desirous of becoming disciples of Jesus.' He made no reply; after a few minutes' silence, he said, 'Teacher, be not in haste; do not think so well of us, be not deceived, we are a wicked, deceitful people; stop till you have been longer with us, and know more of our character, and way of living.' A few weeks having elapsed, again I mentioned the subject. 'Ah!' said he, 'teacher, you don't know us yet. You think because we come to the house of God, and the schools, and do what you tell us, that we are good people, and love God. It is not so; we are deceiving you; there is a great deal of private wickedness committed that you know nothing of. Ere long you will know.' His words were verified, and many of those, whom I had fondly thought had begun to seek the Lord, were clinging to their heathen practices. This discovery led me into a more particular investigation of the private character of those who united themselves to us, and I found that our dear friend had not in the least exaggerated in what he had told me. In inquiring of him, from that time, either privately or publicly, the character of those making a profession of religion, I uniformly found him the same, and do not recollect an instance in which he connived at the sins of any. His word was to be relied upon. Among a people just emerging from heathen superstition and idolatry, such a man is to be ranked amongst a missionary's greatest blessings.

"But the time came when our friend must die. About three years ago his health began to decline, and he was much afflicted with a disease which ate into the soles of his feet, and destroyed the tops of his fingers. He was, however, able to attend to his varied duties, though afflicted with much pain, till within a few weeks of his decease. At length his seat in the house of God was empty, and he was confined to his dwelling. Frequent were my visits to him, and the following notes from my journal will tell the state of his mind, when 'flesh and heart began to fail.'

"Sept. 16.—Spent an hour with deacon Tupe, a tried and valued friend. His days on earth are fast closing; he is very weak. 'It something strange,' I said, 'to observe your seat empty in the house of God.' 'Ah!' he replied, 'it is the will of God it should be so. Here I sit and hear the people sing in the chapel, and, oh! I wish to be there. I give myself to prayer. God is with me. He will not forsake me.' I quoted several passages of sacred Scripture for his comfort, and mentioned the texts and outlines of discourses on the Sabbath. With these he was acquainted, his wife and children having given him particulars. He referred to the great advantages afforded to this people, and asked whether it was not for their sins God was pleased thus to chastise, by cutting off so many by death. He then spoke of the faithfulness of God in the fulfilment of His promises to His people. 'Not one good thing,' said he, 'has failed of all that God has spoken. He promised to Israel victory over their enemies, possession of Canaan, &c., all of which He fulfilled.' After a pause, with much emotion and feeling, he asked, 'Where, oh, where is Pitimani vaine, what detains her?' He thought he should be called away ere her return.

"Sept. 19.—On my way home called to see my faithful friend Tupe. The change is great; not long and he will be seen no more below. He is, I believe, fixed upon the Rock of Ages. His views are clear and

Scriptural. We conversed together on our labours from the beginning, and I said it gave me great pleasure that he had through grace been enabled to hold out to the end. 'Yes,' said he, 'we have hitherto been permitted to work for God. His goodness has been great; His compassion boundless.' I referred to his sickness, and the constant prayers I presented to God on his behalf, and how much I had been cast down at the prospect of our separation; but had been enabled within the last few days to resign him into the hands of God, to do as seemeth Him good. 'That,' said he, 'is well; do so. Grieve not. Detain me not. My end is near:' and he quoted several passages of Scripture. 'Two portions of the Word of God,' he said, 'afford me much delight; that in Isaiah, "Thine eyes shall see the King in His beauty; they shall behold the land that is very far off;" and the words of Paul, "Having a desire to depart, and to be with Christ, which is far better." I have no dread of death. Christ is my refuge.' I said, 'You have greatly assisted me in the work of God, from my coming to Rarotonga, and now we shall be separated.' 'Ah!' he replied, 'salvation is all of grace, through the blood of Jesus. Our work has not been in vain. Here I sit, and think, oh! the teacher, the teacher, who will assist him? then I think God is with him.' Looking up, he exclaimed, 'Oh! Pitimani vaine, Pitimani vaine, I shall not see her face again.' He wept, and I wept; who could help it? I broke silence, and said, 'In our Father's house we shall meet again.' 'Yes,' was his reply, with an effort which almost deprived him of his voice, 'we shall meet in glory.' 'No more,' said I, 'to part.' 'No,' he replied faintly, 'to be for ever with Christ. I long to go to be with Him.' I requested an interest in his prayers, for myself, my partner, the church, and the island. 'I have done,' he said, 'with the world. What remains is to set all in order, and think of the cause of Christ.' I left him with feelings not easily to be expressed, and talked awhile with his daughter in an adjoining room. My soul is cast down, yet rejoicing in the consideration of God's wonderful love in thus employing me as an instrument of good to immortal souls. All glory to God and the Lamb!

"Sept 24.—As I was preparing to go to the out-station, a son of Tupe came to say that his father was much worse and wished to see me. I immediately went, and perceived the messenger of death was come to call him hence. He could not see me, but was perfectly sensible. With great effort, and at intervals, he answered a few questions.

"'How is it with the soul?' 'All well.' 'Do you find your Saviour your support in death?' 'He is.' 'Is the path-way clear?' 'No obstruction, the way is clear.' 'Have you any fear?' 'None. Christ is mine.' 'Your last discourse to the people,' I observed, 'was on the death of Stephen, who saw the glory of Jesus; are you also looking to Him now in your departure?' 'I desire to see Him, and to be with Him.' I said, 'Death is come, you will soon leave us, we shall be left in the wilderness.' 'Yes,' he replied, 'I go, you remain. I am going to God. I have done with the world, we have been long companions, now we part, it is painful—but let the Lord's will be done—yes, the Lord's will be done.' I referred to his family, most of whom were present, and said it was pleasing to see some of them uniting with the people of God. 'Yes,' he said, with effort, 'and the others will come.' 'What,' I asked, 'do you desire for your children?' He answered, 'The Word of God, the blood of Jesus.' He was thirsty, and asked for drink. 'That,' I said, 'is water for our bodily sustenance.' 'Yes,' he replied, 'I shall soon drink of the water of life.' I then read part of the fourteenth chapter of John and expounded it, asking him a few questions, as I proceeded, respecting the mansions provided for the righteous. He said, 'Ere long I shall be taken to mine, and "shall see the King in His beauty."' After commending his soul to God in prayer, I asked him if he heard and understood. 'Quite so.' 'Now, Tupe,' said I, 'in our separation, what shall I say to the church?' As soon as he heard mention of the church, he exerted himself to the utmost, and said, 'Tell the church to hold fast, and be diligent for God. Tell Kaitara [his brother deacon] to be strong in the Lord, and active in His cause; also to Tupai.' Then to me he said, with his dying breath, *Aua koe e taitaiā*, 'Be not cast down.'

"I had not long arrived home ere his son came to say that his happy spirit had fled, to be with Him whom he loved. Thus lived, and thus died, a man of God, the first deacon of the church in Ngatangiia, and the first member of that church at its formation. Few such men are to be found. 'Mark the perfect man, and behold the upright; for the end of that man is peace.'"

The Closing Weeks of 1840.

At the close of this my second year at Rarotonga, I began to be much affected by the return of the hot season. Mrs. Gill was also often very prostrate, especially when north winds prevailed. I was so weak, that had a ship called we should have sought a change by going to Sydney. We sent to Mr. Buzacott, who kindly came, and advised a complete giving up of all work with the natives during the month of November. He promised to send his horse that I might take daily exercise, and he also sent me a supply of medicine.

The first morning I attempted the ride two natives were obliged to accompany me, one to lead the horse and the other to keep me from falling off. However, as the days passed on, this release from all work among the natives, and daily exercise, restored me to health, and at the end of three or four weeks I was again able to resume my labours.

A few extracts from notes at the time will give some idea of daily work during the last weeks of 1840 :—

December 1.—Went to the village of Titikaveka. New chapel in progress. Met the church. Held a business meeting.

December 2.—After school, met an aged female member who for some time has been doing good work in the village; also met another who wished to join the church.

December 3.—At schools. Translating school books. Afternoon, had long talk with Papeiha's wife on native affairs and work. A truly good woman, and helper of Mrs. Gill's work. Evening, writing class and long talk with Ngatikero, formerly a heathen priest, now a good servant of Christ. Formerly never without human flesh on his hook outside his hut, now how changed!

December 4.—At adult and children schools. Afternoon, Bible class. Evening, translating books and writing papers.

December 6, Sunday.—The school and chapel services; also the communion of church members. Evening, household Bible-class and prayer-meeting.

December 7.—Met class of inquirers. Evening, met a general class for conversation on the subjects of yesterday's sermons.

December 14.—Was engaged with the students of Institution.

December 15.—Returned to Arorangi. Preached at 4 p.m. Had singing class at 7 p.m.; then met a young chief who was candidate for communion.

December 20.—Our house somewhat injured by a heavy gale.

December 21.—Went to Avarua to superintend printing an elementary book on geography.

December 24.—Had pleasure in printing the first sheet. Evening, returned to Arorangi. Met the chief and people about police matters.

In this way it was our happiness to close this second year of our work.

At the settlement of Arorangi, we had about 1,400 people. During 1840, 144 deaths, 60 baptisms, adults and children of the families, 25 marriages; 38 members *joined the church*, and 2 were suspended.

Early in 1841 a fine stone chapel at Titikaveka was finished. I have preserved the following report of the opening services drawn up by the Rev. C. Pitman:—

"The erection of edifices for the worship of God is always, to the Christian, a source of unfeigned pleasure. Another temple has been dedicated to the service of Jehovah in Rarotonga. The 11th of last June was the day appointed for opening the new stone chapel at Titikaveka. At an early hour the church members belonging to the different settlements assembled. On entering the chapel I was surprised to see every seat occupied. As two or three hours would elapse before the arrival of Mr. Buzacott, I requested the people to walk about the settlement till it was time for Divine service, but they preferred sitting where they were. I had the pleasure of dedicating the building to God by prayer and reading the Scriptures. An excellent discourse was then delivered by my respected colleague, the Rev. A. Buzacott, of Avarua, from 1 Pet. ii. 5: 'Ye also, as lively stones, are built up a spiritual house.' The hymns were read by Taunga, late superintendent of the school in that place, but now a student in the Institution for preparing young men for missionary labour. May the glory of God be here constantly manifested, and immortal souls renewed and saved for generations to come!

"The Gospel was introduced into these districts in the year 1832. Pity for the wretched state of the inhabitants prompted me to the use of means for their deliverance from spiritual death; for at that time they were living 'without God, and without hope in the world,' abandoned to every species of vice, and many of them notorious for their violent opposition to the Gospel. At first they suspected some political design, but when at a public meeting the native teacher and myself stated the object we had in view, to instruct them in the Word of God, they gave us a cordial welcome, and not long after a great change was perceptible.

"Such has been the origin of the little interest at Titikaveka, and such the result, little anticipated by me, of my first visit. 'The Lord has done great things for us, whereof we are glad.' To Him alone be glory for ever! In this place the Gospel has been constantly preached; and, I hope, much good done. The enemy of souls did not tamely give up his possession—his stronghold of many generations. Various have been his attempts to regain the ascendancy; but 'He who sits in the heavens has laughed' at him, and frustrated all his deep-laid schemes. Hitherto the Gospel has triumphed; yea, and will triumph!

"The village in which it stands is situated on the south side of the island. Behind the chapel is a range of woody mountains, over which, on the left, ascends the peak of Teatukura—the highest point in the island. On the right stand two large Barringtonia trees of many ages' growth. The chapel itself is built of coral-sandstone, which is found on the shores in beds from one to two feet thick; in some parts it is extremely hard and compact, being composed of shells and sand closely cemented together. The building is 61 feet square inside; the walls are 25 feet high and three feet thick; there are 17 windows and three doors, all arched with the same stone. To guard against storms, it is covered with three roofs, supported on four iron-wood columns.

"To be spared to see the completion of such a fine and substantial building for the worship of God is to me a cause of thankfulness and joy, and earnestly do I pray that, in it, hundreds of immortal souls may be born again of the Spirit, and those who have through grace believed, be built up in their most holy faith."

Notice of School Work, 1841.

At this period our daily labours were devoted largely to the schools, the good fruit of which abides in the present adult population.

Our schools are well attended, and, I am happy to state, afford many blossoms of hope. Some of the children were some time since tempted to join in a heathen dance got up by the "Tuteauri," but the majority are constant in their attendance, and make good progress. Several among the teachers have given pleasing evidence of a renewed heart; and others, both teachers and elder scholars, are among the inquirers. I could mention the cases of several, but at the present time will refer only to one,—that of a young man about 18 years old. I do so the more willingly because it has some reference to the labours of our departed brother Williams. It appears as the fruit of a word spoken in season by our brother, the result of which yet remains to be disclosed to him in eternity.

My first conversation with the lad was as follows:—

"I have," he said, "long wished to converse with you."

"On what subject," I inquired, "do you wish to converse?"

"On the subject of baptism."

"Tell me first what you think of baptism."

"I think it to be a sign by which to show that our hearts are entirely defiled by sin, and that except we are renewed by the Holy Spirit we cannot be saved."

"Are all men fit subjects for baptism?"

"No; none but those who hate sin and who have run to Jesus and desire to become entirely His disciples."

I observed that what he had said was in accordance with the Word of God, and inquired whether he had been baptized. To which he replied,—

"No, I have not. When my father was baptized he took me with him to Williamu, who put me back, stating I was too old and too wicked to receive the ordinance until I sought it myself. Some time after I was taken to Mr. Buzacott, who also refused me."

"Do you remember being taken by your father to Williamu?"

"Yes, quite well."

"Were you a steady, thoughtful lad then?"

"No, far from it. I was a very wicked boy. I would not live at home; I joined, as often as I could, a set of wild lads, with whom I used to steal and commit all kinds of sin."

"That was indeed an awful condition," I observed. "Was it really your character at that time?"

"I have not told you all," he replied; "I cannot. I was indeed a very wicked boy."

"But," I continued, "I am surprised at what you say, because since my residence here I have known you as a steady lad in the school. What first wrought a change in your conduct?"

"While I was so wicked I frequently had thoughts of fear in my heart, but they were not lasting, until one day just before Williamu was going to England he came here to preach, and afterwards to address the children; being his last address I was induced to go and hear him. He told us it was an evil and bitter thing to sin against God, and exhorted us to go to Jesus for pardon and salvation. He told us we ought to go at once and not delay."

"Well, how did this address affect you?"

"It caused fear to grow in my heart, because I then saw my sin, and it also excited my desire to speak to Williamu."

"Well, did you speak to him?"

"Yes," replied the young man, "I, with another, went and begged a little book that I might learn, for I did not then know how to read."

"How did you succeed?"

"I asked for a book, and Williamu looked at me and said, 'Are you come for a book? Why, I know you to be a very wicked boy, and, besides, you cannot read; how is it that you are come to beg a book?' I then told him all he had said was true. I was a very wicked boy, but from what I had heard that morning I was full of fear because of my great sins, and now desired to learn, and would try to cast off my former habits."

"Well," I inquired, "what did Williamu say then?"

"He exhorted me to learn to read, and read the good Word of God, and to pray for a new heart."

"But," I continued, "this is a long time since—upwards of six years ago. Have you attended to Williamu's advice and been a praying lad ever since?"

"From that time I have been a steady lad, I have obeyed my father, I have attended the schools and the house of prayer. I used sometimes to pray, but my heart was the same as formerly. I did not hate all evil. I did not desire Jesus with all my heart."

"But do you think that your heart is interested about these matters now?"

"Oh, yes!" he replied, "I feel very different *inside* from now to what I did formerly; my heart is become soft and my eyes are opened."

"Has this been a sudden change?" I inquired.

"No, it has grown very softly."

"But are you sure this change has taken place? What are the signs?"

"I think my heart is changed. This I know, sin is become a very wicked thing to me; I rejoice in private prayer to God; my heart is made light, and I desire to be found in Jesus, that He should be my Lord and Master, and I become His servant."

After some other conversation the young man left with a promise that I would meet him again in some few weeks' time. Doubtless the word spoken by our departed brother was a word in season to his soul. Oh! to be wise to win souls—to sow beside all waters. The word cannot be lost; we have the Divine promise that in due time we shall reap if we faint not. May God ever help us that our faith fail not; that we may continue steadfast in season and out of season, beneath the blaze of prosperity or the chilling influence of adversity, and, after having done all with patience, wait for the glorious revelation of the Last Day.

I cannot refrain from adverting to the joy which was manifested by our destitute orphan children when they received the garments sent from England last year. Long before the day of distribution arrived many of the children wrote short letters on their slates, begging that they might not be forgotten. The number of orphans is so great that the new garments given them made quite a difference in the appearance of the children on the Sabbath. One would almost think them little English children. Since they have received the garments many letters of thanks have been written to us. Thinking it would be pleasing to our friends to see the expressions of their gratitude, I transcribe the following three letters as specimens:—

(Translated from the native language.)

1.

BRETHREN AND SISTERS IN ENGLAND,—Great is the joy of our hearts—the destitute, and the fatherless—because of your compassion to us.

This is from one portion of the children of Rarotonga, at the settlement of Arorangi. This is that by which we know your great compassion to us;—you formerly prayed to God for us, and your prayers were prosperous;—God heard them, and His good Word grew quickly here in Rarotonga. Now you have given cloth to the fatherless and great is our joy, because our appearance in the house of prayer was formerly very dirty, but now we shall think continually of God's love, and we will also pray to Him for you, that His great love may grow abundantly with you in your land. This is the end of our word now.

Napa, *a teacher.*
Papaa, *a scholar.*

2.

Brethren,—Because of your great love to us our hearts greatly rejoice. This is our word to you. We are a company of destitute children,—we have no property to compensate your kindness to us. May you be rewarded by God! That is our prayer. The clothes you have given us, poor orphan children of Rarotonga, have reached us. Our parents are dead, and you have become our parents, because you have given us many good things with joy and compassion. This is our word,—we will pray for you, and you must pray for us. Now, children of England, and brethren, and fathers, let us love one another as Christ also has loved us; let us also love the heathen lands that yet remain who know not God; and let us make known His great love to the world in giving His only-begotten Son that we may be saved. He is the light and the life of men; there is no other good. May we all be found in Him at the last day. All the teachers; all the chiefs; all Britain; and all Rarotonga; and a great number from heathen lands. This is the conclusion of our word.

Unu, } *Two boys.*
Toria, }

3.

Friends and Brethren in England,—We formerly heard of God's loving-kindness to you, but now we truly know that you have been compassionated by Jehovah, because you have had compassion for us, and sent us the good Word, and slates, and pencils, and teachers, and now you have sent us a great quantity of beautiful cloth, that we may be clothed on the Sabbath. We formerly resembled the worms without cloth. Our mothers are dead—we now dwell parentless—God only is our Parent. We have not been able to attend the house of prayer; the want of cloth has been the reason. Our native cloth soon rots,—it is only the skin of a tree and will not keep good long; therefore we are greatly rejoiced by this English cloth you have sent us that we may be covered. We have no property in our land. We will pray to God for you. May you be saved by the Messiah. This is all our word.

Tepairu, } *Two girls.*
Miri, }

CHAPTER XII.

VISIT TO MANGAIA, 1841.

On the 9th of June, 1841, we left our station at Arorangi, amidst the tears and prayers of an affectionate people, and embarked next day for Mangaia, accompanied by the native assistant, Maretu; Rupe, from the seminary, and his wife; Medua-aru-toa, a native deacon, from the church at Mangaia; and Setephano, the young chief of Arorangi. We had hoped to reach Mangaia within two days after our embarkation, but our God, by whose hands the wind and the ocean are controlled, had otherwise appointed: contrary winds sprang up by which we were kept at sea nine days.

Mangaia lies about 120 miles south-east of Rarotonga, and is from twenty-six to thirty miles in circumference. From the extremities, north-east to west, is a bold shore of perpendicular, barren coral rock, twenty to sixty feet high, thickly indented by deep, huge caverns of most grotesque appearance, into which the sea beats with awful grandeur in the season of its rage. The other side of the island is preserved from the inroads of the mighty billows by a coral reef, about half a mile from the shore, which contains no opening large enough to admit a boat.

The roughness of the weather prevented our landing on the day we made the island; several of our companions, however, ventured on shore, and communicated the intelligence of our arrival. In the course of the afternoon Numangatini (the chief of the island) and a few native Christians came in their canoes to welcome us.

Early the next morning a canoe came alongside, and having descended into it, in less than a quarter of an hour we were landed on the reef. The majority of the church members were then waiting to receive us; and, as the canoe touched the edge of the reef, several rushed forward and dragged it in haste to the land, and, with acclamations of joy, bore us, canoe and all, to a house prepared to receive us. The scene was most overpowering. The crowds of people—old and young—the unintelligible shouts of some, and the mute amazement of others, exceeded anything I ever saw or heard.

After recovering in some degree from the excitement of the morning, our friends from the vessel took leave of us, to proceed on their way to Tahiti, whence they hope to return in three months.

June 20.—At Oneroa, the chief settlement, situated on the north-west side of the island, there are not less than 2,000 inhabitants. At six in the morning, the natives held their early prayer-meeting, and from 700 to 800 persons attended. At nine the children were assembled in the school-house, or rather shed, as it has neither sides nor seats, being merely a roof supported by a number of low posts. More than 1,000 children were present, sitting in rows on the ground so close together that it was with difficulty I made my way to a rudely constructed pulpit erected in the centre. Every eye was fixed on me while I gave them a short address, and stated that the object of our visit was, among other things, to devote as much time as possible to the schools. Every countenance beamed with an expression of joy, too forcible to be misunderstood by the heart of a missionary, when they were informed that I had brought a sufficient supply of school-books for all the children on the island, and that at an early period we would meet them, and arrange them into classes.

After singing and prayer, the children walked in order to the chapel, where the adults had been some time assembled. The chapel is 130 feet long by 36 feet wide, the wonder and admiration of all who visit the island. The numberless rafters of the roof, each neatly covered with native paint, are supported by twelve or fourteen pillars of the finest wood, carved in the most ingenious manner. How affecting the scene from the pulpit! To see this large and skilfully constructed native building, not only full, but overflowing, crowded on all sides by attentive listeners to the words of life, who, but a few years ago, walked with the children of darkness, devoted, like their fathers, to idolatry and sin. While my spirit rejoiced at the scene before me, my heart sunk at the awful responsibility of my situation. The subject of our meditation was 1 Cor. ii. 2—a crucified Saviour the glorious theme of the Gospel ministry. In the afternoon the children again assembled to be questioned on the morning sermon. Another public service in the chapel closed the labours of the day.

June 25.—This morning left Oneroa, with a party of natives, to visit Tamarua, a station about seven miles distant. Our path lay over barren hills, and through fertile vales, bounded on every side with perpendicular piles of coral rock, from 50 to 100 feet high. As the day advanced we entered a lovely valley of taro and cocoa-nut trees, when we espied in the distance a newly finished house of prayer; as we approached, the natives in great numbers ran to meet us, and with smiles and hearty congratulations welcomed us to the place. On reaching the settlement we were led to a native house, which had been neatly prepared for our reception; clean grass had been strewed on the ground, and a bed of rude construction had been put up, hoping that we should remain a few days. Upon learning that this was only a hasty visit, and that we intended returning in the evening, one person pleasantly proposed that they should fetch the "*Rope of the Judges*," and make fast our feet; but, upon being informed of our intention to visit them two or three weeks hence, and make a longer stay, they were pacified, and consented to let us go.

In the course of the forenoon, I proposed to meet the members of the church who reside at this station, for the purpose of settling them here. Hitherto they have been in the habit of assembling with their brethren at Oneroa; but it has long been their desire to have a native missionary settled over them, and to observe the ordinances at their own place. On entering the chapel, which is very large, and most pleasantly situated on a rising eminence in the valley, the emotions of our hearts were inexpressible. Truly the isles wait for Thee, O Lord! We thought of the prophecy: "He shall prolong his days, he shall see his seed, and the pleasure of the Lord shall prosper in his hands."

The members of the church, about seventy in number, were waiting to receive us. Among them were some aged fathers, from the dark caves and dens of this once heathen land, and from the yet darker regions of sin and depravity, the reign of which is now trampled beneath the feet of Him, whose is the Kingdom and the Power and the Glory. Others were just in the prime of life, whose countenances expressed the gratitude of their hearts that they had been delivered from the thraldom of him who held their fathers in bondage. Some were yet young; and their softened manners, earnest attention, and glistening eyes, whose light was half lost in the rising tear indicative of the affection of their hearts, filled the soul with adoration to that Saviour whose love and grace is all triumphant; and excited the pleasing hope that the good work would continue to advance.

After singing, prayer, and an address, I questioned them as to their desire to be separated from the church at Oneroa, and settled at their own station; and finding them unanimous, it was arranged that henceforth they should observe the ordinances of the Christian Church among themselves: four of the most active, pious, and intelligent men were then selected to act as deacons. After distributing a few hymn-books, we commended this infant church to the gracious presence and blessing of the Saviour, and dispersed.

A fuller account of this visit is recorded in "Gems from the Coral Islands."

After more than three months' residence at Mangaia, we returned to Rarotonga, and our people received us with gladness.

We received from Mangaia arrowroot contributions which realised £50 for the Bible Society and £16 for the London Missionary Society.

The natives of Rarotonga contributed, also, £50, making a total of £116—no mean sum, raised principally by hard labour on the part of our *poor people*, as a token of their gratitude to the Bible and the Missionary Societies.

The following letter, in the form of a journal, written by Mrs. Gill to her parents, gives a graphic history of our visit to Mangaia:—

"June 9th.—This morning we left Arorangi amidst the tears and prayers of our people. They feel our leaving much. It was quite affecting to hear and see them; some said, 'We shall look at your house, but our "Oromedua" is not there, and we shall feel lonely;' others said, 'We shall be like children whose parents are dead;' others said, 'We will not cease to pray that God may preserve you and watch over you while you are absent from us, and bring you back again.'

"June 11th.—Sailing with a strong, but contrary, wind.

"June 16th.—The strong wind and currents have carried us on to the edge of the tropics, consequently we are, with light winds and calms, almost as far from Mangaia as the day we left Rarotonga. It is most wearisome both to ourselves and the many natives who are with us.

"June 17th.—Early this morning we arrived in sight of Mangaia; but owing to the strong wind, together with a heavy surf rolling in, it is questionable whether we shall be able to effect a landing to-day.

"This island has on one side a bold shore, and on the other a coral reef, so that it would be dangerous to land in boats; we shall therefore be obliged to send everything on shore in canoes. Evening—Many canoes have been to our vessel to-day, and most of the natives who came with us are gone ashore. The chief, Numangatini, has been on board. He came, according to the native custom, with the intention of waiting until we could accompany him; but, feeling a disposition to sickness, he was obliged, somewhat speedily, to take his departure.

"June 18th.—This morning, almost as soon as it was light, our ship was surrounded by canoes; our attention was directed to one as having been sent by the church expressly to take us on shore. The sea being less troubled than yesterday, we were handed down the side of the vessel, and soon found ourselves seated in the canoe ankle-deep in water. In this we were paddled about two miles. As we approached the shore we saw a great number of natives standing on the reef; these, we were told, were members of the church waiting to receive us; and as soon as our canoe rose with the wave to the reef we were instantly lifted over, before another rolling surf had time to break. The canoe was then dragged a long distance inside the reef, until we arrived at the head of the settlement; here we expressed a wish to get out and walk the remaining distance; but our request was positively refused, and the people insisted upon our sitting still. A signal was then given, when instantly we, with the canoe, were hoisted on the sable shoulders of forty or fifty individuals, and carried through the settlement; to attempt a description of the scene is utterly impossible. When we reached the teacher's house, we found it literally crowded with natives, who, as soon as our canoe was put down, hastened to offer us their congratulations.

"Sunday, 20th June.—At 9 A.M. the children were assembled in a kind of shed, their school-house having been blown down in the late gale. I should think at least 1,000 were present. W—— gave a short address; after singing (if singing it may be called) and prayer, they were dismissed to the chapel, which, however, was so filled with adults that not half the children could enter. The chapel is very long, and narrow, about 126 feet by 36 feet; the sides are very low, but the roof is lofty; the centre is supported by eighteen large pillars, and other smaller ones, ingeniously carved, which look exceedingly beautiful, and show great industry on the part of the natives. The people listened attentively to the sermon from 1 Cor. ii. 2. After service the children flocked around us in such numbers that it was with difficulty we could proceed home. I appeared to be the principal source of attraction—they would run a little before me, and then walk backwards; others got upon large stones; some, more bold than the rest, came quite close in order to look at me.

"Monday, 21st June.—To-day the men and women of the classes have, according to their custom, brought us a present of native cloth, food, &c., &c., and the usual ceremony of shaking hands was gone through, a most formidable affair where there are 400 or 500 individuals, though much to be preferred to *rubbing noses!* It was amusing to hear the old native teacher telling the people to be very gentle in taking the foreigner's hand, and to be sure to give us the *one* they had *washed* (?). One individual spoke for all; he said the presents we saw were brought as a proof of their love, and also of their joy that we had come to teach them the Word of God.

"Tuesday, 22nd June.—This morning several members of the church came to see us. Evening—Attended the church-meeting. Upwards of 500 members were present. We are surprised to find so many; but we understand that they are consistent and diligent disciples.

"Wednesday, 23rd June.—Engaged this morning with several female members, endeavouring to instruct them in household matters. I find, alas! that here, as well as at Rarotonga, these duties are little understood and very inefficiently performed. We feel very solicitous about the native children and young people; they have been too much neglected. W—— had a meeting with their parents, and urged upon them the necessity of erecting a new school-house, if possible, during our stay; to this they cheerfully consented.

"Friday, 25th June.—Visited Tamarua, a small village three miles distant; a chair was fitted up for my accommodation, in which I was carried. The roads here are bad, owing to the 'makatea' (or coral rock) of which the island is formed; this, jutting above the surface of the soil, renders walking exceedingly painful. Our path lay across sterile mountains and fruitful valleys; the mountains yield little beside a wild fern, but the valleys grow cocoa-nuts, bananas, mountain plantains, and taro. Soon after our arrival at the settlement, W—— met the members of the church, when, in compliance with their wishes, they were separated from the church at Oneroa. It was also arranged that Rupe, from the Native Institution, Rarotonga, should be appointed their teacher. At this village we were much pleased with the neat chapel; it reminded me of some country place of worship in England. I could scarcely feel convinced that we were indeed in a land where, but a few years ago, the inhabitants were all heathen. Truly God hath blessed these poor people, and the ends of the world have seen His salvation. In the afternoon we had the children collected under a shed, and W—— gave them an address, and distributed books. About two hundred were present, but only one girl and six boys could read. When the children were dispersed, the adult classes met in the chapel to hold their usual Friday evening services, after which we took our departure, with hearts filled with gratitude for what we had been permitted to see of Gospel work among these interesting people.

"Monday, 28th June.—Early this morning we left Oneroa for the village of Ivirua, on the eastern side of the island, about eight miles distant. We arrived here about 11 A.M., and, according to native custom, found food prepared for us, and laid on the *floor*. A piece of native cloth was spread for us to sit on. About 1 o'clock the members of the church were assembled, when, like those of Tamarua, they expressed a wish to be settled at their own village. Taking into consideration their number, the long distance from Oneroa, and the bad roads, it was thought well to comply with their desire. The church was then formed, and three deacons were chosen to conduct its services until a teacher could be appointed. This evening the house was crowded with natives who came to gaze and talk.

"Tuesday, 29th June.—This morning we attended the schools, and separated the children into eighteen classes. To each child was given a book, and to many of the teachers slates and pencils; but we had only twenty-four slates to distribute, so that many were left without. At 10 o'clock we met for public service in the chapel, after which we returned to Oneroa.

"Wednesday, 30th June.—The people have commenced the new school-house to-day, 92 feet by 45 feet. This afternoon I met a class of women, and arranged to meet a class every day for instruction, and also to teach them cutting and making garments.

"July 2nd.—Morning—Met all the female teachers in class for instruction, and distributed to them books on geography and arithmetic. I engaged to instruct some of them four days a week, in order that they may be better able to teach their classes.

"Monday, 5th July.—Morning—Met the teachers in class, and afterwards cut out a dress for a native woman. Afternoon—Conversing with two church members. Evening—At missionary prayer-meeting; the chapel well filled.

"Wednesday, 7th July.—A small vessel hove in sight this morning. The captain came on shore. He is from Huahine, and has brought letters and a few Tahitian books. This afternoon, met a class of women; and evening, attended service.

"Thursday, 8th July.—Morning—Met the female teachers for writing and arithmetic. They have not the least idea of writing figures, so that I fear they will not make much progress during our stay. Afterwards I was engaged in cutting out a pair of trousers for Maretu's son.

"Friday, 9th July.—This morning W—— attended to the men on one side of the chapel and I to the women on the other. After reading and writing they were questioned on Scripture, geography, and the multiplication table. Afternoon—Met a class of adult women; and conversed freely on their responsibilities as parents. Some said they had indeed been guilty in reference to their children, and had neglected their instruction; but they pleaded want of time and ability.

"Saturday, 10th July.—This afternoon we left Oneroa for Tamarua. We have heavy rains, which make our *reed house* damp and uncomfortable. The people were quite pleased when we told them of our intention to stay a few days amongst them.

"Tuesday, 13th July.—Attended the school. There were seventeen classes of boys and twelve classes of girls; several of the former could read, but only one of the latter. To four classes of boys and one class of girls we gave copies of the Acts of the Apostles; and among the remainder we distributed elementary reading books. In consequence of the inadequate supply of books the children have been taught by *rote;* hence their ignorance. I went into all the girls' classes, and found the teachers (without exception) reading, and the children repeating, at the same time not knowing a letter. I gave them our method; but it was so foreign that I fear it will be some time before they adopt it.

"Wednesday, 14th July.—Arrangements were made last evening for the purpose of setting apart Rupe as native pastor over the people at Tamarua and Ivirua. The deacons and other members of the church at Oneroa, together with those of Ivirua, arrived at an early hour this morning—about eight o'clock we assembled. The service was commenced by singing and prayer; W—— gave an address explanatory of the object, and Rupe answered several questions, simply, but satisfactorily. Another prayer was then offered, and W—— preached from 1 Cor. ix. 22: 'I became all things to all men; if by any means I might save some.' The ordinance of the Lord's Supper was then administered to about one hundred and forty communicants. The services being concluded, the people sat about in groups round the chapel, and partook of a feast prepared for the occasion. This evening we left for Oneroa: the new school there being in a state of forwardness, and the people not knowing how to proceed, W—— was needed to superintend the work.

"Thursday, 15th July.—Morning—Engaged with class of teachers. Afternoon—I had a class of adult women; the teachers are very anxious to learn writing and arithmetic, but we had no slates. Fourteen young persons joined the inquirers' class.

"Friday, 23rd July.—The last few days have been exceedingly wet and gloomy. We have kept all the wooden windows and doors shut, and had a lamp burning all day; we have also been obliged to wear our cloaks. We feel the damp much in the native house.

"Tuesday, 27th July.—This evening, at the church-meeting, Setephano, with Atuia, natives of Rarotonga, and Tauiri, of Mangaia, were received into church fellowship. We were much pleased with the account Tauiri gave of himself. He said:—'Brethren, by the love of God we are met together in this place. You know me, and are well acquainted with my former character; it was evil, very evil. I lived in sin on shore, and when on board ship I did the same there. I went to Tahiti, and to other lands; I was the same there. I lived some two or three months at the station of Avarua, and then went to Arorangi, the same wicked man. My first Sabbath at Arorangi I entered the house of prayer where the message of God was delivered, "Behold the days approach that thou must die;" then I first felt the solemnities of death, death of the body and of the soul. I was afraid, and began to pray to God. I joined the classes for instruction, and attended constantly the house of prayer; but I was not a truly changed man then. On one Saturday morning in the year that is now lost to us, a ship hove in sight off the island. At the proposition of Setephano, the chief, I made one of the party to go to it. In haste we left the shore, taking with us a little fresh water and one bunch of bananas, with a few cocoa-nuts. Before we could reach the vessel God sent a strong wind, by which the ship was soon blown out of sight; and we, tossed upon the waves of the great sea, tried to make the land, but all efforts were vain. Before night the land was quite lost to us. On the Sabbath the storm continued, and our fears began to grow; thus we continued, day and night, without seeing land, until the following Sabbath. One or two of our company had become quite helpless; and we all expected to be buried in the sea. We thought of our sins, and confessed to each other our guilt; and we made a covenant with the Lord that, if He would in love save us, we would be His. We had no hope, however, for it appeared to us that death was near. But Jehovah had compassion; and when we were helpless He Himself brought us in sight of Rarotonga, and gently brought us to the shore. From that day to this I cannot forget my covenant; and my hope is, *that* season of death has proved the means of my life. I am a great sinner; but the sinlessness of Jesus is all-sufficient for me. This is all my hope and prayer—to be saved by Him who died for me.'

"August 2nd.—This afternoon, W—— proposed that the church here invite the church members of Tamarua and Ivirua to the opening of the new school-house on Wednesday next. This proposition was agreed to, and two deacons were appointed to take the letter of invitation.

"August 4th.—Early this morning the people were busily employed in bringing food for the feast at the opening of the new school-house. At 9 o'clock the children were assembled; not less than 1,200 were present. The place was quite full, so that only a few of the adults could find standing room. The children listened with the deepest attention while addressed from 1 Kings iii. 5–9. At 11 A.M. we took our seats at the feast. It was a new scene to them. Never before had parents and children united in a feast of this kind. At 2 o'clock both parents and children again met in the chapel, the school-house not being large enough. After singing and prayer, from twelve to fourteen short speeches were delivered by deacons and others. An old man, once a heathen warrior, but now a true Christian, said: 'This is a new day, the like of which we or our fathers have never seen, a day of great love; yes, God has loved us, and we love one another. Formerly, during Satan's reign, we prepared food, and were weary with carrying it to our idols, where we left it to rot, without advantage to ourselves or others; but to-day our own mouths have eaten what our hands have prepared. Formerly, the children were kept at home to take care of our lands, and the women ate food after the men were satisfied; but to-day we have all met, not afraid to leave our lands, nor ashamed to look at our wives; and now, you, our children, look at this new school-house, built on purpose for you. Let us, adults, hold fast that which is good; do not let the children have any excuse on our account. And you, children, see that you regard well your instruction.'

"Friday, 20th.—Little of importance has transpired during the past fortnight. I have attended daily to the teachers and adult women. This evening we gave a dinner to the chiefs, six in number, *served up in English style*. All, of course, were expected to use knives and forks, and some were rather awkward; but, considering this was the first attempt, we thought they succeeded pretty well.

"Saturday, 21st.—This evening finds us at Ivirua, whither we have come to spend the Sabbath. We are now sitting in a native reed house; the floor is strewed with clean dry grass; in one corner stands a rude bedstead, covered with native cloth, and in another a cooking apparatus; on the opposite side, partitioned off with native cloth, is a place for the servants, while in the other corner are three fowls. The wind is whistling through the reeds in all directions; happily, there are no windows.

"Monday, 23rd.—This morning we attended the children's school, and were glad to find them in tolerably good order. I distributed a few bags among the teachers, with which they were much pleased. At noon attended a meeting of the church.

"Tuesday, 24th.—Much gratified with the progress of the children during the past six weeks. Conversed with several candidates for church fellowship. At noon attended service, and in the afternoon we returned to Oneroa.

"September 3rd.—Early this morning the people from the two inland stations, with those of this settlement, assembled to celebrate the third anniversary of their auxiliary to the London Missionary Society. The meeting was commenced by singing and prayer. Numangatini, the chief, was then re-appointed to the office of treasurer, and Taki to that of secretary. Many of the natives then addressed the meeting, after which the following articles were contributed:—Arrowroot, native cloth, thirty-five fathoms of fishing nets, also twenty-eight 'kumities,' or bowls, two carved axes, twenty-four cocoa-nut cups, and 8s. 6d. in money, the value of these articles amounting to about £17.

"Thursday, 9th.—Early this morning we left Oneroa to visit a heathen settlement. We were received kindly; had a long conversation with the heathen. They listened attentively to all that was advanced. One old man said he would not go to the Christian settlement,—his mind was made up to continue where he was until he died; but his two wives and a large family attend the schools. After resting a little time we went with a company of natives to see a large cavern—I should think more than a mile long; the people of this district were accustomed, in time of war, to take refuge in this place. The spar in some places was very large, and presented the appearance of massive stone pillars; in other parts it formed a rich drapery; in others it was like a bed of snow, and in others like beautiful icicles. When we had gone about half-way through, the smoke from our torches became so unpleasant that we were obliged reluctantly to retrace our steps; we, however, succeeded in breaking off a few stalactites to send home to our friends. As we returned we again called at the heathen settlement, and it was proposed to engage in prayer with them, to which they made no objection.

"Friday, 10th.—Morning and afternoon engaged with the school-teachers' wives, showing them how to make bonnets.

"Monday, 13th.—To-day the people went to plant arrowroot for the Missionary Society. About a fortnight ago I came to the end of the adult classes, twenty-two in number, and in all nearly 400 women. I now meet only one class a week.

"Saturday, 25th.—Early this morning we heard the cry, 'A ship! a ship!' About noon the ship came off our station. At two o'clock Mr. John Williams came on shore, and expressed a wish to get off in the evening; he said certain indications around the sun portended a storm, which he wished, if possible, to avoid. We immediately commenced packing, and at sunset were on board. Our departure was so sudden that scarcely any of the people knew, for they were at their plantations. We have with us three natives for the Institution, and three who are to live with us at Arorangi. We leave these people with deep regret, but duty is plain. We bless God if He has permitted us to do anything for their advantage and improvement, and desire more than ever to devote ourselves to His service.

"Monday, 27th.—Yesterday we were near Rarotonga, but the weather, being hazy, prevented us seeing the land. Near midnight we encountered the anticipated gale; it continued several hours; the thunder and lightning were terrific; but, strange to say, I scarcely heard it; the fatigue on Saturday, together with sea-sickness, laid me quite prostrate. This morning the wind was high and the sea rough; we, however, were anxious to get on shore. Mr. John Williams and ourselves got into a little boat, and landed in safety at Ngatangiia. Mr. Pitman was waiting on the beach to receive us.

A messenger was despatched directly to Avarua, and soon Mr. Buzacott arrived to welcome us.

"Tuesday, 28th.—This evening finds us at Arorangi, surrounded by our good people here, who are overjoyed at our return. I cannot describe our feelings on finding ourselves again in our *own house at home.* As we review the past few months, the dangers to which we have been exposed and the varied scenes through which we have passed, we are constrained to acknowledge that goodness and mercy have followed us. To our heavenly Father be grateful praise."

* * * * *

The remaining three months of the year, after our return from Mangaia, were chiefly devoted by myself and Mrs. Gill to our church, and school, and station work at Arorangi.

At this time there were about 3,600 people on Rarotonga, 1,000 of whom were at Arorangi. At Arorangi, during the year 1841, there had been 90 deaths, 40 births, 16 marriages; 24 adults and 26 children were baptised, 28 members were received into church, and 300 adults and 400 children were in our schools.

* * * * *

It will give an idea of the Bible intelligence of these natives at this early stage of the mission if I transcribe a list of texts, or subjects, I preached from on successive Sabbaths for three months,—January to March:—

"Remember all the way the Lord hath led thee."
"Let us go unto Christ, outside the camp," &c.
"One God, Jehovah, the only Being to worship."
"Those who walk in pride, God will humble."
"Those who shall shine as stars in the heaven."
"Those whose goodness is as the morning dew."
"We are encompassed with a cloud of witnesses," &c.
"Those who sleep in Christ, God will bring," &c.
"God's book of remembrance."
"The golden rule."
"Christ will give His disciples a white stone."—Rev. ii. 17.
"They all began to make excuse."
"The pastor's watchfulness and labour."
"The crown of glory laid up for believers."
"Thou hast in love delivered my soul.",
"Foundation laid on the rock."

"The dead shall hear the voice of the Son of Man."
"Being in gall of bitterness and bonds of death."
"God's love manifested by the preaching of Jonah," &c.
"Why God does not answer prayer."
"The new song and the singers in heaven."
"The evil of the impenitent heart."
"Despise not the goodness of God's love," &c.
"He, Christ, has entered into heaven for us."
"The Lord working with the apostles."
"The prayer of Jabez."
"The good old way."
"The committal of Jesus by Pilate."
"The prayer of the penitent thief."
"The heavenly house not made by hands."

Sermons on these subjects were listened to with interest by a congregation of 1,000 people, more than half of whom would meet, in classes of twelve to fifteen persons, in the village after service to talk over what they had heard. The plan had been introduced by the native teachers from Tahiti, and we found it work well, both on the minds and the lives of the people.

Amid this advance in the mental and spiritual progress, the people were encouraged by us to improve their dwelling-houses. Twenty years before this, when they were first visited, their huts were miserable reed hovels, damp and dirty, and very unhealthy, especially in the rainy season.

The building of the new stone chapel at Titikaveka had created a very general wish in the people to build stone houses. This I encouraged, and did all in my power to assist. During this year some eighteen neat, suitable *stone houses* were built in our settlement, besides one good-sized house, with large verandah, by the chief. It was my habit, whenever a house was being built, to visit the workmen once or twice a week, and this I found to have a good effect.

In the midst of these varied labours Mrs. Gill had classes of girls four mornings a week, besides a class of adult females three days a week. The following is a letter written to friends in England by Mrs. Gill during this year:—

"The good work is still going on amongst us, and a steady increase to the number of the faithful proves, I trust, that our labours are not in vain in the Lord. Our schools are also well attended, and the desire of the children for instruction is very pleasing. Some time ago I selected from the upper classes a few girls whom I taught to write on paper. I have sent home some of their copy-books, that you may see their first attempt—the paper is bad, but we had not any other at the time. I hope their second books will be better done. They are also making progress in arithmetic and geography, having committed nearly the whole of their text-book, of the latter, to memory. If some kind friends in England would send us an entire set of 'Pinnock's Catechisms,' they would be acceptable. We could make selections, and have them translated for the use of our schools.

"Last May we held our annual meeting with the children of this station and those of Avarua. Early on the morning of Wednesday, May 17th, they all assembled in the chapel; when, after singing and prayer, Wm. addressed them from John: 'Will ye also become His disciples?' When the service closed, the children partook of refreshments prepared for the occasion. After singing a hymn they were formed into ranks; and, with their native banners, painted all colours, and decorated with leaves and feathers, they marched in procession from one end of the settlement to the other. On their return we again met in the chapel, where several addresses were given by teachers and others, expressive of their joy on the occasion.

"One of the deacons who attended the meeting—an old man, once a heathen—engaged the attention of the children by reciting, in a vehement manner, an ancient invocation to Tangaroa, their idol; he said:—'Children and youths, listen to me; these were our words, and this was our manner, in the days of your fathers, who are dead; yes, they are dead. Oh, if they had lived! if they had lived! how happy would they be to see what I see! I greatly compassionate you, my dear children, and greatly desire that you should know the great deliverance you enjoy. Often you have heard me tell of the dark deeds practised formerly, before the great love of God reached our land. I will not say much to-day; but listen to me a little while, and I will just tell you of one little child whose fate I knew when I was young.

"'We were often at war, one chief with another. At a certain season, some time before the great Word of God shined on us, we were at war—the people of Avarua with us of Arorangi. No one was safe at that time; if a man, woman, or child went out in the morning, perhaps they would be killed before night. During this war of which I speak a father and mother left their house in yonder mountain, and went somewhere by the sea-side towards Avarua. They took their little child with them, and being weary they sat down under a tree to rest; when all of a sudden they saw two men of your station not far from them. Ye children of Avarua, listen to me! What to do they did not know; in a moment, however, they resolved to put the child up in the tree, and run themselves to the bush, and thus escape their enemies, and in the evening return for their child; but, alas! the little child was seen in the tree by the men. Was it compassionated? Was it saved? No; the two Avaruans took it, and with wild shouting brought it and dashed it down on a heap of stones, when in an instant its bowels gushed out. But this did not satisfy their rage. They took up stones and crushed it to powder. Alas! alas! that child, that child! if the good Word of God had come just before his time, he would have lived, and would, perhaps, now have been in our midst—my heart weeps. You, little children, and you, older youths, weep for that child, and for the dark deeds of your fathers! Blessed are your eyes, for you see this season—here you are, the children of Avarua and the children of Arorangi, united in love! Be diligent, be attentive, be followers of God as dear children!' The old man then sat down, but the impression his speech produced was not soon forgotten.

"How true, my dear friend, is prophetic testimony concerning the heathen: 'Their habitation is full of cruelty, and their feet are swift to shed innocent blood.' Oh, cease not to pray for the heathen!—there are yet hundreds of islands in this vast ocean, whose wretched inhabitants are still living, as these once were, unblest by the light of Divine truth, but who, through the increased efforts and prayers of the churches at home, soon might, like these, enjoy all the blessings of our common salvation."

I wrote to the Directors the following, dated August 27th, 1842:—

"The letter from the Directors to our churches, inviting them to assist by all possible means in the great work of making known the Gospel to the heathen beyond them, was fully appreciated both by ourselves and the people of our charge. It is, however, but little that the poor natives of Rarotonga can do towards filling the treasury. A goodly number of those, who have tasted that the Lord is gracious, are not only willing, but anxiously desirous, to give *themselves* to you and to the work of the Lord. These and many others assist you by their constant supplications to the throne of Him who values obedience more than sacrifice, and whose ear is ever open to the cry of His people; but of this world's goods they have not much. Those of the natives united in classes for instruction have been diligent during the past year in planting and weeding their patches of arrowroot for the benefit of the Society.

"On the 15th of June last, we held the Annual Auxiliary Missionary Meeting at Avarua—the station of Mr. Buzacott. At an early hour of the morning most of the people at this station assembled in the chapel. After singing and prayer, Makea Davida was re-appointed as Treasurer. Several speeches were delivered by natives, testifying their gratitude to the churches at home, and their love to the Saviour for the blessing of grace so richly enjoyed by them. The captains of two American whaling vessels lying off the island attended the meeting, and gave some account of the revivals in America, together with the growing interest in missions there; exhorting the people by every practical means to seek the extension of the blessings of the Gospel to the heathen beyond them.

"Rio, one of the first native teachers to the island, gave an address, which was listened to with great interest. He said, 'Blessed are our eyes, that we see these rays of light. Our fathers were born in darkness, and in darkness their years fell behind them. The various generations of chiefs have died without seeing those days; but we are now rejoicing continually in the light from heaven.'

"Addressing the young, he said, 'You ought indeed to exalt your voices high in praise to Jehovah. He has saved you from the pit of heathenism. We, your fathers, know the character of that pit. Some of you were born there; but now you resemble stones dug out of darkness and filth, and built up, by the love of Jesus, into a house of light and glory. You do not know what we know. The reign of Satan is a dark reign—a reign of death. We, your fathers, have lived under his dominion. The place in which we are now met was once a fearful place—a place of murder. We lived in the mountains, and hid ourselves in the holes of the rocks and in the caves of the earth. Our spear was our companion—our stones of murder our choicest property. *Aue! aue! aue!* (Alas! alas! alas!) we ate flesh—human flesh—and *drank blood;* but *now* we are saved. Great is the love of God! Let our hearts be glad—let our voices be exalted—and let us do what we can to send the Word of God to those who *are* as we *were*. The churches of Britain are doing much now; and they call on us to help them; we have no real property, but we all have land, and we all know how to plant. Let us plant—continue to plant—arrowroot, to assist in this great work; and what we do with our hands, let us see that our hearts be there also; that will be well pleasing to God.'

"After the meeting, the arrowroot prepared by the classes was weighed—it amounted to 1,400 lbs. (two years' subscription). The people of this station, Avarua, were prevented from preparing their arrowroot last year, owing to their building a new school-house, their old one, together with their chapel, being blown down by a fearful hurricane in March, 1841.

"A few days after the above meeting, one of a similar kind was held at our station, Arorangi, at the close of which 900 lbs. of arrowroot were subscribed, together with three dollars and twenty-four bundles of dried banana. The people of the station, with the children of our school, have planted for the ensuing year, and by their cheerfulness in the work give proof of their desire to aid, as far as in them lies, the holy cause to which they owe so much."

I sent also the following translation of letters from the native officers of our Auxiliaries at Arorangi and Mangaia, addressed to the Directors and friends of the Society generally:—

"Our friend and brother, he who writes sends greeting. This, my letter, is concerning the growing of the Word of God and His Church at Arorangi. We are greatly rejoiced while thinking of your compassionate love to the heathen, and the great work you are doing by your Society. Ours is a land of no property; nevertheless we have contributed arrowroot, and, for the three years now fallen behind us, we have assembled at one place. No ships have come to buy until now. Now Mr. John Williams has come, and we have given over the property to him.

"We were heathens formerly, and then we neglected this good work; but when Williamu came and brought our first teacher, whose name was Papeiha, we found life, and the darkness fled. It was as Paul has written, 'We were once darkness' (Eph. v. 8); and, as John says, 'The light shined in the midst of darkness, and the darkness comprehended it not' (chap. i. 5). Then it was we knew that good was the Word of God. Then were our idols abolished, and now we are thinking that thus shall be the growing of the Word of God in the lands yet remaining in darkness, who know not the salvation and loving-kindness of God.

"The arrowroot (2,306 lbs.) has been sold to Mr. Williams for money, amounting to £24 0s. 5d. There is joined to it £6 17s., making in all £30 17s. 5d., which Mr. Williams will forward to the Society through Dr. Ross, Sydney.

"This is the conclusion of my letter. "NA SETEPHANO."

"Mangaia, *September* 10th, 1842.

"FRIENDS, BRETHREN, AND SISTERS,—Blessings on you from God, and from the Lord Jesus our Saviour! We were heathens formerly, when Williamu first came to us in his vessel. They brought to us the Word of God, but we took the teachers and ill-treated them, and their wives. We scattered their property, and took the books they brought us as ornaments to our heathen dances. This we did in our blindness; but when we knew the Word of God we greatly wept. The Word of God has grown very great among us, and the word spoken by Isaiah has been fulfilled (chap. ix. 2). Through your compassion and prayers we have obtained the knowledge of Jesus our Saviour. Our former gods were wood and stone, and great in number; each family had a separate god, but now we have one God, as was written by Paul (Ephes. ii. 13). Look you at that passage!

"Brethren and Sisters, we send the property we have collected to assist you and the churches of Britain. It has been subscribed by the churches at Mangaia—but it is very little. Ours is a land of no property. This is the amount of what we have subscribed: £11 12s. 6d. It is not ours—it is yours.

"Brethren, here is another little word of ours to you; we are much in want of slates, paper, pens, ink, and pencils. We have learnt to write on sand and leaves, and we greatly desire that you should give us a supply of the things mentioned.

"We are greatly rejoiced at the testimony of Paul (2 Cor. v. 18, 19). By that word we know our former state of blindness, and that now we are reconciled to God. Because of the great love of God, our war-clubs are laid aside, and we are become brethren.

"This is all we find to say at present.

"NA NUMANGATINI, who collects the property at Mangaia for the Society.

"NA SOLOMONA, who writes at Oneroa, the Great Settlement."

SPEECH OF A RAROTONGAN CHIEF.

At a meeting of the Australian Auxiliary to the London Missionary Society, held at Sydney, in August, 1842, the following speech was delivered by Makea, a native chief of Rarotonga, then upon a visit to the colony with his respected pastor, the Rev. A. Buzacott, who acted as interpreter on the occasion:—

"Sons and daughters, and those amongst you who are chiefs and members of the churches, your attention I crave while I deliver to you a little speech. I think you will not despise me in consequence of my colour, but will have patience while I tell you something of what God has done for me and my people. I wish to make known some of the evils which formerly grew in my own land. The evils of which I wish to speak first are wars; then of cannibalism; then of the plurality of wives which prevailed in my land; and the way in which God has been pleased to remove these evils. I do not wish to dwell upon them, because they are now abolished, but to make known to you how God was pleased to send His messengers, who came with the Word of Life in their hand, and said, 'This is the Word of God'—though we did not know what was meant by it. After Papeiha, Mr. Williams, who is now dead, arrived among us, and idolatry was abolished; but not the evils connected with it: they still remained, and were practised secretly in a very great degree. When Mr. Williams arrived, he explained more fully the love of God in sending His Son Jesus Christ; still we were in partial darkness as to these great and wondrous things. When the teachers explained more fully the true God, some of the people said they were deceiving us, that Jehovah was a deceiver, and that their gods of wood were true gods; but now these things are more clearly revealed to us, and we have abandoned our gods of wood and stone. You understand what I have already said, that the gods we formerly worshipped were deceivers; but it was not soon that we could abandon the evil things connected with idol worship, and, had it not been for the power of Jehovah, these things would still remain: this power has operated, not only in an outward manner, but in showing us the evil of our nature, and in leaving us to abandon our evil courses. I hope you will bear with me while I endeavour to explain the means God employed in causing the good Word to grow in our land, and in destroying the evils which remained.

"The people had embraced Christianity in name, but knew little of its power; but they have been visited by affliction, and these afflictions have been great, and they have been sanctified. After Mr. Williams left us, God was pleased to make Mr. Buzacott an instrument of explaining more fully the love of Christ in dying for sinners—this has been the means. Here I stand before you as a Christian, and to what are we to attribute it—to your love! to your compassion! No; it is in consequence of the love of God—the mercy of a Saviour—that I have been made a Christian, and stand before you this day as an evidence of what the work of God has been among us. You are well acquainted, dear friends, with that passage of the Word of God spoken by Paul, and which well applies to us, 'We were once darkness, but now are we light in the Lord.' Formerly we had bad gods; we were bad men; had bad clothes, bad bread, bad water, and lived in bad houses; but now we know the true God, and have good clothes, good food, good water, and good houses to dwell in. You are white—you know the good God, and have good clothing, and everything good—these all follow in the train. But, though we are of a different colour, God does not look at that. He has not prepared heaven for one colour only—we shall not be rejected in consequence of our colour—God is no respecter of persons. He looks at the heart. Why is it that *you* have not understood the command of Jesus Christ, 'Go ye into all the world, and preach the Gospel to every creature.' England has sent the Gospel and missionaries that have taught us respecting the true and living God, and by this means we have become His professed people. Who has observed the command of Christ—who has obeyed it among you—'Go ye into all the world!' How is it that none from Sydney have been sent—that none from the church here have been qualified for this great work! Why leave it to ignorant natives, such as myself! We may do very well to go before, to prepare the way, but missionaries are wanted. At every land we come to the door is open; every one is saying, 'We want to know what is the Word of God'; let them not die for want of help.

"I have one little word more for you, and shall then have done. I am much delighted to look upon your faces; I have seen something which neither my father, my grandfather, my great-grandfather, nor any of my ancestors, have seen; they all perished in darkness, and only saw evil, such as killing and eating each other; but, in consequence of knowing Jehovah as the true God, I stand before you, and see this beautiful house—these beautiful lights—which your hands have made, and behold these friends who make my heart rejoice. I have only one little word more to say; that is, I commend you to God and the word of His grace. Do not forsake the Word of Life—do not follow that which leads to death;

but every one of you seek that which leads to life—and again I commend you to God, now and for ever."

Previously to sitting down, Makea's attention was called to the money lying upon the table, in reference to which he observed:—

"This is what I have to say—these are the subscriptions from the churches at Rarotonga—it is very little; but we have not money as you have—what we get we are happy to give. Mr. Williams told us something about what the people of England did: how they collected money for the Society to send forth the Gospel; when we knew this, our desire began to grow for other heathen lands who knew not the true God; and, therefore, having been told how we might set to work, we planted some land, and sold the produce. This is the result—the sum amounts to about £90."

We had been now about three years on the island, and we were happy in our work. Many trials, and some inconveniences, were, of course, experienced. The "*Camden*" had had its route disarranged by the death of Mr. Williams, and our want of supplies was being felt rather heavily; hence we were glad indeed this year to receive a visit of the "*Camden*" direct from Sydney. Our boxes had been lying in wet cellars some twelve months, and when they came to us they had been packed some two years. But, alas! on being opened, almost every article of clothing, barter, and food was completely spoiled; most of the things were as rotten as tinder. Two or three large packets of letters from parents and friends lay in the middle of one of the boxes, but crumbled to dust as we touched them. This was most trying. It was the only time I ever saw Mrs. Gill give way to sorrow.

But the charge of the two stations which devolved upon us took off our attention from being too much absorbed in our troubles, for our friends, Mr. and Mrs. Buzacott, had been appointed to visit the out-stations in West Polynesia, and also to visit Sydney. For nine months Mrs. Gill and I had to attend to the two stations, Avarua and Arorangi, and undertake the care of the students in the institution, besides the superintendence of the printers and press.

Before I left England I had never been in a printing-office, and knew nothing of practical printing; but by this time, by frequent visits to the native printing-office, I had become pretty well able to attend to its operation.

Native young men, whose fathers had been heathens, had learnt at Tahiti all press work, and were able to perform all its branches with wonderful correctness, though rather slowly.

CHAPTER XIII.

SECOND VISIT TO MANGAIA, 1842.

WHILE thus fully engaged in the work of the two stations I had again hastily to visit the island of Mangaia. The following is an account of the cause, and of the work done on the island during this hasty visit :—

An American whaler had called at Mangaia, and had taken in a supply of hogs, yams, potatoes, &c.; the captain had shown much kindness to the people. On his taking leave, they asked him to favour them by giving two or three volleys from the "pupui maata o te pai"—big guns of the ship—the report of which they had heard was like thunder. Getting on board he gratified this desire; the *thunder* report of the great guns wonderfully astonished and pleased them.

To return the compliment, Maretu, the teacher, filled his double-barrelled gun with powder, and fired a salute; in doing so the barrels burst, and one of his hands was completely shattered, and the poor man fell, as dead, to the ground. A canoe was immediately sent to the ship to give information of the accident; the captain went on shore, and, after giving all the assistance in his power, he sailed for Rarotonga to communicate the distressing intelligence.

A small schooner had just come to Rarotonga from Tahiti. This I chartered and sailed for Mangaia, which I reached a week after the accident. Getting near to the shore, several natives came off in their canoes, calling out as they approached us, "Praise be to God! You are come; hasten; Maretu still lives, and has been praying to see you." Poor fellow! His hand was fearfully lacerated, and he was in a high state of fever.

Detaining the vessel several days, we did our best to subdue the worst symptoms, but concluded that in order to prevent mortification it would be necessary to amputate some part of the arm. Not wishing to undertake this responsibility alone, I resolved to remove him to Rarotonga; this was done, and the good man recovered, re-entered on his labour, and is now one of the fathers among the native pastors of the islands.

Previous to our leaving the island, I visited the *third* settlement, Ivirua, and was much gratified with the evident marks of industry. The land is sterile and unfruitful, compared with the luxuriant richness of Rarotonga, whose mountain summits and lowlands are alike covered with rich variety of verdure; but here the well-watered and cultivated valleys form a striking contrast to the surrounding barren hills.

The houses which form this village are built on rising ground in one of these valleys, surrounded with taro and yam plantations, and shaded with the wide-spread branches of the lofty cocoa-nut trees. The population was about 500, *sixty* of whom were in church communion, and two hundred children were in the school.

During my stay I had frequent conversations with the people respecting their former heathen state, and the blessings of the Gospel which were now enjoyed by them. The older natives gained new vigour while they related, in language of deprecation, the facts of their idol-worship and their heathenism. The last of those who had seen Captain Cook had died a month or two before my first visit; but most of the present population remember the accounts respecting him and his ship, as given by their parents; and they preserve with great sacredness an axe and two or three knives, which were left on shore by this discoverer of the island.

It was interesting to witness their emotions of sorrow while they told us of their cruelty towards Papeiha, the teacher whom "Williamu" wished to leave among them, and of their subsequent affliction, by which they said God prepared their hearts to receive Davida. They also told a singular instance of their heathen ignorance and superstition. When Davida landed on the island, he brought with him a pig. Having never before seen any animal larger than a rat, the people looked on this pig with emotions of awe; they believed it to be a representative of some invisible power. The teacher did all he could to convince them that it was only an animal, good for food and for trade; but they were determined to do it honour; they clothed it in white-bark, sacred cloth, and took it in triumph to the principal temple, where they fastened it to the pedestal of one of the gods. For some time the beast resisted such honour, and made attempts to get at large, but all efforts to escape proved futile; for two months her degraded votaries brought her daily offerings of the best fruits of the land, and presented to her the homage of worship. At length, however, she repaid the devotees by "a litter"; and for a while the young ones were considered as sacred as the mother: they were kept within the precincts of the temple, until, becoming more unmanageable than their *dumb* gods, they were left to the privilege of a wide range over the land. The teacher, who had not ceased to ridicule their folly, succeeded now in having the sow returned to him, which he killed, cooked, and ate! Thus was the spell broken; and since then the posterity of this honoured ancestor of the pig tribe have been left to their natural state, administering no small gratification to the people at their feasts; and, by barter, are now the principal means by which they obtain property from ships that call at the island.

During the twelve months since I had left them, the people at Ivirua had built a large and commodious chapel, and my present visit was made an opportunity for opening it. It was an interesting day's service. The sound of the chapel gong echoed from valley to valley, in the place where, only a few years before, all the people were idolaters. Company after company came over the hills and through the plantations to enter the new house of God. My text was Isa. lvii. 7: "A house of prayer for all people."

Thus ended 1842.

CHAPTER XIV.

MISSION WORK IN THE ADJACENT ISLANDS—HERVEY GROUP.

THE first Sunday in 1843 saw us back at our own station, and we were pleased to see signs of much success in our work; eighteen natives were received into the fellowship of the church, and seventeen were baptized.

Early in January Mr. and Mrs. Buzacott returned from Sydney. We were cheered also with a visit from Mr. and Mrs. Royle, from Aitutaki, who were, after four years' isolation and trial, needing rest and society.

As soon as practicable, Mr. Buzacott and I arranged to meet two or three days a month to revise the manuscript and native-printed proofs of the Rarotongan Bible—a work we had commenced before he left for Sydney, and which we now desired to finish, that it might be sent to England for printing at the first opportunity.

As the people were advancing in civilisation they wished for more frequent visits of ships to the island. To encourage such visits market-houses were built near the harbours, and a native salesman was appointed to take charge of each, and market laws were printed for the regulation both of sellers and buyers. These laws were introduced from Tahiti, and all these improvements were made mostly under the conduct of the natives themselves. From seventy to eighty whaling and other ships were then visiting the island yearly for supplies, from America, France, New Zealand, Tahiti, and other places. We only had visits from four English ships all the years I was on the island.

Two efforts were made by natives of this group to build small vessels—one by the people of Aitutaki, who, in heathen times, occasionally visited Rarotonga in large double canoes for purposes of war and bloodshed; the other by the people of Avarua, who desired to emulate the enterprising traders who came in small vessels from Tahiti. Both these vessels were finished, but only made one voyage each, when they were wrecked.

At this time the missionaries were the only foreigners residing on the island, and we untiringly rendered all help at our command to develop the industry and commercial enterprise of the people. We encouraged them to cultivate the growth of cotton. Coffee we had introduced, and we now urged them to plant it out freely. Arrowroot also was generally grown and prepared for sale. I planted pips of South American oranges, and in subsequent years I had the satisfaction of seeing them grow and bear fruit. Fire-wood was largely bought by ships. Yams, potatoes, bananas, &c., &c., were in much demand, so that even at this early period the people were getting well supplied with foreign goods and with money.

During this year we commenced a weekly native periodical, called the "*Puna Vai*" (Fountain), intended to be a record of events on the island, and to give general information gained from the outside world. This little work was paid for in arrowroot, and had a large issue, and the people much appreciated it. In after-years the "Fountain" was laid aside, and a newspaper called the "*Manu Rere*" (Flying Bird) was printed; this was a more pretentious production, and had a wider circulation.

Besides these varied efforts for the improvement of the people, the church at Arorangi built a school-house on my premises, where I had from twelve to fifteen native youths in training. This school engaged much of my time, but was successful, and after a while several young men grew up who were able to take the oversight of it, and greatly to aid in the general work of the station.

About the middle of 1843 it was decided that Mrs. Gill and I should pay a visit to all the islands of the group, to see the churches, and to arrange plans for our native teachers residing on them—these islands had native teachers only, except Aitutaki. It was also planned that we should go in search of an island reported to be a day's sail to the south-east, called Tuanaki, and then remain six months on Mangaia.

The little Samoan-built schooner, "*Samuel and Mary,*" came to Rarotonga just at the time, and this we chartered. On the 29th of May we embarked, with several teachers and natives going to the islands. After a three days' voyage we reached Aitutaki.

Aitutaki.

Rev. H. Royle landed here in 1839. He had experienced very much trouble and danger during his four years' residence, but now the people were all under instruction, and Mr. and Mrs. Royle were reaping the fruits of former years' labour and suffering. A hurricane had recently devastated the plantations, and the poor people also were suffering severely from dysentery when we arrived. For some time most of the people had been living on roots of shrubs and trees, which are only resorted to in extreme famine. While in the midst of these troubles the heart of the missionary was cheered and encouraged by an ingathering to the church of some who had been the most wicked and abandoned on the island. No fewer than *fourteen* of such were in one year convinced of their sin, and enlightened in heart; and these, by a subsequent consistent Christian life and conversation, proved the genuineness of the change which they had undergone.

Two of them had been ringleaders in an outbreak which took place some years before, and had sought to destroy the life of the missionary. In speaking of them, Mr. Royle says: "I shall not soon forget the emotions with which the members of the church listened to their confessions of sin and guilt; and from my own eyes, I am not ashamed to confess, they drew copious tears." These converts learned to read well, and some of them became useful teachers in the schools! This class of natives, it will easily be imagined, were looked upon by the missionary with peculiar interest: in the days of their ignorance, when they little understood the benevolent intentions which actuated him, or the genius of the Gospel which he taught, they had done many evil deeds; but now they were as docile as they had been formerly wild, as truthful as formerly deceitful, and as useful as formerly injurious.

During our stay on Aitutaki, we were enabled to realise the fruits of Mr. Royle's devoted labours. We had heard much, but the half had not been told us. In the settlements and houses, and in the persons and manners of the natives, we were pleased to see a total absence of everything which characterised their former rudeness. The schools had the daily personal attention of the missionary, and upwards of *one hundred members* were united in church communion.

But Mrs. Royle's health failed, and relief from labour, with change, was deemed essential to her recovery; the natives, therefore, began to build a small schooner, with a view to bring her to Rarotonga. Happily, however, before it was completed an American captain called at the island, and, as previously mentioned, the mission family went to Rarotonga, where they rested awhile from their labours.

Many of the natives accompanied them. During their stay it was pleasing to see Papeiha and Tapairu and the Aitutakians often grouped together, talking of the incidents of their early lives. At a public meeting, held to welcome the strangers, one of the Aitutakians, an old man, addressed the assembly as follows:—"Brethren, let us praise God to-day that we, who once lived in idolatry on Aitutaki and Rarotonga, are now worshippers of Jehovah, the true God. Oh, the love of God! How great it is! Let us rejoice that we are met together here to talk about that love. We have been brought across the soft path of the sea, and now in this house of prayer we look at each other with wonder. We, the old people, know the dreadful state from which we have been redeemed. Let *us* talk to-day; do not let the young men speak, but let us old men rise up and tell what the 'Evangelia a Jesu' has done for us. Brethren, my heart is full. Suppose we at Aitutaki had built a vessel in our heathenism and had come to you. How should we have been treated? What would have been the result? We should have been murdered, and you would have taken our property and ship as your own. But how different is it with us now! We are safe, our property is safe, and you call us '*Brethren*'! All this comes out of the love of God. The great sea we have crossed is become a sea of love; the air we breathe is full of love; from the top of the mountains, down to the valleys, there is no more heard the sound of war, but the voice of love; the church of Aitutaki is come to salute the church at Rarotonga, and you have embraced us in love. Brethren, let us praise God; He is the Author of this."

These delighted and grateful people returned to Aitutaki much refreshed in heart and strengthened for Christian duties. In the year 1846 I again visited them, and nothing was more palpable than the advance which they had made in knowledge and civilisation.

With a view to show the importance of having a ship in those seas *exclusively devoted to the service of the mission*, I will narrate a few facts connected with missionary voyages in *other ships*. Mr. Royle had been waiting some time on a neighbouring island for an opportunity to return to Aitutaki. At length one occurred; and, agreeing to give a fair remuneration, it was gladly embraced; but it was attended with circumstances of discredit to the captain and danger to the missionary. Arriving off Aitutaki, they found the sea running so high as to render landing all but impossible. Uncomfortable, however, as circumstances were on board the ship, yet, for the sake of safety, the missionary proposed to lay off the island until the next day; this being denied by the captain, he signified his willingness to be taken on to the port whither the vessel was bound, but this was refused, and he was reluctantly compelled to descend into the boat and to attempt a landing. On reaching the reef the surf was rising so high that another effort was made to prevent what appeared to be a most foolhardy act: pointing towards the passage in the reef, through which the boat would have to pass, "Do you think you can enter now you see the real state of the sea?" inquired the missionary, who was anxious for the safety of his wife and children with him in the boat. "I mean to try," was the answer of the man who had charge of the boat; and instantly he ordered the crew "to pull smartly;" but a mighty billow swept over them which rendered their oars as useless as straws, and, gunwale deep in water, the boat was carried out to sea. "Take us back to the ship," the missionary said; "we dare not make another attempt to land in the present state of the surf." "I will not detain the ship," was the reply; "you *must* land!" By this time a numerous body of natives had come to the reef, some of whom swam off to the boat, and, finding that the captain was determined, they, at the risk of their lives, rendered all assistance in their power, and succeeded in effecting the landing of the mission party.

On another occasion, returning to Aitutaki from a visit to an island a hundred miles distant, trials and dangers were undergone which Mr. Royle described as follows:—"It was many hours after we left the shore before we reached the vessel; and when we came on board we found the mate, part of the crew, and some of the passengers in a state of intoxication. We were *nine days and nights* making a passage which, by proper management, ought to have been made in *thirty hours.* During this time I do not think I was two hours in the cabin. In fact, it was some time before any cabin accommodation could be gained for us, and, when gained, I used nightly to see my family into their berths, and then return on deck, where my mind was frequently and severely pained by the most obscene language ever uttered by human tongues. We must have passed Aitutaki the second night, but the excesses of the crew led to its not being seen." These notices require no comment; they will show that, apart from other service rendered by the "missionary ship," it is essential to the well-being, if not to the continued existence, of our older missions.

While at Aitutaki a whaling-ship came for supplies, and the captain gave us more information about the island of Tuanaki, which we purposed to go in search of after visiting the islands of this group.

On leaving Aitutaki we sailed for Atiu, and *en route* made two small uninhabited islands, Akaatea and Manua.

Manua was once inhabited, but now is only occasionally visited by natives who go to feed pigs and make cocoa-nut oil. At Aitutaki we saw a woman who was the only survivor of the tribe who formerly lived on Manua: she is married. Once a year she and her relatives on Aitutaki used to visit this island of her ancestors. She, with twenty-four other natives, took canoe the day before we left Aitutaki, intending, so they said, to take possession of this small but fertile little spot.

Passing these islands, we came to

ATIU.

This island was discovered by Captain Cook. When he visited *Watcoo*, he found three natives of Tahiti, who had been drifted there in 1765. Forty-five years after Captain Cook's visit Christian teachers were placed on the island. Their lives were spared, but they were very ill-treated.

On our landing, several hundreds of the natives came to give us welcome. The village was situated on the hill, and was about two miles in extent, in the centre of which were a large chapel and school-house. The chapel was an old building, and in bad repair, but it was well filled on every service during my stay. Copies of the New Testament had been taken to the island about three years before, and we were gratified to find that the people had purchased copies to the amount of *twenty-six pounds*. The desire of the natives for the Word of God, and their intense delight in listening to its exposition, gave me much delight.

Walking through the village one evening, I saw a young man—a conceited Tahitian—just come to the island, who had induced the chief to have a *body-guard* of soldiers, after the manner of the French Governor and Queen Pomare; these soldiers were being drilled in military style; they were about fifty in number, and armed with sticks instead of guns and swords. The chief appeared much ashamed at our remarks on this foolery, and said he had merely given his consent to please the young people. Returning from our walk, we met the deacons of the church. Thirty-nine members had been admitted, five of whom had been suspended for improper conduct, and four had died, leaving thirty in communion.

It was encouraging to see the children's school under the care of the native teachers. No fewer than 246 boys and 164 girls were present, of whom one-fourth could read well.

I had a long conversation with the chief of Atiu, explaining to him the wonders that had taken place on his own island since the people had burnt their idols and embraced the doctrines of Jesus Christ.

The chief and many of his people listened with much interest to these statements, and determined to give more heed to the words of their teacher than they had heretofore done. This chief was especially interested and instructed by an exposition of Psa. cxv. and Isa. xlv. 9–20; and even with the small glimmering of light which he then had received, he expressed himself surprised that he and his people should have been so long deceived by dumb idols of wood, stones, and feathers. A Tahitian teacher was left on the island, and, according to his ability, he instructed the people. A goodly number of them received the "Word of God," and rejoiced in the salvation it revealed; school-houses were erected, and were well attended, and a church was formed of those who were thought sincere in their professions of Christianity.

Occasional visits were made to Atiu by the missionaries of Tahiti, who, from time to time, were pleased with its progress under the superintendence of the teachers. There were, however, serious evils in connection with the social life of the people, which it was felt could only be overcome by a prolonged residence of an English missionary; and as this could not be speedily gained, Papeiha was appointed to live there two or three years. During his stay he gave attention to everything connected with the progress and purity of the mission, and the people were much benefited by his experience.

In 1842, the Rev. E. Krause came to Atiu from America. Having a letter of introduction to the people from one of the missionaries on Tahiti, he landed on a part of the island where neither man nor habitation of man could be seen. The boat returned to the ship, and he kneeled down on the lonely beach, and implored Divine guidance and blessing. After some time a youth came to the spot, to whom he gave his letter of introduction, and soon after a number of people came to him from the settlement, who gave him a kind reception. But the circumstances of his landing were most unfavourable, and calculated to excite suspicion; the letter of introduction was thought to be authentic, but it was some time before they would give full credence to his being a missionary; this, together with the evils which he set himself to reform, retarded his success. But in time he was enabled in a great measure to overcome the prejudice of the people, and his labours were useful both to the teacher and the natives, until the illness of his wife compelled him to leave the island before his plans had taken full effect on the population.

The next missionary visits were made by the Rev. H. Royle, who frequently remained many months at a time with the people, and he endured much persecution from a disaffected party, strong in number and influence. A code of laws was adopted, but they were too feebly enforced to secure general order and justice to the community. The doubtful character of the chief, together with that of the native police, rendered it almost impossible to bring the perpetrators of crime to punishment. As a specimen of the outrageous conduct of some of this party I may state that, one Saturday night, some of them secretly entered the chapel, and covered the bottom of the pulpit, ankle deep, in mud and filth. This was not discovered until Mr. Royle entered the pulpit on Sabbath morning. Doubtless there were some of the miscreants in the chapel, expecting to be gratified by a disturbance of the service, but in this they were disappointed by his quiet forbearance. He conducted the worship, standing in the mire, without uttering one word of reference to the indignity. The moral effect of this forbearance on the hearts and opinions even of the ungodly was most beneficial and lasting, and resulted in a triumph which could not have been gained by any act of retaliation.

Visit in 1845.

My second visit to Atiu was in the "*John Williams,*" 1845. I was pleased to find that the teacher had prospered in his work. The schools were well attended, and the whole population were more enlightened. A service was held; I preached from John xiii. 34—Christ's love our joy and example. Eighteen members were admitted to the church. I was accompanied by two elderly natives from Rarotonga, and on the evening after the service we were walking on the cliffs, looking across the wide extending sea, when we were joined by some old men of the island who entered into conversation with the Rarotongans; both parties became much animated as they talked about incidents connected with their former heathen life, and praised God, who had spared them to meet "*i roto i tona aroa*"—in His love. Numerous deeds of fame done by ancient heroes were spoken of. One was concerning a man who had a desire to voyage to other lands—a thing quite novel in the condition of the people at that time; he built a large double canoe, and visited most of the islands of the Hervey Group, and returned to his own island in safety. During the remainder of his life he was deified by his fellow-countrymen, and was worshipped after his death. His head was embalmed and preserved for many generations, and, in after-years, prior to undertaking a voyage of any length, the natives would pay homage to it to ensure safety and success.

* * * * *

On my voyage to Samoa, 1846, I again visited Atiu, and was pleased to find that the people had built a new chapel, which, considering their limited means, was a most wonderful achievement. The settlement being some distance from the shore, lime-stone was scarce, but in order to make up the deficiency the people had cut down large "tamunu" trees, which they had dragged to the site of the building; some planks they cut were twenty feet long, two feet thick, and six feet wide; these were placed round the building at distances of six feet apart, and it was calculated that not less than 3,200 feet of this beautiful wood, which much resembles mahogany were in the walls, and more than a thousand feet of it were used in the floor of the chapel.

As this "*are pure anga*" (house of prayer) was nearly finished, the people made arrangements to have it opened during my stay. Nearly the whole population came together; two sermons were preached—one from Rev. xxi. 3, the other from 1 Tim. ii. 5; eight members were admitted to the church, and the communion of the Lord's Supper was commemorated. Many of the old people who had been the first to receive the Gospel on the island had died, but it was pleasing to see a goodly number of young people rising to occupy their places.

It cannot fail to interest the friends of missions to know the history of the present *native teacher* who has charge of the island of Atiu. Tapairu, a woman of the royal blood of Rarotonga, being at the time a heathen, landed, about the year 1820, among the heathen people of Aitutaki. Her rank introduced her to the families of the chiefs, to one of whom she became wife. Rupe, her son, was born just about the time Papeiha was received by the people; it was his privilege to be instructed in his childhood, which introduced him to the blessings of the Christian dispensation. On the return of Tapairu to Rarotonga, Rupe remained with his father on Aitutaki. When the Rev. H. Royle took up his abode there this lad was among the most active and intelligent of his generation. He early attached himself to the missionary, and gave evidence of early piety. He continued to grow in stature and in grace, and, after having devoted himself some time to the active service of religion in his own island, he was sent, with a view to the ministry, to the Institution at Rarotonga. Here he made great proficiency, and in 1846 he was located at Arorangi, where he discharged the duties of the station with diligence and success, and thence was removed to this island of Atiu as the teacher of the people and pastor of the church. Thus, as in many other instances, we see the children of those who were instrumental in the overthrow of idolatry on these islands are now raised up to be helpers in the Mission, and to occupy positions that make native agency essential to its very existence—an agency at once the reward and the glory of our early labours.

Another illustration of this is afforded in the fact that Atiu itself, where no European missionary has ever had a permanent residence, has sent its quota of aid to mission work. Besides sustaining all expenses connected with its home affairs, and contributing to the funds of the parent Society in England, it has supplied *men*, of whom Katuke has been for many years, and continues to be, one of the most laborious, consistent, and efficient evangelists on the island of Mangaia. In 1852 Mr. Royle had under his care seven young men from Atiu, who were candidates for mission work. As an out-station for forty years under native care and control, Atiu yields much encouragement. It is one of those numerous islands in the Eastern Pacific where idolatry has been *entirely* abolished and Christianity has gained a glorious triumph.

MITIARO.

The island of Mitiaro is thirty miles from Atiu. Owing to contrary winds, we were three days making it. It is one of the smallest islands, only three miles in circumference, and has only about one hundred inhabitants.

Okotai, the native teacher here, was soon on board our ship, and assisted us in landing, and at once we commenced our work among the people.

The first settlers on Mitiaro came from Atiu; cruelties of heathen war drove them to this place of exile, and now to its present inhabitants it has all the enjoyments and endearments of *home*.

The poor people told us heart-rending tales of the cruelty of the Atiuans, who in past years were wont to man their war canoes, and to come in battle array to Mitiaro—tales of cruelty and bloodshed too atrocious to be detailed. As soon as opportunity presented, the Atiuans conveyed the knowledge of Christianity to the Mitiaroans, whom they had formerly so cruelly oppressed; the chief of the island himself led the way. On his arrival at Mitiaro, he told the people what he knew about the "new religion;" he exhorted them to renounce idol-worship, to place themselves under the instruction of a Christian teacher, and to build a "house of worship to Jehovah." The ignorant, bewildered islanders listened with astonishment, and somewhat of suspicion, to these propositions; and under fearful apprehensions, exclaimed,

"What! forsake our gods!—Destroy their temples!!—Burn the Sacred One!!!—Shall we not die?" "No," replied the visitors; "No, you will not die; those are false idols—blocks of wood—they cannot kill; we have been deceived in calling them gods; forsake them! commit them to the flames!" Thus did this once savage chief preach to the people of Mitiaro, and was the means of overthrowing the system of idolatry of which he himself, in former years, had been the head.

A Tahitian teacher was at this time left on the island; the people commenced learning the truths of Christianity, and since then they have been advancing in knowledge and civilisation; for *eighteen years* did this their first teacher live among them, receiving only an occasional visit from the missionaries of Tahiti.

When I first visited the island I was much pleased and encouraged at the advanced state of the mission. A number of consistent men and women were united in church communion, the whole of the children were under instruction, and the entire population were living in order, peace, and social propriety. Much to their gratification, I left among them a good supply of slates, pencils, pens, and paper; and also many books for the use of the schools.

In 1845 I again visited this island, and perceived a greater advance in the people. *Twenty* members had been added to the native church; nearly all the young persons on the island could read the Scriptures, and a neat building had been erected as a chapel.

In 1849 the teacher wrote to me, saying:—"I am desirous that you should know the true state of the people of Mitiaro, and therefore will write all I know. There are many men of God here, who love Him and serve Him; but there are also others whose hearts are dark and hard. Yet the Word of God is growing; many of the wicked are subdued by it—the powerful Word of God. There are at present twelve whose hearts are pierced, and who are coming to me to inquire about salvation. These were all, a short time ago, living in ungodliness—they were loving sin, and were a trouble to us; but now they are very different; their minds are light, and their hearts are soft. True is the testimony of Paul: 'The Word of God is life, it is power, sharper than a two-edged sword.' This is a true figure to illustrate these inquirers; and in them I have joy. Pray for me, that I may be assisted in this responsible work. I must also tell you that the former chapel built here is not substantial—the people wish to have a stone chapel—they are burning lime, but hardly believe it can be done. I do hope soon to get tools for this work—'Kia ora na koe i te Atua'—Blessing on you from God."

There are many points in such communications as this which illustrate the character of the teachers, the work they have to do, and the manner in which they do it. The following translation of a letter from the teacher's wife will be found equally suggestive and characteristic. Writing to Mrs. Gill, she says:—

"My Friend,—Blessings on you from Jesus Christ. During this season of our absence from you, I and my husband are frequently thinking about you, and of our dwelling with you. Rauraa has sent you word about our joy in the prosperity of our work here. This is true, all true. But now I must tell you concerning some sorrow that I have in my heart. *Smoking tobacco* is much practised here, not only by the men, but, alas! by the *women* too! This is very bad, especially in women who *make a profession* of religion. Rauraa has exhorted them to leave off this practice, and he is firm with those who are in adult classes, and who are in the church. Some of them have received this advice, but others are still obstinate. We have, therefore, sought other means to do away with this bad practice. Rauraa has a book in which all who are willing to leave off smoking write their names to a pledge, and the thing is done. This has been a good plan, the obstinacy of many has been overcome, and many of the women are reclaimed. My heart is glad to tell you that the people are kind to us; one side of my heart is joyous, thinking we are doing good, and that our work is prospered, but the other side of my heart has many fears."

The practice of tobacco-smoking prevails to a very injurious extent amongst most of the natives of these islands;

and efforts, both by precept and example, are constantly made by the missionaries either to prevent or to moderate its use; but where this teacher gained his idea of "a pledge" I am at a loss to conceive, for nothing of the kind, that I am aware of, had been introduced by the missionaries. The success, however, which attended his efforts must have been encouraging and beneficial.

At the Institution, Rarotonga, we endeavoured to give the students, during their residence there, a knowledge of those arts and usages of civilised life which might make them useful to the people among whom they labour. Hence Raurua, the teacher on Mitiaro, while teaching the people in the schools, was desirous to aid them in building stone houses, and encouraged them to begin with a chapel—an undertaking about the accomplishment of which they had some doubts. Their first teachers had burnt stone into lime, and had built plastered houses, but how stone on stone could be so fixed as to be raised many yards high, and become so firmly cemented as to bear a heavy roof, was a mystery not to be believed until seen.

Early in 1850 sufficient lime had been prepared, and the teacher fondly hoped that before the end of the year the chapel would be finished. A public meeting was convened, every proposition was acceded to, and all bade fair to end peacefully, until it was proposed not to build the chapel on the old site, but on one more convenient and appropriate. This was strenuously opposed, and so strikingly illustrates their superstitions, that I cannot refrain from noticing it. The old chapel stood a little inland from the beach, opposite that part of the reef which formed their most successful fishery. By some means they had conceived a notion that the sacredness of the spot where the chapel stood and the constant good supply of fish were connected and inseparable! "What!" they exclaimed, opposing the views of a more enlightened party, "What! remove the chapel to another spot, and thus deprive us of our principal food! No, we will never consent to that; if that be decided on, we will never join in the work!"

The teacher attempted to show the folly of such notions,

and to reason the matter with them. It was, however, of no avail; their minds were made up—the building should not be removed. "Alas!" exclaims the teacher, "that these people are so slow to leave off their old thoughts and ways! so slow to *receive* the whole truth respecting God! He is *everywhere* present, doing good to all, and the whole earth is full of His goodness. What profit can there be in mere place? But I fear the majority of the people will have it their own way; my heart is sorry, not on account of the place, but because of the wrong thoughts of the people about it. We have decided not to begin the building yet. We must first let these errors and troubles fall behind us. I am grieved, but I am trying to be patient."

Many of the church members on Mitiaro made an arrangement to take a voyage to Mauké, to have a conference with their brethren. The teacher accompanied them on this visit, and they reached Mauké after twenty-four hours' sail. Here the party remained a month, during which time many religious and social services were held; the old people refreshed their memory respecting deeds of bygone years, while they encouraged each other to gratitude and praise for the new state of things which they now enjoyed, and they exhorted the rising generation to hold fast the "Word of Life," to which they were indebted for the happy change.

On their return voyage to Mitiaro this party had well-nigh lost their lives. They embarked on board a native-built schooner, and were overtaken by a storm, which kept them at sea nearly a week; at length, however, they made the island of Aitutaki. Here they attended the missionary May meetings. Not long after their return the people, improved in temper and refreshed in spirit, began to build the new chapel. By a little mutual yielding a site was fixed on which pleased all parties; and in giving the dimensions of the house, the teacher says, "It is 72 feet long, 40 feet wide, and the walls are 20 feet high. It has ten windows, and is enclosed under two roofs; every man and woman on the island did something towards the building, and even the children helped us; they assisted in bringing stones and lime, and in drawing the timber to the place of building." "It is now finished," con-

times Rauraa in his last letter, "and the people sit and look at it with wonder and delight! My heart is glad, and I thank God, who has assisted me in doing this work. His love is great! His power is great!"

For three months after the completion of this chapel, the teacher and people anxiously waited the arrival of a missionary to conduct the opening service; but, being disappointed, they sent messengers to Mauké and to Atiu for some of their friends on those islands to come over and unite with them on the occasion. One native teacher read the Scriptures, and another preached from 1 Kings viii. 10, on "Solomon's Prayer," and the whole service was one of devout joy. The fathers of this people had never dreamt of seeing so glorious a change in their children.

As on other islands, the people are now, by their prayers and contributions, aiding, according to their ability, the spread of the Gospel to other lands. Their money and their arrowroot are cheerfully given towards this good cause. "It is but little we can do," they say; "our land is small and we are poor, but we cannot deny ourselves the pleasure of doing something to spread abroad the Word of God, to WHICH WE OWE OUR ALL."

MAUKÉ.

Leaving Mitiaro, we voyaged to the island of Mauké. It is a *reef-bound* island, and has no landing-place except through *the surf* that rises, with great violence, over the reef.

We came in sight of Mauké about noon, but, owing to light winds, were unable to make up to it, and at nine miles' distance I embarked in a boat. The sea was beautifully smooth, and we rowed cheerfully onward until, when the moon arose, we were within half-a-mile of the reef; here, to our surprise, was heard the roaring sound of heavy breakers, and as we advanced we heard the deep, long, rolling swell of the surf. Our native pilot paddled ahead in his canoe, but we dared not follow; and in this situation, so near danger, so far from the ship, and at night, we became perplexed as to what plan to adopt. We had, however, but just decided to lay on our oars all night when we were cheered by seeing a large blazing fire on the beach. Perceiving some of the natives adjusting their canoes inside the reef, we ventured to row nearer; they made signs for us to go forward in our boat, but it being heavily laden we remained some distance at sea until, about midnight, the teacher came off to us. He was sorry to find that we had left the ship so late in the evening, but had made arrangements to land our boat's company, one at a time, in a large canoe. I shall never forget the wildness of the scene, and the roar of the surf, as we came near the reef; but, waiting a favourable opportunity, our canoe mounted one of the highest waves, and we were borne in safety to the shore. On landing, a number of the natives led us to the village, situated about two miles from the beach. On reaching the teacher's house the crowd had increased so much that all our party could not be admitted; the verandah, therefore, was lighted up with torches, and there we took our seats, in the midst of more than two hundred people, giving to them an account of the state of the islands whence we had come, and of what we purposed to do during our stay at Mauké.

Being somewhat exhausted, I proposed to retire to rest. This was opposed by the assembly; they said we could sleep when we returned to the ship. In the first place, they wanted to hear about the growth of the Word of God on Rarotonga; and then, as they knew the Rarotongans were good singers, they wished to learn some of their tunes. Having brought a supply of hymn-books, I made arrangements for the Rarotongans to teach them some new tunes, which the delighted people practised until the dawn.

The next day we held services in their pretty chapel. In the afternoon 1,830 lbs. of arrowroot and 84 lbs. of twisted cocoa-nut cord were collected as subscriptions to the London Missionary Society, and at evening we left the island grateful that our native teachers had been so helped and blessed in their work.

Having finished our visitation of the islands of the Rarotongan Group, we decided that before taking up our abode on

Mangaia we would engage the vessel to go out a few days in search of *Tuanaki*, the heathen island said to be about a hundred miles south-east of Mangaia. We had not been out two or three days, when the winds became stormy and the sea very rough, and many of the natives on board became very ill from dysentery, and our little vessel showed signs of imminent danger; so that, after a week's unsuccessful voyage, we held consultation, and decided to return to Mangaia.

It has been found, in after-years, that the reported island was *Easter* Island, due east of Rarotonga.

We reached Mangaia in safety, and the little ship sailed direct to Rarotonga, where, almost without any warning, its rotten timbers broke up. The wonder was that it had held together during the high winds and rough sea it had encountered during our recent voyage. In mercy our God watched over us and our fellow-passengers.

CHAPTER XV.

THIRD VISIT TO MANGAIA.

As stated at the close of the previous chapter, we returned to MANGAIA. It was my *third* visit, and I remained there six months, and gained much information respecting the state of its churches, schools, and stations, which, upon the whole, was peculiarly gratifying, as the result of *native* instrumentality. One of the most pleasing features of the island at this time was the prosperity in both the adults' and children's schools. No fewer than ninety male and female teachers were daily instructing nine hundred children. With these teachers I had four, and sometimes six, classes a week, giving them lessons in history, biography, geography, and Biblical expositions. Besides these, I met, every other day, adults in church fellowship, and others under instruction, of whose attainments the following figures will give a pretty correct idea:—

An adult *male* Bible-class, 23 in number—19 able to read well; 6 had Testaments, 17 had leaves of books only. Another *male* class, 17 in number—4 only not able to read; only 1 had a complete Testament. In a third class, 19 in number—14 could read well; each had a Testament. In two other classes, 49 in number—37 could read well; 42 had Testaments. In the adult *female* classes, conducted by Mrs. Gill, it was gratifying to find that a decided improvement had taken place. But much more remained to be done before they attained a proper mental or social position. In a Bible-class of *female* adults, 14 in number—3 only could read, and 12 had portions only of books. In another class, 20 in number—4 only could read, and three only had complete books. In two other classes, 39 in number—18 were able to read, and 8 only had Testaments.

In accordance with arrangements made in 1841, no members had been admitted to the church, but all candidates had been formed into Bible-classes, receiving weekly instruction from the teacher; and now I found seventy candidates for church fellowship, some old, others young. Many of the members of the church had also united together into an Association for visiting the careless and ungodly. The following were the resolutions agreed on by themselves, under the superintendence of Tairi, an excellent Rarotongan teacher:—1st. "That compassion towards our brethren who are living in unbelief and sin leads us to unite in this plan for their good." 2nd. "That we purpose to visit such at their house weekly, and also on Sabbath evenings, for conversation, reading, and prayer." 3rd. "That we meet the first Wednesday of every month at the teacher's house to report, and for consultation and prayer."

The general statistics of Oneroa, the principal station, in 1843—*not twenty years* after the landing of the first Christian teacher—were, inhabitants, 2,000; number in adult classes, 306; boys and girls in children's school, 900; number in church fellowship, 360. For the year ending September 30, 1843, there were 65 births, 40 deaths, 22 marriages, and 45 infants, and 4 adults were baptized.

One afternoon I passed over the low hills which separate two districts to visit one of the heathen families. In a long, low reed hut I found the father of this family seated on a stool. He was tall in person, well clad with native cloth, grave in manner, and about forty years old; numerous ornaments of shell and human hair were suspended at the lobe of each ear; his own hair hung dishevelled on his back, and about thirty of his children, and children's children, sat around him. "Friend, I have come to see you," I said.—"Blessing on you!" "What is your name?"—"My name is Tira," was his reply. "Are these your children?"—"Yes, most of them are my children." "How many wives have you?" I enquired.—"I have only one wife now living; three are dead," he replied. "Is this your dwelling-place?"—"Yes; here my father, and my father's father lived, and here I live with my children, and here I intend to die." "Friend," I continued, "the light of the Word of the true God has now been shining a long time on you in Mangaia. Have you no desire to attend to instruction in that Word?"—"No," he replied; "but sometimes I hesitate." "You are getting old, my friend," I said, "and death may come and find you destitute of that good which alone prepares for another world."—"Yes, death may come," he replied, "and then there will be an end." "An end!" I exclaimed; "but you believe in a future state, do you not?"—"Yes," he continued; "but who knows the truth about it?" Here I tried to explain the truths of the Word of God, about sin and salvation, this world and the world to come. These things were evidently not new to him; but he became sullen and slow in his replies, and concluded the conversation by saying that he had seen the folly of idol-worship, but that he still believed in the religion of his forefathers, and that he intended to remain in his present state until death. Finding that he could read a little, I sent him a New Testament, expressing my hope that he would read it; but, to the dismay and grief of all, he returned it, saying he had made up his mind to do without it. This was the *first and only* instance known in the history of Mangaia of refusing to accept a book, and it produced no little anxiety in many of his children. This man was frequently visited by the members of the church, but he lived on in obstinate unbelief; and the native teacher, speaking of his death, says: "Tira lay ill a long time, and became very unhappy. *His mind was light, but his heart was hard.* He was full of fear, and trembled continually. He told his children not to follow him in unbelief." His eldest son became an excellent Christian man, and, with many of the younger branches of his family, joined the Christian village.

A fatal epidemic was, about this time, brought to the island, and many of the natives were cut off in the prime of life. Among these was Ngatai, one of the teachers; but the joy and peace which he experienced in death did much to comfort and instruct the people; not that we needed this to assure us of his fitness for heaven, for his life had been a perpetual evidence of his faith; but his dying experience was peculiarly appropriate to the afflicted circumstances of the people. His words of consolation to the godly, and his exhortations to the ungodly, were blessed for much good. His last words were: "The billows of death are breaking over me, but my vessel is safe; it is fixed by the anchor which entereth within the veil, where Jesus, my forerunner, is. MY HEART IS FIXED—MY HEART IS FIXED ON HIM!"

The people of Mangaia, in their heathenism, knew no animal larger than a rat. I have previously referred to their ignorance and superstition at the first pig that was taken on shore. I will now give a brief account of the introduction of another animal.

On my voyage in 1843, we were accompanied by many natives, among whom was a young man who was returning from Sydney. This young man was taking home a rabbit: it was a fine creature, and much thought of by the owner, and by the natives on board. One day while on deck, fondling his rabbit, and thinking what notoriety he would gain among his countrymen for taking it on shore, the young man was accosted by an elderly man, a friend of his, who was a deacon in the Mangaian church—a man of known piety and integrity, and, moreover, honourably connected with the bench of magistrates. "Friend," said this worthy man, "that is a pretty creature; what is its name?" "It is a rabbit," replied the young man, "and," he continued, "they are very numerous in foreign lands." "Numerous are they?" replied the old gentleman; "allow me to nurse it awhile." The rabbit was immediately handed over to him, and for some time he continued to stroke its head and back playfully, and then, in a moment, to the distress of all who stood by, he wrung its neck, and cast it into the sea! Astonished and irritated at this unprovoked conduct, I united in condemning it, and in demanding an explanation. But, finding myself too much vexed to institute a calm inquiry, I turned aside, leaving the enraged young man to discuss the matter with his friend, who was provokingly easy, and, withal, apparently kind in the midst of the storm of angry words which bore down upon him.

Some time afterward I seated myself in their midst and asked an explanation, assuring the deacon that I thought he had done wrong. "Oh, no," he replied; "it will be all right when we get on shore. I shall report it to the magistrate, the thing will be justified, and the young man will receive property more than the value of the animal." "Indeed!" I inquired; "how so?" "Last year," the old man replied, "a ship came to our land and put on shore two beasts much like that rabbit. At first we were all pleased with them, but very soon they became the plague of the island. They took up their abode in the hills and bush, and so rapid was their increase, and so ferocious and wild their habits, that they had well-nigh destroyed all our poultry." "Tell me what kind of beast it was," I asked. "It was much like that rabbit," rejoined he, continuing his conversation with an air of consciousness that he had done right. "These animals became so destructive that the chiefs and landholders held a council and resolved to hunt them to death, and that no such animal should again be permitted to be brought on shore." "What do you call it?" I inquired. "We call it Kêao," he answered. "Kêao, Kêao," I repeated again and again; "whatever can it be?" "Oh! it is a real savage beast! You will soon see it," was the reply. About a fortnight after a terrible uproar was heard at midnight in the settlement. On making inquiry I saw a multitude of half-naked natives armed with sticks and stones, and carrying flambeaux, and was told it was a Kêao hunt. In a short time shouts of victory were heard, and the hero of the night was seen returning through the settlement holding up a *large cat* by the tail! Yes, it was poor puss! She had been landed among a people who did not know her quiet, domestic habits; circumstances had driven her to the bush, where she had become wild, and had occasioned these grave incidents in the island life of the people of Mangaia! The young man to whom the rabbit belonged received property, by order of the chief, from the public store, which more than remunerated his loss, but which did not overcome his regret that his quiet and pet animal had been supposed to have relationship to the Kêao tribe!

Among the laws made by the people of Mangaia the one

prohibiting tattooing was the occasion of more trouble and annoyance to the police than any other. The natives here more generally practised this art, and were more proficient in its execution, than those on the other islands of the group. I had frequently questioned the propriety of imposing a penalty on its practice; not that I thought its continuance desirable, but from an opinion that the individual who tattooed himself committed no public wrong, and that a sense of propriety, induced by a continued course of proper education, would in time do away with the custom. The native authorities, however, who knew the design of the practice, were determined to attach a severe fine to its execution, which occasioned a large majority of the young men to be brought into the criminal court before the age of twenty, which doubtless did as much, or even more, injury to their moral feelings than the act for which they were judged. Thus, in things of which the native law takes cognisance, the missionary often finds opposition to his advice for prudence and moderation, and has much difficulty in showing the people the difference between discipline of the church and laws for the establishment of national order in a general and mixed population. Caution is therefore necessary in advising tribes just emerging from heathenism respecting the adoption and enforcement of laws, lest they increase and perpetuate the very crimes which they desire to subdue.

I well remember an address given by a young man on his admission to church fellowship. He said that between the years of fifteen and twenty he had often been publicly tried in the criminal court for tattooing, and had been degraded and heavily fined. At first he felt the degradation most severely, but he afterwards became hardened, until he found himself destitute of any desire for that which was good. Thus he grew deeper and deeper in sin, until one Sabbath afternoon he thoughtlessly came to chapel. A sermon was preached from Rom. vii. 9, concerning the *spirituality* and extent of *God's law*. "It was then," said the young man, "that I felt for the first time the nature of the *law of God*—I felt that it was above me, and under me, and around me, and *in* me. All my sins, of hand and heart, came to my view, and I became as a slain man. At first I desired to die. It is this that has *driven* me to Jesus as my Saviour and refuge; now I have peace in Him; He alone is my joy and trust." In this way the efficacy of the Gospel most illustriously appears in the *regeneration* of these degraded tribes—*translating* them from the kingdom of Satan into the Kingdom of *righteousness*, and peace, and joy.

At the same church-meeting at which the young man was admitted, another man from among the heathen gave an account of himself. He had been brought to see the error of his way by a different means from his companion, but the effects of the change were the same. Standing before the members of the church, he said:—"Brethren, my heart is wondering at the way by which I have been brought from my sin, and led to seek fellowship with you. You know that I have been one of the most vile young men in this village. It is true I frequently used to come to chapel, but all I heard there I laughed at, for I *loved folly*, and after it *I ran*. But one day, while fishing outside the reef, a shark upset my canoe, and for some time he held my thigh in his mouth. I had no hope of life; my pain of body was great, but a shining light burst into my mind—all my former life came up to my view. The shark still held my thigh; I felt his teeth go to the bone, and I expected it to be bitten off, but God had mercy on me. I did not cry for mercy at the time, for I had nothing but horror and despair in my heart. A companion, who was also fishing, came to my assistance, and helped me on shore. I lay ill a long time; many members of the church came to see me, who talked and prayed with me, and I was led to see that Jesus was the Saviour I needed. I have given myself to Him; He has brought me in your midst to-day, and my heart is full of wonder and praise."

During our stay on Mangaia we visited Ivirua, and then proceeded to Tamarua; our path lay over hill and dale—sometimes we were on the summits of the hills, whence the whole island and the sea lay open to our view; at other times we were passing through dales, which were richly shaded with groves of cocoa-nut trees. Our company would have afforded no small amusement to an English spectator. Owing to the badness of the roads, E. was borne in a chair on men's shoulders; I followed, and then came, in single file, a motley group of merry natives, carrying our beds and boxes, and other articles necessary for a temporary sojourn at Tamarua. As we proceeded the old people pointed out many spots renowned for heathen cruelty. One of these in particular excited our attention. It was a valley at the foot of two low hills; on reaching it, an old man, as if awaking from a reverie, exclaimed: "This is a spot of ancient fame—this was the devil's ground!" We halted awhile, and another of our company related a sad tale of heathen wickedness and horror not often surpassed, even in cannibal heathen life. On an occasion of general peace, about six or eight years after the visit of Captain Cook, an aspiring chief, who had been defeated in former wars, conceived a plan of wholesale slaughter before unknown. Sending his messengers to all the tribes on the island, he gave an unlimited invitation to a feast in commemoration of the peace. The day was fixed on; a large quantity of food was prepared, and on the morning appointed an immense number of the people came together. An oven of extraordinary dimensions was heated, which consisted of a large deep hole dug in the ground, filled with stones heated till red-hot. But when all was ready, and each man was about to arrange his food in the oven, a host of warriors, under the chief who had given the invitation, rushed forth at the sound of a preconcerted signal, and, with fiend-like fury, drove hundreds of the visitors into the flames of the oven. For many days the sky was literally darkened by the ascending smoke of this gigantic funeral pile! The old man who gave us this account was, at the time it took place, a little boy, but is now a consistent deacon of one of the village churches. "Let us rejoice," he said, addressing those who stood around him, "that those dark days are passed away, never to return; the bright Sun of Righteousness has arisen upon us with healing beneath His wings; let us rejoice in His light and salvation!"

In the evening a missionary prayer-meeting was held in the chapel of Tamarua; and it was indeed cheering to hear the praises and the prayers of those who were once in a state of heathenism; they were sensible that they were indebted to the Gospel for the privileges of their changed condition, and were anxious to extend the same blessings to the heathen beyond them.

One of the oldest men in the settlement, giving an account of his experience, said :—"Listen to me, my brethren; I am an old man, and, as I have now taken upon me the Word of Life, I will say a little about my former history. I was born a heathen; my father was a great warrior, and he determined that I should be one too. I remember, when I was young, he frequently led me out to see the bodies of the victims he had taken in war, and he taught me to eat human flesh. As I grew older, I was always with my father; he taught me the customs connected with idol worship, and he gave me a war-club, and a spear of his own making; and when he knew I had killed N——, of yonder settlement, he was much rejoiced; a great feast was prepared on the occasion, and afterwards I became wise in all the practices of the priesthood, and my heathen greatness continued to increase until the teachers, the men of Jehovah, came to our land. Some people of Oneroa received them, but we despised them; I was full of pride and anger towards them, and more than once I led my people to fight against the Christian party. Many of our tribe went to live near the teacher in order to be instructed, but I, and my wives, and our children remained here, at Tamarua. About three or four years ago I went to the teacher's village to see my brother; there I first listened *quietly* to the meaning of the Word of God, and afterwards Maretu came to preach in this place; he visited me, and explained to me all about myself and salvation. I then began to attend to the Word of God on the day of the Lord, and my mind became enlightened. I felt that my heart was as old in sin as my body was old in years. I have truly been very wicked, but I am now looking to Jesus; He is my Saviour—a great Saviour for a great sinner!" Turning to the members of the church, he said:—"Brethren, in the name of Jesus, receive me as one of His saved ones."

Coming from Tamarua to Oneroa, we prepared for our return to Rarotonga. An American captain chanced to touch at Mangaia, and he offered us a passage. It was Sabbath morning when he landed; in the afternoon our arrangements were complete, and I preached a farewell sermon. The large chapel was crowded to excess by a congregation of more than two thousand natives, who listened with deepest attention to a discourse from Rev. iii. 11: "Hold fast that which thou hast, that no man take thy crown." The expressions of affection of the people were beyond description. Nearly three thousand of them accompanied us to the beach, while a few of the most sturdy and expert took charge of the canoe which bore us to the ship.

As we sailed away from Mangaia our hearts were full of wonder and praise at what our eyes had seen, and what our hands had been permitted to do, in the moral elevation of a race of men who, less than a *quarter of a century* before, were savage, heathen idolaters, and scarcely known to the world, but who now, by *native teachers' instruction* and our occasional visits, had attained a position in intelligence, morality, civilisation, and Christian character that suffered nothing by comparison with missions of older date. The word that Isaiah, the son of Amos, saw concerning the mountain of the Lord's house has come to pass: it is exalted on the TOP OF THE HILLS, AND ALL THE PEOPLE FLOW INTO IT.

CHAPTER XVI.

BUILDING OF INSTITUTION AT AVARUA, AND CHAPEL AT ARORANGI.

ON returning to Rarotonga we were welcomed with gladness by our people, and we devotedly laid ourselves out, for the welfare of the stations. E.'s health had, for some time past, shown signs of weakness. The past year's privations, labours, and voyages in little vessels had wrought an evident change, which caused us no little anxiety. We were glad, therefore, to have the prospect of a few months' residence at Arorangi, with occasional intercourse with Mr. and Mrs. Buzacott, from Avarua.

At the close of this year, 1843, we were able to tabulate, with a correctness which failed in former years, the population and results of Christian labour among the people after about twenty years' missionary effort.

The population of the group was 10,250. There were in all—

12 Villages or Settlements.
4 English Missionaries.
8 Native Pastors.
1,115 Church Members.
3,600 Adults in Schools.
4,300 Children in Schools.

The mission was now so far advanced as to require an institution for the special preparation of students for mission work. I had had, in common with the Rev. A. Buzacott, two or three young men under instruction who had gone out as teachers to other islands; but we now felt the necessity of larger premises, so as to accommodate a larger number of students. From the experiences of those who had thus taken part in pioneering work, the natives were fully alive to the importance of the object we proposed. Feeling how much the generations of their own land had lost by delay, their zeal would have led them beyond prudence during the first years of their knowledge had not their isolated position and limited means kept them in check. Tuanaki, Maniiki, Tongareva, Samoa, and other islands were constantly mentioned before God in prayer, and not a few of the natives qualified for the work offered themselves, saying, "O Lord, our God, Jehovah, here are we, send us. Let a ship come to our help in this work. We feel the heathen to be our brethren. O Lord, let us be the means of saving them, in this world, from the teeth of the savage, and of leading them to Jesus, the Saviour." Such was the language of their prayer; and no hymns of praise were sung with greater fervour or sincerity than those which had reference to the salvation of the heathen. The following are almost literal translations:—

"Mourn for the heathen,
In blindness they sin,
Bound as in prison,
By Satan their king."

"Let all the idols perish, Lord,
False every whit are they;
Thou, and thou alone, art God,
Evermore we worship Thee."

"Shall we who have knowledge,
And life from above,
Shall we hide this knowledge,
This life-lamp of love?
It is life, yes, 'tis life!
Oh sound it abroad;
Let all the world know it,
And live by this word."

"Ye messengers of Christ, sent forth,
Many are your foes and strong;
But Jesus is your shield and strength,
By Him the victory is won;
And the crown of everlasting glory, yours."

An extensive and suitable piece of land was now bought of the chief, and a good-sized mission-house, with class and lecture rooms was built, besides small stone cottages as separate dwellings for the students.

The work of this Institution was begun in 1844, and it was arranged that I should go from Arorangi twice a week to share the work with Mr. Buzacott. This plan was carried out during the year, and it gave us opportunities of revising together the Scriptures.

During 1844, in the midst of the varied duties connected with the general schools, boarding-school, visiting the institution at Avarua, and revising the manuscript of native Scriptures, it was resolved by the natives of Arorangi to build a new stone chapel, which, as architect and general superintendent, demanded from me much time and attention. I gave out all the plans for the building on the first day of the year; but the building of such a place was a great work for these unpractised natives, and it took twelve months to complete. Its inside dimensions were 60 feet long, 50 feet wide; walls 30 inches thick, and 24 feet high.

The work was undertaken by the members of the adult classes, and, after burning many tons of lime, I made preparation for laying the foundation. The day of this ceremony was one of peculiar interest. In the morning, while Mr. Buzacott and I were selecting a stone in which to place a sealed bottle containing a written statement of the time and circumstances of its erection, we were met by Tinomana, the chief of the station. On being asked whether they were wont in heathenism to observe any kind of ceremonies at the erection of their "maraes" (idol-temples), he said, "The day of commencement was always a great day. He had seen many built, and the occasions had always been connected with the slaughter of many a bloody human sacrifice. The things of importance were the posts of the house; these were always of the best wood that could be found. They were wrought by special workmen, and, the least imperfection being discovered, were laid aside. When prepared, these posts were brought with great ceremony to the site of the 'marae.' Wide and deep pits for the posts were then dug, into which native cloth, axes, poe, and other articles were thrown, and a man was buried alive under each post as an act of propitiation."

While relating these things, the old chief seemed to become young again, and several times exclaimed, "These were days of darkness, and the deeds done then were suitable to the devil. This is a season of light, and we are all rejoicing in the light."

A numerous meeting of natives, including many church members and deacons of the other village churches, was held at the station. Makea and Pa, formerly rival chiefs in heathen times, but now loving helpers of each other in the Gospel work, together performed the ceremony of fixing the centre stone of the building; a hymn was sung, a prayer was offered, when good old Tinomana, the first chief who burnt the idols of the land, gave a short address. In making reference to the mode of building the temples of idolatry he repeated what he had previously stated, saying, "The principal pillars were always erected with offerings and sacrifices; food and human beings were placed at the bottom of the pit, where the pillar was to be placed, which was called a 'tarangaara,' or propitiation to the gods."

Appropriate use was made of this fact by subsequent speakers, and the service closed, forming one of those happy events which contrast so strikingly with the former habits of this once heathen, but now simple-hearted and grateful Christian, people.

The walls of the chapel were of sawn block coral. It was built to seat 1,000 people, with galleries round three sides, and vestry behind. The galleries were supported by ornamental pillars. The pulpit was of native wood, stained and varnished to represent rosewood, and was furnished with a velvet cushion and fringe sent out by friends connected with Barbican Chapel. The day of opening was a time of peculiar interest. On the previous evening the whole of the people from the settlement of Avarua and Ngatangiia arrived near Arorangi, where they encamped for the night.

At the appointed time the members of the different churches, more than four hundred in number, seated themselves in the body of the chapel, leaving the galleries and raised seats under the galleries for those in the classes. Every foot of room was occupied inside, and for those who could not gain admittance seats were placed in the vestry and round the doors and windows of the building. I should think 1,500 people, at least, were present.

After the usual devotional exercises of reading the Scriptures, singing, and prayer, Mr. Buzacott preached a most encouraging discourse from Psa. lxxxvii. 5: "And of Zion it shall be said, This and that man was born there: and the Highest Himself shall establish her." At the close of the sermon we united in the celebration of the Lord's Supper. It was a hallowed occasion; we had before us more than four hundred souls, the greater part of whom were heathens a few years ago, living in the daily practice of everything that is vile and degraded, given up to idol-worship, and accounting it their greatest and most praiseworthy achievement to kill one another in sacrifice on the altar of their god. How changed the scene! *Then* they were afar off, without hope, and without God in the world; *now* they are brought nigh, are separated and sanctified by the blood of the Atonement, and, we trust, are *growing* in the knowledge and love of Christ; *then* they were hateful and hating one another; but *now* have learnt that new commandment, even that they love one another as Christ has loved them. These were our meditations on this sacred occasion, and we felt that it was a season of refreshing from the presence of the Lord. "This is the Lord's doings, and it is marvellous in our eyes."

CHAPTER XVII.

ARRIVAL OF THE NEW MISSION SHIP, "JOHN WILLIAMS," AND STATE OF THE MISSION IN 1845.

ONE morning, the first week in 1845, I was engaged with the boys in the boarding-school, when the arrival of the new mission ship, the "*John Williams*," was announced. To our great joy my brother George and his wife had come out in her to take up their abode on the island of Mangaia. Thus, seven years after leaving England, we were permitted to meet and unite in mission work in these islands.

The new ship had been provided by the churches in England to take the place of the "*Camden*." The following notes will show the joy we had at its arrival:—

"It was our happiness, early in January, to hail the arrival of the missionary ship, and to welcome our brethren, for the work of the Lord in these islands. It was a noble effort—worthy of the children of England—to purchase so fine a vessel as a thankoffering to the God of the fathers and founders of the Society, and to our God, at the close of the fiftieth year of the Society, and as a pledge of future attachment and effort in the cause of the Redeemer. To us it was one of the most welcome sights we had beheld since the departure of the '*Camden*' for England.

"We are encouraged to find that the spirit of missionary enterprise, in some degree, keeps pace with the flight of time. The '*John Williams*,' as a missionary ship, and viewed in connection with the spirit of the churches in sending her out, exceeds the '*Camden*' by as much as 1844 is in advance of 1838. The interest is a growing one, and must be so, until the little one becomes a thousand, and the whole world is brought to give homage to Him in whose name we labour."

The arrival of the new mission ship at this period was most opportune, as was the appointment of my brother as missionary to Mangaia.

The taking of Tahiti by the French a few years before

placed our island in constant danger, and caused no small alarm to the natives. It was known to be the design of the priests of Rome to avail themselves of the earliest opportunity to introduce Popery to these islands.

The following has been preserved as a record in brief of the act of the French in taking possession of Tahiti, and as it much affected our mission work in 1845 I give it here:—

"On the 1st of September, 1842, the French frigate of war, 60 guns, the '*Reine Blanche*,' Admiral A. Dupetit Thouars, arrived at Papeete, the principal port of Tahiti. For a few days all appeared quiet on board, and professions of peace were extensively circulated by the French. On the 5th, messengers were despatched to the Queen, who was staying at Eimeo (*daily expecting confinement*), and also to the principal chiefs, requesting them to come to Papeete, that the Admiral might pay his respects to them; and, in consequence, all understood that his errand was of a friendly character.

"On the 8th, the principal chiefs arrived and dined on board with the Admiral; and, upon the same day, we had the first intimation that a meeting was to be held between the chiefs and the French. The same evening the British Vice-Consul and the American Consul received an official document from the ship, stating that differences existed between the Tahitian and the French Governments which would probably lead to hostilities, and all British and American subjects were therefore warned to take means for securing their persons and property. Early on the following morning, we learned from Mure, the chief speaker, that the *expected meeting had been anticipated by a secret one, held during the night between four principal chiefs and the French.* At this meeting a document was signed by the four chiefs, of which the following is a literal translation:

"'To the Admiral A. Dupetit Thouars.—Because we are not able to govern in our own kingdom in the present circumstances, so as to harmonise with foreign Governments; lest our land, our kingdom, and our liberty should become that of another, we, whose names are written below, viz.: the Queen and principal chiefs of Tahiti, write to you to ask that the shadow of the King of the French may be thrown over us, on the following conditions:—

"'1st. That the title and the government of the Queen, and the authority also of the principal chiefs, remain in themselves, over their people.

"'2nd. That all laws and observances be established in the name of the Queen, and have her signature attached to them, to render them binding upon her subjects.

"'3rd. That the lands of the Queen and all her people shall remain in their own hands, and all discussions about lands shall be among themselves: foreigners shall not interfere.

"'4th. That every man shall follow that religion which accords with his own desire: no one shall influence him in his thoughts towards God.

"'5th. That the places of worship belonging to the English missionaries, which are now known, shall remain unmolested; and the British missionaries shall continue to perform the duties of their office.

"'6th. Persons of all other persuasions shall be entitled to equal privileges.

"'On these conditions, if agreeable, the Queen and chiefs solicit the protection of the King of the French. The affairs concerning foreign Governments, and also concerning foreign residents on Tahiti, are to be left with the French Government, and with the officers appointed by that Government, such as port regulations, &c., &c.; and with them shall rest all those functions which are calculated to produce harmony and peace.'

"RAIATA, *Speaker to the Queen.*
"UTAMI,
"HITOTI, *Principal Chiefs.*
"TATI,

"The 9th was a day of painful suspense. The Queen's consent was not yet obtained. The Admiral demanded her signature, or 10,000 dollars for injuries alleged: if neither signature nor money was yielded in twenty-four hours, he declared his intention of planting the French flag and firing his guns; thus formally taking the island and making his own conditions. All saw that the islands were virtually taken, and of two evils it was thought best to choose the least. The Queen *signed just one hour before the firing was to commence.* Proclamations were issued, of which one clause states, 'That any person who shall, either in word or deed, prejudice the Tahitian people against the French Government, shall be banished.' A supreme Council of three Frenchmen was appointed. Beyond *them* there was no appeal but to the King of the French. Universal liberty was proclaimed to Protestant ministers, priests, or any others who choose to teach. Feasts were given, and plays were acted. The priests have built a large brick house and erected a cathedral.

"Since the arrival of the intelligence in France, the public journals of that country have teemed with the most glowing and gratulatory accounts of the annexation of the Society Islands, including Tahiti, to the French crown. In these papers it is stated that the act of cession, on the part of the Queen and chiefs of Tahiti, was purely spontaneous and unsought, and that the naval commander, Dupetit Thouars, in taking possession of the islands, only complied with their earnest solicitations to be admitted to the enjoyment of French protection. A few words will be sufficient to expose the gross and absurd misrepresentations involved in these statements.

"The nocturnal meeting, at which this compulsory and deceitful treaty was made, was held without the knowledge of the Queen, and was utterly at variance with her supreme right and authority: accordingly she manifested the utmost reluctance, and refused to sign.

"It will be seen that the French commander attempted to cover his treacherous and arbitrary conduct in yielding to the request of the chiefs that the island should be placed under French protection, 'because they were not able to govern in their own kingdom in the present circumstances, so as to harmonise with foreign Governments,' and 'lest their land, their kingdom, and their liberty should become that of another.' But this language is at variance with the whole case. The chiefs would not have visited the French commander unless he had commanded their attendance, and no danger to their liberties and government ever arose, or was even apprehended, from any power but the arms of France. The fact, also, that these proceedings were conducted clandestinely, at midnight, without the knowledge of the sovereign, and by foreigners with whose language the natives were entirely unacquainted, must produce the conviction that the conduct of the Tahitian chiefs was the result of terror and constraint, or of motives excited by secret and unworthy means.

"It might be inferred from the articles of the agreement that it was honourably intended to secure the civil and religious rights both of the natives and foreigners; but these, especially as it respects the latter, are neutralised by the last clause—'The affairs concerning foreign Governments, and also concerning foreign residents on Tahiti, are to be left with the French Government, and with the officers appointed by that Government.'"

The inhabitants of Rarotonga became much discouraged at these reports, and the war between the English and natives of New Zealand. Every captain and ship's crew who visited the island was strictly and separately questioned, and on reports thus gained the people formed their own opinions. Sometimes, prejudicially to their own interests, they were evidently suspicious lest the establishment of Christianity on their island should ultimately lead to such disasters as those of which they now heard in other islands. Hence the authorities convened a meeting, and resolved not to sell any land to foreigners, neither to allow them to marry native females, concluding, from what they had heard, that these were the begetting causes of the evils which they dreaded.

At this period we were much distressed at the great mortality among our people. January, 1845, we commenced with *one thousand orphans* on the island of Rarotonga. Most of their friends died in Christian faith and hope, and this gave us joy in the midst of our sorrow; but our anxiety for the provision of the poor children was great.

The following is a record of the end of a Christian woman, one of many who died in Christian faith:—

A rapid decline marked her with unerring precision as an early victim for the tomb. She entertained no delusive hopes, from a consideration of her youth, or the flattering compliments of her numerous friends, but evinced a calm preparation for death, of the certain approach of which she had an abiding conviction.

From my first entrance upon the Mission she was noticed to be of a thoughtful mind. She was early received as one of a select number who attended, with our domestics, a catechetical exercise on the Sabbath evening. Her attendance was not in vain: like Lydia, her heart was opened gradually to the instructions of her teacher. As an anxious inquirer, she was directed to Jesus, whom she eagerly and cordially embraced as her Lord and her God. She continued to attend upon all the means of grace, until confined, by increasing debility, to her lowly mat, where I found her on the occasion of my first visit.

Frequently have I seen her, on my way to the chapel, seated against the trunk of some overshadowing tree, utterly exhausted from her earnest attempts to reach the house of God. I kindly advised her, in her extreme debility, to desist from attendance, assuring her that it was not required by Him who loveth mercy better than sacrifice; but I satisfied myself by close inquiry that it was from an enlightened attachment to Divine ordinances, and not from any superstitious feeling, she thus acted. In like manner she cherished a warm attachment for her fellow-members. "Tell them," she said to me at one time, "to come and see me. Tell them I do not wish for their property," alluding to a native custom of making presents when visiting the sick; "a word, a prayer, an exhortation, I will value more than all the property they could bring me." Her diligent attention to the means of instruction was correspondingly blest by the Divine Spirit in the maturity to which she attained in Christian knowledge and experience. Comparatively a child in years, she made rapid advance in the Divine life; and, as death approached, she evidently ripened for an abundant entrance into heaven.

On entering her cottage one morning, when her end was near, I found her supported by one of her family, as she was too feeble to sit erect by her own strength. I said, "Well, Martha, I am glad to see you once more; how is the state of your mind this morning? what turn have your thoughts taken since my last call?" "There is only one direction," she answered, "in which my thoughts now go, and that is to Jesus! I have visited the Cross—there I have been able to leave my burdens. Oh! how sweet are those words: 'He bore our sins, and carried our sorrows.' I have indeed been a Martha, cumbered about many things which I ought long ago to have left to the disposal of my heavenly Lord. I have been waiting for His coming, but I was not ready—I lacked one thing; my canoe was safe, but I had not made fast my anchor; I was in a current, still safe. Jesus was my anchor; Jesus is my refuge; Jesus is my all! My course is finished; I am now ready."

The destitution of so many orphans led us to apply to friends in England for help, especially in clothing. This appeal was made, and commended to the consideration of friends by the Directors, who wrote: "We would invite the attention of our friends to the appeal of Mr. Gill on behalf of his schools, in the hope that it will receive from many prompt and generous consideration."

"This month closes our seventh anniversary at Rarotonga. In reviewing the past, we feel we have abundant cause to take courage and go forward. We owe a large debt of gratitude to our dear friends for all the sympathy and acts of kindness shown towards us; but, above all, are we encouraged in our work by the measure of success which has followed the labours of our hands. The church of Arorangi has increased two-thirds during our residence among them, and others are continually coming to ask what they must do to be saved. While we have had to mourn over some who have made shipwreck of faith, we have to rejoice over many more who continue to walk according to the Gospel of Christ. This evening, at our church-meeting, we are to admit fourteen members to communion, most of whom have been making a consistent profession for the past two years. Seven adults are also to be baptized to-morrow.

"Our land is full of young people. The fathers have been prematurely swept away during our years of affliction. We have hope, however, that the arm of the Lord has been revealed to us for good. Last year our deaths only exceeded by two our births, and property collected for the relief of the *sick* has been given as presents to native teachers among the heathen.

"The present state of society demands diligent, active, and constant effort for future good; but in the discharge of our duties, we meet trials of no ordinary character. We have encouragement in many; but there are others who are constantly giving trouble. We must have schools, and be assisted by friends at home with school materials. The liberality of friends also towards our numerous orphans we appreciate much, and it will turn in most cases to good account as soon as the Scriptures are put through the press. It must be devoted to the printing of books for the use of our juvenile population."

Having received a liberal supply of garments and stuff to be made up, the children wrote the following letter of thanks:—

"Brethren and Sisters in England,—Great is the joy of our hearts, the destitute and fatherless, because of your compassion to us. It is this by which we know your love to us. You formerly prayed for us, and your prayers were effectual. God heard them, and His Word grew quickly on Rarotonga; and now you have given clothing to the fatherless. We shall now think continually of God's love, and we will also pray to Him for you, that His love may grow abundantly with you in your land."

The Jubilee of the London Missionary Society.

It was now fifty years since the London Missionary Society commenced its missionary work among the South Sea Islands. We thought it therefore a suitable opportunity to call the special attention of the natives of this group to the history and progress of Christianity in the islands that had received it. So we arranged to hold a jubilee service. An aggregate meeting was held at Avarua. As the people could not be accommodated in the chapel, the service was held under the shade of large Tamanu trees near.

The arrival of the missionary ship at this time added to the interest of the gathering. Captain Morgan came on shore and gave an account of his recent voyage to the westward islands and the landing of native teachers on some of them. We also gave details of the work in the nine islands in the Tahitian group. Some of the old men spoke gratefully of the introduction of the Gospel to Rarotonga, telling us what they were in heathenism, and of the blessedness they now had in the Gospel era. This grateful people manifested their joy in a practical manner on this occasion. They contributed as subscriptions to the London Missionary Society:—

Arrowroot—	
Yearly contribution	1,602 lbs.
Extra for Jubilee	989 „
	2,591 lbs.
Money—	
Yearly contribution	$25.37c.
Extra for Jubilee	$10.50c.
	$35.87c.

One old man said that in heathenism sacred men had been raised up who reproved the abounding iniquity of the times, and who exhorted their fellow-countrymen to live orderly, honestly, and peaceably; they taught the people to pray to the gods, and to expect a time to come when good should prevail over evil, and happiness abound over misery. Among the sayings of these sages I was much struck with one, often referred to as having been now fulfilled. It is as follows:—

"Takatakai marie, e,
E aku au potiki e!
Aua e oro pu i te kino, e,
E, i te tamaki, e mate ei e!
Takatakai marie, e,
E aku au potiki e!
Te vai ra tetai inapotea e!
Kia ora, e aku potoki e!
Kare teia e mou."

A heathen prophet is here exhorting the young men growing

up around him not to ruin themselves by acts of vice and war. It may be translated thus:—

"O sons beloved!
Tread gently in your course.
Run not rashly to do evil,
Or into deadly war.
O sons beloved!
Tread gently in your course.
For seasons bright,
Of shining light,
As full-moon night,
Are yet in store.
And may you live,
My sons beloved,
Forgetting days of yore."

The first time I heard these lines this old native, who for many years had been a consistent member of the church, said: "Thus did my father, when I was young, exhort me, and blessed, indeed, are my eyes, for now I see these 'seasons bright, of shining light,' of which he spake. Jesus is *that* light, and we rejoice in Him."

CHAPTER XVIII.

VISIT TO MANGAIA, 1845, WITH NEWLY APPOINTED MISSIONARY.

MY brother George had now been on Rarotonga six months, which he felt to be of great advantage in acquiring a knowledge of native character, in learning the language, and in making various preparations for his residence on Mangaia. The arrival of our missionary ship gave an opportunity for his voyaging to his appointed island, and it was arranged that E. and I should accompany him and our sister, and introduce them to the Mangaians, and remain with them two or three months till some passing ship gave us opportunity of returning to Rarotonga. We availed ourselves of this visit again to call at most of the islands of the group to see the teachers and people.

We first made the island of Atiu. We went on shore, and remained three days in assemblies with the people, the church, and the schools, and were much pleased with the progress made. Leaving Atiu, we sailed for Mauké. It was a lovely South Sea morning, and, it being Sunday, we were desirous to get on shore to hold services with the people. But Mauké being a reef-bound island, we could not land without the aid of canoes. But no canoe came off; not a native was to be seen. This much surprised us, as we were sure the ship was seen by the people, though the settlement was a mile inland. After waiting some time in more than anxious suspense we fired one of the ship's guns, but this did not bring any of the people to the beach. We fired again, and, to our great relief, we now saw a small canoe bounding over the surf, having on board *one* native. In order to meet it we lowered one of the ship's boats, but no sooner did the native see this than he turned his canoe towards shore, and paddled away from us with all his might.

Somewhat annoyed and confounded at this unusual treatment, the crew of our boat rowed in pursuit, and overtook the runaway near the reef. On seeing a Rarotongan in our boat, he was evidently relieved, and conducted us to the beach. By this time a great number of the people had assembled, and, on inquiring the cause of their mysterious conduct during the morning, they said that when the ship was first seen they were holding their early morning prayer-meeting; and, it being a new vessel, they did not know it was the mission ship. While wondering what ship it could be, the report of the gun was heard; this, they said, made *their hearts like spilt water;* having heard of the doings of the French in Tahiti, they concluded it was a French ship of war, come to add their island home to the possessions of its nation. "Alas!" they exclaimed, "what shall we do?" "Do not let any one be in haste to go off to it;" and then they resolved to protract their prayer-meeting, in order to call upon God to deliver them from evil, and to be their refuge in this day of their supposed distress. At the close of this meeting the second firing was heard, and they thought it wise to send their bravest man to see who we were, and what we wanted; this was the man who, coming near to us, had turned away in fright.

Their fears were now passed, and we hastened to the village, where we held an afternoon service; and never, I suppose, was there a quicker or more perfect transition from dreadful apprehension to peaceful quietude, from deepest sorrow to highest joy, than that experienced by this people that day. The whole population came together in the chapel: hymns were sung, the Scriptures were read, prayer offered, and a sermon preached, after which we united with the church in commemorating the Lord's Supper. The whole service was one of interest and delight; and the truths of the Gospel, received through these ordinances, were as water to thirsty ground. In the evening a prayer-meeting was held in the teacher's house, and many of the people remained until midnight, reviewing their past history, listening to reports about the churches in England, and asking questions about heathen islands yet to be visited. After meeting the deacons of the church, and making arrangements for the classes and the schools, I located among them Itio, a pious, intelligent native missionary from Rarotonga, and again left this interesting station.

These small islands of the Hervey Group will never have a resident European missionary, neither is it necessary, for the teachers are, in character and labour, all that is required for such stations; and it is a matter of thankfulness that we have such raised up for the work.

The year following, the people of Mauké were visited by natives from Atiu and Mitiaro. Speaking of the occasion, Itio, the teacher, says, "We have had a joyous gathering this year: our brethren and the teachers of the other islands came to visit us, and our people have not had such a meeting here since the Word of God came to these lands. The old men told us of the days when Satan reigned over them, when they were enemies, and rejoiced in the evils of heathenism; and the young people rejoiced in the dispensation of Gospel love into which they had come. Truly it is as is written in the Word of God: 'Old things are passed away, and, behold, all things are become new!'"

There are on Mauké fifty members in church communion, and nearly as many others who are in the Bible-classes. Let the reader realise these island scenes of intelligence, civilisation, and Christianity in contrast with the ignorance, anarchy, and heathenism that prevailed thirty years before, and the warmest sympathies of his heart will be more than ever enlisted in the cause of Christian missions; by fervent prayer and enlarged liberality he will give his influence to extend the blessings they communicate TO EVERY TRIBE OF THE WORLD.

Leaving Mauké, we sailed for Mangaia. It was a lovely day when we came in sight of the island, and the sea so calm that the waves broke with more than ordinary gentleness on the reef. We embarked in the ship's boat, and on approaching the land we heard the shouts of the joyous people, echoed from the coral rocks, "Ko te Pai Oromedua teia! Ko nga tavini o te Atua teia! Kua tae mai! Kua tae mai ia!!" (It is the missionary ship! Here are the servants of God! They are come! They are truly come!) Rowing the boat near to the reef, it was seized by a number of natives, who bore it, with us in it, to the teacher's house. At a meeting held about two weeks after our landing, for the purpose of giving public welcome to their missionary, the following characteristic speech was delivered by one of the natives. Addressing the people, he said: "Brethren, God is truly a hearer and answerer of prayer. We have prayed to see what we see this day. God has heard us, and here is our missionary in our midst. He is going to live with us. But, brethren, do not let us leave off praying. Let us ask God to assist him in learning our language. This is the first thing, and then to assist him to do his work, and then let us be prepared to receive instruction. Pray also for his wife, and for their child, now so young; and ask that he may live and become a missionary to our children. We all rejoice that our teacher has come. Now, this is my thought: let us see to it that not one lock of his hair be ruffled—I do not mean by the winds of heaven, but that his heart be not grieved by our evil conduct. Let us go to his house frequently, and inquire of him about things of which we are ignorant, and about the Word of God. Remember he is neither *an angel nor a spirit*, that you should not go near him. He is come to live with us as our brother, companion, and friend. If you see his face and hear his voice on the Sabbath only you will not receive much good. *You must have intercourse with him* DAILY, and he with you. Let us praise God for His love to us! May we remember what I have said! And may the Holy Spirit prosper our missionary in our midst!"

With a view of giving an idea of what missionary work is at such a station, I will here copy a few notes from my journal for the month.

"August 2. Morning—I met the parents of a number of children who were to be baptized on the morrow. Noon—With the deacons of the church for conversation and arrangement of matters about the church and settlement. Evening—At the church-meeting.

"August 3. Lord's-day. Morning—I preached in Oneroa

chapel, two thousand persons present. Text, Dan. xxxii. 25: 'Shoes of iron and of brass,' or Divine grace appropriate and sufficient to daily labour and trial. Afternoon—Public administration of the ordinance of the Lord's Supper to more than three hundred church members, in the midst of the great congregation. Evening—United prayer-meeting with native preachers and their families in the class-room of our house.

"August 4. Morning—At adults' early school. Forenoon—At the children's school. Held a meeting with some of the principal people of the station, who are desirous to build a stone chapel. Noon—Assisted in making some alteration in mission-house—my brother having brought from England some *glass windows.* This was the *first glass* the natives here had seen, and it caused no little wonder to them. Afternoon—Visited one or two sick persons.

"August 5. Morning—Held missionary prayer-meeting in the chapel; read to the people letters just received from two of their own countrymen, who are teachers on the distant island of Tanna. Forenoon—Met the teachers of the adult classes. Evening—Had Bible-class with young men.

"August 6. Forenoon—At the children's school. Afternoon—A public service. I preached, John iii. 8: The influences of the Holy Spirit in conversion. Evening—Held a meeting with the visitors of the Christian Instruction Society. Increased their number for that village from twelve to twenty.

"August 7. This morning attended the monthly prayer-meeting of the teachers of Oneroa schools: forty-eight male teachers and fifty-one female teachers present. Noon—Assisted natives in mission-house work, and preparing books for inland stations. Evening—Church members' Bible-class.

August 8. Attended the teachers' class this forenoon. At noon a schooner arrived off the island from Tahiti—brought information of the surrender of the Queen, which occasioned much remark and sadness among the people. Afternoon—Went to the village of Tamarua, and held public service in the chapel there.

"August 9. Morning—Visited the sick; met candidates

for baptism, and had private conversation with the deacons of the village. Native teachers' labours had been blessed to the people, schools were well attended, and upwards of *fifty* candidates for church communion.

"August 10. Lord's-day—I preached in Tamarua chapel. More than seven hundred persons present. Text, Phil. ii. 12: Fear and trembling connected with securing salvation. Afternoon—Public service; text, Psa. li. 11: 'Take not Thy Holy Spirit from me.' Evening—Attended a prayer-meeting in the native teacher's house.

"August 11. Early morning adult school; three hundred present. Noon—Dined with the chief of the village. Afternoon—Met the deacons; made arrangements to locate a teacher here, whom we had brought from Rarotonga Institution. Evening—Visited two of the caverns.

"August 12. Forenoon—At children's school, after which selected a singing-class of young people; all delighted with my brother George's ability to teach singing; much room for improvement in them, but they are diligent and willing learners. Afternoon—At church members' candidate class. Evening—Church prayer-meeting. Night—Met several young men, who wish to go to Rarotonga Institution.

"August 13. Morning—A preaching service; text, Deut. vi. 12: Necessary caution while in the possession of privileges. Forenoon—Took leave of the people of Tamarua, and journeyed to the village of Ivirua. People gave us a hearty welcome. Evening—Preached from Ps. lxxxix. 15: The blessedness of hearing, and attending to, the joyful sound.

"August 14. Forenoon—Distributed books to the people. Afternoon—Visited some of the heathen party.

"August 15. Morning—Instructed the teachers of the children's schools. Noon—A native teacher came with his proposed bride to make arrangements for their marriage. Evening—Conversed with a member who had been suspended from the church for disorderly conduct.

"August 16. Forenoon—Met the deacons of the church at Ivirua; added an excellent and tried young man to their number. Evening—Meeting of the church; six candidates admitted.

"August 17. Lord's-day—Public services were well attended; sermons from Job xlii. 5, 6: Knowledge of God necessary to true repentance; and from Isa. v. 20: Delusions and punishment of sinners. Brother George made his first attempt to speak publicly in the native language, by reading the Scriptures and offering prayer.

"August 18. Attended children's school, and took our return journey to Oneroa.

"August 19. Forenoon—Had private conversation with Maretu about texts which he had selected for sermons. Noon—A little girl, having fallen from a precipice, was brought with fractured limbs to be dressed. Afternoon—Church prayer-meeting. Evening—Young men's Bible-class. At night a little boy was brought, whose stomach, while he was asleep, had been dreadfully mutilated by a savage pig; it was dressed, but the poor fellow died.

August 20. Drawing plans for proposed new stone chapel. Afternoon—Married Tangiia, the native teacher, to Miriama. Evening—Preached from text, Gen. xxviii.: Jacob's journey, trust, and vow.

"August 21. After attending to children's school, was with natives marking out the foundation of new chapel, ninety feet long by sixty-two feet wide, which was partly dug out in the afternoon. Evening—Church members' Bible-class.

"August 22. Teachers' classes in arithmetic and geography. Noon—Conversation with candidates. Afternoon—With carpenters, who have commenced window and door frames for new chapel. Evening—Public service. Night—Conversation with one of the native teachers.

"August 23. Preparation for Sabbath services.

"August 24. Lord's-day—Large chapel full; subjects of discourse: 'Zeal for God's house,' Neh. ii. 20; and Zech. iii. 2: 'A brand plucked from the fire.' Evening—Household prayer-meeting.

August 27. Public service on the site of the new chapel; upwards of two thousand persons present. Brother George gave out a hymn; I read a portion of Scripture; Maretu engaged in prayer, after which I gave an address. The foundation-stone, in which were placed native books, and writings respecting the circumstance and date of the building, was then laid by Numangatini, the chief of the island."

Mangaia had been frequently visited by foreigners, some of whom had taken up a temporary abode there; none, however, had permanently resided on the island, except one Frenchman and an American; these had married, and had conducted themselves with propriety. Two or three others had also married, but after a time they had left their wives and families, which had occasioned no little trouble to the people. Hence the authorities, as at Rarotonga, made a law to prohibit marriage of native females to foreigners, and also the sale of land.

Some little time before I reached the island—1845—two Frenchmen, and an American who gave himself out to be a Mormon, came from Tahiti. They brought a letter, purporting to be from the French Consul, to the chief, of which the following is a copy:—

"Papeete, April 22nd, 1845.

"To the chief, and those in power at Mangaia,—Blessings on you! Certain Frenchmen are now going to your land, and the Governor desires that you should treat them kindly, and with justice, like other foreigners. No evil will be to your land. But if you ill-treat these said foreigners, or any other Frenchmen who may hereafter come to you, evil consequences will be to you. Blessing on you!"

On their arrival, the strangers delivered the above letter to the chief of the island, and they were treated with courtesy; but, on being assured that the people intended to abide by their law, not to marry their females to foreigners, nor to sell any land, they left the island in the same vessel which brought them.

The general statistics of the island in the year 1845 were: adult males, 655; adult females, 676. Young persons and children of parents then living, 1,789. Young persons and children whose parents were dead, 447—making a total of 3,567 population, of whom 1,429 were females and 2,138 were males. Five hundred persons were in church communion, besides whom there were six hundred in adult classes receiving instruction. For the year ending December, 1845, there were on the island 101 deaths, 156 births, 99 baptisms, and 50 marriages.

Just before leaving the island I attended a public service at Tamarua, where one of the elders gave an address, in which he unburdened his grateful heart in language so appropriate that a few sentences of it cannot fail to interest my Christian friends. "Brethren," he said, "I am an old man, but to-day I feel young again with joy; the darkness and distress of our heathen life are passed away—that season was indeed a dreary winter season, but it is past—we now have light, and joy, and peace; and I have been thinking of one of our prettiest heathen songs, which exhorted the people to be glad on the approach of spring; it is as follows:—

"'The sky is bright, and the storms are o'er,
The bud and the fruit reward the sower;
The birds are singing, and the trees rejoice,
The winter is past; exalt your voice!'

"This," continued the speaker, "was never properly fulfilled in heathenism, but it has now come to pass. *This* is a season of sunshine. Our storms are now blown leeward. The messengers of God now sing in the land. We have begun to eat the fruit of summer, and a rich harvest of knowledge and love yet awaits us. Let us rejoice!" In concluding his remarks, he said, "But, my friends, in the midst of this joy I have a little trouble; we have not yet reached the heights to which we aspire, but we are still climbing upwards. Oh, let us not resemble those who, climbing up the hills, hold by the tufts of grass, and suddenly fall backwards. I mean, let us not merely hold on to the outward forms and bodily doings of Christianity, but let us hold to Christ Himself, and we shall be safe."

The following are letters written during our stay on Mangaia, and, as they recount incidents not mentioned elsewhere, they may be of interest:—

"*September* 14, 1845.

"My dear Father,—At the conclusion of the Sabbath-day's services I find myself all alone at this our inland station. The different families who live here have just dispersed after holding a united prayer-meeting, and, not knowing the day when the '*John Williams*' may arrive on her way to Sydney, I embrace the hour that remains before rest to hold a little converse with you. I scarcely know how it has been, but lately I have had so much writing to do that I have been obliged to leave a letter to you for the last hurried moments before a vessel's leaving and then fill it with matters of business. But I am desirous that this sheet should narrate the good work in which we are so delightfully engaged. Through the goodness of God we landed here about two months ago, and have had the pleasure of settling George and his wife among a people prepared of the Lord to receive them with all gladness. From the first we have felt much attached to these people, and that attachment has increased as we have known more of them. It has been our pleasure to witness a steady improvement in them for the past five years, and we now rejoice in being permitted to give them over to the superintendence of a beloved brother and sister. May they soon acquire the language and so delight in the work as to feel a growing interest in the welfare, present and future, of the people. Without this there can be no hope of permanent usefulness. Novelty soon dies away. In their case I feel confident that the more they mingle with the people, the more they will feel interested in them ; and, if they have our experience, will never wish to leave them ; it is a fine field of labour. For comfort's sake, it would be pleasanter to have a companion in labour here, but the interests of the mission do not require it, and the present state of other fields will not allow it. George will reside at the principal station, and will have two excellent and devoted native teachers for the inland settlement, and by visitation, and general superintendence, will be able to conduct all well. About four weeks ago we all visited the stations, and were much rejoiced to find them prospering even beyond our expectations. This is my second visit. We like going about among the people. On Friday last we had a most interesting meeting with the deacons and native teachers of the several stations—a kind of 'Congregational Union.' It is a quarterly meeting established when we were here two years ago, and has proved the means of much good. The number at our meeting on Friday was as follows :—Six deacons from the church at Oneroa, four from Ivirua, and three from Tamarua; the three native teachers of the different settlements, Davida, the first teacher, landed here by Tyerman and Bennett, who introduced the Gospel among the people ; Tairi the 'youthful convert,' noticed some time ago in the '*Chronicle*,' who was left here by us, on our last visit, in charge of the school ; and a deacon of the church at Arorangi who has come with us this time. These, with George and myself, composed the assembly. After singing, prayer, and an address, the senior deacon of each station gave a report of the most important occurrences during the past three months. One from Oneroa said that, soon after the last meeting, they received letters from 'Miti Gilo,' Rarotonga, stating that 'Gili,' his 'teina,' had come as missionary for Mangaia. At these tidings they were greatly rejoiced, and, as they were told he had been supplied by the church in England with goods for the erection of a new chapel, they determined to follow the example of Rarotonga, and have a stone house of prayer. They immediately began the work, and are now happy to find that they have enough time to finish the chapel and build the teacher's house too. He stated that the walls were raised all round, and in some parts finished. He said it was a work of much pleasure, and exhorted them to do likewise. During the last three months two members had been excommunicated for immorality, and twelve were admitted last month. At present there were six in the candidates' class, and a goodly number of inquirers.

"The deacon from Tamarua said that, as we, the missionaries, were present, he would state for our encouragement that our work in the Lord during the past visit had not been in vain. Tamarua had been a troublesome station, but now love was reigning in their midst, and where love was there must be peace. Our brother deacon, Rota, whom 'Miti Gilo' left at Tamarua two years ago, was a good man, and the word he had preached had been like a strong hurricane, which levels to the ground all that opposes it. He said, the heart of the church was sore every day with weeping after Rota, who has been removed to Rarotonga, and succeeded by a teacher from the Institution. But the sign of Rota's labours could not be removed. There was a class of candidates, ten in number, to be admitted on Sabbath next, and the number of inquirers was sixty. He further stated that since the residence of Tangiia, the new teacher, there had been a great revival in the schools; that the adults' morning school was well attended every day at sunrise, and that the number and attention of the children had much improved; that many who had been formerly very wild were joining the school classes for instruction, and it was hoped that the good Word of God was growing in their midst; they had doubtless heard that the devil had succeeded in troubling them; that was nothing new. One of their number, a deacon of long standing, had fallen, and, together with an inquirer, had made shipwreck of faith.

"The deacon from Ivirua said his heart was much rejoiced that we were all assembled at their station to-day, and hoped that such meetings would continue as long as the church should continue at Mangaia. He had to report that since the last meeting three members had died. About six weeks ago ten were admitted to communion, and there were ten others in the class of candidates who received weekly instruction in the Bible-class from the teacher. Those who had been admitted had been well tried, being among the number of those who began to seek God two years ago, when 'Miti Gilo' was here from Rarotonga. There were still two or three influential men in the settlement who were disaffected, one of whom had lately been punished for ill-treating his wife. This course of justice had wounded his pride, and he had left the settlement and was trying to annoy it in various ways. Many of the teacher's articles had been stolen by members of his party. This made them very sorrowful, because he was a brother from another land, and had come there to do them good. The teacher was a man of much patience, and told them not to make much ado about it. He thought it a good thing to advise the wild 'Tutacauris' and young men at the heathen stations, who are visited every week by members of the church, to get married, for they had had many instances lately of young men who had been the pest of the place formerly, but on getting married came to the chapel, and were now living steadily.

"Katuke, native teacher at Ivirua, confirmed the statements made by the deacons. Towards the close of his 'little speech' he said, 'When I came here last year I thought I should be very lonely, for there are but few people (500), and those scattered, but I have found it quite the reverse. I rejoice in my work every day, and wonder at the love of God who has made me His workman.' Pointing to a pretty new lime house just built by the people for him, he said, 'That house which has lately been finished gives me much pleasure, not only because it is so comfortable, and adapted to my work, but because I see in it the desire of the people towards me, and their willingness to receive instruction.'

"Tangiia, the teacher just stationed at Tamarua, said, 'My brethren, this is the first time we have met together; a little time ago we had not met, but now we meet fellow-labourers in the Church of Jesus our Lord. I felt very strangely on leaving my own land; I did not know where I should be left; I gave myself into the care of the missionaries, and placed the confidence of my heart in God. A little time after we landed I was stationed at Tamarua; it is but a short time since, and I am not well acquainted yet with all the people; but I already feel that I am among brethren. I have commenced my work with much joy and hope; much good will be the result; this is my little word of exhortation, Let us help one another by our prayers and counsels.'

"Ngatokoa, a deacon from Arorangi, in the course of his address, said, 'I am a stranger, and I have been thinking how very different we are now from what we were a few years ago; we were then indeed strangers. If we had met then we should have either joined in the works of the devil, or have met as enemies. I have lately been to see all the churches in the lands near us, and find they are all one; they are all at peace, and these lands, which were once the property of the devil, are now become the possession of Jesus our King. I wish to tell you that the Church of Jesus has grown very much at Rarotonga. The Waters of Life run about us in rich abundance, and we are drinking continually. There are still many who do evil, but the Word of God is all-powerful—it is a hammer—it has broken in pieces many of our hard, strong hearts, and we are striving together that it may still be very prosperous. Do not you forget us. Many of our fathers who first embraced the Word of God have died, but God has not left us. He has chosen others to do the work they left, and we know the Church of God must grow, until all people be gathered together in Jesus.'

"Other interesting addresses were delivered, but I must conclude with a few words of Maretu's. He came here when the '*Camden*' arrived from England, and now that George has come among the people he is to return with us in a few weeks. He is one of the most excellent of the earth, and has been of eminent good at this station. The closing remarks of his address were as follows :—'I have been thinking very much about God's dealings with me, in bringing me to this land ; formerly the church at Rarotonga sent me in compassion on a visit, just to see the churches here. It was blowing a gale of wind when the vessel arrived off Oueroa ; we could not land there. "Wiliamu" said to me, "Maretu, we must land you if possible, it will not do to take you on ; there is a great work to be done on shore, and you have only six weeks to do it in." The ship then went to the other side of the island ; here the surf was very high ; "Wiliamu," however, lowered the boat ; as we came near the reef I was much afraid, for the gale was very great. I said to "Wiliamu," "Put me back a little while, we shall all be lost in this surf." In reply, he said, "Don't fear ; if there is much danger we will not land you, but we must not mind a little." We went on, and in a little time we were landed in safety, and, I often wonder at it, not an article got wet. On arriving at the settlement I found some false reports had spread abroad about me—that I was come as a spy. It was then just the daybreak of the Word of God among you. I was treated very badly for some time ; the teachers and the people would not look at me. I should have been very sad if I had not remembered a word of exhortation "Barakoti" (Mr. Buzacott) gave me as I left Rarotonga. He said, "Maretu, you are going to Mangaia ; it is likely the people there will treat you at first as they did me on my first visit to Atiu—that was very badly ; but be patient ; don't soon be angry ; do not express surprise at public meetings ; give a word of exhortation as a member of our churches ; and what you have seen and learnt of 'Pitimani' that teach the people in a quiet way." I thought of this advice, and it did me good. After some little time I spoke at one of the Friday meetings. I merely gave a simple address on a portion of God's Word. That night I shall never forget. I came home and was followed by a few people ; they came to hear the Word of God explained as I had learnt it at Rarotonga. Soon after others came, and others ; at length the house was so full that they made me go outside the door, and there the people asked questions on all the texts they had heard since the introduction of the Gospel. They did not leave before the morning light came upon us. It was then I knew the Word of God was power, and light, and love. These things did not soon cease ; month after month found the people as earnest as at first for the Word of God. What wonders has the Word of God done for us ! How has the church grown ! Then, there were only sixty in communion at the Lord's Supper ; at Tamarua they were heathens ; here at Ivirua there were one or two who had begun to pray to God. We have surely entered the noon-day light of the Word of God. Instead of living six weeks among you, I have been seven years, and this is my last word: Do not leave off seeking into the Word, the good Word of the Gospel of Jesus. Blessing on you for ever.'

"Thus you see how God advances the interests of His Kingdom among us. I have been particular in all the details of the meeting, because I believe it will interest you and give you a better idea than anything else I could write of the state of the people. I did intend, when I began, to say something about Rarotonga, and our labours there; but I am sure you will excuse me now."

* * * * * *

"My dear Mother, "*September* 21, 1845.

"We have just been thinking and talking about you at our supper-table on this the anniversary of our wedding-day, and in our prayers we have supplicated for you a continuation of those mercies which have so freely and so suitably been granted unto you during our separation from each other. Last Sabbath evening I was alone at our inland station, and wrote to dear father; and now, although weary in body by the labours of the Sabbath-day's duties, I am desirous at least to begin this to you. I will, however, first just give you a sketch of the day's engagements.

"This morning, after breakfast, Elizabeth and I went to the children's schools. These were assembled in the school-house, not far from a thousand in number, while the adult population were going to the chapel. We commenced by singing a beautiful hymn to the good old English tune 'Whitby'—

"'Taki aere tatou
Ki to Siona ngai
Kia kite tatou ta Jesu
E akakite mai.'

TRANSLATION.

"'Let us all go
To Zion's place
That we may know
What Jesus will reveal.'

A teacher then engaged in prayer, at the close of which a few words of exhortation were given, founded on 1 Sam. iii. 10. This service occupied about an hour. We then met in the house of prayer, each class being led by its teacher from the school-house to the door of the chapel, where the 'tiakis' or superintendents take charge of the children and arrange them in their seats; the whole congregation then united in singing—

"'Kua rauka tikai ia tatou
Te ra meitaki nei;
No tona aroa kia mou
I omai ana nei.'

I then read the 98th Psalm, and also part of the 22nd chapter of the

Book of Numbers—the history of Balak and Balaam's confederacy against Israel. After the reading of the Scriptures the whole congregation bowed in prayer. Often do I wish you could witness this inspiring scene. It would excite your wonder and your gratitude, and inspire a feeling of holy devotedness throughout the whole soul to the service of God and the extension of His Kingdom, until all people and kindred and tongues shall be blessed, even as these are blessed, with the light of the Gospel. After prayer we again united in praises, and then meditated on the 23rd chapter of Deuteronomy, 5th verse: 'The Lord thy God turned the curse into a blessing unto thee, because the Lord thy God loved thee.' Our minds had been led to this subject by the present trials of the churches in Tahiti, and with a view to inspire our unshaken confidence in the Lord who will do all things in the exercise of infinite love and wisdom for His people's good and His own glory. At the close of the sermon we sang—

"'Atua mou i te rangi nei,
Iehova mana mou;
Kare rava e tu ke
Te Atua no tatou.'

Thus ended the morning service. At half-past two E. and I went to the children's school, where the children and teachers were assembled, as is their custom every Sabbath afternoon, for examination on the morning subject. This exercise occupies about an hour. We then assembled again in the chapel as in the forenoon. George commenced the service by giving out a hymn. The sermon again devolved on me. Our text was Luke x. 42. At 6 p.m. this evening we held our united family prayer-meeting in a large room at home. George presided. This practice is observed every Lord's-day evening by all the inhabitants on the island. Two or three families who live near together meet at the same hour for the purpose of prayer and talking over the subjects of the sermons. These services are over at 8 o'clock, when the native police strike the wooden 'pateis' or gongs, and all persons seen out after this are taken up and fined, except they can give a good account of themselves. The public engagements at the two inland stations have been very similar to those at this station. A teacher has preached twice at each settlement and attended to the schools. Besides these services three members of the church, who belong to a visiting society founded when we were here before, have been one to each of these districts where there are yet a few old obstinate men and their enslaved wives and families who continue to refuse to attend the ordinances of the Gospel at the settlement. These have been the engagements of the day, and will give a view of our Sabbath duties. I am sure you will be gratified that we have to record the goodness of God which has followed us every year since we left you. Our every want has been supplied. Yea, our cup has overflowed. Our health has been preserved more than we could have expected. We desire to be grateful for past mercies, and especially for those blessings which have attended our labour. In this we have had peace and prosperity. It is our happiness to feel an increased attachment to our daily work ; still we say—

"'Be all our life and all our days
Devoted to His single praise,
And let our glad obedience prove
How much we owe, how much we love.'

We are at present enjoying the society of dear George and Sarah. They are also quite happy ; and I hope, as they know more of the language and the people, they will be interested in them and be willing to be spent for their salvation. Their dear little boy is a fine fellow, and will I doubt not be a great comfort to them in their solitary, but inviting field of labour. We are now daily expecting the '*John Williams*' from Tahiti when we return to Rarotonga. Our friends Mr. and Mrs. Buzacott came with us round the islands, and spent two nights on shore here, when they returned. We continue to find in them all we could wish as friends and fellow-labourers. I rely on your kindness towards my brother Henry. I hear it is probable that he will go to Hackney and follow us, his brothers, in the preaching of the Gospel of Christ. How great is this privilege and honour, and what a pleasure it would be to meet him as brother-missionary in this group. We are in want of another labourer for the islands of Atiu, Mauké, and Mitiaro, and have sent to the Directors on the subject ; but as to Henry's suitability to the station I, of course, can be no judge. I doubt not the providence of God will direct him. I hope to write to him soon. I feel confident that in Mr. Tidman he will have a wise counsellor and kind friend. I must now conclude, as E. has promised to fill up the remainder of this sheet. I am obliged to you for your long and kind letter to me. I like to have one of my own. You will not, I am sure, forget us *this day* ; and you with dear father will doubtless express many kind and affectionate wishes on our behalf. May we in mercy experience them in our persons and in our labour. May the God of all grace still comfort you in our separation from you, make up by His consolation much more than we could supply. If it be His will, may we on some future anniversary of this day be permitted to be together. This I still hope may be the case, especially if we get *another* missionary vessel. In the meantime let us live and labour as those who are looking forward to a more sure, more happy, more lasting meeting where we shall cease to measure life by years, where the union and the joy will be eternal."

• • • • • •

During the last three months of 1845, on our return from Mangaia, E. and I spent as much time as possible at Arorangi among the people of our station. The schools, classes, and general visitation fully engaged our time. The work of the mission was prospering and hopeful.

CHAPTER XIX.

DESTRUCTIVE HURRICANES.

THE year 1846 commenced with our usual New Year's Meeting. The whole day was devoted to services in the chapel and examination of children in the schools. A rapid advance had been made in the social and domestic habits of the natives, and it was felt by all that the new era of Christianity was fast putting out of practice, and almost out of memory, the customs of heathenism. This was a joy and reward to the missionary's heart, and excited gratitude and praise. Still the future was anticipated with no little concern. The greater part of the elders who had received the Gospel and inaugurated the new national life were fast dying and leaving us the young people, many of whom were intelligent and good; yet many, very many, were only externally affected for good, and were yielding to the evil of their own nature, and were easy victims to the bad influences of evil-disposed foreigners and natives from other islands. Ships were now more frequent in their visits to the island for trade; the people were fast entering upon an enlarged scale of commercial intercourse; the missionaries, Pitman and Buzacott, were much out of health, resulting from past years of trying labour. All these things made us feel anxious. The transition had been more than usually quick from heathenism to civilisation; and with increasing success we felt the weight of increasing responsibility.

In the midst of our varied labours and anxieties we were overtaken by a dire calamity such as had not been known for twenty years.

On the morning of 16th of March, 1846, I had attended

the adults' and children's school, and had held in the forenoon a conference with the chiefs and people as to the best means of restoring the settlement, so as to repair the injuries of the gale in February.

The weather had been very threatening the whole of the day, and, expecting another storm, we did all in our power to secure the roofs and windows of chapel, schools, and our house. At 8 p.m. we assembled the boys in the boarding-school for worship; but we had scarcely closed service when a strong gust of wind burst open the door of the windward side of our house. As soon as possible we replaced the door and began to put away books, &c., in boxes.

While thus engaged a tremendous gust of wind broke on the roof, part of which fell. In a moment all was alarm and consternation. As soon as possible I went to the storehouse; the roof was gone; the terrible wind was still increasing. E., I found, by feeling rather than by sight, was crouched down by the side of a box. We and the servants then took refuge in the boarding-school, but were soon obliged to quit; and during the whole of that terrible night we had to remain exposed to the fury of the hurricane. The following is a record of the circumstances sent to our friends in England:—

"A few days since we forwarded letters, &c., in reference to the increasing trials of our brethren in Tahiti and the Society Islands. Little did I then think that I should so soon have to give you an account of our own calamities. My heart is so heavy at the scene of desolation which now surrounds us, and so burdened by a sense of the trials which await ourselves and our people, that I feel it difficult in the extreme to collect my thoughts for writing, and utterly impossible to convey to you a correct representation of our present circumstances. For the past few years we have enjoyed much prosperity. The good Word of the Lord has had free course among the people. Our schools have been well attended, and were cheering our hearts with prospects of much fruit. Our settlements were in good condition; many good stone houses have been built; and our chapels were our glory and delight. But, alas! in a few hours—a few awful, never-to-be-forgotten hours—our prospects have been blighted, and our hearts left to mourn in anguish over a desolation before unknown to these people.

"Up to the evening of the 13th, I had been staying at Avarua with Mr. Buzacott revising the Scriptures; but, having a meeting to attend at Arorangi, I then returned, leaving Mrs. Gill to be brought on the following day, the rains being so heavy. On the 14th (Sabbath) the weather was so unfavourable that it was with difficulty we held our morning service. The following day, at six a.m., we held a previously appointed meeting with the principal people of the station to make arrangements for burning lime, collecting stones and wood for a new school-house, and for other improvements in the settlement. Here we were detained some time by heavy rains. During the day the wind increased very much, but, continuing steady from the east, we did not apprehend danger, especially as our stormy months had passed by, and we had had two severe gales within the last six weeks.

"At sunset (15th) we had the doors and windows of the chapel fastened, and, after putting away several movable articles of furniture, we assembled for family prayer. We had scarcely risen from our knees when all was sudden consternation. The fury of the wind had burst open a door. As soon as possible it was again secured, with all the windows in the direction of the wind. By this time it was evident we must prepare for the worst. Calling together the servants and natives who were near, we began to remove books, medicines, papers, &c. While thus engaged, a dreadful gust of wind beat on the house. Mrs. Gill fainted. We found it impossible to remain any longer. Our storehouse, which stood near, and had been more recently built, we made our first place of refuge. We had scarcely got inside this house before the thatch was blown off, and we were deluged with rain. Seeking shelter a little time by crouching down by the side of a box, we were soon obliged to fly. The bursting open of the door admitted the wind, which blew with such force that before we could tell what to do the windows and sides of the house were blown out.

"During this consternation a native ventured to carry Mrs. Gill to a small detached school-house on the premises. I remained with a few of the people to fasten up the windows, in order to preserve, if possible, a little of our provisions, continually looking with intense anxiety toward a light still burning in our dwelling-house. About this time (midnight) the wind shifted from east to west-south-west. This, having full play on our settlement, was destined to complete the awful devastation. While taking shelter under the broken door of the store-house, our servant, who up to this time had been staying in the house, came running, crying in the most piteous strains. Calling for me—for nothing could be seen, only as the awful lightning shed a momentary gleam on us—he cried, 'Where is the teacher? Where are you? O listen to my voice! Our house is down to the ground! We shall all die! We cannot live out this night.' On hearing this I gave up all for lost, and hastened, in a crawling position—it was impossible to stand upright—to Mrs. Gill. The moment I left the storehouse the roof fell in. My wife, I found, had been obliged to leave her first place of refuge in the school-house, for it had fallen; she was standing, supported by a native woman, by the door of a small sleeping-room, the only place that now remained on our premises.

"Here for a moment we encouraged each other to exercise confidence in the Lord. Just then the most fearful blast was experienced: the lightning flashed incessantly, the earth trembled, and the repeated crash of rolling thunder which rent the air was all but lost in the still more terrific roar of the wind. Leaning on the arm of a native, Mrs. Gill and I now fled unsheltered to the open field. To flee to the mountains was unsafe, for uprooted trees were flying around us in every direction. To escape to the settlement was impossible, for the floods had risen to the verandah of our house. Thus exposed, and in most awful suspense, we almost despaired of life. While in this predicament the gale moderated a little. Looking towards the shelter we last left we saw that a part of the wall was still standing, and a few pieces of thatch still remaining on the roof; we returned, and, with much trembling, watched for the morning. As soon as the path to our house could be seen, natives came from the settlement, from whom we learnt that the chief's reed-house was standing. Mrs. Gill was taken there. The native women came to render all the assistance in their power; taking off all her wet garments they laid her in one of their blankets on the dry grass of the house.

"To give you a description of the scene presented by the morning light is impossible. Our house in ruins; furniture injured; clothes and provisions spoiled; box after box, as opened, only increasing our trouble; most of our valuable books completely destroyed; and our little store of sugar and flour swimming in water. All this, however, we could have borne with comparative resignation; but when the natives ventured to tell us that Zion, our holy and beautiful house, was in ruins, we felt we had lost our all. This is our chief trial. The poor people weep at the sight, and on every mention of it exclaim, 'Alas! alas! Ziona, our rest and our joy! What shall we do? Who shall comfort us?' The scene is most heart-rending. The poor people have at least two years of famine before them! This, in their present weakened state, we fear, will deeply affect their constitutions. Our only hope is in the Lord. May His mercy still comfort us and His power still assist us; then we may yet rejoice in the light of His countenance. We also rely much on the sympathy, prayers, and assistance of the Directors and our friends at home. We know you will be deeply afflicted on our account; we trust you will not despair, but still continue those expressions which never fail to encourage us and our people.

"I fear the valuable subscription of arrowroot for last year is all spoiled; this year there will be none.

"On Saturday last, after putting up a little shed for a temporary abode, accompanied by all the male church members, I visited the different settlements on the island. Ngatangiia and Avarua have been deluged by the rising of the sea. Everything is desolate. Our friends,

Mr. and Mrs. Pitman, with their sister, in running from their house, fell into the water which surrounded it ; and, but for the assistance of a native woman and a gentleman residing with them, must have been lost."

Hurricane at Mangaia.

The hurricane extended its ravages to the Island of Mangaia, 120 miles eastward of Rarotonga. It reached that island four hours later than Rarotonga. My brother George gives the following description of its ravages :—

"At four o'clock on Tuesday morning, 17th of March, we were disturbed from sleep by the bursting open of all our windows with great violence. The wind was roaring like thunder, and the sea was dashing furiously upon the reef. The whole village was alarmed and in great confusion. In the darkness of the hour the foam of the billows and the waves gave us light. How dreadful was our suspense in watching and waiting for dawn ! As dawn appeared the wind and sea increased in violence, and everything seemed to be doomed to destruction. The stones from the beach, carried by the wind like hail, fell upon us, and the whole house itself was rocking. Mrs. Gill with our dear babe hurried outside, and for more than an hour were supported by natives surrounding them, as it was impossible to stand without help, or to seek a shelter, in consequence of the violence of the wind.

"There we stood, in dreadful anxiety, drenched to the skin, and watching the falling of houses and trees and the rolling of the sea. Who can describe the anxiety of that hour ! Our dwelling-house was roofless, and the gable ends had fallen. The house in which we kept our stores was also shivered and rocking, and almost roofless. The rain fell in torrents ; we were without shelter, and trembling with cold. The natives gathered around us for comfort and counsel ; but I was unable to speak, either to direct or console. Just at this time there was an awful shriek, which rent the air, and seemed to be louder and higher than the roar of winds and waves. The natives observed that the wind had changed, and had assumed the character of a whirlwind ; every part of the village was caught by its violence, and the tallest trees, with more than fifty houses, fell in a moment. Still all was not over ; the winds again roared, and the waters thundered ; trees, as they were broken, were tossed in the air, and were seen turning rapidly like wheels.

"I had left the tree near to which I was standing to take my position at another whence I could command a longer view of the village. I observed the sea again rushing upon the shore, and with it came a stronger gust than we had yet felt ; the very land seemed to shake. Seven large houses fell, with the school-houses and the *old* chapel, which was more than 120 feet long and 36 feet wide. I was blown down, but, recovering, I seized a young tree to support myself, and, looking around me upon the beach, I could see no house standing. I looked towards the *new* chapel on the top of the hill, and greatly rejoiced to see it standing, although I perceived the roof was much injured. But another moment—and another gust—and it was not! the building rocked and I saw it fall! Alas! alas! my heart was just broken.

"The hurricane extended around the whole island; the two inland stations are desolated; the chapels, the schools, and the dwellings of the natives are all levelled to the ground. The plantations of food are greatly injured, and the arrowroot, which they had stored up as contributions to the Society for the year 1846, is destroyed. But He, who rides upon the wings of the wind and directs the fury of the storm, said—Peace! be still! and the tempest of the morning was followed by an evening unusually placid and serene. In our store-house, half full of dirt and water, we laid us down to rest, though not to sleep. Throughout the night we watched the broad expanse of the starry heavens through our roofless house; and, if we did not feel as comfortable as we could have wished, we still felt peace. The sea was again calm—like a lake; the winds were gentle; the stars thickly and brightly shining; and we looked on them with gratitude and confidence, as they led our thoughts to Him 'who spake the promises.' In Him we have a refuge from every storm that blows, and in the security of His pavilion we will abide until these calamities be overpast. They are designed to humble us, and to teach His power and dominion; and we will humble ourselves under His mighty hand, that He may exalt us in due time."

The Church at home very generously responded to an appeal which the Directors made on our behalf. A sum of £3,000 was raised, and a large supply of useful goods sent for the use of our poor people. In acknowledging the receipt of the goods, the chief sent the following letter to the Directors of the Missionary Society:—

"Friends, brethren, and sisters in Britain! Blessing on you from our Lord Jesus Christ, throughout continual ages. Our hearts have been greatly rejoiced at this season by your compassion towards us under our sufferings, on account of the famine of this land, caused by the great hurricane of the year that has fallen behind us. You have heard that the houses were blown down, and all the trees; nothing stood. The desolation cannot be described. But we are now wondering at your compassion to us: it is very great. Our fathers are dead—they knew not that there remained such great love in store for us. We now know and rejoice in this dispensation. What is the origin? Let us think! Why are we thus compassionated? This is the root of it

—the love of God. This is the only source: there is no other. We need not seek any other. Only this—the compassion of God.

"Now the food you sent us has reached us. It was made known that the churches in Britain had sent it to the churches in Rarotonga. It came here in a ship from Sydney, and was divided among the people of the settlements. Our division was eight bags and a half of rice and five bags of biscuit. This was given out to the chiefs and governors of the district, and they divided it among the households of this station (Avarua). We were filled with joy and wonder. We are truly a privileged generation. We did nothing but wonder.

"We then asked our teacher how we were to cook the rice. When he told us we were much amused. Having received our portion, we began to cook it; some baked theirs in the native oven; some boiled it in pans; and others tied up portions in the leaves of the Ti-tree, and thus cooked it. There was no measure to our joy. You would have thought we were children, thus eating our rice and biscuit.

"After the gale, we had nothing but pumpkins, which we used to eat with the roots of the 'ti' and the 'te' plants. Such was our food after the gale. We then planted potatoes and taro. No one sat still—all were diligent in planting; so that we now have bread-fruit, banana, plantains, &c. We are still planting, and should another gale come this year it will make an end, and we shall have nothing left. This is a strange land—there can be no other like it—gales come one after the other—there is no ceasing. It is, however, well. It is not man, but God Himself, and He is Lord of heaven and earth. Man can do nothing; but with God all things are possible—whether to bring to naught or to increase. He is Lord of all.

"We have written this that you might know the joy with which we have received your compassion. We are truly leaping with joy through you in this dispensation of love.

"*Written by the* CHIEFS, GOVERNORS, *and* LANDHOLDERS."

It will readily be seen that these difficulties laid heavy work on our hands and much anxiety on our hearts. The first thing to be attended to by us was the erection of temporary houses, so as to set the people free to attend to their planting.

The first Sunday after the gale was one of great trial. Our new and beautiful chapel was a wreck. We met on its ruins, and amid much weeping held a service of prayer. I preached from Isa. xxvi. 20. In the afternoon six assemblies were held at different places in the settlement.

While in the midst of our work at Arorangi the missionary ship arrived from Sydney. It was a most welcome visit, for we were much in need of supplies. The only drawback was that it took away Mr. and Mrs. Buzacott, who were much out of health, to visit Tahiti; they were to be absent for three months.

The charge of the two stations, with their churches, schools, and the Institution, now devolved upon ourselves. Happily, we were able to make use of several able and trustworthy natives as teachers and helpers. E. and I took up our residence principally at Avarua, so as to be near the students for daily classes, visiting Arorangi once in two weeks. During the three months of Mr. Buzacott's absence all teaching and services had been renewed, and the settlements were put in as good order as possible.

The good old chief Tinomana, who was forty years old, and a heathen, when the Gospel was first brought to this land, was still living; and his firm adhesion to Christianity, his simple faith and consistent loving behaviour, were a source of much pleasure to us. A friend of mine in London had sent him a few presents, and the following is his own letter sent in acknowledgment of the kindness, and is highly characteristic of the style in which the more educated Christian islanders are accustomed to speak and write. It gives me real pleasure to preserve this letter, for I knew him so well and loved him:—

"FRIEND,—I am about to make known to you my former character. It was darkness—evil and savage. Ignorance is the author of all evil. The reign of the devil is an evil reign. Two tribes came formerly, before the introduction of Christianity, and made war with me. I fled to the mountains, because they were many and we were few. Afterwards we made peace; but the peace of heathen chiefs is not of long duration.

"When my father died, the kingdom came to me, and I governed under the savage king, the devil. War again grew, but my enemies did not overcome me. The name of one party was, 'Takitumu' (*completely tear up*); the name of the other, 'Taareotonga' (*the Southern Reign*). The name of my party was, 'Buangi Kura' (*strength of the bread-fruit*). The enemy obtained guns from a foreign ship, fired upon us, and three were killed: all my people were greatly distressed, because we had not before been accustomed to the firing of guns. If we ran to the mountains we were not safe—guns are strange weapons. We kissed each other again, and again dwelt in peace.

"Not long after, war grew among themselves. Makea, chief of Avarua, was driven to me for shelter; and we were dwelling together, when a ship came and brought the Word of God to this land. I believed, and received the thing the teachers taught. They told us to cast away our gods, to burn them in the fire; saying, 'Jehovah is the true God, in whom is salvation!' I asked, 'What is that new doctrine? who is that God?' Papeiha then said, 'Jehovah is God: Jesus is the Lord!' I then asked, 'Will wars cease? will my head be safe? will my children and my people live?' It was answered, 'There will be no more war, no death, but peace and life will grow: the reign of Jesus is a good and lasting reign.' I then burnt my gods—they blazed in the fire. I put away my many wives (seven in number), and put down all heathen practices.

"Friend, this which I have made known is a part of my former character when I did the savage work of the devil. Now I know the true God, who made the heavens and the earth, from whom cometh the dominion of kings in this world. I am now dwelling in the reign of Jesus: often am I thinking of my former days—the days of my youth. Now I am old, my joy is the great love and goodness of God, and that I should know the peace of Jesus.

"The eye-lengtheners (spectacles) you sent me have reached me—they are now with me. I am rejoiced, while I look through the glasses, to read the Word of God, because my eyes are misty with age.

"This is the conclusion of my letter. May you be saved by the true God!

"Written by my daughter-in-law, Stephano Vaine.

"My own hand writes:—

"TINOMANA, Chief of Arorangi."

CHAPTER XX.

VISIT TO THE ISLANDS OF WESTERN POLYNESIA, 1846.

EARLY in July the missionary ship returned, and, although Mr. Buzacott's health was improved, it was evident that he ought to leave the mission for prolonged rest and change. It was therefore decided that he and Mrs. Buzacott should proceed to England on the vessel's next visit.

Under these circumstances it was thought desirable that we should go for a six months' voyage and visit the out-stations in Western Polynesia, some 3,500 miles distant. This was a most unlooked-for arrangement, but the present and future of the mission required it, so we fell in with it. Selecting four or five native teachers, we soon got ready for the long voyage, and set sail on the 18th of July, 1846.

On our way through the Hervey Group we called at Atiu. Since my last visit the people had built a fine chapel. The pillars and floor were of fine Tamanu wood, and would seat a thousand people.

Leaving Atiu, we reached Aitutaki, whence, after four days' sail, we came to a small island of the Samoan Group—Manua. I landed, and had a service with the people through the interpretation of an English sailor, Matthew Hunkin, now an assistant missionary teacher. At night I returned on board. Next day we saw two other islands—Ofo and Olosenga—both inhabited and having Christian native teachers. We then visited Tutuila and Leone, and had two days' pleasant intercourse with Rev. A. W. Murray and Rev. T. Bullen.

It was seven years since I first saw these semi-heathen natives on my arrival from England, and very gratifying it was to witness the great advance of the people in Christian knowledge and behaviour.

Leaving Tutuila, we sailed for Upolu, and, after two days' rough passage, cast anchor in the harbour of Apia. A trading vessel was there, the captain of which told us that, in sailing from the west last week, he had passed through sixty miles of dense smoke and ashes, evidently the result of some volcanic eruption.

While at Apia a general meeting of the missionaries was held, at which the whole staff met, thirteen in number. The business of the convocation continued three days. Reports of the Samoan teachers, the translation of the Scriptures and printing first copies at the mission press for correction by natives, and visitation of distant islands were the subjects brought under consideration. The whole mission seemed to be growing rapidly. In company with some of the brethren, I visited various stations round the island, and was pleased indeed to find the people so advanced and prepared for further improvement.

It was arranged that the Rev. H. Nisbet should accompany me to the Westward Islands. Having held services with the natives and the sailors, we bade our friends at Upolu farewell and set sail for Savaii, the last island of the group—a very large and thickly populated one. We went on shore at Matautu, the station where the Rev. Mr. Pratt was labouring. After intercourse with Mr. Pratt, his family and people, we sailed westward, taking with us fourteen native teachers to locate wherever doors might be opened for them, and also a native of Savage Island who was anxious to return there.

Visit to Faté, 1846.

In October we reached Faté. The day before sighting the island our ship had passed inhospitable Eromanga; thick clouds were resting on its mountains, and thicker clouds of heathen delusion and degradation enveloped its savage population. Drawing near Faté, however, we had in view a land of hope, and all nature seemed to animate and encourage us. It was one of those lovely South Sea mornings of which people who live only in northern climes can have no conception; the sea was smooth, the sky clear, and a fair "trade wind" bore us nearer and nearer to Faté's extensive and fertile shores.

We were happy in the hope of cheering the hearts and relieving the wants of our devoted native brethren, who had been left so long without visitation. On nearing the shore the two teachers were soon alongside, and were taken on board. Their unbounded joy at again seeing the ship, after eighteen months' residence in much suspense, can better be imagined than described. In the embrace of their brethren they fell prostrate on the deck; sobs gave relief to the joy of their overflowing hearts, and, as soon as they could speak, words of praise were the first sounds heard. "Faafetai i le Atua! Faafetai i le Atua i tona alofa tele!" (Praise be to God! Praise be to God for His great love!)

Many of the incredulous heathen, especially the warriors and priests, had long since taunted the teachers and the party attached to them "that their '*religion-ship*' would not return," and "that they had been deceived by the foreigners, who only wished to gain possession of their land."

It was not deemed safe for us to go on shore; yet there was no danger apprehended by our coming to an anchor in the harbour. This we did towards the evening of the day, and the ship was immediately surrounded by more than a hundred canoes, each carrying from four to ten natives, many of whom were admitted on board. As might be imagined, there was much wildness and confusion in their conduct; but we were desirous to reciprocate the friendly disposition they seemed willing to manifest; and, this being done, at sunset we gave them to understand that we should like them all to leave the ship until morning. This intimation was given through one or two of the leading men, and in an instant scores of these unseemly looking savages were scrambling down over the sides of the ship in utmost confusion, amidst hideous yells and shouts; each, however, understood what he was about, and, getting into his own canoe, paddled to the shore.

Left alone with the teachers on board, I spent most of the night in listening to a report of the various incidents that had occurred during the protracted absence of the ship, and in gaining an account of the habits and customs of the people.

It was found that, in common with all the Polynesian tribes, they believed in the existence and dominion of a god, which they called "Maui-tikitiki." They had no carved idols or images, but had many objects and places connected with events and persons which they held sacred; they also rendered worship to their departed chiefs and renowned warriors. They believed in a state of future existence, and made some preparation to enter it happily by attending to certain rites and ceremonies. When asked where the happy place is whither they desired to go at death they invariably pointed towards the west, and called it "Lakinatoto."

The population of the island is numerous, and is divided into tribes numbering from one to three hundred people. Each tribe is governed by its own chief; hence constant jealousies occur, which frequently lead to war. Cannibalism, polygamy, and infanticide were found to prevail beyond restraint in their most barbarous forms.

The people were very averse to strangers penetrating into their country. One day, however, as a great favour, gained through the kindness of the Bishop of New Zealand, a party from his vessel was permitted to visit the spot where the teachers had erected a house; they were not, however, allowed to go along the shore, but were conducted by an inland route. The native houses were of tolerably large dimensions, oblong in form, with curved roof, closed at the sides, but open at the end. The first of these seen was taken for a temple; from the rafters were suspended human bones, supposed to be offerings to the gods. On reaching the village they were ushered into a large building, 100 feet long by 25 feet wide, having the whole of one side open, and the interior of the roof also entirely concealed by ***bundles of bones***, vertebræ of pigs, joints of their tails, merrythoughts of fowls, and bones of birds and fishes mingled with lobster-shells and sharks' fins. These, I learnt, were more or less connected with their religious ceremonies.

I was gratified, by the testimony of the teachers, to find that Sualo, the celebrated Samoan chieftain, continued steady in his attachment. He was still a heathen, yet desirous to lend his influence in aiding the establishment of Christianity throughout the island. Each teacher had been permitted to build himself a house, a part of which was appropriated as a place of instruction to the people. The first day of the week had begun to be observed by many as the Lord's-day—a day of rest; schools, adult and juvenile, had been established; and more than a hundred persons at *each* of the stations where the teachers resided had nominally renounced the practices of heathenism.

This success, however, created a struggle in which the powers of darkness aroused the natives to more than usual activity and strength. One deadly conflict had been engaged in by the tribes among whom Christian truth and light had become an antagonistic power. The conflict continued for weeks, and many were the slain of both parties.

The cruel practice of burying alive old and infirm people and new-born infants, especially females, was found to exist to a fearful extent, but against it the benign influence of Christianity had exerted its power successfully.

Having heard this report, we resolved to have a public service on board the ship the following day. Messengers were sent on shore to announce our wishes, and in a very short time the deck was completely crowded with a company of tall, black, naked, wild, yet attentive people. Taking our seats on the quarter-deck, and having near us the teachers and principal chiefs, we expounded, through our interpreters, the doctrines of the Gospel. On board the mission ship, at sea, surrounded by such a congregation, we "were fishers of men," letting down the Gospel-net into the abyss of deepest moral degradation, and bringing up to heaven's light many thickly encrusted pearls of inestimable worth, which, when polished, are to be gems of eternal splendour in the crown of Jesus the Saviour.

At the close of this service the people desired that we would not only leave amongst them the former teachers, but that we would add to their number. Four tried young men were therefore set apart to reinforce this mission, and they were instructed to prudently make a tour of the whole land, and to locate themselves at stations as opportunity should occur.

Amongst the assembly above alluded to there was an old and influential chief, called Ngos, who, with his tribe, inhabited a small island situated in the bay where our ship was lying at anchor; and, after having made arrangements to locate *four* teachers on the mainland, Ngos requested, with great importunity, that we would allow one to reside with him. I was much pleased with this request, but to comply with it was a difficulty. Already we had drawn too largely from our limited number of teachers, and, having yet to visit other islands in the group, felt unable, from those who remained, to select one for Ngos.

While, however, hesitating what to do, a young man, a tried, consistent junior deacon of my church at Rarotonga, came and said that he had been spending the previous night in prayer to God for himself and wife to enter on missionary labour amongst this people, and that now they were not only willing, but anxious to be allowed to go with Ngos. This offer was thankfully accepted, and Tairi was landed on the island of Mele under circumstances of peculiar interest. Tairi was born in Rarotonga just about the time the Gospel was introduced to that island. His father was a great "mataiapo," or independent landholder, in one of the largest districts, and was the son of one of the most savage warriors, who gained pre-eminence in deeds of cruelty in times when idolatry and war were rampant. Tairi's father was one of the first of his tribe who gave attention to Christian instruction, and who publicly professed his having received "the Word of Jehovah" as his guide and portion.

Tairi himself was among the group of heathen lads who first attended the schools established at Rarotonga by Papeiha, and, in 1832, he received from the hands of Mr. Williams the first book which he could call his own. He gave heed to instruction, made good progress in reading, writing, arithmetic, and geography, and was soon distinguished in the midst of his companions as a thoughtful, pious youth. At the age of eighteen he made profession of his attachment to Jesus by uniting himself to the church, and henceforth he gave his time and talents and influence, with constancy and zeal, to the work of instructing his fellow-countrymen. Three years after joining the church he was set apart as an assistant missionary to Maretu, the native pastor, who had charge of Mangaia; for two years he filled this office with ability and success. On the appointment of an English missionary to Mangaia, Tairi returned to Rarotonga, was elected a deacon to the church at Arorangi, and, surrendering his claim to a large inheritance of landed property in favour of his younger brother, he gave himself to theological and general studies, with a view to the office of the ministry.

Such was Tairi's character and position in 1846. He was truly one of the numerous gems gained from Polynesian tribes—the fruit and the glory of our missionary enterprise. His Christian excellency shone with a steadily increasing strength. In the church, in the settlement, and in the schools he was loved, and in the light of his instruction and example both the aged and the young delighted to follow where he led the way. We hoped his life would be spared, and that in future years he would be an efficient pastor over one of the Polynesian churches. On the arrival of the mission ship, in which we were to visit the distant tribes of the New Hebrides and Loyalty Groups, Tairi and his excellent wife expressed their desire to accompany us, but did not disclose their intention in reference to missionary work until we were at Faté, when Ngos, the chief, requested a teacher for his tribe. It was then that Tairi came and told us that he and his wife had been praying to God to open to them some field of labour in a heathen land, and that they had both made arrangements not to return to Rarotonga; in proof of which he showed us a basketful of mallets and other tools for making "bark cloth," which he said his wife had brought with her to teach the heathen how to make cloth. Finding that I hesitated to accede to his desire on his parent's account, he said, "My father understands and approves of my intention. On bidding him farewell I said, 'Father, do not again think of me in reference to our land; give me up to the work of Jesus amongst the heathen.' My father said, 'Well, my son, if it be the will of God, I do give you up. I, and your fathers before me, have done much service for Satan during his reign over our country; go, my son, I give you up; go, and may you be a good warrior in the service of Jesus.'"

Tairi died of fever brought on through want. His attached and faithful wife was spared the pains of disease to fall under circumstances still more distressing. She was in health at the time of her husband's death, and soon expecting to give birth to her first-born child. The other teachers were at their distant stations, but arrangements had been made to remove her to one of their stations as soon as possible. Some time, however, elapsed before this could be accomplished, and she was left alone. Taking advantage of her desolate and unprotected condition, these degraded people, prompted in the first instance by good motives, proposed that she should be given to one of the chiefs, who already had many wives, with whom it was proposed she should live. This proposition she, day by day, strongly opposed, until one night a party of savages came to her house, and said that they were now resolved to accomplish their object by carrying her off to the chief's house; she succeeded in resisting them until morning, and then ran into a narrow part of the sea, which divides Mele from the mainland of Faté, hoping thereby to escape, and gain the protection of the other teachers. She was pursued, and, getting out of her depth, she sank and was drowned—thus preferring death to degradation! We do homage to the noble spirit of this Christian woman, and to God's grace, which made her what she was.

Visit to Eromanga, 1846.

Eromanga is an island about a hundred miles in circumference. Its coast is for the most part rugged and barren; its mountains are of moderate height, and its valleys, even in heathenism, were in a state of comparative cultivation.

The first acquaintance of the English with its inhabitants was made in 1774 by Captain Cook. On nearing the shore his ship ranged the west coast, keeping about a mile distant. Numerous inhabitants were seen, who invited the strangers to land. Detained by contrary winds and currents, the vessel did not get near the land until the fourth day. Two boats were lowered, and Captain Cook, commanding one of them, began to seek a proper place for landing; but, not finding any, owing to the rocks which everywhere lined the coast, he merely put the boat's bow to the shore, and distributed various presents to the natives, who became so desirous that he and his party should land that they offered to haul the boat over the breakers. Finding that their offer was not acceded to, the excited people directed the "papalangi," or "heavenly foreigners," to row farther down the bay, while they ran along the shore. At length the captain landed, on a fine sandy beach, in the midst of a vast concourse of natives, having nothing in his hand but a green branch of a tree, which he had obtained from the people, and by which he signified his peaceful intentions.

In all probability this navigator was the first white man who had come in actual contact with the Eromangans. What they thought of him we know not; but he was evidently much charmed with their behaviour. He says they received him with "great courtesy and politeness;"—they brought him cocoa-nuts, and yams, and water, and a chief successfully exerted himself to keep the crowd in order, making them form a semicircle round the bow of the boat. Nothing in their manners on this occasion gave indication of unfriendly feelings; only that they appeared, what they were in reality, a heathen people, in a degraded condition, armed with clubs, spears, and bows and arrows.

* * * * *

About the time when Williams fell, there were two native boys, one on the island of Aitutaki, and another on the island of Rarotonga, who, in the days of their youth, gave themselves to God, and were raised up to be the honoured instruments favourably to commence the good work on the island.

* * * * *

In the year 1840, I was one evening sitting in my study, at Arorangi, Rarotonga, when a little boy from the settlement came and knocked at the door. On being admitted, I asked him his errand, and, in reply, he said that he had been thinking a long time past that he would like to do "angaanga no te are O te Atua"—some work for the house of God. Rather surprised at such a proposition, I asked him what he thought he could do. He replied, that he would like to *ring the bell.* At that time we had no metal bells, but a kind of wooden gong, which answered the purpose. A piece of hard wood, about three feet long, and eight inches in diameter, was hollowed out, which, being struck by a small stick of iron-wood, makes a sharp shrill sound, heard from a mile and a half to two miles distant. This gong was used to announce the time for worship in the chapels, and also to gather the children to the schools, and it was to this that the lad referred when he said, "That he would like to do something—something for the house of God," and he desired to begin by striking the gong.

Two years afterwards I formed a boarding-school on our own premises for the education of lads of promise who were in the settlement school. The evening after these lads had been selected, Akatangi came to my house, looking very sorrowful, and, on my inquiring the cause, he said: "Alas! my heart has been crying all day." "And why so?" was my question; to which he answered, "You were at the school this morning, and you selected Tekao and Nootu, and others, to come to your new school. All the time you were there I kept looking at you, and thought I would like to have come with them; but you said that the number was complete, and when I heard that my heart began to cry, and has been crying all day." "Are you, then, very desirous," I asked, "to come to this boarding-school?" "My desire," he replied, "is very great." Knowing his family, I said: "But how can you be spared from home—your mother is dead; you are the eldest of your family, and are needed by your father to assist in his plantations?" To this he quickly rejoined: "I think my father will give his consent if you will allow me to come." Akatangi returned home that night with a lighter heart then he had brought. Inquiries were made; his teachers recommended him; his father gave him up, and before the end of the month this lad was a resident in my boarding-school in the settlement of Arorangi.

He gave diligent attention to reading, writing, arithmetic, geography, history, and other branches of instruction, but did not give up his office of "bell-ringer." Every morning he was seen beating the wooden gong, calling together the children of the settlement school, and attending it himself. Two or three years passed on, and he became known as a youth who loved reading the Word of God, and who daily observed private prayer.

One night, when he was about fourteen years old—he always came at night when he had anything to say about himself—he visited me, and said that he had a "manga manoko iti"—a little thought—which he wished me to know. I inquired what it was; he replied that he would like to become a "tangata no te Atua"—a man of God. I assured him that was no *little* thought, but a great and a good desire. After further conversation, he said: "I have been thinking I would like soon to join the church." I then remarked, "that merely becoming a member of the church would not make him a *man of God*." "No," he replied, "I know that; but I have given myself to God, and now desire to give myself to His people." Akatangi continued his consistent Christian life, and was admitted to communion with the members of the church at Arorangi.

Months rolled on, and his term of scholarship had well-nigh expired, when one night he came again, and said he had now been a long time under instruction; he trusted the advantages he had received had not been entirely "puapinga kore,"—profitless; he felt grateful to God for those advantages, and that he was now desirous to give himself to the work of a missionary among the heathen. If I thought him suitably qualified, he wished to be admitted in the Institution for native teachers and pastors. This was not altogether unexpected by me, but it was the first time we had talked on the subject, and shortly afterwards he was transferred from the school to the College. Early in the year 1852, the missionary ship being expected to call at Rarotonga, on her voyage from England to the heathen lands westward, Akatangi was appointed to proceed in her as a missionary. I well remember the interview I had with him when I communicated this decision. He wept tears of joy, and said "that it had long been his desire to be the first teacher to some *heathen people*, who had not yet heard of the Gospel of Jesus."

About a week had passed, and the young missionary was again sitting by my side. For some moments he remained silent, as though musing on some important subject. After his silent musing, he said "that as his station had been partly fixed on, and the vessel was expected shortly, he had been thinking, if there was no difficulty in the way, that he would like to 'akaipoipo vaine'"—get married. This proposition was as unlooked for by me as it was serious and important to his future history, and, thinking that his station would be somewhere near the island of Aneityum, where European missionaries resided, I expressed my concurrence in his wishes, and inquired whether he had thought of any suitable individual. "Yes," he said, "I have been thinking of Maria." This young woman was a daughter of one of our first native missionaries, and had been educated in the mission-school. I then asked if he had made known his desires to her. With some bashfulness, he said: "No, I have not yet spoken to her, but I have been looking at her for a long time." I rejoined that it was now necessary that something more should be done than merely looking. He replied that he thought so too; and, putting his hand in his pocket, he took out a letter, which he handed to me. It contained the important question for Maria's decision. Feelings of cheerfulness, mingled with a conscious importance of the matter, filled my mind as I read it.

I will transcribe a copy:—

"To MARIA, the daughter of ———.

"I, Akatangi, have been appointed to go as a missionary to the heathen in the dark lands westward. I have been looking at you a long time, and I desire that you will go with me. If you love Jesus, if you love the heathen, and if you love me, let us go together. Think of this, and let me know. Blessings on you from Jesus. Amen. "NA AKATANGI."

A worthy deacon of the church conveyed the letter to

Maria, who, on being told from whom it came, betrayed an expression of countenance which showed that his "looking at her" had produced no unfavourable impression; and, on reading it, she was pleased to signify her willingness to converse with her parents; and, if their decision was favourable, she would give an affirmative to the proposal.

Akatangi and Maria were married, and in March, 1852, the mission ship reached Rarotonga. They embarked; and, after calling at Samoa, they proceeded to the island of Eromanga, and there, in company with a companion teacher, landed, and have been the means of instructing many of the people in the Word of God, and of leading the very men who murdered Williams and Harris to feel their sin, and to rejoice in the blood of Jesus that cleanseth from all sin.

In a letter received from Akatangi, under date Eromanga, 1854, he writes:—

"To my minister, who instructed me. Blessings on you! The letter you wrote to me has come to hand. I and my wife read it with great pleasure, and we wished much to see you; but alas! you are gone to Beritani. We are still here, and are doing the work of Jesus our Master, and He has prospered our work. The chief of the tribe with whom I am living is the man who murdered Wiliamu. He did not know that Wiliamu was a missionary. He is now full of distress when he thinks of what he did. But I am now teaching him the Word of God, and he is gaining knowledge. My joy is great in God, who has assisted me in this work, and who has brought the people to be instructed. * * * The *work is still great; send us missionaries to do it.*"

* * * * *

Early on the morning of the 21st of September we were off the leeward of Eromanga. Seeing a whale-boat sailing along the beach, we hove to. The boat came near, and we learnt from the crew that she belonged to the "*Isabella Ann,*" Captain Jones, then lying at anchor in Dillon's Bay, collecting sandal wood. Calling off Dillon's Bay at noon, the captain and Mr. Nisbet went on board, and had a short interview with

Captain Jones. Captain J. said the natives were continually at war among themselves. He had sailed all round the coast, and seen no other place of good anchorage than Dillon's Bay. He believed the whole population did not exceed 1,000 souls. He found them in a most degraded state, and with but little food in the land. At their feasts they kill their women to eat. Of all South Sea islanders he had seen he thought these the most savage. A few natives came on board, while our friends were there, to whom Mr. Nisbet was able to make a few remarks, through some natives of Tanna, who were on board, and who knew something of the language of Eromanga. The old chief—supposed to be the man seen on the last visit—was some distance inland. The natives were told to tell him who we were, and the object we had in view—what the teachers were doing in other islands, and that at some future time the vessel would again call, and we should be willing to leave teachers, if he would allow us to do so.

Captain Jones gave us information respecting Tanna, which much excited our apprehension for the safety of the teachers. He had heard that within the last two months a disturbance had taken place at Tanna between the natives and the teachers, and that the teachers had all fled to Aneityum. While we were unwilling to give implicit confidence to this report, it made us anxious to go on thither without further delay.

Visit to Tanna, 1846.

Tanna is a large island in the New Hebrides Group, which, when its resources are developed, will hold an important commercial position in Western Polynesia. It is about thirty miles to the west of Aneityum, and is about a hundred miles in circumference. Captain Cook, its discoverer, was much pleased with its appearance and impressed with its importance. The soil is exceedingly fertile. Even the highest mountains are covered with the richest vegetation to their very summits. The cocoa-nut, bread-fruit, and bananas are neither so plentiful nor so good as on the eastern islands of the Pacific; but the sugar-cane, sweet-potato, taro, fig-tree, and yams are not only plentiful, but superior in quality.

The most interesting natural object on the island is a large active volcano, the crater of which forms the top of a low mountain, about three miles inland from Port Resolution. This mountain is held in great veneration by the people, and its precincts are inhabited by the principal men of their idolatrous priesthood. It is sometimes exceedingly troubled, a deep, long, rumbling noise, like the roar of distant heavy thunder, being heard, which is usually followed by the appearance of prodigious columns of fire, and the casting up of great burning stones into the air. At the base of this mountain there are hot-springs of sulphurous water, in which the mercury rises to 190° or 200° Fahrenheit. Pure sulphur is found in quantities near these springs, and the water is used by the natives for cooking purposes.

This island was the first in Western Polynesia visited by Christian teachers, and by the Rev. John Williams, the day before his fall on Eromanga. "When will you come back?" inquired the people as Williams left their shore; "When will you come back?" His murder occasioned a long delay of the missionary vessel's return, which, together with the unfavourable influence of other vessels that visited the island, produced a prejudicial impression on the minds of the people, and gave time for evils to grow which have not been fully overcome. The number of distinct tribes into which the people were divided, the diversities of their languages, their superstitions respecting disease, and the envy and rage of the heathen priesthood were felt to be formidable difficulties, and its occupation by sandal-wood traders led us to decide that it should have English missionaries without delay. The Directors of our Society appointed the Rev. Messrs. Turner and Nisbet to this island, who, with their wives, landed in 1842.

Recording their first interview with the natives, they say:—"After landing, we wished the principal men of the district to come together. They did so, and we explained to them the object we had in coming among them; this they seemed to understand, and promised to hold our lives and property secure from injury. But we have, however, reason to fear that avarice and pride are the ruling motives of their minds; by the Divine blessing even these may be overruled for good. Poor creatures! they are indeed in a degraded state; naked, painted savages as they now are, we look upon them with the deepest interest and compassion." With devoted hearts and active hands, these brethren applied themselves to the arduous and self-denying labours of their station, and in three months they had picked up sufficient of the language to make themselves understood. For a few months things progressed as favourably as could be expected; but it was not long before troubles arose and accumulated, details of which cannot fail to excite Christian pity and prayer.

The first opposition to Christian instruction was raised by the numerous body of heathen priests who lived in the vicinity of the volcano. They saw that, as the "Word of Jehovah" was attended to, they were no longer either feared or fed, and they were aroused to vow death to the "servants of Jehovah." To accomplish this purpose they made several daring open attempts, from which the brethren were mercifully preserved.

Another cause of danger was *a wonder-working little printing-press*, by which the missionaries were multiplying books in the language of the people. At this time books were looked upon as the "*voice* of the foreigners' God," and their chiefs and priests saw that, as the people attended to the books, they lightly esteemed what they formerly held sacred; hence their rage against the press, their resolve to stop its work, and that the missionaries should either leave the island or die. Many anxious days and nights were passed, and, as one succeeded another, danger became more and more imminent. The enraged savages, like ravening wolves, were collecting all their forces, and every day coming nearer to the mission premises. The little party of friendly natives did all they could to protect the missionaries from harm, but they were few in number, and feeble. At length even these lost courage, and the two devoted missionaries, with their wives, accompanied only by two or three teachers, were left alone.

It was known that the missionaries had in their possession a gun; being sure of obtaining this as a means of protection, a few of the natives came for it. "No, no!" was the reply of the missionaries; "we cannot give it up." Strange and unaccountable to the minds of the natives was this refusal. Again and again they asked for the gun; but "No," was the reply. "We dare not be the cause of taking away life. We give ourselves to Jehovah's protection. Live or die, we will not allow you to use the gun on our account." The crisis now advanced. The flames of burning huts and plantations were seen all around. By the light of these flames hundreds of naked savages were seen advancing nearer and nearer to the mission-house. It was a night of agonising anxiety. To remain in the house was certain death to the missionaries, and worse than death to their beloved wives. Under these circumstances what was to be done? They had but one boat; to this they fled, and, followed by the teachers in their Samoan canoe, at midnight they put to sea! About thirty miles eastward was the island of Aneityum, where they might gain a temporary rest, could they reach it; but the contrary winds and waves prevented them from steering for that island. Eromanga was to the north, but its inhabitants at the time would have murdered them. The only alternative appeared to be a lingering death at sea. Alas! in such trying circumstances, how mysterious do the ways of Divine Providence appear! Wherefore should the heathen be permitted to say, "Where is now your God?"

After having resolved to abide at sea for the night, the missionary party were driven from their purpose by a series of contrary squalls, which compelled them to return to the shores of Tanna. Faint with anxiety and toil, they again reached their house, about four o'clock in the morning. At daybreak, however, just as they had commended themselves to God by prayer, and had asked sustaining grace for the events of the day, a fiendish yell or war-whoop was heard, and hundreds of the natives were close upon them; for an hour or two they were kept from striking the fatal blow, and in an unexpected moment shouts of "Sail oh! sail oh!" were heard, from lips which a moment before were vociferating death and destruction. This was "life from the dead" to the mission party. The eye of their unslumbering Protector had been upon them, and in the hour of extremity He honoured their faith and rewarded their hope.

The ship was the "*Highlander*," of Hobart Town. Communication was had with her, and her obliging commander, Captain Lucas, received the missionaries on board, and brought them to Samoa, and thus for a time this mission was abandoned.

* * * * *

More than *two years* passed before the "*John Williams*" came from England. On her first voyage, she was employed in taking back the native teachers to Tanna. Her arrival was hailed with delight, not only by the Christians, but by many of the very men who had excited the persecution in 1843. The war of persecution, which drove them away, had terminated in favour of Christianity, and two teachers were landed; but, not long after, their patience was tested, and the progress of the mission was again retarded, at the season of the year when fever and ague prevailed. Pita and Petelo, two teachers, were laid prostrate: Pita's child died; Rangia was ill and was also laid low, and Vasa Vaine and two other teachers died. At this time the persecution was brought to a crisis by the death of a daughter of a chief of one tribe, the son of a chief of another tribe, and an influential chief of a third; these events inflamed superstition; and vengeance was again vowed on the "servants of Jehovah."

The Christian party, with a good old man, called Viavia, at their head, did all they could to set aside the evil designs of the wicked, and to encourage the sickly teachers; but the storm, already high, rose yet higher, and its first burst fell on the person of Ioane. Recovering from a severe illness, he had gone to the hot springs for the purpose of bathing: while there, a heathen rushed from behind a bush, and, with a blow of his club, struck him to the ground. His death was intended, but, assistance being at hand, he escaped, and gradually recovered; but the day of death was not distant to one of his devoted companions. One evening Vasa, as was his custom, went to the bush, some distance from his house, to pray. While on his knees, a fatal blow was struck, and his distressed brethren carried him to his grave, not knowing who of them would be the next to fall. Writing at this time, one of them says:—"We do not know what a day will bring upon us; we do know, however, that these can only kill the body; the soul is in the hands of our Master."

Before, however, the heathen could finish their deeds of bloodshed, God interposed for the teachers. A merchant vessel put into the bay for supplies. The captain, hearing the teachers' tale of distress, offered to give them a passage to the island of Aneityum. A consultation was held by the teachers and their native friends, and it was decided that they had better retire awhile. They embarked for the passage; but before the vessel got under weigh, the captain sent a boat's crew to a distant station, round the coast, to obtain more yams. While there a disturbance occurred, and one of the crew was killed. This outrage much exasperated the captain, and he, with his men, resolved to be revenged. The ship's fire-arms were prepared, and powder, in great abundance, was measured, to be ready for the attack. Alas! for the poor teachers, that they should have been on board; they endeavoured to dissuade the injured captain from his purpose, but he would not be satisfied without revenge. In the meantime about forty natives, who had not heard of the murder of the white man, came off to the ship for purposes of barter. These were taken prisoners, and put in the hold. Message after message was then sent on shore, announcing it as the captain's intention to fire on their village if they did not bring to him the body of the unfortunate man. But this they could not do, for the very hour it fell into their hands it had been cooked!

The teachers left the island, and abode awhile on Aneityum. But so great was the desire of the Christian party for their return, that they fitted out canoes and took a voyage to that island for the purpose of taking them back; and, when visited twelve months afterwards, the two principal stations had been re-occupied, and others were ready to receive teachers, whom they had formerly ill-treated.

The following is an extract from a letter, written by one of the teachers to the church in Rarotonga in 1850:—

"My brethren, blessings on you all from our Lord Jesus the Messiah. I and my companions are still alive on Tanna. We are continuing to do the work of Jesus in this dark land. Our hearts are often crying because of the wickedness of the people, but we are not quite destitute of joy. Our work is a work of joy, and Jesus is fulfilling His word, 'Lo! I am with you even to the end of the world.' We want more brethren to help us. I am now ill. I cannot say what will befall me, whether I am to live or to die. Oh, pray for Tanna, and send us more help!"

This excellent young man died soon after writing the above, and one of his fellow-labourers wrote the following letter to his father; its record is an evidence of the piety and intelligence of these native brethren:—"My friend Tiotekai, the father of Tumataiapo, and you, his brothers and sisters, may you all be united to Jesus the Saviour, from whom come streams of consolation. I, Obedia, now write to you. I, and your relative, Tumataiapo, have dwelt together in this land; but now he is dead, and I am left here at my station alone. He lay ill a long time, but Jesus was near him. My friends, this is my message to you; receive it. Do not grieve on his account. He is now in the beautiful mansions of heaven with his Master. He has rested from his work; he has gained his reward. Do not grieve for him. Like him, may you all be united to Jesus as branches in the true vine; then you will again see him in joy and glory, which will abide for ever."

Reports of the happy change on Aneityum so interested the people of Tanna that many of them recently visited that island, and they were much gratified at what they there saw and heard. They made a tour of all the stations *without club or spear*, and returned in delighted astonishment at what they saw and heard of the influence of Christianity, and were prepared to do all in their power to promote its advance on Tanna.

The time has now come when the claims of Tanna, with those of Aniwa and Espiritu-Santo, and the numerous islands of the New Hebrides, demand the presence of resident missionaries. To this demand the Presbyterian Church of the Lower Provinces of British North America, together with the Reformed Presbyterian Church of Scotland, have attended with promptness and liberality.

On Wednesday, the 23rd of September, 1846, at noon, we entered Resolution Bay. Before we had cast anchor our fears were increased by the unusual quiet the bay presented. We saw numbers of natives sitting in groups on the beach, and in the bush, but all were still—no canoe put off, and, above all, the mission house erected by the brethren, Turner and Nisbet, was not to be seen. Waiting some time, we saw two or three canoes put off from the shore, row a little distance towards us, then return. We then waved a piece of white cloth from the boat, and after a little time Lahi, the native who had been taken to Samoa, and who was brought back last year, came on board, and the report we had heard was to our sorrow confirmed. Much disease had broken out among the people, for which the teachers were blamed. Some of the chiefs were well disposed towards the teachers, but were not able to protect them from the violence of the infuriated people.

Niua.

On our way to Tanna, we made the small island of Niua, where we had hoped to see the teachers who were left here on the last visit. On making the island we sailed along the shore until we arrived off the settlement, where the teachers were located. We looked for the teachers house, which formerly stood on the shore, but could see nothing of it—neither could we, for some time, see any natives. At length we saw a few sitting down among the trees, not more than ten or twelve; these, however, made no attempt to come off—nor any sign for us to land. After waiting some time we were obliged to conclude that the teachers were not on shore. We now began to fear that the report we had heard respecting the teachers having all fled was true, and sailed for Tanna, and thence to Aneityum On leaving Aneityum the vessel probably would have returned to Niua, but it was considered by Mr. Nisbet, who well knows the influence the people of Tanna have, that it would not do to leave teachers here while Tanna was abandoned; and, even had we thought it desirable, it was probable no teacher would have been willing to stay, owing to the reported scarcity of food on the island.

Visit to Aneityum, 1846.

On the day after we left Tanna we made Aneityum. Sailing off and on the settlement where the teachers were first left, we were somewhat surprised at seeing no natives about, and were just about to sail for the harbour when we discovered a few natives, and a man among them who had on a red shirt. Hoping it was a teacher the boat went to the beach, and to our joy returned with some of the teachers.

We had hoped to find something at this station to cheer our desponding spirits. This, however, we were not permitted to realise. We were glad to find that the Tanna teachers had reached here in safety, and were all well except Rangia, who was ill before he left Tanna, and has been getting worse since his residence here. There were four teachers placed on Aneityum on the last visit—Simiona and Boti at the station in the harbour, and Apaisa with Apolo on this side of the island. Simiona and Boti gave us to understand that, owing to sickness and other untoward circumstances, but little success had attended their labours. They said, a fortnight after they went to their station Boti's child, who had been left with Apaisa at the other station, was taken ill. Boti was sent for. He and Simiona went to see the child. The child got better, but before they could return to their station they were taken ill themselves. Before they left they began to build a house, and left Apaisa to finish it. Soon after this Ioane and Vasa came to Aneityum from Tanna to pay the teachers a visit. Simiona and Boti came to Apaisa's station to see the visitors. After staying some little time the teachers of Tanna returned, and Apolo, one of the Aneityum teachers, went back with them. Simiona returned to his own station. Then they all became ill of influenza. They all lived together. Boti's wife and child died, as also did a child of Apaisa. Afterwards, while preparing to return to their own station, the teachers came from Tanna. While thus living together they heard a report that some of the people were angry, and designed to kill them. One chief actually beat Boti and Simiona. After this, things got a little better; the people were reminded of the promise made by Messrs. Murray and Turner that a missionary would come on the return of the vessel and live among them. The people said if a missionary came and gave them pigs, and allowed them to use his boat, it would be very good. If not, he should not stay among them. They had constant service on the Sabbath among themselves and the family with whom they lived. Sometimes many others attend. They had made no attempt to collect a children's school. They planted food, and as it grew some of the natives stole it. In these circumstances they had enough to do to provide for themselves.

The above is the substance of information gained from Boti and Simiona. The other two teachers had but little to add. Apaisa said that at their station the people came well together on the first few Sabbaths after their landing. But he reports their only object was to get what they could. On Sabbath afternoons they used to go about to talk with the people. These engagements, however, were greatly interrupted by their frequent illness.

Unfavourable and depressing as this report was, we were pleased to find by the united testimony of the teachers that many of the people were friendly, and that they had no fear whatever as to the safety of their lives. Their non-success may, in a great measure, be attributed to their frequent illness, and, in these circumstances, they were obliged to attend so much to their own wants as to prevent their influence being much felt among the people of the land. This impression was confirmed by an interview we had with some four or five chiefs, or principal men, of this side of the island. They all expressed their willingness to receive instruction, and did not wish the teachers to leave. Under this state of things, we were desirous that some of those teachers who were not disabled by sickness should remain. On proposing this to them, we were sorry to find that previous to the arrival of the vessel they had had a consultation, and had resolved that, if no missionary should come this time, they would all leave. For a time we endeavoured to dissuade them from this conclusion, but they were firm. Placed in this difficulty, we asked some of the new teachers to recommence the work alone. This they refused, on the ground that all the old ones were leaving.

Having come to anchor between the reef and the shore, we were now desirous to get all the teachers on board as soon as possible. This being done, we gave the chiefs before referred to a present, and, telling them they might expect to be visited again at some future time, we weighed anchor, and sailed for the harbour on the other side of the island, for the purpose of seeing the chief of the district where Boti and Simiona were left.

On our passage thither, Upokumanu, one of the teachers from Tanna, and another from Rarotonga, expressed their willingness to stay, if we found the chief disposed to receive them.

The evening we cast anchor we sent a boat on shore to the chief of the station to inform him who we were, and to invite him on board. He returned an answer that he felt too indisposed from the effects of "Kava" to come off that evening, but would see us in the morning.

Early the next morning we sent the boat for him. He came on board, and was quite friendly. We told him our regret at the non-success of the teachers' object who were left with him last year; that now we had, for the time being, removed the teachers from the other side of the island; that we were desirous to leave teachers again with him, and would now select them if he would promise his protection. He replied it was very good; he was quite willing to have teachers to live at his station, and would attend to instruction; but his people were now few, and he could not answer for them. He would, however, mention one evil—perhaps the teachers, after remaining a little time with him, would go away to the other station as they did formerly. We reminded him that sickness was the cause of their so acting. Now there were no teachers on the other side of the island, and the teachers would promise to remain with him, if he would receive them. After this, he gave most willing consent that the teachers should stay.

We therefore appointed Upokumanu and Tumataiapu, and were desirous to secure another Rarotongan, but, he wishing to go on to join Pao at Lifu, another application was made to Simiona, who had been stationed here at the first. After some little time, he said he was willing to stay. Their former resolve being thus broken in upon, Pita, from Tanna, expressed his willingness to remain also. We gladly availed ourselves of these offers, and appointed all four to remain here. In coming to this decision, we were influenced not merely by the claims of this island, but also by a hope that the two teachers from Tanna would, before long, be able to re-occupy that station, or at least to have communication with the people of that island.

About noon, when all the teachers' goods were ready to be sent on shore, we learnt to our surprise that the chief and all his party had suddenly taken their departure. Not a native was left on board. We could not tell what interpretation to put on this movement, but felt sure it indicated nothing favourable. After a little consultation we sent the boat on shore to say the teachers and their things were ready. The chief returned answer that while on board he had received a message from the foreigners, who are living on the small island in the harbour, and connected with the Sandal Wood Company established there, that he was not to receive teachers. He therefore wished us to take a pig to Mr. Murphy, the proprietor, and gain his consent, then all would be well. We returned answer that we had nothing to do with the company on the island—neither with Mr. Murphy—that we had only to do with the chief of the land, and, since he was the chief, we would abide by his decision. This message being taken to him, he came on board, where we again assured him of our sole object, namely, to instruct him and his people in the knowledge of the true God—that we applied to him as the chief of the land to receive the teachers, and give them his protection—and that if he were willing to grant this the teachers were willing to go on shore. The chief then gave his most sincere pledge that he would receive and protect the teachers and attend to instruction. Having secured this, we left the island.

I preserve the following additional particulars copied from "The Gems," &c.:—But few of the people understood and valued the instruction which they had received, and were anxious to retain the teachers; but the majority, with whom were the chiefs and priests, would give no further protection to their lives, and we were obliged to receive them on board. Sailing round to another station, it was not thought well to go on shore; we therefore sent an invitation to the chief, requesting that he and some of his people would come off to the ship. On the following morning a meeting was held. Squatting themselves on the quarter-deck we took our seats in the midst of them, with Petero, Simiona, and Upokumanu as our interpreters; we opened an important discussion—a discussion which was to decide the future destinies of the people. Should the teachers remain, or must they leave?—that was the question. They were willing to risk the consequences of remaining, if the chief of the district would pledge them his protection. Much had been gained during their residence, in the acquisition of the language, in their acquaintance with the customs of the people, in the hold which they had on the hearts of many, and the evidences of conversion in a few; and we felt that this meeting would be the turning-point, either in favour of or against a happy consummation, and that the abandonment of the island at such a time could only be adopted in the last extremity. It was an anxious hour, and I well remember the hope and fear which alternately took possession of my mind as I reviewed with the people the past, and argued on the probable future. Sometimes the chief spoke encouragingly about re-occupation, and at others hesitatingly, until, at length, he decided the matter by saying —"Let the teachers remain; I will do my best to protect them so long as they dwell in *my* district; but if they rove abroad to other tribes they will be murdered. But listen to me," he continued, "this is the great evil: your ship goes away, and moon after moon, moon after moon, rises and sinks, but you do not *return.* Other ships"—sandal-wood vessels, he meant—"come here and go away, and in two or three moons come back again; but you go away, and," putting his head on the deck, he emphatically continued, "we sleep, sleep, sleep, but *you* do not come back again!" The truth of this statement deeply affected us. We would that our friends in Australia, who are only *three weeks'* sail from this land, could have so realised the importance of frequent missionary visitation as to have *then* adopted measures for its accomplishment. We had to explain the cause of the protracted absence of the mission-ship, and were compelled to tell them that it was now about to voyage to England, and that, in all probability, *two years* would pass away before it could return to them. This was a startling statement to these long-neglected yet well-disposed heathen. The teachers, however, had confidence in God—their desire was ardent—their purpose was fixed; and we resolved not to abandon the island. A few supplies of clothing, medicine, books, and school material were got ready; and, commending our brethren and their mission to the guidance and blessing of God, we landed them. We had many fears, but were not without hope that the crisis had turned in favour of Christianity.

Days passed on, and the endurance of the "servants of Jehovah" continued; a part of their own house was constantly used for daily instruction, both by the young and the old; and services were held for prayer and praise and preaching. The instruction given on those occasions was blessed. Rays of Gospel light entered the hearts of many, producing fears and convictions which led to anxious inquiries—"Who is God?"—"What is truth?" and "What shall I do to be saved?"

About this time one of the teachers was walking some distance from the settlement, and was suddenly surprised by hearing a sound of weeping, and language in the tone of distress and supplication. Turning aside, and going towards the spot whence the sound came, he saw, through the bushes, a heathen place of worship. An oblation of food was lying near the altar of sacrifice, and a young man, kneeling on the ground, with uplifted eyes towards heaven, was praying to his god. "Alas!" exclaimed the teacher, in relating the circumstance, "the compassion of my heart was very great when I saw this; and, waiting until he had finished his prayers, I went to him. He knew me, but was surprised to see me there. I asked him whom he had been worshipping. He said the name of his god was 'Natmas;' and, pointing to heaven, he said: 'He is there.' I then inquired if his god heard and was able to answer his prayer, to which he sorrowfully replied that '*he did not know!*'"

How interesting a position for a Christian teacher to find a heathen young man in! We are not told what was the precise burden which pressed so heavily on his heart; but he was in sorrow; he had been praying for relief, and had brought in his hand a propitiation to his god: under these favourable circumstances, the teacher "preached unto him Jesus." While the truths of the Gospel were being expounded, an old man, the keeper of this heathen temple, joined the company. What he then heard induced him to come every Sabbath to the station for the purpose of receiving instruction; his mind became enlightened and his heart changed, and he died believing in Jesus as his Saviour. He was one of the first natives who was buried in the soil of the land. It had been usual, from time immemorial, for the people of Aneityum to cast their dead into the sea.

Reviewing the mission on Aneityum at this point in its history, we see a more favourable position gained, with less difficulties and opposition, than had been known on any other island in that group; and, thus encouraged, the devoted teachers write:—"This work of God is a good work. It causes happiness to grow in the hearts of those who do it. The reign of Satan is giving way, and the Gospel is advancing. Many of the people have cast away their idols, and pray to Jehovah, in their families, at their meals, and in private. This is the work of Jesus."

The success which had been gained on Aneityum, together with its distance from the eastern groups, rendered it important that European missionaries should occupy it as a principal station; and while the native converts of the south were preparing the way, God was raising up in the north a labourer to occupy the field. The Rev. J. Geddie, D.D., of Nova Scotia, about this time was sent out by the churches there as missionary to the heathen. After remaining six or eight months in Samoa, gaining an insight into missionary work, the Rev. Dr. Geddie proceeded to Aneityum, where he landed in 1848. Although much had been done, yet much remained to be done and endured by our brother. Few of the population were willing to receive Christian instruction, and a small minority gave signs that they were really changed characters; but idolatry, superstitious jealousy, and savage cruelty were rampant among the tribes. Having, however, counted the cost, the missionary gave himself to the work. With devoted heart and active hands, he met the dangers and difficulties of the mission; and he has every year had to report growing success. Not, indeed, that this success has been gained without conflict. In measuring the strength of our foes, he writes, "We feel that it is sufficient to vanquish any other than a Divine arm. Satan's seat is here, and he will not yield his dominion without a struggle; but He who is with us is greater than he who is against us."

Not long after this the struggle commenced with renewed vigour. A violent persecution set in against those who adhered to the teacher. Finding, however, that this did not succeed, the heathen party *feigned an interest* in the "new religion," and by subtlety and deceit sought to involve the mission in ruin. The following will illustrate this:—

A crafty inland tribe sent a messenger to the missionary, inviting him to come to them as soon as convenient, stating that they had heard much about the "Word of Jehovah," but, as they did not understand it, they wished to be instructed. The unsuspecting man, delighted with the prospect, made preparation to visit them. The nearest route to the station was by boat on the lagoon, inside the reef. A boat's crew was selected, and all things were ready; but the morning fixed for the journey was too stormy to allow them to proceed, and it was resolved to postpone the visit. Some few days passed away, and the disappointed heathen sent another messenger, expressing their regret that the missionary had not come, but stating that they were desirous to barter some native productions for a hog, which they wished to be taken inland to their village. Terms were proposed and accepted, and four young men of the mission station carried the animal to its purchasers. These were followed by a young Christian who had distinguished himself by his zeal. The Christian party had no sooner got into the village before the savages fell on them with an intent to murder them all. Four of the number escaped, but the other, who was more the object of their hatred, because the more decided Christian, lost his life, and his body was committed to the oven. There can be no doubt, had the missionary gone, he too would have been killed. Among other attempts made by the heathen to overthrow Christianity was setting on fire the missionary premises and buildings erected by the Christians for purposes of worship and instruction. Houses and huts were burnt to the ground, and the chapel was only preserved by the vigilance of a nightly watch. An attempt was made in this manner to destroy the missionary's house, and himself and family in it. He had retired to rest one night, but was aroused by the smell and crackling sounds of burning wood. Rising in haste from his bed, he gave an alarm to his faithful domestics, who, with himself, were just in time to extinguish the flaming fagot.

The custom of strangling widows and others was found to prevail to a great extent. It had its origin in their belief of a future state. Those who were wives must go, they said, when their husbands go, in order to be with them in the other world; and those who were servants here must go when their masters go, in order to be their servants there. This deed was, by law, done by a brother or near relative of the victim, and was not confined to widows and servants, but mothers, on the death of their unmarried sons, would often demand to be strangled, in order to follow the departed.

In one of the sacred groves of the island there stood a public altar to the gods. It was held in high veneration, and the heathen frequently visited it with offerings and homage. A Christian native, young in experience, determined to be revenged on the system which had caused his delusion. Without consultation with his friends, he went to this grove, broke down the altar, and with it made a fire which cooked his evening meal. This gave great offence to the heathen. Another instance occurred with the lads who attended the mission school. In the ignorance of the people it was considered a great crime to eat food which had been placed on the altars as an offering to the gods; such sacrilege was always followed by death. But the boys in the school had scarcely gone beyond the alphabet of learning, before they cast off all restraint in such matters, and many of them wantonly helped themselves to the choicest portions of this sacred food. The teacher censured this conduct, and enforced caution towards the heathen; but it was not in their power always to restrain the conduct of those whose minds were but just enlightened respecting the absurdities of idolatry.

At another time the missionary, assisted by native workmen, was making some alteration in his dwelling-house, and, not having sufficient wood to complete the work, the men went to the mountain districts to cut rafters. In their search for materials they came to a grove where it was supposed the gods resided, and where, but a year or two before, they would not have ventured to set foot. But now, fearless of the gods, they wrought heartily with their axes, and, having cut down all they wanted, returned to their work in the village. The thing soon was noised abroad, and the heathen became so filled with horror and rage that they threatened to take away the lives of the party concerned.

These facts show that while the early converts, from principle, abstain from war and other offences against the heathen, yet it is often difficult to control their feelings of scorn and ridicule towards their idolatrous and superstitious ceremonies. The utmost that can be done is to counsel them, and to show that the spirit of Christianity is incompatible with evil by which such deeds are perpetrated, and that its advance to triumph needs not such aid. This the converts soon understand, and, after the first years of missionary instruction and example, they generally exhibit forbearance under provocation, courage under persecution, and love to their enemies.

A young man and his two sisters had become impressed with the folly of heathenism, and, in order to be instructed in the Word of God, had taken up their abode with the missionary. This much exasperated their relatives, and every inducement was presented to cause them to return to their former faith and practices. Failing of success, their mother, an old heathen, came to the mission-house, armed with a murderous club, vowing vengeance on her children, in the name of her gods, if they would not come with her to a heathen feast. The children were grieved at the folly of their mother; but they feared God, and would not comply with her wish. She became enraged, and, had not the missionary interposed, would have fulfilled her wicked intentions. She was told that her children were free to act for themselves; but so long as they decided to remain on the mission premises they should be protected. She then left them with her curse, threatening to murder them as soon as she found them alone.

It must be remembered that the natives, in their heathen state, had no idea of a periodical observance of one day above another as a sacred day of rest and worship. All days to them are alike. Whenever a Christian teacher lands among them, the observance of the *first* day of each week, the "Lord's-day," takes the precedence of the other ordinances of Christianity. Its uniform and careful observance by the teacher, from the first week of his residence with the people, is characteristic and influential—a tangible and unmistakable exposition of Christ's death and resurrection practically set forth before them.

One of the first evidences of the Christian teacher's success among a heathen people is to see a few of their number preparing their Sabbath-day's food on the Saturday evening, and their attendance on the Lord's-day for the worship of Jehovah, and to hear His Word translated and expounded.

In 1852, when I visited this island, after eight years' absence, how glorious was the change in this respect! Each village occupied by missionaries or teachers was adorned with a commodious "house of prayer," in which the people congregated, in increasing numbers, to worship God. At eight o'clock every Sabbath morning a public service was held, at which the people were orderly and attentive. Should any impropriety occur in the conduct of the disaffected, as was often the case in former years, it was now followed by such marks of disapprobation from the audience as to need no remark from the teacher. After this service, the missionary's wife gathered together a class of females for catechetical instruction, while her husband held a class for like purposes with the males. Some part of mid-day was spent in household prayer-meetings, and visits to those who would not attend worship. In the afternoon another public service was held in the chapel. After singing, reading the Scripture, and prayer, a sermon was preached by the missionary, which was followed by a short address by one of the natives. These islanders, whose heathen character I have been describing, are now so far advanced in Christian instruction and experience as to meet in such assemblies, and, with the entire confidence of the missionary, to address their own countrymen on subjects of Christian truth!

Equal in importance to Sabbath-day instruction among such a people is the establishment of *day schools*, and the conducting of them occupies a large portion of the time and labour of the Christian teacher. At first he gets a few persons to meet him in his house, or under the shade of a tree, or on the sea-beach, and there, with limited means, commences writing single letters of the alphabet, repeating their respective sounds in the ears of his astonished pupils, and teaching them how to join letter to letter, so as to form words in their language.

Besides these schools for elementary instruction, each missionary has a select Bible-class of young men, who, twice or thrice a week, receive information which they understand and value, and by which they are being prepared to become assistants in the further advancement of the mission.

It was cheering, on my visit to the island in 1852, to see

three neat buildings erected in the midst of the harbour settlement; one a chapel, another the mission house, and the other a *printing-office*, all built by the very men who six years before were heathens, some of whom were now assisting the missionary in the composition and press-work of books in their own language. In 1855 three thousand copies of the Gospel of St. Mark were printed; and we are called to rejoice to learn that the Bible is now open to another tribe of the human family.

Fotuna.

We visited the small island of Fotuna, which is closely connected with the mission on Aneityum. After the murder of an excellent teacher and his wife by the heathen, the station was left, and before it could be re-occupied the Bishop of New Zealand visited it, and took with him two Fotuna lads from the island, to be educated in New Zealand. These lads returned home in 1852; on which occasion the Bishop writes:—"To-day we have landed our two Fotuna scholars, and have left them in the hands of their relatives with our prayers, but with great uncertainty as to their future progress, *as there are no teachers now on the island.* This is one of the islands on which the London Missionary Society *has obtained a vested interest, by the death of two of its teachers, who were killed by the natives.* We shall be thankful," continues the Bishop "to hear that others have been speedily placed here." This prayer has been heard and answered. There were converts on Aneityum who were anxious to be sent to Fotuna. Two of these went to the island, and, after a few years' earnest pioneering Christian work, prepared the way for its being occupied as a principal station by Rev. J. Copeland, of the Presbyterian Board of Missions. Thus, the founders of the mission of Aneityum have lived to reap the first-fruits of their labours, and are yet sowing seed for a future and more extensive harvest. The idols are abolished; war, cannibalism, and heathen orgies are things of the past. Aneityum is now added to the trophies of Christianity, and its history is a source of encouragement to human efforts.

Maré.

On Sunday, 27th of September, at noon, we hove in sight of Maré, and near sunset we were off the station occupied by the teachers. A canoe came to the vessel in which were the teachers, Tataio and Iakobo, and a son of the chief came off to the vessel. They remained on board all night, and we obtained information respecting the state of things ashore. We were sorry to learn that the chief and Taunga, with most of the people, were absent on a visit to the island of Lifu, and could not be expected to return until a change in the wind; and that the people were not now in so pleasing a state as formerly, nor were the prospects so promising for the future. The teachers were living with a Tongan family, and these were the only individuals who attended services on the Sabbath. The people had, during the past year, been greatly afflicted—numbers had died, and the people were disposed to blame the teachers. This visitation had also been felt at Lifu, and the chief there had sent a request to the chief at Maré to kill the teachers. The chief of Maré felt disposed to comply with this suggestion, but his sons interposed, and they were delivered. The people were now restored to comparative health, and there seemed cause to hope that better days were at hand. On the Monday morning the principal son of the chief at home came to us. We had a long conversation with him on the state of things, and said we now wished to remove Iakobo to Samoa, and to take back Taunga to New Caledonia. We were also desirous to leave three other teachers, two Samoans and a Rarotongan, to join Tataio, and with a view that two of them should, as soon as possible, go to some other station on the land. The young chief expressed his pleasure at this, and said it was very good, and no difficulty would ensue; that we could put them on shore now, and as we were bound to Lifu we could take the information to his father. Things being thus decided, we appointed Mika, Feli, and Maka. Towards evening they were landed among the people, who appeared to receive them with pleasure.

I transcribe some further particulars respecting Maré from "The Gems," &c.:—

The island of Maré is in the Loyalty Group, Western Polynesia. It is a low reef-bound island, about sixty miles west of New Caledonia, and nearly 3,000 miles from Rarotonga. The native name is Nengone. It is nearly seventy miles in circumference, and has a population of about 6,000 persons. These, when first visited by us, were living in practices of barbarous heathen life, and were amongst the most degraded races of the South Sea Islanders.

The people of Maré believed in the existence of one great unseen power or personage, whom they honoured as god. They had no carved images, but worshipped this superior governing power through the medium of sacred stones and wood, and relics of their departed relatives and heroes.

One of our first Christian teachers on Maré, after describing scenes practised by the people in reference to their cannibalism, which I cannot write, says:—"These things are so bad that in order to believe them you may inquire if I myself have seen them done. I tell you, in truth, I see them every day; I am constantly going about in the midst of them. I dare not tell you all I see of cannibalism here; you could not bear it. Not only do these people eat bodies taken in war, but on occasions of strife and jealousy a father kills his son, a son his father, a brother his brother Alas! alas! they are more like wild beasts than men."

Repulsive, indeed, must have been this state of things which so much distressed a Christian islander, whose own father, only five-and-twenty years before, was accustomed to the same deeds of cruelty. But, looking at the Rarotongan Christian in contrast with the heathen of Maré, we see the transforming power of the Gospel, and also how it fills the heart with a Divine compassion.

I record details of moral triumphs achieved by the united agency of Christian natives from the Samoan and Rarotongan islands. But in tracing the difficult path through which these teachers have had to pass to their present reward, I first record some of the many deeds of cruelty which were committed in the first contacts of natives with white men.

In 1841, a boat's crew of six men, belonging to a small ship from Sydney, went on shore for the purpose of bartering for supplies of yams and other vegetables. The crew landed on the north side of the island, and, under cover of fire-arms, succeeded in concluding their barter on terms of comparative friendliness. As the white men were leaving the beach, the chief of the district expressed a desire to accompany them to the ship. This proposition was resolutely opposed, and in the hurry and bustle of the boat's crew pushing off to sea, one of the oars struck the chief on the head. A shout for revenge was immediately raised by the natives, a fight ensued, and the six unfortunate white men were killed.

At a later date, an English ship touched at Maré. One of the Christian teachers, then on shore, went off to it, told the captain of the former massacre, and urged him not to land. This advice, however, was not heeded; a boat's crew was sent to the beach, and at the same time a number of the natives were admitted on board the ship. A premeditated signal was given, a simultaneous attack was made by the natives, and ten white men were murdered in the affray!

The first Christian teachers who landed on Maré were two educated, intelligent natives from Rarotonga and Samoa. Two years after their landing it was pleasing to find that a favourable impression was being made on the minds of the people in favour of Christianity. The teachers were permitted to build themselves a house, which, being finished, stood in palpable contrast to the wretched hovels of the people. This was the first appearance of civilisation. A large space in the centre of the building was set apart for week-day instruction and Sabbath-day preaching. The teachers in erecting this house were assisted by many of the young men, who saw with wonder how materials so nigh at hand could, by the proper use of the saw, and adze, and plane—tools which they had never before seen—be formed into so commodious a dwelling-place, and also into desirable articles of furniture and domestic use.

In a class of heathen youths gathered together for daily instruction, there were two sons of Jeiue, the old chieftain of the district. These two young men soon became deeply interested in the instruction they received, and were raised up by God to protect their instructors, when the rage of their heathen father would have destroyed them. Before, however, much progress could be made in educating the people of Maré, the teacher had to learn their language. This was no easy task. In the eastern groups there are different dialects of the same language, but in these western groups the language is quite different from the eastern, both in its roots, idioms, and pronunciation.

In 1846, accompanied by several Christian teachers, I left Rarotonga in our ship, and, calling at Samoa, where I was joined by the Rev. H. Nisbet, sailed to Maré. On approaching the island we saw hundreds of the wild, naked heathen population running along the beach, or dancing through the cocoa-nut groves in the utmost state of frenzy, and so loud was the yelling as to be distinctly heard by us on board.

Arriving off the settlement, where teachers had been landed two years before, we were cheered by seeing one of them coming off to us in a canoe, and were glad to find him accompanied by the two sons of the chief. Much encouraging progress had been made, yet it was not deemed prudent for the ship to come to an anchor, nor that we should trust ourselves on shore. The lives of the teachers were safe, yet such was the wildness of the masses of the people that no dependence could be placed on them for the security of life, for even our clothes might present a temptation to them to commit acts of violence. The teachers had learned the language, and the people now better understood the object of our visit.

Gaining much valuable information respecting the people, at the latter end of 1848, Jeiue, the chief, was taken ill, and soon after the attack severe symptoms of dropsy were developed; day by day he grew worse, and, as is usual, alike in uncivilised and civilised lands, the serious illness of a chief was a season of public anxiety. Every available means for Jeiue's recovery was resorted to; offerings of food, and charms, and prayers were religiously attended to by the priests; but they were of no avail; the old man continued to grow worse. The Christian teachers, too, did all they could to relieve his sufferings and to instruct his mind. They said, "Alas! alas! for the parent chief, Jeiue; our compassion towards him is great. We see him every day; we talk with him about the Gospel of Jesus; we give him what medicines we have, but he gets no better; Jeiue must die!"

During this sickness the disconsolate sufferer manifested more mental distress than is usually seen in a heathen. He often expressed a wish that "he had died ten years before." And why? Alas! the light of Divine life and love had been shining around him, but he had opposed its entrance into his heart. He had loved darkness, and now, stung by an upbraiding conscience, he must die!

As his end drew near, the faithful Christian instructors never left him; and to them the self-condemned man unveiled the bitterness of his soul, in the review of his idolatry, his heathen practices, and opposition to the Gospel.

In a moment of comparative repose, he said to his sons, "I have been wrong in my opposition to the Word of Jehovah; attend you to my advice, and continue as you have begun; *let the heathenism of our family die with me*." To questions proposed to him it was pleasing to find that, even at the eleventh hour, the dying sinner acknowledged that "Jesus was the only Saviour:" to every announcement made to him of the love of God, and of His willingness and power to save, he bowed an emphatic assent, and his last words were, "Jesus is the only Saviour." Thus died Jeiue. His sons determined to bury him with Christian burial, and selected a cave in a rock facing the sea as the place of interment. The coffin was fastened to the ground by many lengths of cable chain belonging to one of the English ships, which had been cut off by the old man's commands a few years before.

Soon after the death of Jeiue, his eldest son made known his determination that heathenism and idolatry should no longer reign in his district, that he and his brother had given themselves to Jehovah, whom they believed to be the true God, and that they intended to use their influence to establish His worship throughout the island.

The house of prayer, commenced under circumstances of so

much interest, was finished early in 1851, and the people waited three months after its completion, hoping the mission ship would bring a missionary to take part in the opening services. At length, weary of delay, they resolved to open it themselves. A day was fixed, and an invitation was sent to the tribes of the districts, which was very generally accepted.

Referring to this event the teachers say, "This was a day of much joy; our hearts were glad. Early in the morning messengers were sent to proclaim the joyful occasion, each one calling out as he went, 'Brethren! come, come to the opening of the house of Jehovah; come, the house is finished; the feast is ready, come.'

Obeying the joyful summons, tribe after tribe came to the new settlement, and, with emotions as new and as peculiar as the circumstances, attended the opening services of this house of prayer. At an early hour hundreds of visitors had arrived. More than a thousand entered the building. The honoured teachers were there. Many had been the years of toil through which they had passed, and none can realise the amount of trial and privation which they had endured; and none can know the joy they felt while they stood in the midst of the large assembly in this chapel, raised by their own industry, and aided by a people who, a few years before, were heathen!

In 1848 I printed at the Mission Press, Rarotonga, a number of school books, and Scripture extract books, in the language of Maré. These were invaluable during the years of pioneering work, and, in writing to me, the teachers urgently requested another and a more varied supply. They say, "Our want of books is great. The people much desire to learn. Alas! how long a time we have to wait before we shall get any. Oh, that we had a press near, to print speedily the books we need, in the language of this people!"

One moonlight night in June, 1852, after an absence of nearly two years, the children of England's missionary ship again visited Maré. It cast anchor in a fine bay on the south-east side of the island, near the station where the second chapel was built. A great and good change had taken place on the island since its last visit—a change for which the missionaries had often prayed, and which they now rejoiced to witness. About seven o'clock in the morning, looking on shore from the vessel, crowds of natives were seen travelling along the beach towards the chapel; it was Sabbath-day; they were going to the early morning prayer-meeting. The building, the people, and everything seen from on board the vessel were involved in mystery, until the excellent and faithful teachers came off, and related, as well as their excited feelings would allow, the experiences through which they had passed since the departure of the missionary ship.

The Rev. Messrs. Murray and Sunderland, accompanied by Captain Morgan, went on shore to attend the forenoon service. The missionaries preached by the teachers, who acted as interpreters. Owing to the former desperate character of these people, but few captains of merchant ships had yet visited their shores, hence but few of the congregation were clothed; some of them had a single garment over their shoulders, others had on native cloth which had been sent to them by the churches in Samoa and Rarotonga, but the large majority had nothing but plaited leaves or bark to cover themselves. After the service, the brethren visited the schools; two hundred children were present, being taught by the more advanced young men and women.

Remaining three days at this station, the missionaries went to the settlement where the *first* chapel was built; here the change seen in the character and habits of the people was still greater. A few years ago they were a wild cannibal race, at war amongst themselves, and aiming to murder every white man who approached their shore. Now they are repentant, docile, humble, and anxious to be instructed. Here was a good chapel 120 feet long, neatly seated with good benches, in which were met more than a thousand natives for the worship of God. The service was conducted with the greatest order and attention. Sabbath-day services were well attended; daily schools full of children; thirty-one individuals had been baptized and many others were consistent candidates. Instead of the thorn there had indeed come up the fir-tree, and instead of the brier, the myrtle-tree. The people had built a large, commodious dwelling-house, hoping soon to welcome a missionary from England who should take up his residence amongst them. This house was fifty-four feet long, thirty feet wide; walls fourteen feet high; it had a spacious verandah, venetian blinds, and six convenient rooms—the workmanship of the natives, and built expressly for a missionary residence.

A complete revolution has taken place in the entire framework of society. Hundreds of the people can now read the Word of God; hundreds more are learning, a great number of whom are anxiously seeking the salvation of their souls.

Lifu.

On the morning of the 29th of September we were close off Lifu. We hoped to have seen the teachers early, but a strong wind blowing on shore prevented this. A canoe in coming off got swamped; we lowered the boat to render assistance; and doing this, our vessel got somewhat in danger by being drifted too close to the lee shore.

Towards noon Paó, one of the teachers, came off, accompanied by Bula, the principal chief. Paó gave us an account of his labours among the people.

The teachers have confidence that the Word of God will prosper here; and that even now missionaries might, not only without danger, but with almost sure success, live among the people. The power and authority of the chief are very great, and at present decidedly in favour of the introduction of the Gospel.

In our conversation with the chief, we told him of our pleasure at the present success, and urged him to give all attention to the truths of the Gospel; that it was his duty to use influence to prevent war, and to leave off some of their old customs; that Jehovah is a God of love, and designs His Word to bless *all* people; that therefore our object was not only to do good to *his* party, but bless *all the tribes* of the land. We told him that, if agreeable, we were desirous to remove Jona to Samoa to receive further instruction, and to leave three other teachers to unite with Paó until the return of the vessel. He replied that he was quite willing, and much pleased at what we had told him; I left three teachers on the island.

The first Englishman of whom we have any knowledge as taking up his abode with the people of Lifu proved unworthy of his country. By deeds of appalling depravity he much impeded our efforts to introduce Christianity.

This Englishman was a son of a most respectable Christian family in this country. From his birth he had had the pious example and instruction of his excellent parents, and his character was then as promising as that of many youths in such circumstances. But uniting himself to lads of immoral practices, he became impatient of the restraints of his well-ordered home and of his friends. Efforts were made to check his onward career in vice, but its force accumulated on him, until, to the sorrow of his relatives, he resolved to go to Australia. Mingling with bad company during the voyage, he landed on those distant shores more confirmed in wickedness than when he left his father's house. For some time he remained there, and gave himself up to the excess of vicious pleasure, until at length he engaged himself as a seaman on board a trading-vessel bound to Western Polynesia. On the ship's arrival at Lifu, the reckless young man determined to take up his abode with its savage inhabitants. He landed among them, and gained their favour by giving away his clothes, and adopted their mode of roving abroad in a state of comparative nudity. Without restraint he delighted in the practice of all the abominations of the heathen; he assisted the tribe with whom he lived in their cruel wars, and revelled with them in their feasts! When the missionary ship first visited the island, this *heathen white man* came to it in a canoe, as wild as the wildest, and more detestable to look on than they.

Although not more than one-third of the heathen tribes had been visited, and even the great mass of the people where the teachers lived were still heathen, yet a large building had been erected as a "house of God," in which a goodly number of natives met every morning for Christian instruction, several of whom were sufficiently advanced to take part, in the services of the Sabbath.

One of the most interesting characters I saw was Bula, the chief of the district. He was about five-and-thirty years old; for some years he had been afflicted with total blindness. From the first landing of Paó, Bula had been his friend, and now he had made considerable advance in Scriptural knowledge and Christian experience. Through his example and influence, the first blow was given which led to the overthrow of heathenism and the subjugation of the people to the Gospel of Christ.

Bula much regretted that his tribe would not cease to war with that of the other side of the island, and he was frequently pained with the conduct of the warriors, who brought the bodies of their victims before him, inviting him to do as in former days. These deeds he reproved with indignation, mingled with Christian mildness, always affirming that he had become a "praying man to Jehovah," that he would have no more to do with heathen practices; he assured the people that the time would come when they would mourn over their wickedness and folly. Bula visited the mission ship; I had long conversations with him, and was delighted with his behaviour.

The children of the Samoan mission school, having heard of the love and zeal of the children in England in purchasing the "*John Williams*" as a missionary ship, were stimulated by their example, and resolved to purchase a supply of "missionary canoes," for the use of the destitute teachers in Western Polynesia. *Twenty* of these canoes were put on board the mission ship at Samoa, and, as the Lifu canoes were much inferior to those of Samoa, we gave Bula one. He could not see it, but his mild countenance, made more so by the benign influence of the Gospel, bespoke the feelings of his heart, while, with his hands, feeling over every part of it, he frequently exclaimed, "Alas! the greatness of their compassion to us. This is one fruit of the Word of Jehovah!"

When visited again in 1852, it was indeed pleasing to see the great change which had come over the people—their bodies were clothed, their wildness was subdued, and their whole demeanour bore witness to the civilising influences of the Word of God. It is not easy to describe the feeling of grateful surprise which filled our hearts as we landed in the midst of a well-ordered settlement, where but a few years before deeds of cruelty and bloodshed were rampant, and as we saw the large commodious stone chapel standing on the very spot where Satan's seat was—all the result, through God, of native instruction and labour. The chapel was *one hundred feet long, forty feet wide,* and the walls three feet thick. Besides being well furnished with seats, it had a pulpit, reading-desk, doors, and neat venetian blinds over the windows, all of which was their own work.

As far as their limited means of books would allow, the people were being taught, and a goodly number were able to read fluently. *Three hundred persons* were in select classes for Biblical instruction, whose lives were in outward conformity to the requirements of Christianity; and not a few were engaged in teaching their fellow-countrymen, and in taking part in conducting religious services. In reply to inquiries of an intelligent native about getting a missionary to live among them, he was told that one would come some day; he rejoined, "Say not *some* day—I do not like to hear that word *some* day; why not say *to-day?*" Truly the fallow ground has been broken up—the seed has been scattered; the fields are *already white unto the harvest;* but, alas! the labourers are few. The call for European missionaries to reside on this island, to *advance* the work thus begun, was loud and imperative.

Uvea.

After a day's sail we made the leeward of *Uvea*—an unbroken chain of reef islands, from one to two miles round. There are dangerous openings from island to island. Sailing far round in search of an entrance into the lagoon, at length we resolved to make a trial, and get in between two of the little islands, about four or five ship's lengths one from the other. Just as we got between the islands, our dangers increased. We found the shallows extend farther to the middle than we had expected, and the vessel labouring against a heavy head-wind and a short, broken swell, occasioned by a strong current running against the wind. We were glad, therefore, to back out again, and thankful that we sustained no damage. We were thus obliged to abandon our design of visiting the islanders of Uvea in 1846. Subsequently, however, teachers were landed, and were so successful that for some years it has been occupied by the Rev. S. Ella. The language has been learnt, the Scriptures are being translated, a church has been gathered, and daily schools are well attended.

New Caledonia.

New Caledonia is one of the largest islands of Western Polynesia, being nearly three hundred miles long and seventy or eighty miles broad. It was discovered by Captain Cook in 1744. The first attempts to instruct and to civilise its inhabitants were made in 1841 by Rev. R. Murray, who succeeded in landing two native teachers. The "*Camden*," in which we first went to these islands, was taken out of its intended route, owing to the death of the Rev. John Williams, so that it did not return to New Caledonia for more than two years after the landing of the teachers. Then, to our grief, it was found that one of them, after a few weeks' residence, had died. The other had made good progress in the language, and had gained a favourable hold on the minds of the tribe with whom he lived. He was encouraged by a reinforcement of two teachers. The ship "*Camden*" came to England, and her successor, the "*John Williams*," did not reach the island until two years after. These delays were unavoidable; but it was hoped that the missionary auxiliary formed in Australia would secure more frequent visitation. Could this have been done years ago, I should not have to record the painful reverses, the long-continued struggles, the desolating calamities which overtook this mission.

In recording the events which took place on his landing,

Taunga, a Rarotongan teacher, writes: "The Word of God is growing in this land of New Caledonia. Many of the people have learnt to read, and are attentive to worship every Sabbath. A few days ago a heathen came to me to inquire about casting away his idols. I told him an idol is nothing at all; that Jehovah is the true God; that He made the heavens, the earth, and all things; that He had pitied us in our sins, and had sent His Son, Jesus Christ, to be our Saviour."

This man, after the above conversation, brought his idols to the teachers, and requested that they would burn them. A few of the people were gathered together; the man publicly gave up his false gods, and the teachers addressed the assembly somewhat as follows: "Brethren, you see this your countryman has given up his gods: they are no gods, but idols; he wishes us to burn them." While he was thus speaking, one of the crowd rushed in, and bore away the rejected gods, and thus saved them from being destroyed.

As the idols had been brought to the teachers to be burnt, it was well that they convened this public meeting, for by it they relieved themselves from an act which might have brought on them the revenge of the heathen party. The man who gave up his idols remained steadfast under Christian instruction.

About this time *a comet* was seen night after night rising higher and higher over their land. From time immemorial these "*long-tailed stars*" had been to the people evil omens of disease, and war, and death; and, strange to say, just as the comet now seen became visible on New Caledonia, a very general and fatal sickness prevailed. The heathen, supposing it to be the "fire of Jehovah," vowed vengeance on the teachers of His religion, and combined their forces to extirpate both them and their converts.

On the island known as the Isle of Pines there lived a dominant tribe whose chief, Mathuku, was one of the most wild, savage, despotic men known, even in Polynesia. He had frequently sent his messengers to the natives of the district where the teachers lived, demanding that they should be put to death. Finding his orders were not obeyed, he sent his last command, saying, "If you do not kill the Samoan and Rarotongan men, I will come and kill them and you too." With this intention, he came, followed by a number of his warriors, armed with spears and clubs. Taunga says: "The people of our settlement wished us to flee to the mountains and hide ourselves; but we said, 'No; Jesus is our mountain, we will fly to Him.' On the day appointed, it was arranged that nine or ten of the savages should come to the teacher's house, and commence a discussion about the resurrection of the dead. As the discussion advanced, one of the party, pointing to some graves near, demanded of the teachers, in an angry tone, 'When will these men live again?' With mingled positiveness and kindness, the teachers replied, 'They will live again at the end of the world. Jesus, the Son of God, will come, and all who have lived will live again, and will be judged; those who have loved Him will then live with Him in heaven for ever.' 'By this we know you are deceivers,' rejoined the heathen; 'and we will now kill you. You are liars.'" Upon this, four men rushed forward; one of them seized Noa's right arm in his left hand, and raised his club to strike the fatal blow. Another stood behind Taunga, his intended victim. The teachers bowed their heads, and calmly resigned themselves into the hands of God. All was ready. It was as though the deed was already done. But the man on whose nod it depended silently signified "Not yet," and the crisis turned in favour of the devoted teachers. Would that the missionary ship could have visited this island just as this great conflict began. Many months passed away before it again came; and, when it did arrive, persecution and distress had increased so much that it was not deemed safe for the teachers to remain. They were quite willing to remain—yea, they wept much on being taken on board; but, being assured that the heathen party had fully made up their minds to murder them, the missionary did not see it his duty to consent.

Subsequent events justified the worst apprehensions. Soon after the removal of the teachers, the people of the Isle of Pines maintained a desperate war with those of the southern portion of New Caledonia; they slew nearly the whole of the natives who had professed attachment to Christianity, and the warriors were seen by a captain of a whaling ship returning to their homes in the horrid revelling of heathen victory, with the sculls of the slain stuck on high poles, and their fingers, in almost endless number, hung on strings around the necks of the warriors of the conquering tribe.

As I approached this land, in 1846, having on board the banished teachers, and desirous to renew attempts to bless its people, all was silence and desolation. The entire settlement had been destroyed by fire; the grass, the bush, and even the lofty cocoa-nut trees were yet black as coal, and not a single native was seen. Some distance inland the smoke of fire was ascending, which confirmed the opinion that the district was yet in the hands of the enemy, and that they were lurking in secret to decoy us on shore.

There were on board two Christian natives of New Caledonia, who had followed the teachers. Poor fellows! with the teachers, they refused to be comforted when they found they were not able to land.

On leaving this island we were for some time in great danger. At high tide we had sailed over a sunken reef, which was impassable at low tide, and toward evening we were inside the reef, with little or no wind. We had to sail some three miles to the south before we could get out to the open sea. Had we not gained that point we should have been in the hands of the cruel, blood-thirsty natives during the night. But in mercy we gained the outlet about an hour after sunset.

Isle of Pines.

On leaving New Caledonia we saw the Isle of Pines, and we wish we could have had intercourse with the natives; but the door was not open. The following are notes of its mission history:—

The Isle of Pines is an important island, about thirty miles from the north-east end of New Caledonia. It is covered with beautiful *pine*-trees, from which circumstance Captain Cook gave it its name; the native name is Korie. For some time past it has been one of the principal sandal-wood depôts of Western Polynesia, and it may be considered the seat of political power for the south end of New Caledonia.

The mission ship "*Camden*," five months after the murder of Messrs. Williams and Harris on Eromanga, visited this island; two Christian teachers were landed among its people. Some time afterwards a number of vessels were fitted out, the services of the party referred to were secured, and the quiet little island, hitherto almost unknown, became a scene of bustle and excitement; and in not a few instances the covetousness and immorality of this heathen people were increased before the corrective influences of Christianity had been brought to bear on the population. While, however, we were yet hoping to overtake these evils by our native agency, by more frequent visitation, and ultimately by the residence of an English missionary, a disastrous circumstance occurred which for the time frustrated our plans.

Difficulties having occurred between the natives and some sandal-wood traders, the natives became so enraged that they determined to be revenged on the foreigners by destroying their ship.

An opportunity too soon occurred in which to carry out their purpose. They took to the vessel a quantity of the wood, carrying with them their adzes which they use in dressing the wood. The wood was immediately bought, and the natives were allowed to remain on board to grind their adzes. One of the crew was turning the grindstone, and the captain stood close by; at a given signal, a native swung round his adze, and struck the captain dead on the spot, and in a few minutes seventeen of the crew were killed. The ship was then stripped of sails and rigging, everything was taken out of the cabins, and then it was destroyed by fire. In this massacre our devoted teachers were murdered.

One of the Rarotongan teachers who fell on the Isle of Pines was Rangi. He was the only child of his widowed mother. She, at some sacrifice, being a poor woman, had willingly given him up to the cause of Christ and of His Gospel. When information reached us respecting her son's murder by the heathen, I well remember her heroic Christian devotedness. She wept, and wept much, as any mother would weep; but after the first burst of her distressed heart had been relieved she tried to wipe away the tears as they involuntarily rolled down her cheeks, and she said, "It is not wrong to weep, for he was my son; but I do not weep tears of sorrow for him. No; my Rangi is with Jesus; he has fought a good fight; he is now crowned by his King in glory. Oh, that I had another son! I would give him up to go among the heathen men who murdered my Rangi. They are dark as we were before we understood the Word of God."

Savage Island.

We had three weeks' tedious voyage from New Caledonia before we reached Savage Island. We had brought with us a native of the island, Beniamina, a man who had been taken to Samoa in a whaling ship, and there had been educated and made a profession of Christianity.

As soon as possible we held a conference with the chief from shore on board our missionary ship. It appeared that they could not hastily consent that either a Rarotongan or Samoan should reside amongst them, but that Beniamina had better go on shore, and teach them as far as he knew, then they would better understand what was meant, and be prepared to give a final reply on the next visit of the ship. Thankful for their decision, we acceded to their proposition: a good supply of books, clothes, and tools was given to Beniamina, and, commending him to the protection and blessing of God, he landed in the midst of his wild heathen countrymen. Thus, after sixteen years' repeated visitation and intercourse, we were permitted to leave with this people a Christian pioneer—to teach the Gospel of Christ.

It will readily be conceived that it was not without much apprehension respecting the safety of the teacher that the missionary again visited the shores of Savage Island; but his fears were dispelled; the life of Beniamina had been spared; a little light had entered into the minds of a few of the people through his instruction; and, whilst they had to make much advance, yet they were more kindly disposed than on former occasions, and were willing to receive another teacher as soon as one could be sent to them. This position, however, had not been gained without toil, trial, and persecution.

When the teacher first went on shore, he took with him a box of clothes. This the natives requested should be sent back to the ship, for they were afraid it would bring sickness to their land. "But I am one of yourselves," reasoned the teacher, "a man, and no god; and the wood of the box is the same which grows here." Impatient of restraint, many of the wild crowd gathered around him, and proposed to kill him. With calmness he explained the object of his mission, and, not knowing the moment he would be struck to the ground, he knelt down in the midst and prayed.

A few, touched with compassion, wished to spare him, but others insisted on his being put to death. "Let us do it *now*," they said; "let us do it now, while he is alone; by-and-by others will join him, and it will be more difficult."

After a time, a few of the people ventured to receive him; general confidence increased, and the number who listened to and believed his reports about the Word of God daily increased.

On a subsequent visit, my brother, the Rev. George Gill, reported that things had advanced with surprising rapidity. Good chapels had been built, schools were organised, and the stations were attended to. He gathered the Christians into church fellowship, and, with but very few exceptions, heathenism was abandoned throughout the land. The island is now occupied by the Rev. W. G. Lawes and his brother. There are 1,183 members in church fellowship, and more than 2,500 young people and adults under daily instruction. At this time they sent a contribution to the funds of the London Missionary Society of 13,237 lbs. of picked cotton, 2,934 lbs. of cocoa-nut fibre, 4,374 lbs. of arrowroot, and 1,000 yams, which realised the sum of £340. Their villages are being instructed by their own educated countrymen, and already they have sent two evangelists to the distant Lagoon Islands beyond Samoa!

Such is "*Savage*" Island. *Eighty-two* years ago it was discovered by Captain Cook; for *fifty-six* years after its discovery it was left to its heathenism; the first visit of mercy was made to it in 1830; and, during the space of *sixteen* years, frequent and unsuccessful attempts were made to induce the people to receive a Christian teacher. This was accomplished in 1846; the subsequent *five* years were years of toil and faith in the midst of trial and persecution; and NOW, as a result of those labours, we have, on this once *Savage Island*, the whole of the people under the influence of the Gospel of Christ.

Return to Rarotonga.

Having finished our visitation of the heathen islands westward we set sail for Samoa. We had now been sixteen weeks on board, and had visited most of the islands of New Hebrides, Loyalty, and New Caledonia Groups, and had located twenty-one native teachers among those heathen islanders. We made Tutuila on 29th of October. We were desirous to enter the harbour; but the wind failed us at 4 p.m., and from that time till 10 p.m. we were in imminent danger of being carried by the rolling swell on the reef-bound shore; at one time we had the breakers close to the stern of the ship. The ship's boats were out at the bows making efforts to tow her off; but all without success, till at 10 p.m., just at the extremity of peril, a light wind sprang up, and took us fairly out to sea.

On the morrow and next day we had intercourse by boats with the people at Tutuila and Leone, and then sailed eighty miles to Upolu, and once more cast anchor in Apia harbour.

We remained at Samoa three weeks, visiting the stations and holding meetings with the missionary, giving reports of our voyage, &c.

On the 2nd of December, 1846, we went on board, and received the children of Mr. Hardie and others who were destined for England, and on December 26th we were permitted to land on Rarotonga. We had been absent six months, five months of which were spent on board.

CHAPTER XXI.

MISSION WORK, 1847 TO 1852—REV. AND MRS. BUZACOTT VISIT ENGLAND.

THIS most trying and eventful year (1846) closed by the departure of Rev. Mr. and Mrs. Buzacott for England. On landing, after our long absence, we found our friends quite ready for their voyage. On Sunday, 27th December, we held a farewell service at Avarua, and on the following Tuesday our friends embarked on board the "*John Williams.*"

Our revision work of the Rarotongan Scriptures had been much interrupted during the past year; but it was thought desirable that Mr. Buzacott should take the whole manuscript and printed portions with him, with a view of completing the work, so as to get it printed during his stay in England.

Thus I was practically left in charge of the whole work of the island, with its churches, stations, institutions, schools, and printing-office. The Rev. C. Pitman was at the distant station of Ngatangiia, but was too infirm to take any share in the work of the mission, except in guiding the affairs of his own district.

The prospect often made us fear; but, through the help and mercy of God, we, day by day, were enabled to meet the duties of each as it came.

January, 1847, opened as usual with devotional services at all the settlements; and we began to realise the variety and importance of the work committed to our hands—the restoration of the villages from the devastations of the late hurricane; the care and education of students in the institution; the superintending of the printing-office; the care of the churches and schools, and the general oversight of the people. At first we could not realise that we were to be left to carry on this work alone for more than *five years.* We had, however, been gradually prepared for it, and were much assisted by the kindness and efforts of many of the native teachers and people of the churches.

E.'s feeble health was a cause of great anxiety. For more than twelve months after the departure of Mr. and Mrs. Buzacott, she was often almost prostrate with pain. But God helped us day by day to plod on with our work, and in the review we wonder at the amount got through during these five years, from January, 1847, to January, 1852.

Amid our general mission duties one of the first things that occupied our time and attention was advising and arranging with the people for the rebuilding of chapels, schools, and houses destroyed by the gale in 1846. It must be remembered that the work of each settlement had to be recommenced; every chapel and mission-house, and almost every native dwelling, was in ruins; but before these could be attended to the plantations had to be cleared and replanted, which, with the greatest industry, did not yield a sufficient supply to meet the wants of the people for six or eight months afterwards.

For many months the people at the several stations gave a large portion of their time to their plantations, and at the close of the year were permitted again to rejoice in an abundance of food. The villages, however, were not so soon restored—it was a great work; yet by patience and regular labour it was done. Temporary huts and houses were first erected; but, being convinced of the importance of more substantial buildings to withstand these periodical storms, the people resolved to build strong stone houses, in the accomplishment of which they spared no time or labour. As an illustration I mention one village as a specimen of the whole. The inhabitants did not exceed 800 persons, of whom not more than 300 were available for work; but in three years this handful of people, besides attending to labour connected with providing their daily food, built eighty reed huts, fifty lime and wattle houses, forty strong stone cottages, a stone chapel, and a mission-house. In less than five years after this hurricane, on the islands of Mangaia and Rarotonga there were built twelve large substantial stone chapels and school-houses, three good mission-houses, and upwards of 300 stone cottages, averaging each from thirty feet to sixty feet long, and twenty feet to thirty feet wide.

Towards the end of 1847, while the people were thus busy, but weakened, a very general epidemic of influenza and low fever prevailed on the island. For many weeks some hundreds of the population were laid low. Attention to the sick and the dying drew largely on our time and sympathy. I find in a note made at the time that in one week we made up more than 1,000 doses of medicine, in which work E. was my only assistant.

As soon as this affliction abated, Mrs. Gill and I attempted to resume our regular daily work, which was very much as follows:—While the school for adults was being attended to in the station by the native superintendent, the morning hour from six to seven I was engaged in distributing medicine for the sick; from seven to eight, breakfast; from eight to nine, at the children's schools, or with lads in the boarding school; then, sometimes, we conversed with the workmen or with visitors from the settlement; from ten to eleven, at lectures with the students of the institution; then I would visit the students' workshop, and thence go to the printing-office, where the native printers had been at work since seven a.m. From one to two p.m. was dinner-time. Then some church member, inquirer, or candidate for membership would require attention. Four days in the week, from three o'clock to four, Bible-classes were held with inquirers, or with the teachers in the schools. At most of the stations, public services were held three evenings in the week, from five o'clock until six—one a church members' meeting, another for preaching, and a third, a general class meeting, at each of which I usually presided. From six o'clock till seven we would take walking exercise in the settlement, frequently embracing this opportunity to visit the sick. From seven o'clock to eight I was usually in my study, either reading or translating, or preparing the lectures or sermons, or correcting "proof sheets" from the printers; from eight o'clock to half-past eight was devoted to family prayer with the students, from which time until nine o'clock we engaged in general conversation: and thus closed the *public* labours of each day, with the exception of Saturday, when the natives were employed in personal and domestic duties.

The printing-office was a stone building. It stood on an elevated site near the Institution House, Avarua; it was the first stone building erected by the people of that station, and it has been a means of doing much to promote enlightened views of Christianity, and to extend its blessings throughout the Hervey Group and to islands many thousands of miles distant. The printing-press was introduced to Rarotonga in 1831, and in 1839 the Directors of the London Missionary Society supplied the mission with a new press and a new fount of type. Several native lads became proficient workmen; two or three of whom, in order to be more fully instructed, went to the mission printing establishment in Samoa. At various times we were much aided in this department by grants of paper from the British and Foreign Bible Society, and the Religious Tract Society. Amongst the books printed in the Rarotongan language, from the commencement of the mission, are several editions of first and second class school-books; a large edition of the Pentateuch and other separate books of Old and New Testament; many thousands of small and large hymn-books; numerous editions of "Brown's," "Watts'," and "The Assembly's" catechisms; a large number of James's "Church Member's Guide;" "The Sinner's Friend;" Bunyan's "Pilgrim's Progress;" a good supply of elementary works on Geography, Astronomy, Arithmetic, and Grammar; a small book on *Scripture Characters;* a monthly periodical of missionary and general information; school books and Scripture extracts in the languages of Maré, Lifu, and New Caledonia; a code of laws and regulations for Aitutaki, drawn up by the chiefs of that island; Short Commentaries on the Book of Isaiah, on the Gospel of John, on the Epistle to the Corinthians, on Leviticus, and on the Epistle to the Romans; and two editions, 5,000 each, of the complete Bible: all of which, with the exception of the Bible, the Commentaries, and the *Scripture Characters,* were printed at the mission press on the island.

During the *five* years of Rev. A. Buzacott's absence, ending December, 1851, there were printed 132,500 sheets, containing 1,590,000 pages; 20,350 tracts were sewn in limp covers, and 5,543 books were bound in leather. The whole of this work was done by young men, the first-fruits of missionary instruction, whose fathers had known no letter or sign whereby to represent the sounds of their then unwritten language.

THE INSTITUTION HOUSE, RAROTONGA.

The institution for the education of a native ministry is open to intelligent young men of all the islands of the group, the only requirement being that candidates shall be men of known piety, of active habits, and in membership with the church. Each student is admitted for six months' probation. Each married student has a cottage, and, as far as possible, each single young man has a room to himself. A detached eating-house is built near the institution, where the whole of the students and their wives have two hot meals a day, and each student in rotation gives a weekly superintendence to this department. An hour, from seven o'clock, every morning was devoted by the students to classes in geography, arithmetic, and other school studies. Two hours every forenoon were devoted to theological instruction. A short prayer was offered by a student, who also read the appointed lesson, when ten minutes were allowed for criticism on the manner of reading. The course of instruction to the students included lectures on theology, church history, Biblical exposition, biography, geography, grammar, and composition of essays and sermons.

During the years 1847 to 1852 I prepared for the students translations of Commentaries on the *Book of Isaiah,* on the *Gospel of John*, on the *1st and 2nd of Corinthians;* also a brief *Church History* from the time of Christ, and an exposition of the *Book of Joshua* and the *Judges.* These I brought to England, and 1,200 copies of each were printed and sent out for the use of the students; and in 1876 a second edition of the Church History was printed and sent out.

Late in 1847 a gentleman who had lived many years on the Sandwich Islands visited Rarotonga on his way to America. He sent a report of his visit to the editor of a Sandwich Island newspaper. Coming from a stranger, it may be considered a truthful representation of the state of the island at the time, and, therefore, worthy of preservation. He wrote as follows:—

"In continuing our 'Polynesian Sketches,' quite unexpectedly an interesting account has fallen under our inspection of Dr. W——'s visit at Rarotonga, on his voyage to the United States. We are quite confident that it was never intended for publication, but on that very account the testimony herein given is the more valuable. Would that every reader of Herman Melville's caricatures and misrepresentations (in his late work entitled 'Omoo') of English missionaries in the South Pacific might glance an eye over this sketch of a writer's first impressions at Rarotonga:—

"'We descried the lofty outlines of Rarotonga, forty miles distant. As we approached, it became a beautiful object to look upon, rising sudden and lonely—green and umbrageous from the shore to the mountain top—so pleasant and sunny did it appear, like an emerald set in silver on the bosom of the blue sea. The island is of basaltic structure, and looks more like a great body of land that had been sunk than like a distinct volcanic mass projecting from the bottom of the ocean. On inspecting it, however, you see numerous signs of volcanic action on the sides of the island, as if the lava and conglomerate had been forced above water or near its surface. The peaks projecting here and there, among the more round and rugged summits of the island, were barren, moss-grown, weather-beaten, and needle-shaped. Those and all other mountainous parts and valleys indicated the action of the elements from an unspeakable age of antiquity.

"'I had hoped to see the Rev. Mr. Buzacott, but learned that he had gone to England. The Rev. Mr. Gill, however, was at Mr. Buzacott's station. I had never heard particularly of him, but, presuming on Anglo-Saxon, or rather on Christian, civilisation, I made my way to his house and was received by him and his lady in the most cordial manner, and as an old acquaintance, too—for I found that they had for a long time heard of me, and were expecting me there on my passage home. Some ships had touched there a few days before, and had reported me as having left the Sandwich Islands, and that the "*Atlantic*" would probably touch at Rarotonga on her way home. In all my wanderings I have never known such a hearty and cordial hospitality—and all so simple and homelike too—as was extended to me and mine at Rarotonga. Mr. G. is a fine fellow, and understands the objects of his business very well. He has a great deal to do—a seminary of twenty young men under his care preparing to become missionaries to the unchristianised islands of the Western Pacific; a printing-office and workshop to superintend, and much other business which I have not time to name. He is well and thoroughly educated, possessing much urbanity of manners, well adapted for winning and retaining the love and confidence of the natives, which he appears to have secured. He wished much to receive communications from the missionaries at the Sandwich Islands.'"

During 1839 to 1852, seventy students were admitted to the Institution, thirty of whom were married—making a total of one hundred individuals. It is a cause of devout thankfulness and much encouragement that so few of these have proved unworthy. In the Hervey group of islands, no less than ten stations are efficiently worked by these native teachers; in Samoa, three or four of them have stations, and have the confidence and praise of the missionaries; in Western Polynesia they have proved themselves equal to endure labour, suffering, and even death for the Gospel's sake; in the Maniiki Group, 600 miles beyond Rarotonga, they have introduced the Gospel; and in 1853 one of them was appointed to labour as missionary to the natives of Rarotonga and Mangaia residing on Tahiti.

The expense of each student at this time was £5 a-year, and the entire outlay, or *cost to the London Missionary Society, at the time of my leaving the island*, for educating, clothing, and boarding twenty students, was not more than £3 a-week.

The boarding-school at Arorangi was supported by contributions from our personal friends in England, at the cost of about £3 a-year each boy. The history of those who had then grown up and those who have since grown up is most encouraging. Isaia Papeiha, who in 1877 had charge of that station as the pastor of Arorangi church, came to the school as a boy five years old, and now keeps on the same kind of school, and had twenty boys in it the last time he wrote to me (1876).

Many of those lads we knew and loved we rejoice to think of now as devoted teachers to the heathen in Western Polynesia, or as beloved pastors of churches in islands near their own.

Amid our busy engagements (1849) information was brought to us of the landing, on Manuai, of several heathen natives from the distant island of Maniiki. We had long known of the Maniiki Group, and were now rejoiced at the prospect of introducing the Gospel to its people.

The circumstances which led to this were as follows:—Early in 1849 a large party of these Maniiki natives left their island in canoes, purposing to visit Rakaanga, about thirty miles from Maniiki. They were overtaken by a storm, and but few reached Rakaanga; most of the party perished at sea; only the occupants of one canoe survived.

They had been many weeks at sea, when the captain of a whaling-ship, passing from the North to the South Pacific, saw them *eighty miles* from land. The benevolent man took them on board—five men and four women, some of whom were half dead from exhaustion—and brought them to the Hervey Islands.

The captain intended to land them either on Rarotonga or Aitutaki, but, not being able to make either of these islands, he left them on the small uninhabited land of Manuai.

On the arrival of our missionary-ship she was despatched to Manuai with two teachers; the poor heathen men and women from Maniiki were found and relieved, and brought to Aitutaki. They were landed on the Sabbath, during morning service; all was new to them, and they were lost in speechless amazement at everything which they saw. The people of Aitutaki were their brethren, of the same colour, and spoke the same language as themselves; but how vast the contrast! It was as though some of the old heathen inhabitants had risen from the dead, and, without having had the experience of the past thirty years of Christianity on the island, were permitted to see its results and to contrast them with their own heathenism and idolatry; and the young men of Aitutaki had never before realised the greatness of the deliverance which Christianity had wrought for them, as they did while they looked on these heathen islanders of Maniiki, who had been brought to their shores.

After visiting the schools, the Maniikians attended the service in the chapel; the building and the company were a new world of mystery to their untutored minds. They sat in the midst of *a thousand* CHRISTIAN *natives*, one half of whom a few years before were as heathen as themselves. They listened to the singing of hymns of praise to Jehovah from the great chorus of voices; they looked with astonishment on the congregation prostrated in prayer, and felt that they had entered into a strange world of wonders. After singing and prayer, they heard the story of the Cross of Christ stated and explained, and were told of their own interest in that story. This, indeed, was a day of salvation to them, and they desired that teachers of this same religion should be sent at once to their own land, Maniiki. They remained about a fortnight with the Aitutakian church, and then, accompanied by two teachers, and followed by the prayers of the people, they sailed for their own island, Maniiki.

INTRODUCTION OF THE GOSPEL TO MANIIKI.

On the ship reaching Maniiki the chiefs came on board, and their lost countrymen told them of the wonders they had seen at Aitutaki—of the overthrow of idolatry, and the worship of Jehovah, and of Jesus Christ being the only Saviour. The people were willing the teachers should land; and, under these favourable circumstances, Christianity was introduced to the island of Maniiki.

In giving an account of his early labours, one of the teachers says:—"On landing here, our books, and clothes, and tools were taken from us; but an investigation took place by command of the chief, and they were, for the most part, restored. Many days after we came on shore, the hut in which we resided was crowded by visitors, day and night, and we could not find time to sleep. The people did nothing but listen to what we had to tell them about the folly of idolatry, and the character of the '*evangelia à Jesu.*'"

On my voyage to Sydney, in 1852, I visited this new mission, and it was pleasing to find that the greater part of the young could read and that many of them could write. Five hundred school-books, printed at Rarotonga, had been already circulated among the people, and we left with them more than a *hundred copies* of the entire Scriptures in their own language.

Thus, in the short space of three years, the inhabitants of Maniiki had been delivered from heathenism and idolatry, and were under Christian instruction. Maretu, who had done good service in Rarotonga and Mangaia, went to the island; he formed a church, and superintended the schools, and conducted the affairs of the mission with much success. It is to labours of men like him that such stations are entrusted—and we need no other.

The native teacher who was located there, in less than twelve months reported "that the natives have renounced idolatry and burnt their gods; that at present they are all under instruction, both adults and children, and have already made considerable progress. One of our catechisms has been committed to memory. A place of worship has been erected and the Gospel of Christ preached to them, and the Sabbath regarded."

Thus, in the midst of our abundant labours for the home population on Rarotonga, God granted His blessings on our efforts and those of our native brethren, and gave us encouragement to persevere in our "work of faith and labour of love."

CHAPTER XXII.

COMMERCIAL AND RELIGIOUS PROGRESS.

During these years the increase of merchant and whaling ships visiting the island of Rarotonga was most remarkable. In our early years we were often six or eight months without seeing any vessel from the outside world, but about this time visits began to be very frequent for the purpose of obtaining yams, bananas, cocoa-nuts, potatoes, firewood, oranges, and water. Seventy-five ships came to the island during the autumn and spring of 1850-51, bringing all kinds of goods helpful to the advancing civilisation of the people, and importing money very largely. Fifty-five whale ships that came during the twelve months referred to had on board no less a total than 103,500 barrels of whale and sperm oil.

I record a description of early trading transactions:—

A ship arrives off the island. On its approach a native pilot goes on board to direct the captain, who, on landing, is met by the appointed salesman of the station. Giving the stranger the right hand of brotherhood, he salutes him in the native language, "Kia ora na"—Blessing on you. The captain is then conducted to the "market-house," where are stores of potatoes, yams, bananas, pumpkins, cocoa-nuts, hogs, fowls, &c. A chest of American or English goods is then given to the care of the salesman, who executes the "order," and, paying all expenses, he engages three, four, or five boats, as the case may be, to take the supplies to the ship. The whole business is generally conducted with propriety and satisfaction, and the captain leaves the island with a higher appreciation of the Christianity which has subdued the former cruel barbarity of this people, and has made the island a mart, a refuge, and a home! During two years, ending December, 1851, captains of more than twenty merchant vessels and whalers called at the island, traded with the people, gained suitable supplies for their voyage, and invariably found law, and order, and honesty, and the commercial deportment of the islanders to be such as could not be well exceeded in any port of a more civilised country. In the entire group, not less than one hundred ships annually trade with the natives, and receive produce of native labour in exchange for manufactured wares, amounting to not less than three thousand pounds. In this way industry, civilisation, and commerce follow in the footprints of Christianity, and, deriving from it their security and extension, they should be employed to do universal homage to its power and love; this would always be secured but for the perverseness of man's covetous and wicked heart. Men too often rejoice in the blessings of Christian civilisation, and at the same time ignore (strange infatuation!) the source whence they are derived.

With this increase of prosperity we had to deal with the beginnings of trouble through the landing of foreigners who wished to become possessed of land. The native authorities were, at this time, led to resolve not to sell any land to foreigners, neither to allow them to marry, concluding, from what they had heard, that these were the causes of evils which they most dreaded.

To illustrate the policy with which they carried out this purpose it may be stated that a respectable American captain desired to make the island his home. On landing, he was received by the chief judge of the station as his visitor and friend. Marking out a large piece of unoccupied ground lying between the judge's house and his neighbour's, the captain one day produced a large quantity of cabbage, coffee, pumpkin, and various other seeds. "Fine place this to plant these seeds," said the visitor. "Truly so," replied the native; "let my servants help you." And the thing was done. A month or two afterwards, when the plants had grown, the captain asked and gained permission to put up a fence round the small plantation.

Early one morning, before the judge's visitor had made his appearance, two stout young men were on the spot with wood for framework of a house, and they began to clear this ground for its erection. The captain was soon with them, and commanded them to desist. "No," said the young men; "it is our land, and we are going to build our house on it." "It is mine," replied the angry foreigner, and he would, in all probability, have laid hands on them, had not Joane, the judge, opportunely made his appearance. Depending on his friend's interference on his behalf, he demanded immediate redress, but was answered, with provoking coolness, "that it was bad to be angry, and worse to fight, and that the thing could soon be decided in court before the chief." That day the case was heard, and the foreigner was obliged to relinquish what he supposed he had secured. The two young men were sons of a native who was dead. The spot of land planted had been the site of their father's house, but during their minority they had been living elsewhere; now one of them was about to marry, and he came to take possession of his rights. The matter being thus decided, much to the chagrin of the captain, he inquired about a small coffee plantation inland, which he had planted on the sole ground of friendship, as in the other case. "Very good," replied Joane; "the seeds have grown, the plants are high, and when they bear fruit, the fruit is yours; but the ground is mine, and the trees are mine." "Nonsense," replied the foreigner, "they are both mine, and, when I leave the island, I can sell them to whom I choose." "No, no," rejoined the native; "we do not dispose of our land. As long as you remain you may have the fruit, but the land and the trees are mine."

The men of Rarotonga were now clothed respectably—they wore shirt, trowsers, waistcoat, and coat; most of them have strong rush hats for common use, and finer ones for occasional service, and about one in every twenty completes his full dress by putting on stockings and shoes. The general appearance of the whole population is appropriate to their climate and habits, and in this sense is civilised, decent, and respectable; so much so, that a stranger to their past history, landing in their midst, could not discover, in their present position, any sign of their former idolatry and heathenism, and would scarcely believe that they are the same race, and in many instances the *very same men*, who, only forty years ago, were naked, savage cannibals. The women wear a native cloth wrapper, as inner garment, over which is worn a long flowing robe; they have no shoes, but a bonnet of *finely wrought plait*, neatly trimmed with foreign ribbon, is considered essential to complete their dress. We had the honour of presenting to her Majesty the Queen a bonnet of this native-wrought material, neatly made in English style, for her Royal Highness the Princess Royal. In accepting it, her Majesty was graciously pleased "to express the deep feeling of gratification with which she had received the accounts of the happy results of the teaching of Christianity to this once heathen people." The Hon. Colonel Phipps, in writing to me from Buckingham Palace, also says:—

"I am commanded to state that her Majesty the Queen would be happy to show her desire to encourage the industry of the native women of Rarotonga by ordering some of the sugar-cane leaf plait, which her Majesty would have made up in this country. Perhaps you would be good enough, therefore, to inform me of the extent to which this manufacture is carried, so that I might be able to judge what quantity her Majesty might advantageously order."

I had the honour to communicate the required information, and to receive her Majesty's order for enough material to make twenty bonnets.

With increase of material means it was gratifying to see the willing liberality of the natives to meet the expenses of their mission. At the time of which I write I was able to record that, besides paying for their books, the people of Rarotonga had formed an Auxiliary Missionary Society, with a view to send contributions to the parent Society in England, the result of which, given out of their poverty, will show both their gratitude and zeal. Having then but little money, the larger part of the contributions was given in arrowroot, the preparation of which involves an amount of time and labour but little understood in this country. The seed is planted, and as it grows it has to be frequently weeded; then the root is dug up and is grated;

then it is washed three or four times, and subsequently dried and pounded and sifted; and after this expenditure of time and labour it only yields twopence-halfpenny per pound when sold to the merchant. For many years, however, in this way did these willing and diligent people prepare 4,000 pounds weight of this article for the Society; which, together with money subscribed, amounted to about *eighty pounds sterling a-year.* Latterly, however, they have prepared less arrowroot, but, by sale of coffee and cotton and other produce, have raised more money; so that, in the year 1854, this native auxiliary contributed to the funds of the London Missionary Society no less a sum than *one hundred pounds,* which, added to the amount raised for the same object by the people of Mangaia, Aitutaki, and the other islands of this group, made a total of nearly *three hundred pounds* for the year!

It is with no ordinary pleasure I look back to those years of labour and of the reward in successes then obtained.

But I have also vivid reminiscences of anxiety about the young. All the young men and women thirty years of age knew nothing of heathenism; they had been brought up in the mission schools, but many, very many, at this time, in 1850, gave us trouble, and were a source of anxiety both to their parents and the chiefs.

The site of the village of Ngatangiia had been so destroyed by the gale of 1846 that it could not be built up so as to accommodate the whole of the Ngatangiian tribe. Early in 1850 a few disaffected, evil-disposed young men of the tribe determined to take this opportunity for breaking away from the majority of the people, and forming a new station two miles distant from the original village. This plan was opposed by the chiefs and principal landowners of the district. The contest was carried on between the two parties with such violence and ill-feeling that it had well-nigh caused a war, and proved fatal to the best interests of the whole community. After a long season of anxious suspense, however, the good offices of the chiefs of the other tribes were called in, and the matter was amicably settled by the establishment of a fifth township called Matavera. This party soon built a chapel and school-house for themselves, and have now a native pastor located among them, who is labouring with great success.

Just twelve months after this, a party of ungodly young men came from Tahiti, and secretly taught some of the natives of Rarotonga how to mix and ferment orange juice, so as to make "orange rum." This being prohibited by the law of the land, the parties detected were fined. For some months the right and power of law and order were sharply contended with by those who wished to introduce drunkenness and disorder.

Revival.

Just at this time a blessed awakening took place, followed by a true revival. When we were thus dreading a calamity which threatened to overwhelm us as a flood, the Lord raised up the standard of the Divine Spirit; the billows receded, the plague was stayed, and many, very many, of the most wayward and wicked young persons at every settlement were rescued from misery and ruin.

Among the causes instrumental in leading to this awakening, I well remember the death of a fine, educated, wicked young man. Eighteen months before, he had left the island in a whaling ship for a voyage to the Sandwich Islands. There he associated with most abandoned characters, and on his return to Rarotonga became a ringleader in vice. He was, however, taken ill, and during the first weeks of his affliction he determined to harden himself and companions in sin by opening his house to assemblies for dancing and debauchery. But his illness increased, and with it the viper of his iniquity gained strength, and stung his inner soul with bitterest remorse.

He desired to die. In an awful state of mental agony he was kept alive, almost miraculously, to warn and to exhort those who had been his willing victims in crime. While in this state, he was frequently visited by Christian friends, who desired his redemption, even at this the eleventh hour; but nothing hopeful could be obtained from him—nothing but declamations of self-condemnation—and he died in fearful, convulsive groans, which, he said, were the commencement of everlasting death. The *excess* of his folly was the cause of his death, and his grave was, to his youthful companions, as a beacon of danger, which mercifully prevented their following in the same wild career of destruction.

A spirit of prayer was poured out on the churches; repentance, and desire for religious instruction, were manifested by many of those who heretofore had been scornful or unconcerned. This called out the energies of the godly; domiciliary visits were made, Bible-classes were held, copies of the "Sinner's Friend" were eagerly sought after, and several hours daily were appointed by myself and teachers for talking with those who sought direction and consolation in their newly awakened state.

But, in the midst of this time of revival, there were those who did despite to the Spirit of Grace, keeping themselves back from His influence, and endeavouring to frustrate it in others. Such a case occurred in a young man who had been frequently visited by two aged women for Christian conversation. Always before going to him, they spent a short time together in prayer to God for His direction and blessing; but week after week the wicked young man hardened his heart, and at length became so impudent that these true sisters of mercy resolved on paying *only one visit* more, and the young man had also determined on a daring deed by which to decide that this visit *should be the last.* It was eventide, and, his scheme being arranged, he was sitting on the doorway of his reed hut. "Come in, come in!" he cried to the Christian women as they approached him. Surprised at this unwonted blandness, they entered the house. It was now dark, and the young man requested that they would be seated, while he got a light, saying, at the same time, that he hoped they had brought their books. Seating them near the doorway he appeared to be feeling after the two pieces of touch-wood with which the natives get a light, when, unseen by the good women, he took up his gun, already charged for the purpose, and, pulling the trigger, discharged it over their heads. The flash and report frightened the women; but, finding themselves still alive, they hastened to the village, thankful for their own preservation, yet mourning over the "*lost young man*" as they thought him; but it was not so. Instantly, on their leaving the house, a horror seized his soul; he fell to the ground, and remained most of the night in a state of trembling despair. The extremity of his wickedness was the opportunity of God's grace. His mind was enlightened, his heart was subdued, and, after sorrowing many days, because of his transgressions, he obtained from God peace to his soul.

During the four months of this special visitation of grace, more than *five hundred souls* were brought under anxious concern for salvation, *three hundred* of whom were known to remain consistent disciples of Jesus Christ. It would be easy to notice in detail the history of many of these numerous converts, but I refrain. The following will be an example of many:—A young person wrote: "Blessings on you from God, who is feared by His angels in heaven and by His people on earth, but whom I have not feared. I have sinned against Him, and I now feel that my sins are numerous. I now remember the words of exhortation which you formerly spoke to me, and which I despised. They are now like thorns in my flesh; and my sins are drawing my soul down to destruction. Alas! the fearfulness of that place! I am filled with distress. Oh, that God would compassionate me, and draw my soul out of the net of the devil! My desire is, that you may become to me like Evangelist in the book of the Pilgrim. I had been attempting to take care of my own life, but I have fallen. May the Lord compassionate me, a guilty sinner! I am in shame. I am an orphan, lean of heart, and have no joy; and tears are in my eyes night and day. I am saying, 'Where is God; will He cast me off for death?' Fire burns in my heart; but I am seeking Jesus Christ for salvation. May I not join the 'Bible-class' for instruction? I cannot tell how soon death may come."

The following address, spoken by another of the converts, is amusing, but characteristic:—

"Fathers and brethren," he said, "last night as I lay on my bed, thinking on my present experiences, the cocks began to crow, and all at once a thought came into my mind that they resembled our teachers and missionaries: *they* are always crowing—warning and teaching us. Papeiha came first, and he crowed every morning and evening, making known the sins of the people and the love of God; then came Wiliamu and Pitimani and Barakoti, and they crowed continually. Ah! it was as morning then; and some of your fathers awoke out of the sleep of sin, and you have had a long day, but many of us sleep on. We just heard the sound of the voice, and lifted up our eyelids, but soon folded our hands in folly, and slept on in our sin. It was thus with me; but I am thankful Misi Gilo did not fly away to another land, and leave us to sleep on until death. He remained, and kept on crowing—crowing the Word of God. But, alas! it is noon-day now; my morning has passed; yet I rejoice that I have awakened out of my sleep, and I desire to give the remainder of my day to God and His service."

On another occasion, an elderly native, addressing the church members, said: "Brethren!" and, pausing for a moment, continued: "Ah! that is a *new name;* we did not know the true meaning of that word in our heathenism. It is the 'evangelia a Jesu' that has taught us the meaning of 'brethren.' But, am I here?—here in the midst of the Church of Jesus? What a marvel! I marvel—you marvel. *I am* here! It is the boundless love of God. You all know me." Pointing to a man about his own age, he continued: "Do you not remember so-and-so, whom we killed on yonder mountain, portions of whose body we cooked and ate?" He mentioned three others by name, whom he and others in the church had thus devoured in cannibal feasts; and then, with tears running down his cheeks, he exclaimed, "Oh, the love of God! how far beyond all measurement! These hands have killed eleven men during the reign of Satan here, whose bodies, with those of others, I shared in our war-feasts. And is it true that I am here? Why even you *young* men know me. I was a wild savage long after the Gospel was preached in our land. I was one of the seventy priests who blistered their breasts over the sacred fire of Tangaroa's temple, and I vowed the vow of death to the Word of Jesus. I was among the number who burnt down the houses of those who received the Word; and the chapel, school, and missionary's house we burnt to the ground. But the Word of God Jehovah was more mighty than I, and I *am* here. I think I have loved God some three or four years past, but have not been able to profess that love by joining the church until now. Whenever I have thought of doing so, the *sin and guilt of my cannibalism have prevented me.* This was my great barrier, until, six months ago, I heard Misi Gilo preach from that God's Word written by the prophet Isaiah, which speaks thus: 'I have blotted out thy transgressions as a cloud, and as a cloud of sin. Return unto Me, for I have redeemed thee.' That word was my salvation; my burden was by it removed, my soul was set at liberty; and because of the love and power of Jesus, I, the greatest of sinners, am here."

This gracious awakening was not at one station only, but at each on the island.

Mr. Pitman, writing of these events, said:—"Iro, the teacher at Titikaveka, informed me of the pleasing indications of a great change in some young people who had been very wicked, and who appeared under deep concern for their spiritual welfare, and desired me, as soon as I could, to converse with them. I repaired to Titikaveka, and found it to be as he had stated, and I do hope the Lord has many precious souls in that place. The first who came was a young woman whom I instantly recognised as one of the earliest scholars in our schools, but who had subsequently been 'led captive by the devil at his will,' and had obstinately refused to listen to any exhortation, either from her pious mother or other members of the church who visited her with a view to her eternal interests. She said she hardened herself against reproof, and was determined to have her fill of sin. 'My mother,' observed the young woman, 'frequently warned me of the awful consequences of my guilt, but I stopped my ears to all entreaty. At length my mother said, "Well, my daughter, if you will not hear *me*, prepare for a visit from God, whose wrath against such as you who know better is very dreadful." Soon after this I was visited with a severe affliction, and brought down to the gates of death, when my sins terrified me, and the admonitions of my parent and others were brought to my recollection. I considered myself lost!—an outcast! But, amazing love! God has been pleased to raise me up. Now am I thoroughly convinced "that the wages of sin is death"—the end of the way of wickedness is wrath eternal. Sin to me is now a thing terrific—no longer will I walk in that path; no, I have given up myself to God through Christ, by whom alone I can be saved, in whom alone I trust, though such a great sinner, and hope He will not forsake me.' I reminded her of her wicked ways, and how grieved I was when I made inquiries about her of Iro. She wept, and replied, 'Oh, teacher, if the Lord had then cast me off, my soul would have been lost.'

"The next case was that of a young man, son of pious parents, instructed in our schools, who had formerly been under religious impressions, and was baptized, but afterwards returned to folly. I had been prepared for this interview by his mother, who had previously informed me of his being, through mercy, reclaimed. Coming one day to fetch medicine for a sick relative, such was her joy, ere she could tell me the nature of her errand, that the moment she saw me she cried out, 'Oh, teacher, my son is brought to a conviction of his sins!' 'That,' I replied, 'is good news indeed. How came it about?' 'It was,' she rejoined, 'on the last Sabbath you preached at Titikaveka, from Rev. vii. 9. When I went home after class, he sat very pensively, and did not speak. "Are you ill?" I asked. "Not in body," he replied, "but in mind. Oh, that great multitude—shining robes—palms of victory! But—not to be associated with them! I have forsaken the path they trod, and have turned my back against that glorious place"'—alluding to his return to evil. Having alluded in my discourse to some present who have fathers, or mothers, or near relatives there, and asked, What if you should be refused admission to their joys?—appears to have made a deep impression upon his mind; and he then resolved, without delay, to forsake his companions in sin, and re-unite himself with the people of God."

In my letter to the Directors at this time, I wrote

thus:—"I am happy to state that, up to the present time, we have good reason to hope that, of the hundreds who then were brought to make confession of sin and profession of faith in Christ, the majority will stand firm. You have witnessed our anxiety on behalf of the rising generation. The fathers who *first* received the words of life have died. Since the early days of the mission, daily instruction has been given to the young. This instruction has been attended with evident good, in a social and moral point of view; but still our hope, our only hope, for the future spiritual welfare of Rarotonga has been a change of heart experienced by its favoured population. God has not left us without a witness for good. Since the formation of the three churches of the island, in 1833, more than *fifteen hundred* members have been admitted to communion, one half of whom have died in the faith, whose early years of youth and manhood were devoted to idol worship, and sunk in all the vile degradation of cannibalism. Between seven and eight hundred are now living among us as consistent members of Christ's body, our joy and our crown. During the past year, one hundred and twelve members have been admitted to communion at the three stations. These are fruits of past labours; and, in two or three months hence, we hope to receive a goodly number of those who, in June and July last, gave themselves to the Lord by public profession. Encouraged by these and other tokens of the Lord's favour, we desire to enter on the engagements of the new year in the spirit of gratitude, confidence, and zeal. He hath been mindful of us—He will bless us. Not that we expect to be exempt from trial, or to be able to escape difficulties. But we find that every past trial and difficulty gives an increase of experience, patience, and hope—that hope which maketh not ashamed.

"In this our time of joy we were called to mourn over the death of the most educated and excellent woman on the island. She was a daughter of our principal chief at Avarua, and her years of childhood were advantageously spent in the family of our beloved friends, Mr. and Mrs. Buzacott. Every attention was paid to her moral, intellectual, and spiritual welfare by Mrs. Buzacott; and her decided superiority in mind and manners above others was very gratifying to us all, and led to the hope that her future influence would be most salutary. She had a good knowledge of the English language, in which she could read, write, and converse with much freedom. About ten years ago she married our young and excellent chief of Arorangi. During the first six years after marriage she proved a clever and an industrious woman; but we looked in vain for a change of heart. A conscious superiority, without the influence of subduing grace, led her to manifest a haughty spirit; and, for some little time, a shadow of inconsistency clouded her domestic life, and we feared for her future safety and usefulness. God, however, blessed the efforts made for her salvation. Personal affliction, a parent's death, and a mother's affectionate counsel were made the means of subduing her proud heart, and of leading her to the Cross of Christ as a guilty sinner, and to seek from Him alone pardon, peace, and sanctification. About three years ago she joined the church at Arorangi, and ever since has been a consistent and useful member. Her former advantages were now brought out, and used for the welfare of her household, and began to tell, for good, on the female population of her settlement. Every day she was an active superintendent in the girls' school, and we all thought her course would be long and beneficial. But in an hour of unlooked-for calamity, the opening flower of promise is cut down. After a short illness of three days, she was called to join the number of the redeemed in glory. Her sickness was of such a nature as to preclude much converse. We needed not, however, her dying testimony to sustain our hopes; and she needed not *dying* consolation to *prepare* her for the change. Most of the time of her illness was occupied by prayer and singing. At the close of one of these exercises, she sighed 'Amen!' and her spirit fled, leaving us to mourn her loss."

CHAPTER XXIII.

RETURN OF REV. A. BUZACOTT, AND COMMEMORATION OF THE THIRTIETH ANNIVERSARY.

Early in 1852 we were cheered by the return of the Rev. A. Buzacott and Mrs. Buzacott after more than five years' absence. The growth of the people, the new circumstances in which increasing civilisation was fast placing them, the demand for continual instruction and guidance at this time, together with our isolation and frequent failure of E.'s health, gave us no little anxiety; but we had had much pleasure and reward in our labours, and both our trials and our joys caused us to welcome our friends with gratitude and gladness.

The people also were rejoiced to welcome their first teacher, and a letter written by Mr. Buzacott on his arrival will best describe the circumstances of his landing.

He says:—"We were greatly delighted on finding our station in such an interesting state of spiritual prosperity. During our absence brother Gill had admitted to church fellowship 115 new members, and re-admitted four backsliders. Thirty were waiting my arrival to be admitted, and two days after I had the pleasure of giving them the right hand of fellowship, after having heard many of them give the most delightful testimony to the power of the Gospel; all these were the fruit of the revival in June and July, 1851. The first Sabbath was a season I shall never forget, once more to be in the midst of an affectionate people, numbers of whom were my spiritual offspring; they seemed delighted again to listen to a voice to which they had long been accustomed, while they were addressed from the words of Paul: 'Having obtained help of God I continue unto this day.' The afternoon surpassed in interest anything I had ever witnessed before. The ordinance of the Lord's Supper was administered; thirty new members were sitting down for the first time. Captain Morgan, and several of the crew from the *John Williams*, five of whom we had the pleasure of admitting to church fellowship during our voyage, the missionaries bound for the navigators, and four young men from the Rarotongan college, with their wives, to be set apart as evangelists to the heathen islands to the west. Several addresses were given both in English and the native language, and we found it indeed a season of refreshing from the Divine presence.

"Twelve months since a great revival was experienced both here and at Arorangi, through the instrumentality of brother Gill. Upwards of three hundred were brought under deep conviction for sin, the greater part of whom continue to give pleasing evidence of true conversion to God. Including the thirty admitted on our arrival, we have already admitted eighty-five, and fifteen more stand proposed for next month. Most of them are quite young, and when we left for England in 1846 were children in the school. It is very delightful to hear them give an account of the way in which the Holy Spirit convinced them of sin and led them to the Saviour. The revival happened just after a very trying season to the people of God in this place. Some of the wild young men had been to the Tahitian Islands, where they had learnt to make what the natives call *orange rum*—the juice of the orange in a state of fermentation, which is highly intoxicating. Drunkenness, a new vice for Rarotonga, made its appearance in almost every part of the island simultaneously, and required the strong arm of the law to quell it. This stirred up the people of God to renewed exertion. Earnest prayer, followed by domiciliary visits and other means recommended by brother Gill, was the means, under the blessing of God, of producing the revival. Three very young men, who were taken away by the police in a state of intoxication, to be confined in 'durance vile,' to prevent their injuring each other in their drunken bouts, are now in the church, changed, sitting at the feet of Jesus, clothed and in their right mind. It is our custom to allow the new members, when they are admitted, to give an account of their conversion and subsequent experience. Sometimes as many as ten or twelve have risen one after another to add their testimony that the Gospel is still the power of God unto salvation.

"Various have been the means employed to produce the blessed change. Some attribute their conversion to the visits of the members of the church, many of whom were very active and earnest in the work, and they laboured not in vain. Others came to the house of God, not only careless, but to mock the preacher, and make game of what they heard; in some unexpected moment some word or sentence, like the arrow drawn at a venture, pierced them, and they went away wounded and distressed, until they found peace in the Crucified One. One young man said he came to the house of God as usual, careless and thoughtless, but he had no sooner taken his seat than he became overwhelmed with a sense of the Divine presence—that it was the house of God, and that God, who had been an eye-witness to all his sins, was now looking on him. The ground being thus already prepared for the reception of the seed, on the announcement of the text—'He drew me out of the horrible pit,' &c.—he trembled exceedingly. This sermon, preached by brother Gill, was the means of setting the poor man at liberty, and many others have mentioned it as the means of producing a deep impression on their minds. Everything at present looks well."

The natives on all the islands of the group had been anxiously expecting the complete Bible in the Rarotongan language on the return of Mr. Buzacott. But as the fourth and fifth years slowly moved on, they began to fear they would not realise their expectations.

My brother wrote from Mangaia giving an account of the people's delight on the occasion. Some said, "Surely Barokoti is dead." Others thought, "The Society could not finish the work." At length, however, their apprehensions were put to flight, the missionary ship came, and for two days many able-bodied men were engaged in bringing the boxes of Bibles over the reef, with great zeal and delight. It was with difficulty they could be restrained from breaking open the boxes in order to see the "*whole Bible;*" and when a copy was held up in their midst, they gave utterance to their feelings in a loud and long-continued shout of joy. A box full of the sacred volumes was taken into the chapel, and, after offering praise to God, copies were distributed to those who had *prepaid* for them. At a subsequent missionary meeting, an aged disciple, addressing the assembly from Job v. 17—19, said: "I have often spoken to you from texts out of other parts of the Bible than those which we had, but this is the first time I have *seen* the book of Job in our own language. It is a new book to us. When I received my Bible, I never slept until I had finished this book of Job. I read it all. Oh, what joy I have felt in the wonderful life of that good man! Let us read these new books—let us go to the missionary and inquire into their meaning; let us be at his door before he rises; let us stop him when we meet him, that he may tell us about these new words." And, lifting up his Bible before the congregation, he continued, "My brethren and sisters, this is my resolve. The dust shall never cover my Bible—the moths shall never eat it—the mildew shall never rot it! It is my light! my joy!"

At Rarotonga 5,000 copies were landed of the "whole Bible in the native language." At the several stations religious services were held to commemorate the event, and nothing could exceed the desire of the people, each one to receive a copy for himself. Those who had no money to purchase brought arrowroot, dried banana, coffee, and various other produce, as barter, by which means, in three years, they, with the natives of other islands of the group, transmitted to the Bible Society more than *five hundred pounds* as part payment for that edition.

The people at Avarua, under the superintendence of Mr. Buzacott, built a new chapel. The walls were of coral block, and it was finished in superior style. It would seat one thousand people.

Early in the morning crowds of natives came from all the stations to commemorate the thirtieth anniversary of the landing of Papeiha. A thousand persons got inside the chapel, 700 of whom were members in communion at the village churches. Most of the deacons, teachers, and missionaries from the surrounding islands had come for the occasion. The captain and crew of the missionary ship were there; Rev. C. Hardie, representative of the distant Samoan churches, was there; the Rev. Messrs. Pitman and Buzacott and myself were there; the venerable Tinomana and Pa, chiefs who had lived thirty years of heathen life before the Gospel was taken to the land, were there; the noble chieftainess, Makea, the worthy successor of her sainted parent, was there; Papeiha, the aged and the honourable teacher, who, thirty years before, had landed in the midst of the heathen population, at the peril of his life, was there; and, to complete the hallowed company, Tapaéru, the native woman who was stolen from her island home a heathen captive, and returned a Christian pioneer—the heroine who fought for the life of Papeiha when her countrymen had designed his murder—she also was there.

It was my privilege thus to unite with the people in commemorating the thirtieth anniversary of the landing of Papehia, the first Christian teacher, on the island. It was a day of holy convocation, long to be remembered and worthy to be recorded in my Rarotonga memories. I give these additional *Notes from my Journal at the time:*—

"Nearly ONE THOUSAND native members of the church had during twenty years died in faith; and *seven hundred* were then living, and that day were united in a communion of salvation and love, and partook *together* of the memorials of Christ's death, whose power and grace had translated them from the kingdom of darkness into marvellous light, and liberty, and love. It was a holy day, a sacred occasion, suggestive of numerous reflections, salutary in its various influences, and long to be remembered by the aged and the young, who formed the two generations present that day.

"After praise and prayer, the missionaries spoke of the past history, the present position, and foreign missionary relations of the people; the elements of the communion were then distributed, and afterwards a goodly number of the members gave short and appropriate addresses. The fathers spoke of themselves when in idolatry and heathenism, and in contrast now under the reign of the Lord Jesus; the young people spoke with gratitude for their privileged position, and pledged themselves, by grace, to hold fast their profession, and to do all in their power to extend the blessing of Christianity to those yet in darkness and degradation. British churches were borne in grateful remembrance, and fervent prayer was offered to God still to cause His face *to shine* on them, and to make them a still more extended blessing to the nations of the world.

"Many of the natives spoke with effect. Old Râtâ related events in his heathen history. Once, while living in the mountains with all Arorangi, on account of a determination of other parties to exterminate the people of that village, he ventured down to the sea-side to fish. While there, a party of Ngatangiians came from the bushes, threatening to kill him. He ran towards the sea, was pursued, but escaped.

"Taevao related a story of a woman who said, long ago, that Pouvaru would in future times be a place of light. He applied it to the Institution now erected; and that there the Gospel was first preached.

"One man said, 'We have our dead buried in Tanna, New Caledonia, Eromanga, Maré, Fotuna, Isle of Pines; we must go and take possession. Think of Abraham; he buried his dead in Canaan, and afterwards got the land.'

"A youth said he had given himself to God's work. He had been in the church five years. Three years ago he wanted to give himself to the work of God among the heathen, but his father would not spare him; his father would have him away from the missionary-house. He was obedient and went home; had been home now three years. He had been continually praying to God to cause his father to give him up. He did not know his father's intention, but he again gave himself to God. Here the young man became affected, but before he could sit down his father, who was present, rose up and, as well as able, said: 'My son, I surrender you. I no more keep you back.'

"Tevaevae said, 'Here' (holding up the Word of God)—'here is this treasure; I have it! Now I am reading it from Moses to Revelation. I am being instructed—Oh, to know its meaning!—and, if God will, here now I am ready to go to the lands of darkness.'

"Patoka said he had often eaten human flesh.

"Marama said he had wings, but they were heavy with his family. Reference was then made to five men from Sydney who were murdered here three or four years before the introduction of the Gospel. Four of them were eaten. 'But,' said he, 'the British came, not to kill us; they sent us the Gospel. Their dead were buried here, and now they have taken possession of us in the name of Christ.'

"Last of all, good old Papeiha spoke; tears rolled down his furrowed face, whilst he unburdened the emotions of his overflowing, grateful heart. He said, 'We are still sowing the seed of the Kingdom, we have done it for many years, and we have reaped. Now let us continue to sow.' The good old man gave a brief account of the savage state of Rarotonga when he first landed among them. 'Now,' he said, 'we say the heathen are savages, but they are no worse than we were.' And, holding up in his hand a copy of the Holy Scriptures, just completed in the Rarotongan language, he gave God the praise, by whom alone had been wrought the triumphs they that day commemorated; and, having committed the Word of God as his legacy to the rising generation, he prayed, 'Now, Lord, lettest Thou Thy servant depart in peace, for mine eyes have seen Thy salvation!—this is the glory of Thy people and Thy light to enlighten the world.' Thus terminated the THIRTIETH ANNIVERSARY of missionary labour on the ISLAND OF RAROTONGA."

CHAPTER XXIV.

PREPARATIONS FOR A VOYAGE TO ENGLAND.

I NOW have to record my leaving Rarotonga and the much-loved work there. For some time past Mrs. Gill's ill-health had made it apparent to all around us that a speedy change was necessary. Our love to the natives and our work made it difficult for us to decide on a change, and when we did so it was only contemplated to be for a time.

After due and prayerful consideration of the subject I wrote the following letter to the local committee of the mission:—

"*April 26th*, 1852.

"MY DEAR BRETHREN,—You are aware the past six or seven years have been years of anxiety to me respecting Mrs. Gill's health. At frequent intervals alarming symptoms have appeared, exciting our worst fears. Medical men from whom we have had advice in the islands, and from England, recommend relaxation from ordinary labour and a change of climate.

"This advice you have kindly seconded as you have marked our anxiety. We could not, however, consider it our duty to suspend our labours during the years of absence of our fellow-labourers, Mr. and Mrs. Buzacott. They have now returned in the enjoyment of renewed health and vigour, and may, it is hoped, under God's blessing, sustain the duties of these stations for a few years. This, in connection with the anticipated removal of two or three of our number three years hence, has led me to think that we can better be spared from your midst now than at any future time; and I think, also, that if Mrs. Gill's health can be benefited by a change, the present is the more likely time to secure the advantage than at a more advanced period in life.

"I beg leave, therefore, to submit to your candid and affectionate consideration the following proposition: That on the arrival of the missionary ship from Tahiti, in December next, Mrs. Gill and I proceed to Sydney, and thence to England, with a view of returning to you in the '*John Williams*' on her next voyage. With heart and life devoted to our common work on the islands, desiring your counsel and prayers, and, above all, the Divine direction,

"I am, my dear Brethren,
"Yours affectionately,
"WILLIAM GILL."

The following letter was drawn up and sent to me by the brethren in reply to the foregoing:—

"AVARUA, *April 28th*, 1852.

"To Rev. W. GILL.

"DEAR BROTHER,—We deeply sympathise with you in your anxiety on account of Mrs. Gill's health, the frequent failure of which has led you to the conviction that relaxation and a change of climate are necessary for her restoration. We are quite sure that nothing but a sense of duty would induce either yourself or Mrs. Gill to relinquish, though only for a season, a work to which you have consecrated your lives.

"It is also with the deepest feeling of regret that we are brought to the same conviction that the step you propose is necessary, and therefore must receive our unanimous sanction.

"Though the time proposed is perhaps the most favourable, yet, in a station where so much is to be done and so few to do it, your loss will be greatly felt. We would, however, try to acquiesce in our Master's will, who is now saying to you, 'Turn aside and rest awhile.' We do not, however, anticipate that your absence from us will, if God give you health and opportunity, be one of unbroken rest.

"We rejoice that in your way to Sydney you will have an opportunity of communicating with our brethren of the Samoan Islands, and of visiting the stations westward, and of encouraging our native brethren who are engaged in the high places of the field.

"We cannot but agree to your proposal that, on your arrival in Sydney, and having had medical advice, you proceed at once to England, there to wait the return of the '*John Williams*.'

"We sincerely commend you to the kind attention of the Directors of the London Missionary Society, and hope they will give you a hearty welcome, and while in England, from your experience and the success with which God has crowned your labours, we hope you may be the means of increasing the interest of the British churches in the cause of missions.

"We shall not forget you in our prayers that the voyage may be beneficial to your dear partner, and that in due time you may both return to your beloved work and people invigorated in body and mind.

"We most affectionately commend you both to the kind care of our covenant-keeping God and Father, and remain,

"Yours affectionately,
"CHARLES PITMAN.
"AARON BUZACOTT."

As soon as it was decided that we were to leave, we returned to our people at Arorangi. Several of the young men in the Institution were appointed to proceed with us to the westward islands, to be located as opportunity offered as teachers.

Isaia, the son of Papeiha, had been in the boarding-school under my care for seven years, and was desirous to go with us. At first both Mrs. Gill and I declined, but his desire was very strong, and his father and mother and Tinomana, his grandfather, were all willing; we were, therefore, led to consent. He accompanied us to England, and remained three years before returning home. He afterwards became the pastor of the church at Arorangi.

Towards the latter part of October a farewell meeting was held, in expectation of the early arrival of the missionary ship to take us on our voyage. I preached from the text, "The Lord watch between me and thee," &c. Several of the deacons and elders gave short addresses full of deep affection and concern, and all expressing hope that we soon might be restored to them.

On November 13th the final farewell was made. It was a trying time both to us and to the people. But we trusted in God that we were following His guidance, and we endeavoured to comfort ourselves and the dear natives in His love. We embarked at three p.m. Many boats and canoes accompanied us to the ship.

ATIU AND AITUTAKI.

Three days' sail from Rarotonga brought us to Atiu; leaving Atiu, twenty-four hours' sail brought us to Aitutaki. After spending a pleasant day or two with the people, and appointing four young men to proceed to the Institution at Rarotonga, we sailed on to Maniiki, the island where we had sent teachers two years before. Mine was the first visit of an English missionary to the island. We found our teachers well, and they had had a good entrance for their Gospel work among the poor heathen people. Schools were well attended, many, both adults and children, had learnt to read, a chapel had been built, and several natives had been baptized, and others were candidates for baptism.

It was our privilege to land one hundred Bibles and New Testaments in the Rarotongan language. This island is one of a group of many small low reef islands; it is 600 miles from Rarotonga. The education and Christian advance of the people were most pleasing to witness.

* * * * *

Manuka.

Four days after leaving Maniiki we came to the island of Manuka, the most eastern island of the Samoan Group. Our excellent native pastor, Taunga, was in health and doing well, and was evidently much respected by the people. This island was made a mission station in 1838, when the natives were in heathenism. Here we found a small schooner trading in arrowroot and oil, the captain of which had lost his life by the upsetting of his boat while going on shore only a few days before our arrival. At the earnest request of the crew, we put on board one of our ship's officers to take the little vessel to Upolu.

Leaving Manuka our vessel sailed to Tutuila. Here we took in oil and arrowroot, missionary contributions of the people, and next day took on board the missionaries Messrs. Powell and Sunderland, who were going to attend meetings at Upolu.

We reached Upolu on Sunday morning and cast anchor in Apia Bay. Here we found an Italian brig, which had brought a Roman Catholic bishop and landed the first instalment of Roman Catholic priests on the island of Samoa.

Upolu.

Recent civil disturbances among the tribes had sadly hindered the work of the missionaries. There is no king nor chief. The people live in clans of from 100 to 500 in each, and each clan has its head, and is independent of the others. This political division is a cause of religious disunion; the germs of future evil also are fostered by the presence—in this the infantile Christian state of the people—of Roman Catholic missionaries, and the residence of many irreligious traders of different nationalities.

Our second Sunday at Upolu was spent in services. In the forenoon I preached in the chapel on shore; in the afternoon I held a service with all the Rarotongan natives who were with us and those residing at Apia, about a hundred in all; in the evening I preached on the deck of our mission ship from the text: "I have taken from thine hand the cup of trembling, and thou shalt no more drink it again." I also held a Communion service with some of the crew and other sailors.

Next day, while descending the ship's side to take boat for the shore, my foot slipped, and I fell into the sea. Not being able to swim, I sank, and was drawn by the tide under the ship, and, but for the timely aid of the carpenter, I should have been drowned.

During our stay at Upolu, I visited the institution at Malua, then under the care of Dr. Turner and Mr. Hardie. More than one hundred students and scholars were receiving instruction. A fine piece of land, sixty acres, had been bought for the erection of houses for students and for lecture-rooms. The institution seemed to be prospering, and gave hope for the future of Samoa.

Two or three days were spent at a distant station, Saluapata, in company with the whole missionary staff, in committee. An important movement was set on foot while we were there—viz., the purchase of land at Apia, on which to erect a school-house for the education of half-caste children of foreigners married to native women. The cost was £200.

Leaving Upolu, we sailed to Savaii, took on board five tons of oil—contributions of the natives to the Bible Society and London Missionary Society—and had a pleasant visit to the station of Matautu.

ANEITEUM.

Ten days' sail brought us to the island of Aneiteum. This is the most eastern island of the New Hebrides. My last visit here was in 1846, when the people were all in heathenism, and we were only able to land native Christian teachers. Now, after six years' labour, we were cheered to find a very large proportion of the people under Christian instruction; many had been baptized, a small church had been formed, and Messrs. Geddie and Inglis were residing on the island. Our ship's party spent the greater part of two days on shore, and were cheered and much encouraged by the advance made and the prospects of further success. Here we gained information of the work of the teachers at the islands of Tanna and Eromanga, and, while not so advanced as at Aneiteum, there was progress and hope. The missionary work of the New Hebrides is passed over by the London Missionary Society to the care of the United Presbyterian churches of Scotland and Nova Scotia, under whose auspices the missionaries now there are labouring.

Arrival at Sydney.

On the 5th of January, 1853, we cast anchor in Sydney Harbour. We were soon boarded by Rev. Dr. Ross, Rev. D. Beazley, my old friend G. A. Lloyd, and others interested in our Gospel work. They each, and all, gave us a hearty welcome, and assured us of some weeks of work in Sydney and other places, to rehearse to the people our report of the islands. Our native chief, Setephano, and Isaia, his nephew, were much excited and interested at what they saw in this new world of English life and civilisation.

A programme of meetings was soon made, and I was obliged to begin again to speak English. For many years I had been speaking Rarotongan, and was now thinking in that language, so that I felt not quite at home in English; but I had to begin. Our first meeting was the annual assembly of the British and Foreign Bible Society. I was able to report the progress of Bible translation in Tahiti, Samoa, and the New Hebrides; and, also, the fact that I had in my charge the first edition of the Rarotongan Bible, to be revised and reprinted in England, if I should proceed thither. At this Bible-meeting £300 were collected for the Bible Society.

On the second Sunday was held the anniversary services of the London Missionary Society. In the morning I preached at Pitt Street Chapel: Isa. xli. 14, 15—1. The difficulties of our Gospel work among the heathen; 2. The fewness and feebleness of our labourers; and 3. The precious and ever-fulfilling promise of God in regard to the work.

In the evening I preached at Redfern. On the following day a public meeting was held in Pitt Street Chapel, and a very large attendance gathered. I attempted to give an account of the pleasing state of Rarotonga and Samoa, and the urgent claims of the New Hebrides, and especially the Loyalty Islands, and was much gratified by the response of the people to our appeals—£1,004 were contributed specially to encourage the Directors of the London Missionary Society to send at once two missionaries to the islands of Maré and Lifu, of the Loyalty Group.

I was much interested in visiting Mr. Oakes, one of the Society's first missionaries to Tahiti. He was living at Paramatta, and was in his eighty-fourth year—weak in body, but full of lively interest about the natives and island.

We spent a week in holding missionary meetings at Maitland and other towns some distance up the Hunter River.

We assisted at the Baptist chapel, Sydney, at which £40 were collected. At the Wesleyan chapel service I mentioned that the poor native teacher at Maniiki wanted a boat, and £30 were at once collected to purchase one for him.

Our two months' stay in Sydney and its neighbourhood was marked by a new era in missionary enterprise. There was a revival in the churches of all denominations, and the work and claims of missions, especially to the islands, were brought before the attention of the population as they had not been before.

Leaving Sydney.

The one anxiety that brought us to Sydney was Mrs. Gill's continued ill-health. The voyage from the islands to Sydney had had but little influence for good. She was very ill during the whole of our stay in Sydney, and the decided advice of all the medical men we consulted there was that we should continue the voyage to England.

At length we saw it our duty to decide on this advice, and a passage was taken on board the fine ship *Waterloo.* My old friend George Alfred Lloyd kindly fitted up our cabin, and many friends vied with each other to show us kindness, and thus to testify their interest in our missionary work. After two months' most pleasant change we set sail for England on April 5th, 1853, accompanied by Isaia.

Getting outside Sydney Heads we had a strong contrary wind, and were in great danger for some time of drifting near the shore. We cast anchor in deep water, just in time to be safe. The roar of the surf dashing on the rocks was heard all night. It was in this dangerous place Captain Green lost his ship some ten years afterwards, when he and all on board, save one, were drowned.

The morning brought us a favourable wind, and we set sail for England.

The Voyage to England.

We found our fellow-passengers mostly very agreeable people. It was arranged that on Sunday mornings the Doctor should read the Church of England prayers, and that I should preach on Sunday evenings. This plan was pursued during the whole voyage.

After a few days on board I arranged with myself the daily division of time—various hours for walking exercise on deck; at times free conversation with fellow-voyagers, both passengers and sailors; a pretty regular time for reading; an hour or two daily revising the Scriptures for reprint in England; and at times an occasional writing of sermons and addresses in prospect of work in England.

Thus three months were pleasantly spent on board. Off the Falkland Islands we had a gale, but in rounding Cape Horn we had fine weather, with fair winds. For a week we had to keep a good look-out to escape icebergs, some of which were so near the ship as sensibly to affect the atmosphere. The change and rest from past years' ordinary work quite restored my health, and Mrs. Gill was much benefited by the voyage, and through mercy we were permitted to land in London on June 16th, 1853.

CHAPTER XXV.

ENGLAND—STRANGE FEELINGS.

On landing at Blackwall, after so long an absence, all seemed very strange. I had never seen a railway-train before I left, and the East End Blackwall train waited to receive us. We were more disposed to examine it than to enter. At the ringing of the five minutes' announcement-bell we took our seats, when Isaia, hearing the bell ring again previous to departure, asked if we were going to have prayers before we started.

Arriving at Fenchurch Street Station, we took cab to the Mission House, and had a welcome from our old pastor and constant friend, Dr. Tidman, and then visited our parents at their homes. Dear Mr. Devonshire, Mrs. Gill's step-father, was at the time dangerously ill, which was the only drawback to the pleasure of our return.

For some time we were half-bewildered by the hurry, bustle, and noise of London life after our long residence abroad. Our life had been one of constant activity, but we had less noise and confusion. At first we could scarcely realise that we were so far from the islands and the natives, and had daily longing to return to them. We were soon visited by our numerous kind friends, who all seemed to vie with each other to show us attentions. Calls and letters came from all quarters, and as soon as house matters were arranged we found that plenty of work was at hand to be done.

SERVICE AT BARBICAN CHAPEL.

The second Sunday after my arrival I had the pleasure of preaching, morning and evening, at Barbican Chapel, dear by so many early associations. But, alas! how changed!—Dr.

Tidman had left, the chapel was half-empty, and the schools far from so full as in former years. Still, notwithstanding all the drawbacks, I had pleasure in taking my first public service in England there. My morning text was Gen. xxxv. 3, "Let us arise and go up to Bethel, and I will make there an altar unto God, who answered me in the day of my distress, and who was with me all the way that I went." In the evening, Ps. cxxvi. 3, "The Lord hath done great things for us, whereof we are glad."

As Mrs. Gill was not well, and I had the prospect of being from home so often, we decided for awhile to reside with Mr. and Mrs. Devonshire, who also were able to make room for Isaia.

The Rev. A. Buzacott, on his return to Rarotonga, had taken out the first complete edition of the Rarotongan Bible. This edition was fast being sold to the natives before I left the islands, and I was enabled to bring to England the sum of £230 towards payment to the Bible Society for the outlay made by them for that edition. It was requested that the Bible Society would aid me in putting a second edition through the press during my stay in England. This request was presented and acceded to. I also engaged to attend Bible Society meetings as often as my other engagements would allow.

The first seven months after our arrival in England were occupied in attending missionary meetings in various parts of the country on behalf of the London Missionary Society. During this period I took part in no less than 136 services and meetings. Isaia accompanied me on most of my tours.

In 1854, on the occasion of the annual meeting at Exeter Hall, I had the honour of narrating my missionary experiences to an interested audience, and at the subsequent evening meeting Isaia gave a speech in his own language, which I interpreted as he proceeded. The rest of the year was spent in attending meetings in the provinces advocating the cause of the Society.

In 1855, the second revision of the Rarotongan Bible was undertaken by Dr. Mellor, and I was appointed to confer with him in the work. When completed five thousand copies were printed, and I had the pleasure of presenting a copy to Lord Shaftesbury at the Bible Society's annual meeting in that year. The writing of the "Gems from the Coral Islands" occupied a great deal of my time during the year, which was an exceptionally busy one, for I still continued my deputation work for the Society without interruption.

In the summer of 1855 we received the three eldest boys of my brother George from the islands; they were sent to England to be educated, and remained under our charge until my brother's return home in 1860.

In 1856, the first complete edition of my work, "Gems from the Coral Islands," was published, and it was gratifying to receive testimonies of their appreciation of it from numerous kind friends throughout the kingdom.

At the annual meeting of the London Missionary Society in Exeter Hall in 1856, Isaia again gave an address which I interpreted. He was listened to with the deepest interest, and his speech was not the least important feature of the meeting.

About this time, owing to Mrs. Gill's weak health, we seriously entertained the project of remaining in England instead of returning to the South Sea Islands, and intimated our purpose to the Directors of the London Missionary Society, who fell in with our wishes without any opposition.

This year (1856) saw the severance of my connection with the much-loved London Missionary Society. I will not attempt to describe my feelings when, after so many years of service in the cause of missions, it was decided that we should not return to the field of labour which was so dear to our hearts, and round which hung so many memories yielding pleasure in the retrospection, and exciting thankfulness to the All-Wise, whose hand had shielded us from the manifold dangers we had passed through, and whose love had guided us during our wanderings in those remote parts of the earth.

Woolwich.

In April, 1856, I preached missionary sermons at Ebenezer Chapel, Woolwich, a church which at that time was without a minister. A few days afterwards I received overtures from the deacons of the church to become its pastor, and, after many interviews and much correspondence on the subject, I was led, under God's guidance, to accept the very cordial invitation which was given me. This decision was not arrived at till the beginning of August. We took up our abode in Mulgrave Place, Woolwich, during the autumn.

On the 6th of October I preached my first sermon at Ebenezer Chapel as the pastor of that church.

The church began rapidly to increase, and in 1857, a project, which had often been mooted, was seriously undertaken, and a suitable plot of land was secured by the generous assistance of Mr. Tame, my senior deacon, for the building of a new church to meet the demands of our growing congregation.

On November 3rd, 1858, it was our pleasure to witness the laying of the memorial stone of the new chapel by my old friend George Alfred Lloyd. The following is an account of the ceremony, which appeared in a local newspaper :—

"The ceremony of laying the corner-stone of the chapel about to be erected in Rectory Place, for the accommodation of the congregation now worshipping at Ebenezer Chapel, William Street, was performed on Wednesday afternoon by George Alfred Lloyd, Esq., of Sydney, New South Wales, in the presence of a large concourse of spectators, including several of the ministers of the town, the metropolis, and the neighbourhood.

"The following is a description of the edifice :—

"The buildings will cover an area of 120 feet long by 44 feet wide at the front, increasing to 60 feet wide at the back, and comprise a chapel to seat 850 persons, a week-evening lecture-room to hold 230 persons (this will also be the girls' school-room), a boys' school-room for 130, a separate room for the superintendent, an infant school-room for 65, a gentlemen's committee-room or library 20 feet by 13 feet, a minister's vestry, a deacons' vestry, boiler-room, and store-room, the whole so arranged as to form a most complete and compact building.

"It is designed from the decorated period of Gothic architecture, and will present an imposing appearance ; in the centre of the principal front there will be a tower and spire and three clock faces ; the main entrance will be under this tower, by a handsome doorway with three columns on each side, and deeply recessed and enriched with arch-mouldings and pinnacles. Right and left of the entrance will be picturesque porches in advance of the main wall ; from these the staircases will lead to the galleries ; the floor will be slightly raised as it recedes from the pulpit.

"The form of the chapel is a parallelogram with transepts, and will be 62 feet long in the clear between walls, and 38 feet wide, except at transepts, where it will be 47 feet wide. There will be a gallery on each side and also at the front. The roof will span the whole width between the walls, thus avoiding the necessity for other than small iron columns to support the gallery. Immediately at the back of the chapel, and extending its whole width, will be a corridor 6 feet wide, having an entrance from Rectory Grove; the corridor will communicate with the library or committee-room, the superintendent's room, and school-room, and the minister's and deacons' vestries. At the south end of the corridor will be a staircase leading to the lecture-room and ladies' committee-room. This lecture-room will be 40 feet by 27 feet, and 22 feet high, with open timbered roof.

"The materials used are Kentish rag stone, with Bath stone dressings, &c.; the walls internally will be stuccoed, and the ceiling plastered between the purlins; the pews will have doors, and the whole of the woodwork will be stained and varnished.

"The cost will be about £3,500. The architects are Messrs. Lander & Bedells, of 4, Great James Street, Bedford Row; and the builders Messrs. McLennan & Bird, of Osnaburgh Street, Regent's Park.

"The proceedings were commenced by the singing of an appropriate hymn, which was read by the Rev. J. Hall, of Chatham, after which the Rev. Charles Gilbert, of Erith, read the 132nd psalm, and the 1st chapter, 1st epistle to the Thessalonians.

"James Pearce, Esq., solicitor, of Rectory Place, one of the deacons, then read the following statement of the origin and history of Ebenezer Chapel up to the present time:—

"This cause was originated by Thomas Robert Richardson, James Dadswell, James S. Miskin, William Irwin, Joseph Slack, Christmas King, Thomas Mann, and William Farebrother, eight Sunday-school teachers, who after the most serious, solemn, and prayerful consideration, extending over a period of several months, met on the 5th of April, 1852, and unanimously passed the following resolution, viz.:—'That by the strength and grace of God, we resolve to establish another Sabbath-school, and, if practicable, another Christian interest upon Congregational principles.' The Sunday-school was opened on Lord's-day, April 25th, when no less than 136 children attended. At a committee-meeting on the 26th of April, it was resolved—'That a juvenile missionary association be formed in connection with the school;' 'That a Dorcas society be formed under the management of the ladies;' 'That a library be provided for the use of the scholars contributing ½d. per month.'

"On the 3rd of May it was resolved 'that a Christian Instruction Association be formed in connection with the committee.'

"On the 20th of July a large room, built for an auction-room, in William Street, Woolwich, was hired of Messrs. Church & Son, when Mr. Tame, the chairman of the meetings, kindly lent the necessary amount to fit up the place for Divine worship, such amount to be returned when convenient, without any interest being paid for the same. The room having been fitted up as a chapel, and the name Ebenezer Chapel given to it.

"On the 23rd of August, 1852, a meeting was held in Ebenezer Chapel, when, after devotional services, the following resolution was unanimously adopted, viz.:—'That the undersigned Christian friends solemnly record their heartfelt gratitude and praise to Almighty God for the signal guidance and blessings vouchsafed to them, and feeling that hitherto and thus far the Lord hath helped them, and in humble, but firm, dependence upon Divine grace and assistance for the future, now resolve to unite together in church fellowship, and to form a Christian church upon Independent or Congregational principles in accordance with the New Testament Scriptures to worship God at Ebenezer Chapel, William Street, Woolwich, and they do hereby unite together and form themselves into a Christian church accordingly.'—Signed by forty-two members.

"The friends present having signed the resolution, Mr. Tame intimated that, the church being now formed, the meeting should resolve itself into a church-meeting, and the meeting resolved itself into a church-meeting accordingly, when, amongst other things, it was resolved unanimously—'That six deacons should be chosen at the next church-meeting.' At a church-meeting, held in Ebenezer Chapel on the 3rd of September, Messrs. Tame, Richardson, Smart, Boylen, Saw, and Dadswell were chosen to the office of deacons. The chairman then announced that it had been arranged (D.V.) to open the chapel on Tuesday, the 7th of September inst., and that the ministers who had kindly engaged to preach on that occasion were the Rev. P. Thompson, A.M., of Chatham, in the morning, and the Rev. S. Martin, of Westminster, in the evening. On the 7th of September, the opening services were accordingly held in the morning at Ebenezer Chapel, at which the Revs. T. Timpson, Independent minister, of Lewisham; J. Cox, of Woolwich; P. Thompson, A.M., Independent minister, of Chatham; W. Lucey, Independent minister, of Greenwich; W. M. Thompson, Presbyterian minister, of Woolwich; W. Woodlands, Independent minister, of Woolwich; R. Thompson and Close, Wesleyans, of Woolwich, took part. In the evening the services were held in the Wesleyan chapel, William Street, kindly lent for the occasion, when the Rev. R. Thompson, Wesleyan minister of the chapel; Samuel Martin, Independent minister, and the Rev. Mr. Close took part in the services. On Sunday, the 12th September, 1852, the first ordinary public worship was held in the chapel, when the Rev. A. Stuart, of Palmer House, Holloway, preached morning and evening, and the attendance on both occasions was very encouraging. The church continued to grow, and, having invited the Rev. S. Hebditch, of Ashburton, to the pastorate, on Sunday, the 24th of April, he commenced his stated ministry amongst us; he continued with us, labouring zealously and successfully, till the 21st October, 1855, when, having received a call to Arley Chapel, Bristol, he resigned his pastorate here. God, in His great goodness and mercy, still preserved the church, though it was exercised with many trials till the 4th of August, 1856, when the Rev. W. Gill, formerly missionary, Rarotonga, South Sea Islands, accepted the invitation of the church to become its pastor, and entered upon his stated ministry on Sunday, the 6th of October, 1856. By the blessing of God on his ministry, and the other means of grace used, the church has had added to it from time to time such as shall be saved, twenty-eight members being added to the church during the first year, and thirty-five during the second year of his ministry. The chapel being thus filled to overflowing, great efforts were made to obtain a suitable site to build a larger and more commodious place of worship, God in His good providence ultimately directed us to this spot, when our friend and deacon, Mr. Thomas Tame, now lamented by us as dead, and yet rejoiced over, for 'behold he liveth for evermore,' kindly and liberally gave £1,000 stock, subject to the Government interest only to be paid to him and Mrs. Tame during their joint and separate lives, to enable us to buy the land at a cost of not less than £1,100. At a church meeting held on the 3rd February, 1858, James Pearce, Josiah Smith, and Thomas Robert Richardson were duly appointed trustees, and the conveyances have been made to them, and they have executed the usual deed of trust. On the 13th September, 1858, they executed the contract for the buildings with Messrs. McLennan & Bird, of Regent's Park, London. On the 1st September, 1858, James Pearce, Robert Devonshire, and William Irwin were chosen deacons, and on the 3rd November, 1858, this stone was laid by G. A. Lloyd, Esq., of Sydney, and these particulars, with a copy of the trust deed, were deposited within a bottle in the stone. Architects—Messrs. Lander & Bedells, 4, Great James Street, Bedford Row.

"STATEMENT OF DOCTRINE.

"1. The Divine Inspiration of the Holy Scriptures, and their sole authority and entire sufficiency as the rule of faith and practice.

"2. The unity of God with the proper Deity of the Father, the Son, and the Holy Ghost.

"3. The universal and total depravity of man in the sight of God, and his exposure to eternal death as the wages of sin.

"4. The incarnation of the Son of God, the sufficiency of His Atonement for sin, and free justification by faith alone in Him.

"5. The absolute necessity of the Holy Spirit's grace and power for man's regeneration and sanctification.

"6. The predestination, according to God's gracious purpose, of a multitude that no man can number unto eternal salvation, which in no way interferes with the use of means, or with man's responsibility.

"7. The immutable authority of the law of God as the rule of human conduct.

"8. The immortality of the soul, the resurrection of the dead, and the final judgment, when the wicked 'shall go away into everlasting punishment, but the righteous into life eternal.'

"George Alfred Lloyd, Esq., then received the beautiful silver trowel from the hands of Mr. Devonshire, by whom it had been presented to the congregation, and by them to Mr. Lloyd; the mallet, square, &c., from Mr. Bird, the builder, and the sealed bottle containing the documents from the Rev. William Gill, the minister of the congregation, the presentation being in each case accompanied by a short and appropriate address. The trowel, which is of the value of eight guineas, bears this inscription:—'Presented to GEORGE ALFRED LLOYD, Esq., on the occasion of his laying the Inscription Stone of Rectory Place Chapel, Woolwich, November 3rd, 1858.—Rev. W. GILL, Pastor, late of Rarotonga, South Sea Islands.'

"G. Alfred Lloyd, Esq., then rose and said—The position I occupy this morning demands some explanation why a comparative stranger should accept an office which would have been so much more appropriately performed by one of the members of this church and congregation. I resisted the invitation of this church as long as I could do so with propriety, but the more I declined, the more determined they seemed to have me and nobody else; and when I tell you the reasons by which they were influenced, you may feel that possibly they had a right to demand my services. The pastor of this church is my oldest friend. It was in his society that I first determined to dedicate myself to the love and service of Christ. It was with him that I first became a Sabbath-school teacher—that I walked to the house of God in company, and listened to the blessed truths of the Gospel from the lips of one whom I rejoice to see amongst us to-day. With him I have frequently knelt in early life to implore the strength which was necessary to resist temptation, the grace that we needed to keep us faithful, and the blessing of God upon our labours as Sabbath-school teachers. When I left this country, there were no prayers more earnest than his for my preservation over the mighty deep. After he had devoted himself to the missionary work, it was my privilege to welcome him in a far distant land, on the way to the scene of his labours; and after he had successfully laboured for years, and was compelled by the failure of his wife's health to return to his native land, he again paid me a visit, and was an inmate of my house for several weeks. On my return to these shores, he took the earliest opportunity of welcoming me by a sermon, which I shall never forget, from the words—'Arise, and let us go up to Bethel, and let us build an altar unto God, who answered me in the day of my distress, and was with me all the way that I went.' If I had the power, I would return the compliment, and preach him a sermon from the same text, than which nothing could be more appropriate on the present occasion. And now I find him the pastor of a church and congregation in this town, where his labours have been so abundantly blessed that it has become necessary to find larger space for the numbers that throng to his ministry. Under these circumstances, you will, I hope, admit that I may be pardoned for taking so prominent a position as I now occupy. I proceed, then, to lay this foundation stone, and in doing so I congratulate you that God has put it into your hearts to erect a house to His glory. I shall not dare to touch upon subjects which will be so much better brought before you by the gentleman who is to follow me, but I may say that I lay this stone with confidence, because I believe that within these walls nothing will be preached but the pure, simple doctrines of the Gospel as it is in Christ Jesus our Lord. Because here I believe that the pastor will have but one object in view—and that the grandest object for which a human being can live, namely, to be made instrumental in the conversion of souls—and because I believe that, as God has blessed him in days that are passed, so He will continue to bless him in days that are to come. And while we lay this corner-stone in faith and prayer, may the blessing of God so rest upon those who shall be engaged in raising the funds, and His watchful care so preserve those engaged in raising the building, that when the top stone is brought forth we may all have reason to unite in shoutings of grace, 'Grace unto it!' And when in days to come you assemble within these walls to lift up your hearts in praise and prayer, may the influences of the Holy Spirit constantly attend you; may the blessing of God the Father, God the Son, and God the Holy Ghost ever abide with you; and, as one after another of those engaged in this noble work shall be called to their great account, may it be with a 'Well done, good and faithful servant, thou hast been faithful in a few things; I will make thee ruler over many things; enter thou into the joy of thy Lord!' I receive this handsome present with many thanks, and shall hope to hand it down to my children as a token of your kindness, and a memorial of the interesting events of the day.

"Mr. Lloyd then deposited the bottle in a chamber beneath the stone, and the stone was then lowered into its proper place, Mr. Lloyd using his trowel, mallet, and square in an artistic manner. He then declared the stone laid in the name of the Father, Son, and Holy Ghost. The stone bears an inscription recording the event.

"The Rev. Dr. Spence said they had been engaged in a work the results of which would be beneficial to mankind in ages to come. The question might arise from a stranger to their object who might be present, 'What mean ye by these services?' and to this the answer would undoubtedly be that they had been laying the corner-stone of a new sanctuary. They might then be asked, 'Are there not already many churches for the worship of God in the land, and why have you resolved to have your own church, pastor, and office-bearers?' He would answer that it was for the sake of Evangelical truth, for the sake of voluntary religion, and for Congregational church fellowship. The doctrines of their faith were man's ruin, redemption, and regeneration, these being the essential principles of the Gospel of the Lord Jesus Christ. The erection of any number of churches could not be an injury, for the multiplication of good could do no harm, and, unless they had a sufficient number of such places of worship, what guarantee had they that the Gospel would be faithfully preached in after-years in those already in existence? The erection of this church would be an example of their principle of voluntary religion, for the funds required would be raised by no tax on the inhabitants, but its unostentatious spire would seem to say to the passer-by, 'God loveth a cheerful giver;' and his people are doing this work with the means God has blessed them with, without any Act of Parliament to make a compulsory levy. God received the gifts of the poorest beggar and the richest nobility only as they were given voluntarily. The movement was for the sake of church fellowship, congenial souls being drawn together on equal terms, operating for their general good, and the advancement of Christ's Kingdom, appointing their own pastor and office-bearers, thus forming themselves into what they believe to be a Christian church. But, though differing in minor matters with Christians of other denominations, they loved all who loved the Lord Jesus Christ, and rejoiced at the multiplying of all places where His name was proclaimed. He wished this place every prosperity, though such a desire might be deemed a superfluity so long as they had their present estimable pastor among them, and fervently hoped that the sanctuary to be raised on the spot where they then stood might ere long be thronged with a crowd of worshippers, and might be the birthplace of many souls to the Lord God Almighty.

"The Rev. W. Lister, of Lewisham, then offered prayer, and a number of the Sabbath-school children who were present having sung a hymn, the proceedings were concluded by prayer by the Rev. C. Dukes, of Dalston.

"The weather was beautifully fine, and a spacious marquee erected as a protection in the event of rain was only serviceable to screen the ministers officiating and a portion of the spectators from the rays of the sun, which shone out brightly and warmly during the whole proceedings.

"At five o'clock, a tea-meeting was held at the Town Hall, William Street, when about three hundred persons sat down to a comfortable repast, and about seven o'clock, the tables being removed, a public meeting was held. G. A. Lloyd, Esq., was appointed chairman, and there were also on and around the platform the Rev. W. Gill, minister of Ebenezer Chapel; Rev. H. Crassweller, Revs. Messrs. Woodland, Dukes, Lister, Dr. Tidman, Smith, Gilbert, and Lucey; Messrs. Pearce, solicitor; R. Devonshire, J. Gill, Jackson, Boylen, Elkin, G. Cann, and several other ministers and gentlemen.

"Prayer being offered by the Rev. W. Woodland,

"The Chairman said an arrangement had been made among the gentlemen who would have to address them that evening that no speech should occupy more than ten minutes, and he would set an example of brevity by confining his remarks to five minutes. He was not accustomed to reading written speeches, and that afternoon while conducting the ceremony in which they had been engaged he had nearly failed in the attempt. He would here remark that it would be, in his opinion, exceedingly advantageous if all ministers would abolish the practice of reading written sermons. They had that day been engaged in a most important work the beneficial results emanating from which none of them could properly estimate. Amongst the thoughts which had been suggested to his mind by those services he had been led to reflect that he was in a town in which was situated the Arsenal of this nation, in which were constructed the munitions of war for the destruction of human life; while they, on the contrary, had been engaged in commencing a structure the object of which was the spread of peace and life. In the Arsenal were also made the rockets and lines which were used for the preservation of life from shipwreck, he having this week made application there for such an apparatus for the country to which he belonged, New South Wales. In a like manner, in the building of which they had that day laid the corner-stone, their pastor would throw out the lines of truth for the salvation of souls. They were close by a mighty river, the centre of the world's commerce, on which were employed many sailors, and, as he reflected that those sailors gazed towards the lighthouse which guided them home, he was led to contemplate that in the building which was now being erected would be held forth that light which would save them from the rocks and quicksands which beset this life, and guide them at last into the haven of happiness and peace. Whenever he saw a soldier his heart glanced with warmth towards him, for he felt that he was under an obligation to him for the protection and peace which his family enjoyed. He was happy to see many of the military present on that occasion, and trusted that they would be represented by a goodly number in the congregation of the new sanctuary. He concluded by wishing their enterprise every success.

"Mr. Richardson said he had been deputed to lay before the meeting an outline of the history of this movement, and he would proceed to do so in as concise a manner as the brief period in which he was allowed to occupy their attention would admit of. Between seven and eight years ago, a Christian community in the town became unsettled, and the harmony and happiness which had for years been enjoyed by the congregation was disturbed. A crisis at length arrived, and eight young men (Sabbath-school teachers), feeble in numbers and position, but strong in purpose, considered their duty to God and the Church demanded that they should withdraw from the fellowship. On the 5th of April, 1852, after an hour's devotion, these young men rose from their knees impressed with the conviction that it was their duty to form themselves into another Christian community. They established a Sunday-school at the lecture-hall, the use of which the proprietors honourably granted at a mere nominal charge. On Sunday, the 25th of April, the school was commenced, when it was attended by 136 children, the numbers gradually increasing until they now maintained a school of about three hundred. The originators of the movement were assisted by many others, amongst whom was their late kind, pious, and excellent friend, Mr. Tame, by whose advice they solicited and obtained the sympathy of many of the ministers in the neighbourhood. On the 20th of July they resolved, at a meeting called for the purpose at Queen Street Chapel school-rooms, to form another interest on Congregational principles. They obtained a room in William Street, used as Messrs. Church's auction-rooms, for which they agreed to pay a rent of £50 per annum; and £147, which Mr. Tame generously advanced without interest, was spent in fitting it up. On the 2nd of September their first service in the new building was held, and from that time until April, 1853, their pulpit was filled by many of the most accomplished ministers of the metropolis and neighbourhood. At that time the Rev. S. Hebditch was appointed pastor of the congregation, and it was resolved to look out for some site for the erection of a building more commensurate with the wants of the increasing congregation. In 1855, however, Mr. Hebditch was removed to Bristol, and they were without a pastor for nearly twelve months. But their pulpit was never empty, and not one member of the congregation left the flock. On the first Sunday in April, the Rev. William Gill, whom none of them had previously seen, but of whose reputation all had heard, came down at their desire to preach on the occasion of the anniversary of the Missionary Society. The result was love at first sight, although at the time they had no expectation that he would remain in England. As soon as it was heard, however, that there was a probability of his doing so, a unanimous invitation was given to him, and on the 25th of July he accepted it, officiating as their pastor for the first time on the first Sunday in October. He was sure he spoke the feelings of the whole congregation when he said that their love was even warmer and stronger towards him that day than when they first met him.

"May he and his partner long live to be instruments of good amongst them, and as God had hitherto blessed him in his undertakings, so may he continue to be prosperous in all his undertakings, and be the means of turning many souls into the way of salvation. Mr. Richardson then alluded to the fact that one of the eight Sunday-school teachers by whom the nucleus of the congregation was formed was at present amongst them in the person of the Rev. James Dadswell, who had lately been ordained to a ministry in Berkshire. He also stated that, in the six years in which they had been established, the aggregate of the receipts for the support of the church itself, the schools, the dorcas and missionary societies, but exclusive of the sum raised for the new sanctuary, amounted to £2,046 19s., and 174 persons had been added to their numbers. These facts showed that God was in their midst, and to Him be all the praise.

"Mr. Pearce then proceeded to lay before the meeting the financial position of the undertaking, stating that the ground where the site of the building had been fixed had cost £1,100, and the contract for the erection had been taken at £3,000; but, as this did not include many expenses connected with it, the whole cost might be estimated at not less than £5,000. Of this, the congregation intended to find £2,000, of which they had already collected £1,360, and he thought they could make up the remainder without difficulty. From the Christian public they had received subscriptions amounting to £324, so that they looked to them for only £2,676 more. Messrs. Wilson and Finch, of Tunbridge Wells, have kindly lent £1,500 on mortgage, and the London Chapel Building Society have promised £200 and the "Kent Fund" £100. Messrs. Wilson and Finch have promised £50 each if eight others will do likewise; three of these have been obtained, and it was earnestly hoped that others would come forward in aid of this object. Thus about £1,000 had to be raised before the completion of the work, so as to open the chapel with the burden of the mortgage only.

"The Rev. G. Smith said he had great pleasure in taking a part in these services, if it were only for the opportunity it gave him of wishing prosperity to their pastor and their cause. Any one who had heard the interesting narrative of its progress which had just been laid before them could not doubt for an instant that they had been led on by Divine grace. He rejoiced at the preaching of the Gospel by Christians of other denominations, to whom this building was not intended as an opposition, but as Congregationalists they were convinced that their principles were right. The manner in which they had set about the erection of this building was the most legitimate they could adopt. Its cost would not be defrayed by a compulsory church rate, they would receive no grant of land from Government, nor would they obtain any contribution from the public exchequer, but, like the Israelites of old built their tabernacle, each brought his offering for the common cause. He thought all the inhabitants of this locality of whatever denomination who were favourable to the prosperity of their country and the extension of truth should rejoice at this movement, for were not patriotism and piety intimately connected? Protestant Dissenters were warmly attached to their country, and all loved their Queen. They prized those liberties of which their fathers laid the foundation in troublous times when they were driven by persecution and bigotry on a thorny path into heaven. They had received an heirloom, and were bound by many obligations to transmit the same to posterity. The church they were about to build was for the simple worship of God. They acknowledged no negative theology, nor attached themselves to any name; but they were nevertheless not ashamed of the name of that great, though much calumniated man, John Calvin. He trusted that through the instrumentality of this church many sinners would be brought to God, consolation would be given to the afflicted, and protection to the orphan.

"Alluding to the ornamental nature of the building, the speaker said their parents had been compelled by circumstances to build their places of worship of a mean and common character, but they had no need now to be afraid of the light of day. All things were progressing rapidly, and was this a time when the house of God should be inferior in appearance to the houses in which they dwelt? Therefore he thought they should make their churches attractive, and concluded by expressing a hope that the hand of God would rest upon their undertaking.

"The Chairman announced that Sir Culling Eardley, the Revs. Dr. Campbell, S. Martin, W. M. Thompson, C. Hawson, and several other gentlemen, were prevented from being present by illness and other unavoidable circumstances.

"The Rev. Mr. Gilbert, secretary to the Chapel Building Society, then addressed the meeting, appealing to all persons, the warm friends of religion generally, and the residents in the town especially, to contribute towards the work in hand. This was a portion of the metropolis the rapid growth of whose population rendered an imperative necessity an increase in the number of their houses of God. The population of the metropolis was equal to that of the entire kingdom of Scotland, and was daily increasing, and it had been estimated that, if all the churches in its limit, of every denomination, were crowded to excess, there would still be more than a million persons unprovided for. He rejoiced then that another church was about to be added to the number. He expressed his concurrence in the remarks of the previous speaker respecting the beautifying of their places of worship, and, alluding to the donation of £1,000 given by Mr. Tame, exhorted others to a combined effort for the accomplishment of the object they had in view. He perceived that they were a people of faith from the fact of the document placed beneath the stone that afternoon, stating that this place of worship would be opened for Divine service on the 1st of June, 1858, and he hoped that the people of Woolwich would rise and determine to accomplish this undertaking as patriots and as Christians; and trusted that the day of opening would be also the day of complete emancipation from all pecuniary claims.

"Mr. George Reece, deacon of a chapel in Sydney, New South Wales, said this day's proceedings were the most gratifying to him of any he had experienced during his sojourn in this country, and put him in mind of an anecdote which he had once heard of two ministers, one a Calvinist and the other a Baptist. The Calvinist was riding furiously along, when the Baptist said to him, 'A merciful man hath mercy towards his beast,' to which the other rejoined, 'Whatever thy hand findeth to do, do it with all thy heart.' This seemed to be their motto, and he hoped that ere long they would be free from all incumbrance. The chairman would be able to confirm his statement that, when a cost of £2,000 was incurred in providing additional seats for a chapel in New South Wales, the sum of £1,600 was raised in one day. He hoped and believed that this work would be accomplished, if not so easily, as effectively, and that by the 1st of June they would be clear of debt.

"The Chairman then introduced the Rev. Dr. Tidman to the meeting as one whom both the respected pastor of the congregation and himself were under the deepest obligations to in earlier years.

"Dr. Tidman said it gave him great pleasure to stand forward as the old friend of the Rev. W. Gill and Mr. Lloyd. The recollection of his earlier associations with Mr. Gill afforded him exceeding gratification, and he had watched his progress through life with unbounded pleasure. Should he be spared, he would still remain a faithful minister of Christ, and his prosperity would be multiplied year by year. He was quite alive to the necessity and advantages of having a good edifice in which to worship God, but he thought it was just possible that their attention might be absorbed by the external appearance too much to admit of proper care being taken of that which was of far more importance,—the spiritual structure within. He hoped that all who had the power would largely support their object, rejoicing at the opportunity afforded them of contributing to the means of extending the glory of God and His salvation to perishing souls around. He valued the congregational system of worship, because he considered it was calculated to work out the principles of the New Testament in the freest manner, and he was happy to see that their principles were not confined to themselves, but were rapidly being adopted by other denominations, and by none more than the National Ecclesiastical Church. Mr. Smith had told them that they had done this work without asking for a State endowment, but, although this was creditable to them, it was not so much from the fact that they could not have obtained such endowment if they had applied for it. But, nevertheless, he believed that they were better without such assistance, which might only do them harm, as a man who was not in the habit of using his limbs would be apt to get stiff as he advanced in years. He did not intend to join in the crusade against the doctrine of negative theology or any other objectionable creed, believing that the best way of getting rid of such evils was not to aggravate them. He should rejoice if every place of worship in the country were filled, whether they belonged to the established or any other denomination, provided God's truth were preached in each, for he was sure the result would be the advancement of the glory of God. On the 1st of June, he hoped he should see Mr. Gill look as happy as he did on this occasion, and that he would have even more friends around him, feeling confident that, however large their numbers, he deserved them all.

"The Chairman said, as Dr. Tidman had referred to State grants, he would just mention that in New South Wales they had refused an offered grant of land and the payment of their minister, but had themselves set to work, and in two days raised the sum of £20,000.

"The Rev. W. Gill said, as the chairman would now be compelled to leave them, he would announce that he had munificently given them a donation of £50, for which, and for his kindness in conducting the ceremony of the afternoon and that evening's proceedings, he would in the name of the meeting tender their hearty thanks.

"The Chairman acknowledged the compliment, expressed his regret at being obliged to leave the meeting, and said a friend of his, also from Australia, had that morning given him £5 towards the object they had in hand.

"A collection was then made in the hall, and

"Mr. James Pearce, being voted to the chair, announced the receipt of a donation of £10 from Mr. Baker, and a like sum from Mr. George Cann, the owner of the house adjoining the new building, and who, although connected with a different denomination, had kindly shown them every courtesy in their work.

"Mr. Devonshire said they had hitherto experienced much encouragement, and, if they continued in the same spirit, the enterprise must prosper. He in common with many others had found it a difficult matter to swallow a steeple, but, when men of such superior wisdom were strong advocates that such an ornament should decorate their new building, he had felt compelled to determine on doing all he could to promote it. He proceeded in a humorous manner to describe the progress of his labours on the previous day, stating that from several Churchmen he had received liberal donations, and more than one £5 for the steeple in addition. He had also received half-a-sovereign wrapped in a piece of paper, on which was written, 'For the benefit of the good work of the Society of "Independent" Christians.—Enonemus.' In the day's work he obtained £15 19s. Unfortunately, he came after the great guns of the evening, which made his powers of oratory the more insignificant, but he could assure them from his heart that he loved them as well as the best.

"The Rev. W. Dadswell said it had been his privilege to be associated with this movement in its infancy, and he rejoiced at the answer which had been given to their prayers offered by a lowly few in a lowly room, and with a lowly spirit. The smile of God had, however, rested upon them, and like the grains of mustard seed they had grown and flourished. He prayed that the blessing of Christ would still rest upon them, and, should a cloud of darkness ever fall upon them, that they would remember in whose hands they were, and put their confidence in Him. He alluded to an incident in his own experience, when in the hour of disappointment and trouble God raised him up a friend whom he had never seen before, and on whom he had no claim, and exhorted all to believe that they could accomplish all things by faith.

"The Chairman said it might be gratifying to know that the amount of subscription during the day, including the sum collected at the laying of the stone and in the hall, realised £117 5s.

"This sum was afterwards considerably increased.

"The Rev. W. Gill said he perceived from the countenances of those before him that they had been refreshed by the proceedings of the day, a fact which was the more gratifying to him as the meeting was composed of Christians of all denominations, for whatever he did in precept or in action was on the broad basis of 'Love to all who love the Lord Jesus Christ,' in which principle he hoped they should all grow as they grew in strength and numbers. He could not expect the meeting to enter into his feelings at that moment. Twenty years since he left his dear friend Dr. Tidman, and his native land, to go twenty thousand miles away, and labour amongst a nation whose inhabitants were a few years before amongst the wild and uncivilised on the face of the earth. His acquaintance with Mr. Lloyd had commenced before that, when four young men (like the eight of whom they had that night heard) were in the habit of meeting together for prayer. One of these became a missionary, and died at his post in Jamaica; one was now deacon of City Road Chapel, London; the third was Mr. Lloyd, and he was himself the fourth. He hoped these instances would be an encouragement to young men to give themselves to God, who would open the way before them, giving them peace of mind which passeth understanding, and make of them chords vibrating to the glory of God in heaven. He was one of four brothers, three of whom were in the ministry. He concluded by moving a vote of thanks to Mr. G. H. Graham for kindly granting them the use of the forms and tables, and also the flowers with which the hall was decorated.

"This was carried unanimously; and, after a vote of thanks to the chairman, the happy and successful meeting was closed by prayer and the Benediction.

"Exclusive of a donation of £20 from W. Greig, Esq., London, the collection of the day amounted to £130."

"LETTER FROM THE WORKMEN.

"To the Editor of *The Kentish Independent.*

"Sir,—Will you be so kind as to insert in your journal the following letter from the workmen engaged in building the New Congregational Chapel, Rectory Place, to the Building Committee of the said chapel, and oblige the undersigned.

"'New Congregational Chapel, Rectory Place,
"'Woolwich, Nov. 3rd, 1858.

"'We, the undersigned, artisans employed in building the above chapel, under Messrs. McLennan & Bird, builders, beg most respectfully to express our grateful thanks to the congregation and committee for the kind manner in which they have behaved to us on this day, at the time of laying the foundation stone of the edifice, by presenting each of us with a New Testament and five shillings, which we beg to assure them shall be ever duly appreciated by ourselves and children; and we heartily wish the chapel may be a blessing to us and rising generations.

"'William Richardson.	Thomas Sughrue.
Richard Colegate.	James Gaggon.
John Spearman.	John Roach.
David Bloomfield.	Daniel Carrick.
John Collins.	William Hayes.
George Pane.	George Allen.
Edward Biscombe.	James Morris.
Richard Robins.	James Callihan.
W. Cross.	George Smith.
W. Bugg.	W. Muckle.
L. Taylor.	Charles Bonney.
E. Taylor.	Robert Hollands.
W. Bugg, jun.	H. W. Ralph.
Michael Butler.	J. Wood, &c., &c.'"

On the 28th of June, 1859, the chapel was opened; and the following is an account of the proceedings from a local source:—

"The new Congregational chapel in Rectory Place, built for the congregation hitherto worshipping under the pastorate of the Rev. William Gill, in Ebenezer Chapel, William Street, was opened on Tuesday last by special services.

"Considering that the nucleus of this church was formed but eight years since, and consisted then of but eight Sunday-school teachers, its rapid growth and eminent success must be a source of great thankfulness and of much gratification to the people. The early successes of the congregation, in a large degree, were the result of the Christian liberality of the late Mr. Thomas Tame, whose munificent generosity had contributed so largely to the funds for establishing the original church in William Street, and also for erecting the present building.

"On Tuesday the proceedings were opened by a prayer-meeting at seven o'clock in the morning, followed by Divine service at twelve. The services were commenced with prayer by the Rev. C. Dukes, M.A., followed by a hymn, in the singing of which the congregation were aided by the organ and a well-trained choir. This was succeeded by the reading of appropriate passages of Scripture by the Rev. Thomas Aveling, and singing and prayer. After a third hymn,

"The sermon was preached by the Rev. Samuel Martin, of Westminster, from the 9th verse of the 19th chapter of the Gospel of St. Luke—'This day is salvation come to this house.' From these words the rev. gentleman preached a most eloquent and effective discourse, comprising a narrative of, and commentary on, the whole history of man, his falling into sin, and his redemption.

"A liberal collection was made, and, a hymn being sung, prayer was offered by the Rev. J. Mannering, who afterwards closed the morning services with the Benediction.

"At half-past two an excellent dinner was served in the lecture-room (provided by the ladies of the congregation, and served up under the efficient management of Mr. Gregory Browne), to which about one hundred and fifty ladies and gentlemen sat down, the attendants consisting of the servants from the families of the several members of the church. Amongst numerous friends, we observed the Revs. S. Martin, J. Stoughton, C. Dukes, A. Morris, T. Aveling, J. Robinson, J. Adey, A. Buzacott, W. Lucy, T. Waterman, J. Mannering, S. Hebditch, H. Crassweller, C. Box, C. Hawson, W. Woodlands, J. Laxton, and others; also Messrs. J. Finch, E. Smith, P. Belamy, T. Saddington, R. Mullens, White, Whiteman, and numerous other townsmen of the several denominations.

"The chair was taken by W. Greig, Esq., and the Rev. Wm. Gill suggested that, it being the anniversary of her Majesty's coronation, they should drink the health of the Queen.

"The Chairman said he was sure no queen ever sat on the throne of England, either as the monarch or queen consort, who had shown such sympathies with her subjects, and had given such cordial assistance to all objects which tended to their advancement, as Queen Victoria. She had shown an example of virtue and liberality of sentiment which he believed was followed in a large degree by others of her sex. She was an ornament to her country, she had an intelligent mind, and he believed she had the fear of God in her heart. During the twenty years she had exercised the regal authority of the throne, she had assiduously performed her duty, meeting the toils of her office more like a Trojan of old than a woman of the present day—and this was saying a great deal, for there never was a time when women were held so much in esteem as now. Her name would be handed down to posterity as 'The Queen of England,' and he knew that there was not a good heart in her realms which would not respond heartily to the prayer, 'God save the Queen,' and join in the hope that she might be blessed with peace and happiness on earth, and, at the end, eternal joy in the realms of bliss above.

"The toast was honoured, and the National Anthem sung.

"The Chairman said they had met that day in a good cause, to give 'Glory to God in the highest, and on earth peace toward all men.' They lived in glad times, which formed a marked contrast to the days when he was much younger, when few, even of the supporters of the Church of God, were followers of the Gospel. There were happily some few good exceptions, which shone the brighter for their rarity, but in the present day they had manifold instances of not only love to God, but benevolence to man. There was a time when riches were never devoted to their proper use; but now the affluent gave of their stores to feed the poor, founded dispensaries and asylums, and relieved every species of want. Happy was the man who thus disposed of the riches with which he had been blessed, for at the last he would be received by the Son of God, who would say, 'Inasmuch as ye have done this for the least of these My brethren, ye have done it unto Me; enter into the joy of thy Lord.' He considered that this congregation was much blessed by having so excellent a pastor. Years ago he had read of Rarotonga, where the savage inhabitants attacked every stranger, and not only killed but devoured him. It was to this place that Mr. Gill and his wife went to do the mission of their Saviour. They found the people and the country in a state of degradation, wretchedness, and misery scarcely conceivable. For twenty years they laboured there, and they left it a place far better than they had found it, for the blessing of God had been upon their efforts, and His cause had triumphed. Now they had Mr. Gill in Woolwich, where he had been greatly influential in raising that most elegant and commodious chapel, in which he would preach faithfully the way, through the Lord Jesus Christ, to heaven. Mr. Gill had on all occasions endeavoured to aid him in any object in which his assistance was asked, having attended missionary meetings at Mile End New Town whenever requested. He was one who deserved well of his congregation, and without doubt the Saviour would in the end receive him with 'Well done, good and faithful servant.' He (the chairman) did not set much value upon works as a means of attaining heaven, but he knew that faith without works was useless, and he therefore exhorted them to look to the poor, of whose fearful condition so many of them knew nothing. He would leave £5 for the poor of this district, and he hoped that others would not be unmindful of their claims upon them, but, while attending to the spiritual welfare of the humbler classes, they would also minister to their worldly requirements. He trusted that he should meet them year by year, and learn of the good they had in the meantime accomplished.

"The Rev. W. Gill said he hoped they had all met there that day resolved to merge themselves in the great work which they had begun. It was twenty-one years since he went abroad to the island of Rarotonga in the South Seas. The chairman had made a mistake with respect to the beauties of that island, its natural beauties being great, and the beauties of the Church there being such as would warm his heart to see here. After sixteen years' labour there he returned to England, and he then had the offer of the pastorate of Ebenezer Chapel. He hesitated long, and a serious conflict arose in his own mind as to what he should do, and he anxiously prayed to learn the will of God concerning him. When, therefore, the Directors of the Missionary Society asked him where he would go, he said, 'I have asked God to direct you where to send me; and where you send me I will go.' He and his devoted missionary wife, having consulted a physician as to the state of her health, forwarded a certificate to the Missionary Society, asking if, in the face of that, he would be required to return to the South Seas; for, if so, they would go. As the Directors would not decide, he thought it was his duty to remain in England, and at about that time he received an invitation to accept the pastorate of this church and congregation, and his reception was of so unanimous and so loving a nature that he consented, and on last Sunday three years preached his first sermon as a 'supply.' He found the church happy and united, but small and poor; but they did not publish their poverty—each did his utmost to support the institutions of the Gospel. He took the pastorate under the agreement that as soon as the deacons could find a site for a church they would commence to build.

"Some twenty sites were inspected; but, the most favourable being leaseholds at about £65 per annum on a ninety-nine years' lease, they determined to wait. They did wait until the time came when they were enabled to purchase the *freehold* of the site on which the building was erected. The cost of this site was £1,100, for freeholds were exceedingly expensive in Woolwich. They had many trials, with the repetition of which he would not now detain them; the congregation and himself had worked warmly and happily together, and he knew of nothing which could be considered as a shadow of reproach from one to another. The whole cost of the building was about £5,000, and their good friend, Mr. F. Finch, whom he was glad to see present, had been one of the principals in enabling them to build the chapel, he and Mr. Wilson having readily responded to their application for a loan of £1,500 on mortgage; and the building committee were now anxious to reduce their outstanding debts to this amount, apprehending that the amount could be cleared gradually by instalments. The rent of the building which they had lately occupied was £50 per year, with about £10 per year for the Sunday-school room. Therefore, it was clear that, if all but the mortgage was removed, they would be able to go on smoothly and clear from debt. With the promises they had already, it was estimated that, to do this, they would not require more than £650, and it was earnestly hoped that this would soon be obtained. He then called on Mr. Pearce, their honorary treasurer, secretary, and sub-architect, to read the accounts.

"Mr. James Pearce then read the balance-sheet, in which it was shown that the cost of the freehold was £1,100; cost of building, &c., £3,500; lighting and warming, £200; architects and surveyors, £300; printing, stamps, and stationery, £150. A list of subscriptions was also read, and it appeared that £1,000 had been promised from different sources. The only debt upon the chapel fund now was the mortgage of £1,500, and other accounts amounting to rather more than £600. Mr. Pearce also announced the receipt of a cheque for £10 10s. from Mr. Peake, as a substitute for himself, he not being able to attend.

"The Rev. W. Gill said he had received from the Rev. Mr. Kennerly, of Eltham, an excuse for his absence, and a subscription of £1. Mr. Tiverdie had also given £2 2s.; himself and Mrs. Gill had done their best, and had subscribed an additional £5; and Mr. Greig, who had previously given £20 to join with others in raising £300, now had offered to be one of five to raise £10 each.

"Mr. Finch being about to leave, the Rev. W. Gill expressed the thanks of the congregation for the assistance he had given their work, which was acknowledged in suitable terms.

"Mr. E. Smith, of London, also took his leave, having first subscribed £10 10s., and an additional £10 towards the list proposed by Mr. Greig.

"The Rev. W. Gill expressed thanks to the architects for the zeal and ability, and, at the same time, the urbanity, they had exhibited throughout the progress of the works. He thought they had had more than usual interference while on this work, the committee having been constantly about the spot, seeing every stone laid and inspecting every piece of timber. Alterations had been suggested, which must have been exceedingly troublesome, but they had been received with a good grace and an amount of courteous attention which was quite astonishing. He was pleased to see Mr. Landor was present, and could with pleasure inform him that he and Mr. Bidell had the respect and good wishes of all with whom they had come in contact during the progress of this work. To the clerk of works, Mr. Necton, also, a large amount of praise was due. He had been constantly at his post, watchful and careful; and there was no doubt that the building would owe much of its stability and good workmanship to his care and conduct. He begged to acknowledge a further sum of £2 2s. from Mr. Landor.

"Mr. Pearce said he believed he had been the greatest tormentor of the gentlemen just named, and must take the opportunity of acknowledging with thanks the courtesy he had received from them on all occasions.

"Mr. Landor said in the first place he wished to correct an error. The £2 2s. had been subscribed by his brother, and not by himself. He acknowledged gratefully the complimentary terms in which his name had been mentioned, and could assure them that, although an architect always took an interest in the progress of his work, he had taken a still greater interest in the erection of this building for many reasons. That was a day of congratulation, and he congratulated the pastor and congregation on the accomplishment of the work to which they had so long looked forward. They had begun in harmony, but it frequently happened that, however harmoniously a work might be commenced, however full of promise it might be, dissensions and disagreements sprang up; but in this case he was happy to say all such unpleasant occurrences had been avoided. In the progress of the work he had made many friends with whom he hoped to be long acquainted, and to meet eventually in a better building—a building not made with hands. On behalf of Mr. Neeton, he would say that to him they were greatly indebted for the satisfactory progress of the works, and too much credit could not be given to him for his constant attention, assiduity, and courtesy.

"The Rev. W. Gill said, although Mr. Landor had disclaimed the donation just mentioned, it must not be forgotten that he had been a subscriber in another form, having agreed to erect the spire at a cost of £70 instead of £120. Mr. Gill having alluded to the Rev. S. Martin, and his early connection with that gentleman,

"The Rev. S. Martin said, as he had to leave for London to attend his own church, he desired to say a few words previous to his departure. The building in which they were assembled was one which, by its external appearance, invited any one to come in, and when inside it plainly invited them to stop, and nobody could desire a building to be clothed in better characteristics. One word for the spire. He hoped that it would not be inferred from his words that he was harping after a steeple for his own church, but he must confess that he liked its appearance. A building constructed in the simple Italian style did not advertise itself. It might be the town-hall, mechanics' institution, court-house, public baths, or any other building; but a church built in an ecclesiastical style could not be mistaken. It might possibly whisper to the passer-by that there was a God, and might be the subordinate means of saving souls; therefore an ecclesiastical and religious face upon it was an advantage. He was inclined to defend the spire from the bottom to the top. Alluding to the pecuniary difficulties under which the church now laboured, the rev. gentleman said he had been trying to raise fifty pounds, and thought he should succeed; but, in Westminster, there were so many claims upon them that their labour was ceaseless. He had left his home at twelve years of age, and had met in Woolwich many friends. Indeed, the abundant kindness he had met with here made him think that he had more friends lying in the graves at Woolwich, Plumstead, and Charlton than at his own home, for he missed so many from around him. There was one friend in particular who seemed to have been mixed up in all the important events of his life, who had been to him more as an affectionate father than a mere friend. He had passed away after giving £1,000 towards this chapel, but he felt that he (alluding to the late Mr. T. Tame) was still with them, for the Saviour surely would not let him be in ignorance of this event. Christ had whispered to him that the work was finished. After alluding to an elegant basket of flowers which had been just presented to him by another of his old friends, the speaker concluded by stating that he should ever hold that day and that event in pleasant remembrance. Mr. Martin then took his leave.

"Several other subscriptions just received were announced, including five guineas from Messrs. Josiah and John Smith; £1 from Mr. Gill; a guinea from Mr. Rixon; A Friend, £5, &c. Mr. W. Campbell Taylor said himself and Mr. Watts would subscribe £5 each if eight others would do likewise. Another £5 was subscribed by Mr. Elkin.

"The meeting then separated, re-assembling in greater numbers at tea, at half-past five o'clock, when, notwithstanding the multitude of the company, the ladies presiding, with their numerous and assiduous satellites, continued to perform their rather difficult task with great credit to themselves and satisfaction to those who surrounded them.

"In the evening, at half-past six o'clock, Divine service was resumed in the chapel, when, a hymn having been sung, the Rev. R. W. Betts read from the 2nd Book of Kings the beautiful prayer of Solomon in the Temple, and afterwards offered up an eloquent and appropriate prayer. Another hymn having been sung,

"The Rev. John Stoughton preached from the words, 'Be ye doers of the work, and not hearers only, deceiving your own selves.'—James, 1st chap. 22nd verse.

"A hymn having been sung, prayer was offered by a minister from America, who closed the services with the Benediction.

"A portion of the congregation afterwards partook of supper in the lecture-room, and, a meeting being improvised immediately after, some brief addresses were delivered, and, a subscription being set on foot, about £50 was almost immediately collected, making altogether upwards of £200 collected during the day."

First Anniversary.

In the following year, 1860, my brother George and his family returned to England from the South Sea Islands, and we had the pleasure of welcoming them on the 30th of June, the day before the first anniversary sermons were to be preached in connection with the chapel. Under these circumstances nothing could be more opportune than his taking one of the services on the following day.

Appended is a report of these services, copied from a local newspaper:—

"On Sunday, July 1st, the Rev. William Gill preached from Isaiah lvii., 15 v.—the greatness and condescension of God in relation to the exercises and experiences of worship. Much interest was added to the afternoon school and evening services by the presence of the Rev.

George Gill, who had just reached this country from the South Sea Islands, after an absence of sixteen years in the service of the Gospel among the islanders. The Rev. George Gill preached in the evening from Nehemiah ix., 38 v.—giving a review of God's providence and grace towards His people, exciting in them renewed consecration to His will and service. At the Communion, several members were received into the fellowship of the church; and the people connected with this growing congregation concluded the services of this their first anniversary with expressions of gratitude to God, whose guidance and favour they seek, and with thanks to the friends of the town and neighbourhood who have rendered them sympathy and help. The total collections, donations, &c., of the united services were little less than £200."

. . . .

During the next two years the church progressed in every branch, and a large number of children were added to the Sunday-school. Although my time was largely occupied with home affairs, I was not idle in the cause of missions, for I visited almost every part of the kingdom on behalf of the Missionary Society.

In 1863 I had arranged to preach Sunday-school sermons at Sheerness on Sunday, October 18th; and some four days before, Mrs. Gill and I went to visit our friend Captain O'Dwyer, of the reserve ship *Orion*, lying off Sheerness. On Saturday we made signals for a steam-tug to take us in from the boat, and to take us to Sheerness, a distance of two miles. In attempting this we met with a fearful accident; the tug ran into our boat; Mrs. Gill and I were in the water some fifteen or twenty minutes, and were in greatest danger of being drowned. The local report of the accident was as follows:—

"Alarming Boat Accident.—An accident of a very alarming character, which providentially ended without any fatal result, occurred on Saturday last in the River Medway. It appears that the Rev. W. Gill, of Rectory Place Chapel, Woolwich, was last week paying a visit to Sheerness, having exchanged pulpits with the Rev. J. Samson, of that place, in which Mr. Gill was to preach on the Sunday following. Mrs. Gill accompanied her husband, and they spent the afternoon and night of Friday on board the *Orion*, steam ship, lying in ordinary, on a visit to Mr. and Mrs. O'Dwyer, formerly members of the congregation at Rectory Place Chapel. On the following afternoon (Saturday) Mr. Gill, Mrs. Gill, Mr. O'Dwyer, the wife of a seaman, and four sailors got into the *Orion's* boat and rowed out into the stream, waiting for the screw steam gun-boat, which calls off every ship in ordinary, for the purpose of conveying passengers to the pier. By some misconception of orders the helmsman of the gun-boat turned her in such a position that she came stem on upon the small boat, cutting her down to the water's edge, and throwing all the occupants into the water, in which they were struggling for at least ten minutes. Mrs. Gill, after the lapse of a considerable time, caught hold of the life rope attached to the gun-boat and was rescued, though not without sustaining some severe bruises; but Mr. Gill, who could not swim, was almost exhausted, and would undoubtedly have perished had not Mr. O'Dwyer, seeing his sinking state, supported him until both were rescued.

"A boat belonging to the Hood put out to the rescue, and ultimately the whole of the persons were saved. Mr. and Mrs. Gill and Mr. O'Dwyer were in a very exhausted condition, and were taken on board the *Orion*, where, by the judicious use of warmth and stimulants, they were so far recovered that Mr. and Mrs. Gill were enabled to return by train from Queensborough to Woolwich the same night, where they arrived shortly after 11 o'clock. An official inquiry has taken place, and the result has proved that the man at the wheel on board the gun-boat (who mistook the signal) was the sole cause of the accident, by turning towards the boat instead of from it, as directed by the captain of the gun-boat. We are glad to say that all parties are recovering as well and as fast as may be expected, considering the shock to which they were exposed, and it is hoped that Mr. Gill will be able to officiate at the morning service in his own chapel to-morrow."

* * * * * *

For a year or two previous to this date I had had a great desire to form a Young Men's Undenominational Christian Association. After various and unexpected difficulties in connection with the denominations, I had the pleasure of seeing this infant institution established. The following is a brief description of the first lecture given early in 1864:—

"WOOLWICH YOUNG MEN'S CHRISTIAN ASSOCIATION.—This useful association has grown up under the influence of a few townsmen who are interested in the religious and intellectual welfare of the young men of Woolwich and its neighbourhood. The first of a series of lectures intended to be delivered during the ensuing winter in connection with the association was given on Thursday evening last, at the lecture-hall adjoining Rectory Place Chapel, by the Rev. W. M. Thompson, of London, on the 'Life of Martin Luther.' The Rev. W. Gill, minister of the chapel, presided. The lecturer gave a most lucid and eloquent sketch of the leading incidents in the life of the great Reformer, illustrating them by views given by a powerful oxy-hydrogen apparatus, and was listened to by a highly interested and enthusiastic audience. We were pleased to notice that the lecture was well attended by young persons, for whose benefit the association has more especially arranged the lectures, and we trust, from the highly interesting character of the lectures announced to follow, and the low scale of admission—viz., 1s. for the entire course—to find increased interest awakened towards the well-being of the society. During the last twelve months the meetings of the association, to which all young men are welcome, have been regularly held on Sunday afternoons at three o'clock, and on Wednesday evenings at nine o'clock, in the lecture-room of Rectory Place Chapel, and both the number who have attended and the interest manifested have been most gratifying. Upon the committee of management are included the names of well-known gentlemen representing nearly all the leading denominations of the town. The second lecture is to be delivered on Tuesday evening, December 6th, by the Rev. J. Hiles Hitchens, F.R.S.L., of Peckham, on 'The Tower of London: its Tenants and Treasures.' The hours at which these lectures commence (eight o'clock) is rather early for such a business town as Woolwich. We cannot, however, but hope that many young men may have the opportunity of attending, and that they may also be induced to avail themselves of the Sunday-afternoon and Wednesday-evening classes."

Beyond engagements connected with these public institutions, the weeks of the year were occupied with the ordinary routine of pastoral work—viz., with visitation two mornings or afternoons a week; children's class from three to four every Wednesday, at which forty was the average attendance (none admitted above the age of thirteen); two weekly Bible-classes on Mondays and Wednesdays; and weekly individual interviews with candidates and members.

My principal recreation during these years had been attendance at London Missionary Society's committees, and Hackney College committees, and the meetings of the London Ministerial Board, and London Missionary Society's and Bible Society's deputation meetings.

During this year the church at Rectory Place was asked to take charge of a small chapel cause at Welling. This with all willingness we attempted to do, but found the distance and other difficulties too great to be overcome. But we were more successful in a preaching-station which we were able to establish with the assistance of some of our young men at North Woolwich.

The anniversary meeting connected with the building of

the chapel, held in July this year, was one of great gratification to us all, inasmuch as it celebrated the clearing off of the debt from the chapel and schools, the actual amount of which was somewhat more than £6,500, or, together with interest on borrowed money, &c., &c., increased the outlay to £7,500. We were pleased to have a small balance after all liabilities were paid, and the friends generously resolved to add donations to this balance to the amount of £20 in order to give every child of the Sunday-school a memorial medal commemorative of the event—having on one side the chapel in relief, with the words: "Rectory Place Congregational Chapel, Rev. William Gill, Pastor," and on the reverse side "To Commemorate the Extinction of the Debt on the Chapel." The following is a short account of the gathering of the Sunday-school taken from the *Kentish Independent*:—

"Rectory Place Chapel, Woolwich.—On Thursday last, the children belonging to the Sunday-schools of Rectory Place Chapel were treated with tea, and each child was presented with a medal in commemoration of the clearing off the debt incurred in building the chapel and schools.

"At five o'clock nearly five hundred children met in the upper and lower rooms, and were supplied, to their hearts' content, with tea, cake, and et ceteras, and after an hour's unrestrained recreation they were assembled in the chapel. Before the distribution of the medals, a brief religious service was conducted by the Rev. William Gill. A beautiful hymn, called 'Christ the Children's Friend,' was sung, after which a simple prayer was offered by Mr. Gill, which was audibly responded to in short sentences by all the children. Another hymn was then sung, entitled 'The Better Land,' then a brief history of the schools was given, which was followed by a few appropriate remarks from Mr. Thomas R. Richardson, the esteemed superintendent. The children again united in singing another of their hymns, 'Sweet Rest in Heaven,' and then each class, with its teacher, was called out in order, and each child was presented with a medal. The medal, both in design and execution, was much admired, having on one side a beautifully executed raised outline of the chapel, encircled with the words: 'Rectory Place Congregational Chapel,' 'Woolwich,' 'Rev. William Gill, Pastor.' And on the reverse side the record:—'16th January, 1866,' 'To Commemorate the Extinction of the Debt on the Chapel,' 'Erected 1859, at a Cost of £6,500.' The names of the deacons of the church then follow, and the whole is encircled with the text—Genesis xii., 2 v.—'I will bless thee, and thou shalt be a blessing.'

"A goodly number of the members of the congregation and friends were present, and the whole proceedings were characterised by a spirit of cheerfulness and praise which, we think, will be remembered with interest for many years to come.

"It had been previously arranged by the teachers of the school to entertain their superintendents and secretary, with their pastor and Mrs. Gill, at a supper; accordingly, at nine o'clock, the party assembled in the lecture-room. A well-provisioned table was spread under the superintendence of Mr. Leach, and the engagements of the occasion were happily terminated by friendly intercourse and reciprocal good-feeling and good-will, which, we trust, may long mark both the schools and congregation of Rectory Place Chapel."

During the year 1867 I had frequently been feeling unwell and unequal to the discharge of the varied duties of my position; and this indisposition was much increased during January and February by a succession of colds, thoroughly relaxing the head and chest, so that, in conversation with the deacons on the last Saturday in February, I was led to intimate to them my deepening conviction that I should have to resign the pastorate. During my twelve years at Woolwich, besides attending to the various things mentioned previously, I had preached 1,329 sermons (Sunday and week-day) in Rectory Place Chapel; and London Missionary Society and Bible Society meetings and sermons at various churches during the same period were 403, making a total of 1,732 services. There were reasons also connected with individuals and individual action which no doubt more affected me in my weakened state of health than they otherwise would have done. Thus, very much to the surprise of the deacons, I made known my conviction about resignation simply, and in the first instance privately, to them. I frankly stated that I wished this communication to be strictly private, for if during the next month it became publicly known to the church, it would materially determine me to abide by my conviction.

Early in March I visited Brighton; but the doctors prohibited my stay there, and ordered me to Hastings. While at Hastings, I found that my conversation with the deacons in some way had become known, and that most of the people were thinking that my temporary absence at Hastings was only preliminary to my resignation. I returned to Woolwich in the last week of March, and, under all the circumstances, was led to give in my resignation to the church.

Thus closed twelve years' service at Woolwich. Seventy-five members were in communion when I took charge. Four hundred and twenty-five were admitted during my pastorate, *of whom two hundred and fifty were in monthly communion at my resignation.*

During the autumn of 1868 I employed myself in revising and curtailing "Gems from the Coral Islands" for a cheap Sunday-school edition, of which 5,000 copies were printed, making the total of all editions of the work 11,000 copies.

1869.

Early in 1869 my esteemed and generous friend, Miss Portal, of Russell Square, kindly offered to pay all expenses of a tour for Mrs. Gill and myself to accompany her, with two or three other friends, to France, Germany, and Switzerland. Accordingly in July we commenced a long and interesting tour, visiting Paris, Strasbourg, the St. Julian Pass and the Abbula Pass, Samaden, St. Mauritz, and other towns of the Engadine; St. Galle, Zurich, Lucerne, Schaffhausen, Freiburg, Heidelburg, Frankfurt, Homburg, Wiesbaden, Cologne, Aix-la-Chapelle, Brussels, Field of Waterloo, &c., *en route.* This thorough change and recreation completely restored my health, so that during the autumn I was able to take general services both in London and in the country.

1870.

Four Years at Robert Street. 1870—1874.

Robert Street Chapel, Grosvenor Square, was the oldest Dissenting place of worship in the west end of London. The building as it now stands was built by Seth Smith, and for many years in its early history had the services of the well-known and then popular preacher, Rev. J. Leach. But during the last twelve years, owing to the death of some of its members, the removal of others, and unfortunate settlements of ministers, the place had become neglected except by a few devout, but poor, people, who could do little either to support or increase its efficiency. It was thought, however, that if I would undertake the work, with my restored health and with the sympathy and material assistance of friends outside, which were promised, that the cause might so revive as to encourage the church to build a new chapel, the frontage of which should be in Oxford Street. Several ministerial and lay friends strongly advised my attempting the work, and hence I was invited to preach, and did so on the 16th of January.

On the 4th of April the following invitation was sent to me from the church to become its pastor, which invitation I was led to accept. This invitation was signed by all the members of the church, numbering 115.

"18, Bentinck Street, Manchester Square,
"*4th April*, 1870.

"Reverend Sir,

"It is my pleasant duty to inform you that, at a church-meeting held in Robert Street Chapel the 28th ult., the three following resolutions were unanimously adopted after a report of our conversation with you had been read to the meeting :—

"1. That the Rev. W. Gill be affectionately and earnestly invited to become the pastor of the church.

"2. That the church pledges itself collectively, and the members pledge themselves individually, to use all possible means within their power towards the enlargement of our present chapel towards Oxford Street, on the building of a new place of worship should a suitable opportunity offer itself, to keep this object constantly in view, striving with all prayer towards its accomplishment.

"3. That the church guarantees to the Rev. W. Gill a fixed salary of £200 per year for the first two years of his pastorate.

"I also have the pleasure to subjoin the two first resolutions signed by all the deacons and 109 members of the church, and have no doubt we should have obtained more signatures had we kept the paper a little longer to submit to absent members, but we thought that the number that had signed would be sufficient to show you the unanimity and earnestness of the church in supporting the resolutions.

"Trusting that you will give our affectionate invitation your serious and prayerful consideration, and with the earnest prayer that the Spirit of all wisdom may guide you to such a decision as shall most redound to the glory of our Divine Redeemer,

"I am, Reverend and Dear Sir,

"T. van der Ben, Secretary.

"Rev. William Gill, Camden House,
"The Glebe, Blackheath."

As soon as I was able I made arrangements to go up from Blackheath three times a-week—Mondays for visitation and evening Bible-class; Wednesdays, for visitation and evening preaching service; Thursdays, Bible-class in the evening with young women and teachers in the school. The Sunday-school was one of the most interesting features of the place. There were about four hundred scholars and twenty-five to thirty teachers. As soon as things were a little consolidated I began to look about for a site where with any probability we might ultimately secure a new chapel. The first place under consideration was a timber-yard which could have been purchased, and concerning which I wrote the Rev. J. H. Wilson. Another site was in Oxford Street, belonging to the City Lands Committee. Another plan proposed was to purchase two houses at the rear of the chapel which would open into Oxford Street.

Concerning these plans I wrote to Mr. Samuel Morley, who said, in reply, he would be willing liberally to help us in the building, but he could take no responsibility. Secondly, I wrote through Lord Shaftesbury to the Duke of Westminster respecting the houses at the back of the chapel or any other in Oxford Street. In reply the Duke said that there were nine or ten years of most of the leases yet unexpired, and at the expiration of which he would have to sell them at a marketable value. Thirdly, I had two or three interviews with the Committee and Sub-Committee of the London Chapel Building Society. They expressed themselves glad that I was undertaking the thing, advised me to begin at once, and as the thing proceeded they would render help. Alas! I considered this but poor encouragement, although I told them I had promised towards the work the whole of the salary that I received—viz., £200 for five years. Fourthly, I then, through J. Faring & Son, architects, applied to the City Lands Committee respecting the site in Oxford Street. The Committee were kindly disposed to treat with me, and promised to grant eighty years' lease instead of forty at a rental of £150 a-year. We were assured by the architects that, when the building should be complete, the cellarage would yield an income of £200 a-year. The Lands Committee, of course, required some four or six gentlemen who, as trustees, should become responsible for the fulfilment of our agreements. The whole of these arrangements were fully presented to the church, and a month was given for the members to say how much they could promise towards the seven or eight thousand pounds' expenditure in five years.

At the end of a month it was found that £500 was the utmost that could be promised in the five years. Under these circumstances of difficulty we were led to close the year, as far as building purposes were concerned, without the slightest hope of success.

1872—1873.

Having given up all hope respecting the new chapel, I devoted myself simply to the ordinary duties of the various institutions during these two years with very little incident to record, except the uniform kindness of the people, and their sympathy with me in the evidence that nothing more could be done for the place but to make it a kind of mission station, requiring the labours of a minister who was able to do that kind of work, and who lived nearer to Robert Street than Blackheath.

Hence, at the last church-meeting in December, I gave in my resignation (in the following terms), which was to take place on the last Sunday in March, 1874:—

"*To the Church Assembling at Robert Street Chapel.*

"My dear Friends,

"It will soon be four years since I came among you, and I trust in the review it can be seen that our labours have in some degree been fruitful of good, both to yourselves and to the institutions of the church.

"But with all the good results and the happy co-operation which have marked our labours, it is painfully apparent that our losses by death and removals have not been supplied by anything like a satisfactory or hopeful increase of attendance.

"For some time past my growing conviction has been that a change of ministry is required, alike to meet your circumstances as a church and the character and habits of the population around you.

"It is evident to my mind that the success of your institutions among the people of the immediate locality requires more evangelistic mission-like services and visitation than we are rendering. Therefore, after mature and prayerful consideration, I feel it my duty to tender my resignation as your pastor. I had purposed that this should take place on the last Sunday of this year, but, thinking it will give you time and opportunity to develop plans for your future welfare in the choice of another minister, I defer leaving you until the last Sunday in March next. In leaving you I desire to record my gratitude to God for any prosperity which has marked our labours among you, and I would acknowledge the kindness I have received from you during my pastorate. I shall take with me pleasing memories of you personally, and as a church, and it will always give me pleasure to hear of your increase and prosperity.

"Commending you to the guidance and blessing of our Lord and Saviour,

"Believe me, yours very truly,
"WILLIAM GILL."

This resignation was given in such a manner as to lead the people to see that it was a final decision, and they were compelled reluctantly to accept it. For the three months—January to March, 1874—things went on pretty much the same as during previous years, and in March I preached my farewell sermon, and on the following day a public farewell service was held in the school-room, of which the following is a brief report:—

"ROBERT STREET CHAPEL.—RETIREMENT OF THE MINISTER.—For the last four years the Rev. William Gill (formerly of the South Sea Islands Mission), as minister of Robert Street Congregational Church, Grosvenor Square (one of the oldest, we believe, in London), has been doing a work of great usefulness, labouring with growing success over church and congregation. The rev. gentleman is now about to withdraw from his present sphere of action, and on Wednesday evening made his last appearance as the pastor, a *soirée* being held by his church and congregation on the occasion. The school-room beneath the chapel was most tastefully decorated with flowers and flags, presenting a charming appearance, all connected with the place, the Young Men's Mutual Improvement Society, the Choral Society, and church and congregation generally, co-operating in the work—Mr. Smith, the secretary, and Mr. van der Ben, jun., especially exerting themselves. A series of choice engravings, kindly lent by Mr. Jennings, of Duke Street, adorned the walls, and a picturesque grotto-like arrangement of cork and flowers by Mr. John van der Ben attracted a good deal of attention. An excellent tea, at which between three and four hundred persons sat down, commenced the proceedings, after which the chair was taken by the Rev. William Gill, supported by the deacons. The opening hymn, 'Jesus, Lord, we look to Thee,' having been sung and prayer offered, the rev. gentleman stated the circumstances that had arisen to make him think it well that his connection with the church as its pastor should cease, but assuring them that he should always keep them in affectionate remembrance, and expressing his hope that the recollections of that night would be pleasing to their memories for all the future. Various readings and recitations were then given by Mr. C. H. Dyke, Mr. R. Barber, and Mr. J. Allen, jun., the latter gentleman's recitation, 'The Child's Prayer,' being especially well given, and several choruses by the Choral Society—an institution connected with the church, under the superintendence of Mr. Stephen Kilbey, who is also the organist. An interval for refreshments having taken place, Mr. J. Allen (one of the deacons) rose for the purpose of making a presentation in the shape of a very handsome silver inkstand, in the name of the members of the church and congregation, as a small mark of their Christian esteem and regard to their retiring pastor. He (Mr. Allen) hoped it would be as kindly received as it was presented. The rev. chairman, in accepting the present, gratefully assured the givers that he should not merely in the future look upon, but constantly use it. It bore the following inscription: 'Presented to the Rev. W. Gill by the church and congregation on retiring from the pastorate of Robert Street Chapel, March, 1874.' Mr. J. van der Ben then, in a few kindly words, presented in the name of the Dorcas Society a silver paper-knife to the chairman for Mrs. Gill, as a token of affectionate remembrance. It bore this inscription: 'Presented to Mrs. Gill with Christian affection by the members of the Robert Street Dorcas Society, March, 1874,' and the monogram 'E. L. G.' The chairman having again returned thanks, and Mr. Beesley and Mr. Copeland, jun., having made a few remarks, the chairman desired to express personally his thanks to his young friends for the very handsome way in which they had decorated the room. The closing hymn, 'Each other we have owned,' having been sung, and the Benediction given, the proceedings terminated."

Thus closed my four years' work at Robert Street. During these four years, eighty members had been added to the church, and the various institutions, at great sacrifice of the poor people, had been sustained. I shall have affectionate regard for all whom I knew there, and wish them every blessing needed for prosperity and enlarged success.

CHAPTER XXVI.

CONCLUSION.

From 1874 to the close of his life, Mr. Gill undertook no settled charge. But his heart was in his work as much as ever. He was always ready to serve the Lord and Saviour, whom he unfeignedly loved. His activity was chiefly devoted to the London Missionary Society and the British and Foreign Bible Society.

His last public services were conducted at Beccles on behalf of the institution to which his affections were so long and so devotedly attached—the London Missionary Society. He little thought that he was saying a farewell to his laborious public life. If it had been left to his choice to determine to what society the last service of his forty years' consecration to the Kingdom of Christ should be rendered, most assuredly he would have preferred his beloved London Missionary Society. After services at Beccles the illness commenced from which he never recovered. Upwards of four months of prostration and increasing languor were allotted him, and he passed to the rest in Christ for which his soul longed. On the 14th of August, 1878, he joined the "great multitude which no man could number." He laid down the weary burden of mortality. His last tear had been shed. Among the things which he did just before his illness was to hand over £2,000 to the funds of the London Missionary Society. He had a large and a loving heart, and many remember his generosity with thankfulness. Poor ministers, students without resources, orphans, and many in penury, all unknown to the world, were recipients of his bounty.

The funeral took place at Abney Park Cemetery on Monday, August 19th, the service in the chapel being conducted by the

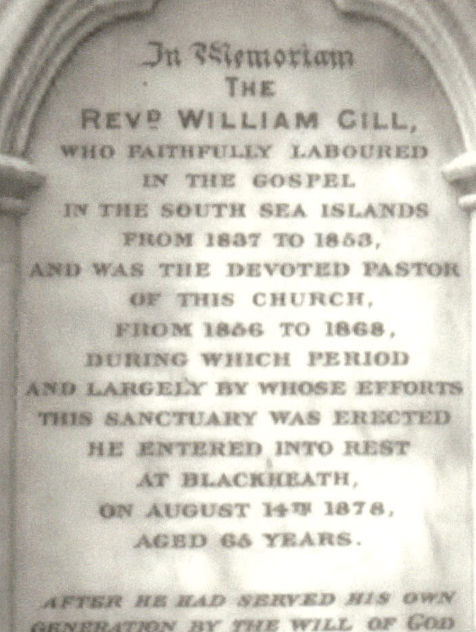
In Memoriam
THE
REVD WILLIAM GILL,
WHO FAITHFULLY LABOURED
IN THE GOSPEL
IN THE SOUTH SEA ISLANDS
FROM 1837 TO 1853,
AND WAS THE DEVOTED PASTOR
OF THIS CHURCH,
FROM 1856 TO 1868,
DURING WHICH PERIOD
AND LARGELY BY WHOSE EFFORTS
THIS SANCTUARY WAS ERECTED
HE ENTERED INTO REST
AT BLACKHEATH,
ON AUGUST 14TH 1878,
AGED 65 YEARS.
AFTER HE HAD SERVED HIS OWN
GENERATION BY THE WILL OF GOD
FELL ON SLEEP. ACTS XIII 36.

Rev. Henry Batchelor, and the Rev. J. C. Whitehouse officiating at the grave. Among those who attended were the Rev. G. Gill, of Burnley, brother of the deceased; and the Rev. S. J. Whitmee, of Samoa. The churches at Woolwich and at Robert Street were represented by their deacons and several members of the congregations.

A funeral sermon was preached by the Rev. H. Batchelor at Blackheath, at the conclusion of which he said:—

"Our missionary epoch has not witnessed a more beautiful, unselfish, and consecrated life than that of our departed friend. The last morning that I called to inquire for him, to my surprise, the mortal conflict was over. It came to me as a shock, and in the hush in which I listened I seemed to hear the Master's voice, 'Well done, good and faithful servant; enter into the joy of thy Lord.' May we, through the mercy of God, be permitted to follow! A tearless world—that is the goal of our hope. No tears. What a change! Here 'Jesus' even 'wept;' no cheek shall be drenched with grief there. No tear of penitence shall ever fall, because no conscience shall be pierced by the sense of sin. Hope shall shed no tear. How often the eye swims with emotion as it descries the radiance which shines from afar, and casts its inspiring beam into the sunken and dusky valleys of our 'tribulation.' There all shall be near, visible, ecstatic; faith shall become sight, and desire exultation. No mother shall pour forth tears in secret over the waxen features from which the life has fled, whose light has gone from the eye, prattle from the lips, and bounding elasticity from the limb. No father shall stand beside premature remains of a prodigal, and with the descending clod let fall big drops from rigid cheeks, and go forth with a rending heart to the dull monotony of daily care. You shall never look with swollen eyes and quivering features into a father's, a mother's, a husband's, a wife's, a brother's, a sister's grave. Pain shall bow no frame, sickness blanch no cheek, mortal anguish wring no last tear from failing eye and flickering lid. Those that stand before the throne clothed with white robes carry unwithering 'palms' of perpetual joy in their hands, and God shall wipe away all tears from their eyes."

A memorial tablet, a photograph of which accompanies this chapter, was erected by the members of the church in Rectory Place Chapel, at Woolwich, soon after Mr. Gill's death; and, in addition to this mark of public esteem, Mrs. Gill received numerous letters from friends, known and unknown, in every part of the United Kingdom, and also from friends in other parts of the world, including many from natives of the South Sea Islands, all of which, while condoling with the widow in her bereavement, bore testimony to the high personal esteem in which the departed missionary had been held by all who came in contact with him.

FINIS.

London: Yates & Alexander, Printers, Lonsdale Buildings, Chancery Lane, W.C.

www.ingramcontent.com/pod-product-compliance
Lightning Source LLC
Chambersburg PA
CBHW020950030726
47496CB00005B/1448

9783744664646